12^{00}
(3050)

WATCH ON THE RHINE

(*Die Wacht am Rhein*)

WATCH ON THE RHINE

(*Die Wacht am Rhein*)

JOHN RINGO
TOM KRATMAN

WATCH ON THE RHINE

This is a work of fiction. All the characters and events portrayed in this book are fictional, and any resemblance to real people or incidents is purely coincidental.

A Baen Books Original

Baen Publishing Enterprises
P.O. Box 1403
Riverdale, NY 10471
www.baen.com

ISBN-13: 978-0-7434-9918-7
ISBN-10: 0-7434-9918-2

Cover art by Kurt Miller

First printing, August 2005

Library of Congress Cataloging-in-Publication Data

Ringo, John, 1963-
    Watch on the Rhine = (Die Wacht am Rhine) / John Ringo, Tom Kratman.
        p. cm.
    "A Baen Books original"--T.p. verso.
    ISBN 0-7434-9918-2
    1. Human-alien encounters--Fiction. 2. Life on other planets--Fiction. 3. Space warfare--Fiction. I. Title: Wacht am Rhine. II. Kratman, Tom. III. Title.

    PS3568.I577W38 2005
    813'.54--dc22

                                                                    2005011257

Distributed by Simon & Schuster
1230 Avenue of the Americas
New York, NY 10020

Production & design by Windhaven Press, Auburn, NH (www.windhaven.com)
Printed in the United States of America

10   9   8   7   6   5   4   3   2   1

For Anna Glinberg and Mania Halef . . .
and all the others whose names and faces
we will never know.

—————◦◦◦◦———————

Mögen andere von ihrer Schande spreche,
Ich Spreche von der meinen . . .

O' Deutschland bleiche Mutter!
Wie haben deine Söhne dich zugerichtet
Dass du unter dem Völke sitzest
Ein Gespörtt oder eine Furcht![1]

—Bertolt Brecht, 1933

PART I

PROLOGUE

Villers Bocage, 12 June 1944

The soldier wore black. Silver lightning bolts flashed on his right lapel; the three rosettes of a *Hauptsturmführer*—or captain of the *Schützstaffeln*, the SS—shone on the left.

He stood in the hatch of a Tiger I tank, peering with binoculars through the gloom of the battlefield. Arising out of the gloom he saw the rising smoke from the engines of an enemy armored column halted on the road below. The soldier counted twenty-five or so enemy vehicles, mixed half-tracks and tanks. There were likely more, unseen. So much he suspected, in any case. He was unimpressed.

Though he stood alone, and though his tank was alone, the black-uniformed soldier knew no fear. If he had ever known true fear there were no witnesses to tell of it. His comrades had never seen it and few of his enemies could have detected it, even had they lived.

Neither, so far as the soldier could tell, had the enemy detected his tank.

It took him scant moments to reach his decision. With a roar hidden by the mass of the enemy's idling engines the driver started the engine and headed for a cart track to the left of the enemy column. Already the gunner, Wohl, was swinging his turret to the right.

"Take the first one, Balthazar," ordered the soldier, the commander.

"The half-track?" asked Wohl, incredulously. "It can't hurt us."

"I know. But by blocking the road it can help us."

"Ahhh . . . I *see, Herr Hauptmann*," answered Wohl, returning his attention to his sight. He whispered, "Come on, baby . . . just a little more . . ." then shouted into his microphone, "Target!"

"Fire."

The eighty-eight millimeter, L56 gun belched smoke and flame. Downrange, at the head of the enemy column, a British half-track was thrown violently across the road, blocking it. The half-track caught fire and began emitting great plumes of smoke of its own.

Onward the Tiger roared, its gun belching death and destruction at a fantastic rate. Tanks, Bren Carriers and half-tracks were smashed with each round. At this range Wohl *couldn't* miss. The enemy, blocked by the wrecked half-track, could not advance. Neither, given the narrowness of the road and its border of trees, could they easily retreat. Instead, they simply died.

A lone enemy tank swung into the path. In a race against time the two hostile turrets and guns swung towards each other. Though Wohl trembled slightly, the commander did not. The Tiger proved the faster of the two and yet another British machine went up in smoke and fire.

The way into the town was clear. Though built-up areas were death ground to a tank, the commander felt no fear. He directed his driver into the town. There the Tiger met three more British tanks. Boom . . . Boom . . . Boom . . . and they were reduced to charred, bloody scrap.

The road and the town littered with ruined fighting machines and dead and dying men, the soldier, the commander, withdrew to refuel and rearm. The Seventh British Armored Division had been stopped cold by a single tank, more importantly, by a single man's will and daring. Soon, the commander would return with reinforcements to finish off the point of their armored spear.

Though he had a month more to live, it was on this day, by this obscure town, that Michael Wittmann entered immortality.

In the recent past:

Though the smoke in the room came not from tobacco but from incense burnt upon the Altar of Communication, and though shimmering tuniclike garments covered the beings attending the meeting, and even though those beings were elfin, with pointed ears and needlelike teeth, any human corporate CEO would have recognized instantly that here was an assemblage of unparalleled economic and political *clout*.

The beings—they were called "Darhel"—were seated around the low boardroom table. All were senior leaders of most of the leading clans which formed that species. The table, a rare and precious iridescent hardwood from a little known or settled planet, spoke well of the wealth of the assembly. Each board member's chair was individual, crafted by a group of Indowy master crafts-men to suit that member's size and body shape alone. An Indowy servant—given the nuances of the galactic legal and economic system one might as well have said "slave"—stood behind each of the Darhel lords, ready to cater to their every need and whim. Though some Darhel were perhaps aware of it, most were bliss-fully unaware that these servants, never comfortable with their status as slaves, were one of the prime sources of intelligence to the Bane Sidhe, the galaxy-spanning plot to unseat the Darhel as lords of creation.

Holographic projections stood before each chair, visible to that board member alone. Though information was available concern-ing things like loss of life among the inhabitants, mostly the green-furred, humble Indowy, of the planets falling one by one into the fanged maws of the invaders, few Darhel cared to look at them. This was not squeamishness on their part. The Darhel were simply indifferent to loss of Indowy life. With eighteen *tril-lion* Indowy within the Federation, the loss of a few billion, or a few hundred billion, was a matter of no moment.

But profits? Losses? These were the key and critical bits of information played out on the holographic projections.

Studying his hologram intently, one Darhel burst out, "Lords of Creation, the loss of capital to this invasion is unsupportable! Factories lost? Profits squeezed? Trade imbalanced? Staggering! Intolerable! It must not be allowed to continue." Almost overcome by his own unseemly and even dangerous outburst, the Darhel then lowered his head, forced his breathing into a calm, steady, measured pace while reciting a mantra to fight off lintatai, a form of catatonia inevitably resulting in death, to which the Darhel were uniquely susceptible.

The Ghin, first among equals of those present, silently *tsk-tsked*, thinking, *These young ones, and especially of the* Urdan *clan, are so emotional. They must spend half their lives bringing themselves to the very edge of lintatai, the other half recovering from that.* Not for the first time the Ghin regretted the system of galactic control which allowed even third-rate Darhel to amass power and wealth, at the inevitable expense of the Indowy. Not that he cared a whit for the Indowy. But the Ghin was not without some sympathy for the plight of the Urdan. He knew they were very heavily leveraged. And they tended to produce far too many third-rate minds.

Whatever his thoughts, the Ghin knew that a Ghin must lead. "Fear not about losses of capital. Fear instead the extermination of our people if this plague of Posleen is not contained."

The Urdan leader looked up from his attempt to stave off catatonia and death just long enough to ask, "And what are you doing about it?" His head immediately dropped again, his lips playing the life-saving mantra.

"Everything possible," the Ghin returned calmly. "Armies and fleets of the barbarian mercenaries, the humans, are already engaged in holding the frontier, even in rolling it back in places. Projections show that, with current-sized forces, and with the ability to breed more human mercenaries from among their children we have taken as our . . . guests . . . we shall be able to insulate and isolate ourselves until this plague has passed. Look for yourselves."

With a wave of an arm, every hologram changed to show a map of the Federation sector of the galaxy, systems already fallen to the invaders appearing as red in contrast to Federation blue. The map was framed on all sides by statistical indicia, the profit and loss sheets so beloved of Darhel merchants and bankers.

"Obscene," muttered the Urdan. "By what right do you charge us the absurd wages these barbarians demand? I have shareholders and investors to whom I am responsible. The cost of these humans is unsupportable. They should take an Indowy's wage and be grateful for it."

The Ghin rather agreed with that last. The arrogance of the humans was infuriating. Nonetheless, he answered, "It is the fault of the most numerous among the human subspecies, the ones they call the Chinese." A little of the Ghin's own fury at human arrogance began to peek through. He suppressed that fury ruthlessly; lintatai, once entered into, was as much a danger to a Ghin as to any Darhel.

"The humans that are called 'Chinese' did some calculations and determined that the wages we were offering were much less than we would have been willing to pay. They, along with the other barbarians, simply held out and refused us aid until we had given them a better offer." With a smug smile the Ghin concluded, "Not that we would not have paid three times what the humans demanded. But they didn't know that, of course. Rejoice that the cost is so low. It could have been much worse. And rest assured, my expenses were even greater than yours. And I have plans for these Chinese to answer for their effrontery."

Head still bowed, because the Urdan really was dangerously close to lintatai, that Darhel lord raised his eyes back to the hologram and asked, "And that is another thing. I see the frontier plainly marked. But why have the human mercenaries permitted this open sector where the Posleen are pushing through en masse?"

In response, the Ghin merely smiled.

Closing on the present:

The tunneling ship hummed with life and purpose; though that purpose—life for the Po'oslen'ar, the People of the Ships—was death for all who stood in their path.

Athenalras mused in pride and satisfaction, contemplating the thrice-cursed Aldenata instruments few of the People but he could comprehend. Around him bustled the Kenstain, a few Kessentai, and the minimal number of superior normals necessary to the running of the battleglobe. The bulk of the People rested, unconscious and hibernating—most importantly, not *eating*—deeper in the bowels of the globe. All was well and the People were well on their way to yet another conquest in the long and fiery path of fury and war.

"My lord?" queried the Kessantai, Ro'moloristen, with something between respect and awe. "I have the information you demanded."

"Give it, young one," ordered the senior and elder, curtly.

"This peninsula, jutting away from the direction of rotation of the target, looks to be our best unclaimed landing area. It is populous, rich with industry and refined metal, fertile and fruitful. It would be a fitting place for the People of our clan . . . until, of course, it is time to move on again." The Kessentai then hesitated, his chief noted.

"Rich and fruitful, but . . . ?" queried the senior.

"It is a strange place, this 'Europe,' as they call it. United and divided. Wise and senseless. Fierce and timid. Heedless in peace, so say the records we have gleaned, but potentially fearsome in war."

The senior's crest came up. "They are worse than the gray threshkreen of Diess? The metal threshkreen of Kerlen? They are worse than the accursed thresh of the lesser continent, who battered and destroyed our first landing and even now defy the People with fire and blood?"

The younger God King looked deckward, answering, "My lord . . . these *are* the gray thresh, their home. The beings of the lesser continent? They are the descendants of colonists, much like the People, who left their original home for a new and almost empty one, smashing and exterminating the thresh they found there."

The chief bristled, crest unfurling. "So you are saying, young Ro'moloristen, that this place, this Europe, is too difficult a task for the People, too difficult for me?"

"No! My lord, no!" apologized the junior hastily. "It can be done. But we must approach more cautiously than is our wont. We must seize a base . . . or, I think, perhaps two. There we shall build our strength before completing the subjugation of the rest. Look, my lord. See. Here is my recommendation." The younger God King played claws over an Aldenata screen.

Mollified, if only partly, Athenalras glanced at the screen. "I see. You would have us land here, east on the flat open area . . ."

"They call it Poland, my lord."

"Poland?" queried Athenalras. "Barbarous name," he snorted.

"Indeed," agreed Ro'moloristen. "And the reputation among the threshkreen of these thresh of this barbarous place, Poland, in war is no mean one, though they have had scant success."

"And the other major landing?"

"They call that France. Again, their reputation on the Path of Fury is no mean one, and yet, they too have had scant success."

"I do not understand, puppy. We land, so you propose, at two locations where the local thresh are fierce in war but do not succeed in it? I simply do not understand."

Ro'moloristen answered, "Sometimes, my lord, one can be powerful on the Path of Fury, and yet fail because there is one more powerful still." The young God King touched a claw to the screen. "Here. Here is the place. The home of the gray-clad thresh. The place which puts into the shadow the threshkreen of France and of Poland. The place for which we must prepare an assault such as the People have never seen."

"And what is this fearsome place called, puppy?"

"My lord, the local thresh call their home, 'Deutschland.'"

CHAPTER 1

Fredericksburg, VA, 11 November 2004

Snow flecked the cheeks and eyebrows, falling softly to cover a scene of horror with a clean white blanket. White snow fell upon, melded into, the hair of a man gone white himself. He was stooped, that man. Bent over with the care of ages and the weight of his people resting on his old, worn back.

The *Bundeskanzler*[2] turned his eyes away from the gruesome spectacle even now being covered by snow. Bad enough to have seen a once vibrant and historical city scoured from the face of the earth as if it had never been. Worse to see the roll of casualties . . . such crippling casualties . . . from the army of a state in every way more powerful than his own. The *Kanzler* trembled with fear for his country, his culture and his people.

Yet, as badly and as plainly as he trembled, the nausea of his disgust was in every way worse.

Fearing to look at his aide, the *Kanzler* whispered, "It's the bones, Günter. It's the little piles of gnawed bones."

Günter, the aide—though he was really rather more than that, heard the whisper and grimaced. "I know, mein Herr. It's disgusting. We . . . we have done terrible things in the past. Horrible, awful, damnable things. But this? This goes beyond anything . . ."

"Do not fool yourself," corrected the *Kanzler*. "We have been worse, Günter, far worse. We were worse because what we did, we did to our own. Cities burned away. Lampshades. Soap. Dental

11

gold. *Einsatzgruppen*. Gas chambers and ovens. A whole gamut of horror visited upon the innocent by our ancestors . . . and ourselves."

"And Dresden?" answered Günter, with a raised eyebrow and a sardonic air. "Hamburg? Darmstadt?"

"I didn't say, my young friend, that we were alone in our guilt."

The *Kanzler* blinked away several snowflakes that had lodged themselves in his gray eyelashes. "And . . . after all, what is guilt of the past?" he sighed. "Do our own young people now need to be destroyed because of what their grandfathers did? Is it right for our children to be eaten, to be turned into little piles of bare, gnawed bones? How far does the sin of Adam and Eve go, Günter?"

Straightening that old and worn and overburdened back, the *Kanzler* announced, "In any case, it doesn't matter. Whatever we have done, nothing deserves this . . . this abattoir. And whatever we can do to prevent it . . . that shall I do."

Günter, the aide, scratched his chin, absently. "But what we can do, we have done. Production of everything we need for defense or evacuation is proceeding apace. The old soldiers of the *Wehrmacht*[3] have been remobilized, what there were of them, and are being rejuvenated. The conscription is in legal force, and exempts only those whose conscience cannot abide military service. We are doing all we can."

"No, my young friend," answered the *Kanzler*, slowly and deliberately. "There is one resource yet we have not touched. One that I would never have touched, myself, before seeing this nightmare with my own eyes."

One resource? One resource. What could the Kanzler *mean?* Suddenly Günter's eyes widened with understanding. "*Mein Herr*, you can't mean *them*."

Tightening his overcoat about him in the cold, reaching up a hand to brush away yet more of the steadily falling snow, the *Kanzler* looked skyward as if asking for guidance. Not receiving any, still with eyes turned heavenward, he answered, definitively, "*Them*."

The chancellor thought, but did not say, *And anything else I must bring back to prevent this from happening to* our *cities,* our *people.*

Paris, France, 13 November 2004

The crowd was immense; its intensity, palpable. One among half a million protest marchers, Isabelle De Gaullejac felt as she had not since her happy and carefree days as a Socialist Youth.

Though past forty, Isabelle was yet a fine looking specimen of womanhood. Typically French, she had retained her slender shape. Her shoulder-length brown hair was untouched by gray. And if her face had a few more wrinkles than it had had as a young college student, the sidelong glances of men old and young told her she had not lost her appeal.

Then it had been the Americans she had protested; them, and the war they had inherited from France. Now it was France she protested against, France and the war it had seemingly inherited from the Americans.

She was sure, *certain*, that it was all the Americans' fault. Had the aliens, these Posleen, attacked Earth first? No. Foolishly, at American behest, the French Army had gone to the stars, looking for trouble and becoming involved in a fruitless war, against a previously unknown alien civilization.

And for what? To save a crumbling federation of galactics?

France's business was here, on Earth, looking after *French* people.

And now they were talking about increased taxes? To help the common people here? Again, no. It was to grease the wheels of the war machine that the money was needed. Isabelle shuddered with revulsion.

More revolting than higher taxes for lesser purposes, the talk was that universal conscription was about to be expanded. She looked at her two young sons, one held with each hand, and vowed she would never permit them to be dragged from her home to be turned into cannon fodder in a stupid and needless war.

Isabelle's voice joined that of the thronging masses. "Peace, now . . . peace, now . . . PEACE, NOW!"

Berlin, Germany, 14 November 2004

Word had spread; Günter had ensured it would spread.

As the chancellor entered the *Bundestag*, Germany's upper

legislative body, he saw a sea of mostly neutral faces, sprinkled with those more hostile or, in a very few cases, even eager. He wasn't sure which group he feared more—the left that was going to raise a cry for his ouster, or the new right that might raise a cry for him to assume a title he loathed, "Führer."

No matter. He could only persevere in his course and hope that the great mass of legislators would see things as he did. To help them see he knew he must show them.

As he took his seat the chancellor made a hand motion. Immediately the lights dimmed. Almost immediately thereafter a movie screen unrolled from the high ceiling.

For the past four days a specially selected team of newsmen and women had been assembling a documentary using mostly American but also some few other sources. It had been America, however, that sensed a need for Germany to continue as an ally, that had been most willing and able to provide the team of German journalists with everything needed to complete their mission.

Nothing had been censored, no holds had been barred. The German legislature was about to be kicked full in their collective teeth with the horror about to descend upon their country.

Annemarie Mai, Green and Socialist representative from Wiesbaden, had been among those unutterably hostile to the *Kanzler's* idea. As the film began to roll she was by no means displeased to see Washington, DC, in ruins. American policies, from their cowboyish adventures in imperialism to their wasteful and destructive energy and environmental policies to—most damning—their insistence on an outdated economic system that had the infuriating habit of making her own preferred statist system seem inefficient; all these made Washington a loathsome symbol of all she despised about America.

Like many in the world, however, Annemarie liked Americans, as people, just as much as she hated their country.

And so her reaction to much of the rest of the film was quite different. Little children gone catatonic with fright at having seen their parents butchered and eaten before their eyes made Annemarie weep. More horrid still were the children not gone into oblivion, the ones shown who screamed and cried continuously. These made the legislator quiver with terror.

And then there were the soldiers, with their sick, dirty and weary faces. They were white enough to seem no different from the boys and girls of Germany. The shrieks of the wounded, especially, tore at Annemarie's heart.

And then came the piles of meat-stripped bones, human bones, along with separate piles of neatly split skulls, some of them very small indeed. These sent Annemarie running for the ladies' room, unable even for a moment longer to keep down her gorge.

"You must think very little of the strength of the democratic spirit in German hearts to be so concerned about the dangers of rejuvenating twenty or twenty-five thousand old men," the chancellor told a group of hecklers, shouting slogans from the gallery.

If his words had any effect on the hecklers it was something less than obvious. Their chants of "No more Nazis. No more Nazis," even seemed to grow a bit in volume and ferocity.

"They were not always old men," answered one of the legislators. "When young, as you propose to make them again, and when armed and organized, as you propose to make them again, they were a menace, fiends, thugs, criminals . . . murderers."

"Not all of them," the chancellor insisted. "Perhaps not even most. Some were drafted into the war. Others found no place in the *Reichswehr* and went, as soldiers will, to whichever military organization they could find that would accept them. And I intend that no one, not even one, who has been convicted, or even reliably accused, of a war crime or a crime against humanity shall be permitted to join."

"They were *all* guilty of crimes against humanity," the legislator returned. "Every one of them who fought in the unjust war this country waged against an innocent world was guilty."

"Were this true," said the chancellor, mildly, "then equally guilty would be Heinz Guderian, Erich Manstein, Erwin Rommel, or Gerd von Rundstedt. They actually did the higher level planning for that war. The people I propose to bring back were low-level players indeed compared to those famous and admired German soldiers."

"They murdered prisoners!" shrieked another legislator.

"In that war *everyone* murdered prisoners."

And so it went, seemingly endlessly. Opponents spoke up; the chancellor answered mildly. Proponents spoke up, usually mildly, and opponents shrieked with fury. In the end it came to a vote . . . and that vote was *very* close.

All eyes turned to the ashen-faced Annemarie Mai as she mounted the speaker's rostrum. The tie was hers to break, one way or the other. With the images of split children's skulls echoing in her brain she announced, "I have conditions."

"Conditions?" asked the chancellor.

"Several," she nodded. "First, these people are the bearers of a disease, a political disease. They must be quarantined to ensure they do not spread their disease."

"To get any use out of them, I have to use them as a cadre for others."

"I understand that," Annemarie answered. "But that group, once filled up to the military body you desire, must be kept as isolated as possible lest the disease spread beyond our ability to control."

"Then we are agreed," the chancellor said.

"Second, they must be watched."

"They will be," the chancellor agreed.

"Third, they must not be allowed to preach their political creed, even in secret."

"The laws against the spread of Nazi propaganda remain in effect and have served us well for decades."

"Fourth, you must *use* them, burn them up, including, I am sorry to say, the young ones we condemn to their 'care.'"

"That much I can *guarantee*."

"Then, I vote yes. Raise your formation, Chancellor."

The peace of the assembly immediately erupted into bitter shouts and curses.

Babenhausen, Germany, 15 November 2004

There is peace in senility, for some. For others, the weakening of the mind with old age brings back harsher memories.

Few or none in the nursing home knew just *how* old the old man was, though, had anyone cared to check, the information was there in his file. Among some of the staff it was rumored he was past one hundred, yet few or none of them cared enough to check that either. Though he was almost utterly bald, shriveled and shrunken and sometimes demented, none of the staff cared about that. The old man spoke but rarely and even more rarely did he seem to speak with understanding. Sometimes, at night, the watch nurse would hear him cry from his room with words like, "*Vorwärts*, Manfred . . . Hold them, *meine Brüder . . .*" or "*Steisse, die Panzer*."

Sometimes, too, the old man would cry a name softly, whisper with regret, hum a few bars of some long-forgotten, perhaps even forbidden, tune.

It was whispered, by those who washed him and those who spoke with the washers, that he had a tattooed number on his torso. They whispered too of the scars, the burns, the puckermarks.

Everyday, rain or shine, bundled up or not as the weather dictated, the staff wheeled the old man out onto the nursing home's porch for a bit of fresh air. This day, the fresh air was cold and heavy, laden with the moisture of falling snow. What dreams or nightmares the cold snow brought, none ever knew—the old man never said.

At the front door to the home, a matron pointed towards the old man. "There he is."

Another man, one of a pair, clad in the leather trench coat that marked him as a member of the *Bundesnachrichtendiest*—the Federal Information Service, Germany's CIA—answered, "We shall take care of him from here on out. You and your home need trouble yourselves no further."

Unseen, the matron nodded. *Alles war in Ordnung.* All was in order. Already the two men had turned their backs on her and focused their attention fully on the old man. They walked up to him, one crouching before the wheelchair, the other standing at the side.

The croucher, he in the trenchcoat, spoke softly. "*Herr Gruppenführer? Gruppenführer* Mühlenkampf? I do not know if you can understand me. But if you can, you are coming with us."

Some faint trace of recognition seemed to dawn in the old man's watery, faded blue eyes.

"Aha," said trench coat. "You *can* understand me, can't you? Understand your name and your old rank anyway. Very good.

Can you understand this, old man? Your country is calling for you again. We have need of you, urgent need."

Berlin, Germany, 17 November 2004

And my, my don't those two seem urgent, mused the patron of the *Gasthaus* nestled in an alley not far from where that patron lived. As was his normal practice, the patron sat in a dim corner, nursing a beer. *And when will the Gestapo, under whatever name they chose to go by, realize that those coats mark them for what they are as clearly as my* Sigrunen—*the twin lightning bolts—used to mark me.*

The objects of the patron's attention walked from table to table, from customer to customer. The Wirt, the owner and manager of the establishment, looked discreetly at the elderly man, dimly lit in a corner. *Shall I tell them?*

The patron shrugged. Macht nichts. *"Matters not."* You know what they are as well as I do. If they want me they will find me.

Nodding his understanding the Wirt called to the two. "If you are looking for *Herr* Brasche, that's him over there in the corner."

The patron, Brasche, watched with interest as the two men approached. When they had reached his table, he raised his beer in salute. "And what can I do for the BND today, gentlemen?"

"Hans Brasche?" one of them asked, flashing an identification.

"That would be me," Hans answered.

"You must come with us."

Brasche smiled. If he was afraid, neither of the men who had accosted him, nor any of the other patrons, would have known it. He had never been a man, or a boy, to show much fear.

Times were hard and getting worse. The calendar on the wall said 1930. As the boy entered the bare cupboarded kitchen, the expression on the mother's face fairly shrieked "fear."

"Your father wants you, Hansi."

The boy, he could not have been more than ten, suppressed a shudder. This was always bad news. He steeled his soul, raised his ten-year-old head, and walked bravely to where his one-armed father—more importantly, the father's belt—awaited him. He knew he could not cry out, could not show fear; else the beating would be worse, much worse.

Afterwards, when the long beating was over, the boy, Hans, walked dry-eyed past his mother, his walk stiff from the bruises, the welts, and the cuts.

The woman reached out to her son, seeking desperately to comfort him in his pain. All she felt was his shudder as her hands stroked his bruises and wounds. "Why, Hansi? What did you do wrong?"

The boy, he was tall for ten but not so tall as his mother, hung his head, buried his face in a maternal bosom and whispered, "I do not know, Mutti. He didn't say. He never says."

"He was never like this before the Great War, Hansi, before he lost the arm."

The boy could not cry, that had long since been beaten out of him. He shrugged. The mother could cry . . . and did.

Later, in a Mercedes, one of the pair said, "I must say, you are a cool one, *Herr* Brasche."

"I am old. I have seen much. I have never seen where being afraid, or showing I was if I was, ever did me or anyone else any good. Would it now?"

The other, the driver, answered, "In this case you have no cause to fear, *Herr* Brasche. We are here to do you a favor."

Hans shrugged. "I have been done favors before. Little good I had of them."

The times had changed. Plenty and hope had replaced hunger and despair. From the windows, from the street lamps, on the arms of men and women all over Germany fluttered a new symbol. On the radios crackled the harsh, gas-damaged voice of a new hero.

Hans felt his thirteen-year-old heart leap at the sound of his Führer's voice speaking via the radio, to the nation.

"Meine alten Kameraden," began the distant Hitler, and Hans felt his one-armed father, standing beside, stiffen with filial love. "Die grosse Zeit ist jetzt angebrochen . . . Deutschland ist nun erwacht . . ." (My old comrades . . . the great time is now brought to pass . . . Germany is now awake.")

"You see, little Hansi? You see what a favor I have done bring-ing you here?"

To that Hans had no honest answer; nothing from his father came without price.

It was a public radio, one with loudspeakers, intended for the address of a crowd. Uniformed HitlerJugend *patrolled, keeping order mainly by disciplined example. Not that much example was needed for Germans of the year of our Lord, 1933; they remained the people who had fought half a world to a standstill from 1914 to 1918. Discipline they had, in plenty.*

The father observed Hans' eyes glancing over the uniformly short-trousered, dagger-wielding, hard-faced and brightly berib-boned youths.

"Ah, you are interested in the Youth Movement, I see, my son. Never fear. I have arranged for you to be accepted a bit early. They'll make a man of you."

Why, how so, father? *thought the boy.* Do they have stiffer belts? What new favors will you show me, I wonder.

Bad Tolz, Germany, 20 November 2004

"Don't do me any fucking favors," snarled Mühlenkampf.

The *Kanzler*—the Chancellor of the German Federal Republic—ceased perusing the picture of the worn and shriveled shell of a wheelchair-bound man in the file on his desk. He looked up sharply at the brand-new, tall, dark-haired, ramrod-backed and broad-shouldered man before him. To the observer, Mühlenkampf, wearing the insignia of a *Bundeswehr* major general, appeared no more than twenty. Despite this, there was a harshness about the man's eyes that spoke of stresses and strains no mere stripling of twenty could ever have undergone.

The chancellor observed, "Amazing, isn't it, Günter, what taking eighty-four years off of someone's life will do for his disposi-tion?"

Mühlenkampf snorted in derision. Quickly and determinedly he lashed out. "Fuck you, *Herr Kanzler*. Fuck all of you civilian bastards. Fuck anybody who had anything to do with dragging me out of that nursing home. Fuck you for giving me a mind back to remember and miss my wife and children with; a mind with which to remember the friends I have lost. Fuck you for sending me back to a war. I've had better than thirteen years of war in my life, *Herr Kanzler*. And never a moment's peace since 1916. I had thought I was finally past that. So fuck you, again."

Halfway through Mühlenkampf's tirade Günter arose from his chair as if to shut this new-old man up. Mühlenkampf's glare, and the chancellor's restraining hand, sent the bureaucrat reeling back to his seat.

The chancellor smiled with indulgence. "You are so full of shit it's coming out of your ears, Mühlenkampf. What is more, you know you are. A 'moment's peace'? Nonsense. The only peace you've ever known was from 1916, when you were first called to the colors, to 1918, when the Great War ended. Then you had some more 'peace' from 1918 to 1923 in the *Freikorps* . . . Oh, yes, I know all about you, Mühlenkampf. And then you found the greatest peace from 1939 to 1945, didn't you? Get off your high horse, *SS* man. War is your peace. And peace is your hell."

Mühlenkampf cocked his head to one side. He tried and failed to keep a small, darting smile from his lips. "You missed one, *Herr Kanzler*. Spain, 1936 to 1939. Unofficially, of course. That was a *fun* time."

The smile broadened. Mühlenkampf laughed aloud. "Very well, *Herr Kanzler*. Whatever you have done to make me young you must have had a reason. What do you want of me? What mission have you for me?"

The chancellor returned the beam. "We have some problems," he admitted. "How far gone were you in that nursing home?"

Mühlenkampf thought briefly, then answered, "I think I was gone back to about 1921. Speaking of which, what year is it? How am I here? How am I *young*? How is it I have my mind back?"

"*Ach*, where to begin? The year is 2004." Seeing the former officer's surprise, the chancellor continued, "Yes, General Mühlenkampf, you are a sprightly one hundred and four years old. As to *how* you have the body and mind of a twenty-year-old? That is an interesting tale."

The *Kanzler* had long since decided to be direct; Mühlenkampf was known to have been a direct man. "We are about to be invaded, General."

"Germany?" bristled the new-old man. "The Fatherland is in danger?"

"*Everyone* is in danger," answered the chancellor. "The planet Earth is about to be attacked . . . actually has already been . . . by alien beings, creatures from space. As I said they have already begun to land, in the United States and—"

"Bah! Ami trash. And aliens? From space? *Herr Kanzler*, please? I was born at night, but it was not last night."

"Not so trashlike, Mühlenkampf. Restrain your prejudices; the last war is long over. And the Ami's, at least, utterly defeated the first invasion to hit them. Not everyone can say that. Though it cost the Americans frightfully. As for when you were born . . . well, you were reborn about thirty minutes ago. Contemplate, why don't you, the implications of that?"

"Ah," agreed Mühlenkampf, contemplatively.

"But, in any case," continued the chancellor, "those first landings were small-scale affairs, comparatively speaking. What we are facing, commencing in as little as eight months, are five more invasions, each of them ten to fifteen times more massive. You will be briefed in much greater detail on the nature and numbers of the enemy after we are finished here."

Mühlenkampf shrugged. He could wait for the details.

The chancellor interlaced his hands in front of his face. "We have a problem though. It is not too much detail for now to tell you that these five coming invasions will come with weapons superior to ours or that they are mostly . . . infantry of a sort. They will have complete command of the air and space. Each will muster from ninety million to as many as two hundred million combatants."

"That does sound dire, *Herr Kanzler*. Five or ten *thousand* infantry divisions."

The chancellor had done his time. He knew Mühlenkampf was miscalculating based on human norms for combat forces. The chancellor sighed. "No. They have no support forces to consider. One million of these beings—they are called 'Posleen,' by the way—means one million combatants. So no, not thirty or forty or even fifty infantry divisions per million. We are talking about the equivalent of about one hundred thousand infantry divisions, but infantry divisions from a warped scientist's nightmares, dropping on our heads, all of our heads of course, over the next five years.

And we have reason to believe, based on the way these beings act, that Europe's share will be greater than that of any similarly sized area of the globe—say twenty percent, with the possible exception of what may hit the United States'"

Mühlenkampf considered, then objected, "But that is impossible, *Herr Kanzler*. No military force can organize like that. How would they feed themselves?"

The chancellor shuddered, remembering piles of small and gnawed bones in the snow. He shuddered and then found the impulse to enjoy giving the shock. "Why Mühlenkampf, they eat *us*, of course."

Even the hardened SS general was taken aback by that grim news. "You are joking. You cannot possibly be serious. One hundred thousand infantry divisions, advanced over anything we have? Maybe twenty thousand of them against us? With complete dominance of air and space? And they will eat us, eat everyone, if we lose?"

"Not 'if we lose,' Mühlenkampf. When."

Günter, so far quietly sitting at the chancellor's side, began to raise an objection, before being hushed by the chancellor. "'When,' I said, Günter, and 'when' is what I meant. Nothing but that kind of desperation would make me put General Mühlenkampf back in uniform. Though I concede there are degrees of losing, some better than others."

Turning back to the veteran, the chancellor continued, "We let ourselves go, Mühlenkampf. You knew the Communists had fallen?"

"I remember thinking, *Kanzler*, back when I still had some faculties for it, that although the Communists may have gone under I could no longer tell the difference between a Red Russian and a Green German."

Günter, a committed Green and a Social Democrat bridled at that.

The chancellor's party drew much of its support from the Greens. Even so, he had to admit, and would admit it only to himself, that there had once been little difference between the two, at least at the *extremes* of both movements. And yet . . .

"General, we Germans are packed into this country like rats. Do you want someone pissing in your drinking water? Well, every piss every German takes ends up there, you know. Do you want our children born deformed and retarded by the things industry dumps in our rivers, or would if we let them? Do you not think we need trees to make oxygen for us to breathe? And if you like to hunt, General, or to hike to enjoy the natural beauty of our country, do you not think those very animals and woodland scenes need a little protection?"

Mühlenkampf shrugged his indifference. "A political fanatic is dangerous no matter if he wants to hang capitalists or to gas Jews or to make economic life impossible, *Herr Kanzler.*"

"I am no fanatic, SS man," bridled Günter.

"Neither am I, bureaucrat," answered Mühlenkampf, coolly. "I am a soldier and I rather doubt the chancellor brought me here to discuss politics. But to my mind a Red fanatic and a Green fanatic are indistinguishable. And Germany has had more than enough of both."

Ah, well, I didn't resurrect this man for his modern sensibilities, thought the chancellor. He continued, "Yes . . . well, be that as it may, after the Cold War ended we, all of us really, chopped our military forces to the bone. Let most of the rest be politicized, demoralized and castrated, too. Why, did you know, Mühlenkampf, that there is a law here now forbidding our soldiers from wearing their dress uniforms in public lest it upset certain types of *Gastarbeiter.*[4]" The chancellor sighed with personal regret. Currying favor with the left at the time he, himself, had voted for that law.

"All of Germany, before this came up, could field, at most, seven mediocre divisions. Of these, one was almost entirely destroyed on another planet. Filling up that division's losses, and expanding the remaining six upwards to about six hundred divisions, has proven impossible. We have the weapons; that or we soon will. We have the manpower . . . available at least. We do not have the trained cadre. We have called up and rejuvenated every combat veteran of the last war we could find except for you and people like you. And now . . ."

"And now," Mühlenkampf continued, sensing the truth, "now you need *us.*"

"Yes. Your country needs you. Your people need you. Your species needs you."

"What will I have to work with?" asked the former SS man.

"We will fill you up with bodies, good ones, from among the

young men we have. For your cadre there are enough, just enough, rejuvenated SS men to make a decent group for a large *Korps*, about five divisions plus support."

Mühlenkampf thought immediately of a problem. "You wish to give us regular division numbers? The 413th '*Volksgrenadiers*' or something on that order? Regular *Bundeswehr* uniforms?" The general shook his head, "*Herr Kanzler*, that won't work."

"Why not?"

Mühlenkampf shrugged. "It is hard to explain, perhaps. But take me, for example. I was like Paul Hauser . . . or Felix Steiner,[5] for that matter. I was a regular first and joined the SS not out of any political convictions, but simply to be in an elite combat organization. And to fight, of course. I think few of the other ranks had very strong National Socialist political convictions, though some did. But one thing we all shared was a pride in the symbols for what they said about us as battle soldiers."

Mühlenkampf sighed. "And then, of course, we lost the war. Rather badly, as a matter of fact. We went from the top of the heap to the despised of Germany, of the world. Our symbols became shit. People turned their faces away. Our wounded veterans were denied the pensions and care given to other branches of the *Wehrmacht* not one whit less guilty—whatever guilt means in such contexts as the Russian Front—than we were.

"We lost our pride." The veteran finished, "And soldiers cannot fight without pride."

This time Günter was not to be silenced. "Your *Hakenkreutzer*?[6] Your *Sigrunen*?"[7] he shouted. "Your Death's Heads? Those symbols you will *never* be allowed to show."

Mühlenkampf buffed fingernails nonchalantly against his left breast for some long moments. All the time he fixed the aide with a deadly stare. "Little man, do not try me. The SS told Himmler and Hitler—and they had the power to have us shot out of hand—to go fuck themselves so often, so many times, I have lost count. We fought the Russian hordes to a standstill across half a continent. We charged into American and British airpower and naval gunfire without demur . . . even without hope. When all was lost we were still fighting, because that is what we did. *Never* think, little man, not for an *instant*, that we can be intimidated by such as *you*," he ended, sneering.

"Peace, gentlemen," calmed the chancellor. "Mühlenkampf,

Günter is right to a degree. While, I assure you, there are some people, especially down in Bavaria,"—the chancellor rolled his eyes heavenward—"who would welcome the return of the SS with cheers, most of our people would turn away. Moreover, my own political support might well melt away. I cannot let you have all your symbols. Is there something else?"

Mühlenkampf considered. "Our medals? Reissue them, perhaps in a slightly different design?"

The chancellor wriggled his fingers dismissively and said, "We already are, after a fashion." Then he thought of the casualty lists from the planet Diess, transferred his wriggling fingers to tap his lips and added, "Mostly posthumously, I'm afraid. Yes, we can do this."

"And division names," bargained Mühlenkampf. "Give us any numbers you want. But let us go by our old division names."

"What?" snorted Günter. "LSSAH? *Leibstandarte* SS Adolf Hitler?"

"We had other divisions," answered the general, coolly. "*Wiking*? No crimes to speak of to their name. Götz von Berlichingen? A clean record there, too. You said five divisions, *Herr Kanzler*? Okay . . . Wiking, G von B . . . Not Hitler *Jugend* but just *Jugend*? *Hohenstauffen*? *Frundsberg*? Yes, those five. No crimes there except one attributed to *Jugend* but as likely to have been committed by 21st, be it noted, *Wehrmacht*, Panzer Division. And maybe use some of the others as independent brigades within the *Korps*.

"Yes, *Herr Kanzler*. The medals, the names . . . uniforms a bit different than the norm. Maybe even the *Sigrunen* after we have shown what we can do? It is not much to ask for and I can build, rebuild rather, some pride with them."

Mühlenkampf's face lit with a sudden smile. "There is one other thing, *Herr Kanzler*. The SS was perhaps the most cosmopolitan armed force in history, certainly the most cosmopolitan force of its size. We had battalions, regiments, brigades and divisions of Dutch, Belgians, French, Danes, Swedes, Latvians, Estonians . . . damned near every nationality in Europe. We even had control for a while, though they were not part of us, of one Spanish Division, the Spanish Azul, or Blue, Division. Moslems? Lots. I have no doubt but that, had we won the war and some of the Reichsheini's[8] wilder schemes for a Jewish Homeland come to pass that there would eventually have been a brigade of the Waffen

SS that would have sported armbands reading, 'Judas Maccabeus.' Yes, I am serious," the former SS general concluded.

"Your point?" queried the chancellor.

"Just this. Put out the word. Rather, let me put out the word, and we might have a few more former SS men for cadre than you think. And perhaps some new volunteers as well."

"What do you get out of this, *Herr General*?" asked Günter querulously.

"Something you would never understand, bureaucrat."

Berlin, Germany, 22 November 2004

Not even the view of the stunning, busty and leggy blonde gracing the Tir's[9] reception room could lift Günter's spirits. Appalled beyond measure and beyond endurance by the chancellor's decision to resurrect—even in muted form—the hated Waffen SS, the bureaucrat had decided to do the unthinkable, to give his support to the nominally allied but, he was sure, secretly hostile, Darhel.

Still, the SS? It was intolerable. And that the chancellor had ignored him? Insulting.

Worse, Günter was certain, the chancellor would not stop with the SS. With the SS in hand, owing their allegiance to the Chancellor, the bureaucrat could foresee another dark age for Germany. To date, the *Kanzler* had depended upon a loose coalition of moderate and left political streams. With the reborn SS in hand, might he not cast aside that dependence? Günter desperately feared it might prove so.

Remilitarization was not the least of it. How Günter had fought to keep the conscription laws somewhat ineffective. Surely no threat could justify dragging unwilling and enlightened young boys from their homes and subjecting them to the brainwashing that, he had no doubt, was the military's stock in trade. How else but through brainwashing could the military convince sensible young men to do something so plainly not in their personal interest?

Günter, himself, had done his "social year"[10] in something useful to society, assisting in a drug rehabilitation program. He had not wasted that year in some atavistic pandering to a spirit long obsolete.

The future seemed dark, dark.

Günter's reveries were interrupted by the blond receptionist. "The Tir will see you now, *mein Herr.*"

Upon entering the Tir's office Günter was surprised to see several political allies also present, along with one soldier. Their chairs were gathered in a semicircle in front of the Darhel's massive desk.

The Tir's German was grammatically excellent, though tinged with a lisp caused by air passing between his sharklike teeth. Even with the lisp, Günter had no difficulty understanding the alien when he said, "Please, *Herr* Stössel, do sit. I am somewhat surprised to see you after you refused our last offer."

Taking the chair indicated by the alien's pointing finger, Günter sat silently for a long moment. When, finally, he spoke he said, "When I refused your offer it was before the chancellor decided to turn Germany into a Fascist state again. Better we should be destroyed than release *that* horror again upon the world."

In a voice so tinged with vehemence and hate that he was nearly spitting, one of the other humans interjected, "Germany has always been a Fascist state."

Günter ignored the speaker. He was himself a Green and while, yes, there was a strong leftist trend within the Green movement, the speaker, Andreas Dunkel was an outright Red. Every time Günter thought upon the ten *trillion* marks so far spent on trying to undo the ecological damage the Communists had done to the east of the country, he bristled. Even that enormous sum was inadequate; only time could heal the wounds inflicted on Mother Earth by the Communists.

He bristled now too but, suppressing it, turned his full attention back to the Tir.

"Your species is dangerous," the Tir said, "and among your species your people are perhaps the most dangerous of all. While the Federation needs you now, in the long run you are as much a danger to civilization as are the Posleen."

The Tir judged his audience well. Indeed, he had a very complete file on Günter Stössel downloaded into his AID, the Artificial Intelligence Devices only the Darhel produced. Much of Günter's wait in the reception area had been the result of the time the Tir had needed to study the file.

"The Galactic Federation is a peaceful place, or was before this invasion," said the Tir, honestly. "Moreover, it is a place where resources are carefully guarded. We produce few goods but of high quality; this is how we keep our ecologies pure." This last was true enough, but the truth concealed a greater falsehood. Galactic civilization kept resource expenditure low by more or less literally starving the Indowy who made up the bulk of its population, produced the bulk of its admittedly excellent products, and had the least share of its power.

At this point, truth fled for . . . *greener* pastures. "We care for our planets," the Tir lied. "Our projections show that, were humans to be let loose onto the galactic scene, ecological disaster would follow quickly. We cannot allow this. And yet we need your people to defend our civilization. It is a difficult problem."

"What can I do to help?" Günter asked.

Had the Tir had the slightest clue he was being overheard, no doubt his lies would have been even more carefully couched. So thought Deputy Assistant Clan Coordinator, and Bane Sidhe[11] operative, Rinteel.

Listening to the conversation between the Tir, Günter, and the others in the Tir's office, Rinteel's mind kept revolving around one word. *Agendas. The Darhel have one. The humans have another. We have still a third. But ours at least leaves the humans free and frees us. Surely they will be difficult to deal with, so violent, so aggressive, so selfish as they are. And yet, so long as the Posleen exist and are a threat, they will need us . . . to produce their machines of war, to maintain them. They will dominate us, no doubt. Yet my people can have a future in every way brighter under human dominance than ever we have under the overlordship of the Elves. The humans, at least, have some sense of fairness. The Elves have none.*

The conversation in the Tir's office was very difficult for Rinteel to follow. The office was bug proof, the Indowy knew. He had tried to bug it but, alas, without success. The Darhel's AID, unlike those given to the humans so lavishly, was untappable, at least by any means available to the Bane Sidhe.

But every gate has its fence, every rat hole its exit. In this case it was simple sound. Coming from the speakers' voice boxes, the sound vibrated the walls of the Tir's office. These walls in turn caused the air of the surrounding rooms to move. This air, it its own turn, vibrated other walls. In time—and space—the very exterior of the building moved, oh slightly, slightly.

And nearby, and in direct line of sight, a Bane Sidhe listening post picked up those vibrations. A Bane Sidhe computer, constructed by the Indowy but designed and programmed by Tchpth, the deep-thinking "Crabs," painfully translated these vibrations into speech. The translation required intimate knowledge of each speaker's voice. The slightest thing could upset it; a cold, a sore throat. And with new speakers the machine was hopeless until examples of their speech could be obtained.

Thus, while one of the speakers, a new voice, was beyond the computer, the words of the Tir came through clearly.

Listening carefully to the sometimes garbled translation, Rinteel thought, *I must speak with the ruler of these people. Alone.*

INTERLUDE

"What is it about this place, these thresh, that puts them so far forward on the Path of Fury?" asked Athenalras of Ro'moloristen.

"That remains unclear, my lord. The records we have gleaned indicate only great, fearsome ability on the path. Well..." The junior hesitated.

"Yes," demanded Athenalras, crest extending unconsciously.

"Well, my lord...the thresh records indicate great, perhaps unparalleled ability in war...but almost always followed by ultimate defeat."

"Bah. Great ability. Great defeats. Make up your mind, puppy."

Carefully keeping his crest in a flaccid and submissive posture, Ro'moloristen hesitated before answering. "My lord...in this case I think the two may just go together. A defeat seems not to stop or deter these gray thresh. They always come back, *always*, from however stinging a loss, and they are *always* willing to try again."

The senior snorted. "Let them come back after they have passed through our digestive systems."

CHAPTER 2

Kraus-Maffei-Wegmann Plant, Munich, Germany,
27 December 2004

Karl Prael, a goateed, heavyset man of indeterminate years, closed the massive vault door against the ear-splitting and mind-numbing sounds of a tank factory on a frenzy of production. A country that had turned from producing a few hundred tanks a year to over one thousand per month could no longer worry about the niceties of noise-pollution-control measures. The workers in the plant, the much-expanded plant, put on protective ear muffs and soldiered on.

Outside of the plant, of course—this being Germany, Germany being Green, and many—though not all—of the Green leadership having sold out to the Darhel, there was a continuous noisy protest against the plant, the projects it housed, the war effort, the draft . . . the name-your-left-leaning cause.

The din inside the vault was little better.

Prael had come to the project team from a cutting-edge software company. His job was fairly easy, or straightforward at least: produce a software and hardware package to control a light-cruiser-sized tank mounting a single heavy-cruiser-sized gun. This he could do; had nearly done, as a matter of fact. But the rest of the team . . .

"A railgun! A railgun, I say. Nothing else will do. Nothing else will give us the range, the velocity, the rate of fire, the ammunition storage capability, the . . ."

Ah, Johannes Mueller is heard from again, thought Prael.

"Then give me a railgun," demanded Henschel, pounding the desk in fury, and not for the first time. "Tell me how to build one. Tell me how to keep it from arcing and burning out. Tell me how to generate the power. And tell me how to do those things *now!*"

"Bah!" retorted Mueller. "All of those things can be fixed. Half the problem in engineering is merely defining the problem. And you just have."

"Yes," agreed Henschel. "but the other half is fixing it and for that there is no time."

"We do not know there isn't time," insisted Mueller.

"And, my friend," said Henschel, relenting, "we do not know that there is time, either."

Mueller sighed in reluctant agreement. No, they didn't know if there was going to be time.

"If you gentlemen are finished shouting at each other?" queried Prael.

Mueller turned his back on Henschel, throwing his hands in the air. "Yes, Karl?"

"I have some news; several pieces actually. The first is this," and with that Prael began handing around copies of a small, stapled sheaf of paper. "The decision on specs has been made. This is it, and we are going to design it."

An elderly gentlemen, bearded and face lined and seamed with years spent in the outdoors looked over the sheaf. "They've rejected the idea of powering every idler, have they?"

"Yes, Franz, they have. They have also . . ." and Prael gave a brief and irritated moment's thought to the thousands of Greens protesting outside the plant, " . . . they have also rejected powering the thing with a nuclear reactor."

"What? That's preposterous," interjected Reinhard Schlüssel, the team's drive train and power plant designer. "We can't power this thing with anything less than nuclear. That or antimatter."

"We can, we must, we will," answered Mueller. "Natural gas. We can do this."

"I see they have at least accepted the use of MBA"—molybdenum, boron, aluminum—"armor," observed Stephan Breitenbach from where he sat by a paper-laden desk. "That's something."

"*Limited* MBA, Stephan. The stuff is too expensive and too difficult to manufacture to do more than reinforce the basic metal."

Breitenbach shrugged off Henschel's comment. Something was better than nothing. And the weight saved did suggest that natural gas would be an acceptable fuel.

"There is one more bit of news, quite possibly bad," observed Prael with an evil grin. "They are sending us an advisor. Well, two of them actually. One is a man, just back from the Planet Diess, an *Oberst*[12] Kiel. He'll be along in a few weeks at most. The other is—"

The vault door opened. In, stiffly and commandingly, stepped a tall, slender man, dressed in *Bundeswehr* gray under black leather, and sporting the insignia for a lieutenant general of *Panzertruppen*. But the officer seemed much too young to be . . .

" . . . Gentlemen, I am pleased to introduce to you *Generalleutnant* Walter Mühlenkampf, late of the *Reichswehr*, the *Freikorps*, *la Armada de España*, the *Wehrmacht*, and the Waffen SS. Now he slurps at the *Bundeswehr* trough. I see you found your own way, *Herr General*."

Berlin, Germany, 28 December 2004

The *Kanzler* had not yet come. It seemed impossible that he should be lost in this, his city.

As much as an Indowy could fume, Rinteel fumed. *A complete lunar cycle of this people's time I have sought a private conversation with the ruler of these Germans. How many will die for that lack of time? How much more is the cause, are the* causes, *imperiled?*

His human . . . guards? Yes, they were obviously guards. Even so they treated him with indifference. Strangely, this made the solid little, green furred, bat-faced form more comfortable, rather than less. Nothing on this world was better guaranteed to send an Indowy, even a brave one—and Rinteel was regarded among his people as preternaturally bold, into a panic as the sight of those bared carnivore fangs the locals used as a sign of pleasure.

Fortunately, the humans of the BND never smiled. Thus, the Indowy had only to deal with their single-mindedness, their barely suppressed innate violence. This was quite job enough.

In the presence of these barbarian carnivores, Rinteel could not even work out his frustrations with pacing. He could only wait patiently for the Chancellor to arrive.

Bad Tolz, Germany, 28 December 2004

In this out of the way *Kaserne*, home at different times to elite units ranging from German *Schützstaffeln* to American Special Forces, Hans Brasche looked skeptically over ranks of recently arrived, rabbit-frightened recruits shuffling forward in lines to be assigned to their quarters and their training units.

They look bigger and healthier than my generation did. But then I suppose they have eaten better than we did. No Depression for them, no lingering effects of the long British Blockade. The Wirtschaftswunder[13] did them well.

Yet their eyes seem watery, the complexions sallow. There is no toughness in them, no hardness. Too much fat. How are we to make bricks without straw?

Hans glanced away from his charges and looked around the *Kaserne. The Americans kept the old home up well. It has not changed much*, thought he. *Not since I was here as a boy of twenty.*

"*Und so, you wish to become officers of the Waffen SS, do you?*" demanded the harsh looking Oberscharsführer *of the stiffly standing ranks of* Junkerschule[14] *hopefuls.*

I want nothing, *thought Hans Brasche, carefully silent.* Nothing except that my father not beat my mother for my failings that he attributes to her. He would have me here, not I. But for her sake, here I must be.

"*To become worthy to lead the men of the SS*," continued the noncom, "*you must become harder than Krupp's steel, more pitiless than an iceberg, immovable like the mountains that surround us.*" The NCO gestured grandly at the Bavarian Alps clutching at every side.

"*There is no room in the SS for divided loyalties. So all among you who have not yet left the church stand forward.*"

Hans, along with rather more than half his class, obediently stepped forward. From behind the Senior NCO marched forward a number of juniors—beefy men, every one of them.

Hans never saw the fist that laid him out.

✧　✧　✧

That won't work here, he thought, coming back to the present for a time. *These kids hardly know of the concept of a God. Unless, perhaps, it resides between their girlfriends' legs . . . or is to be seen on the television. They have no innocence . . . no naiveté. They have no symbols. They seem to have neither hope nor faith. Not in anything.*

Bricks without straw.

Perhaps the general will have an answer. We have a few days yet.

Berlin, Germany, 28 December 2004

"I have the answers you have sought, *Herr Bundeskanzler,*" Rinteel said, simply.

Long, long had the Indowy waited. Long had he been forced to push away and conceal his terror at the near presence of so many vicious carnivores. When the chancellor had finally—in secret—arrived, the Indowy was filled with relief. *Here,* at least was one barbarian who did not completely tower over him. Though the white-haired "politician's" smile was even more fearful than the blank stares of his guardians.

"What answers, Indowy Rinteel? What answers when I do not have even the questions?"

Rinteel forced his eyes to the chancellor's face, no mean feat for one of his people. His face twisted into the mode, *Honesty in Word and Deed,* automatically, though he knew the human could not recognize or understand it.

"Then let me offer the questions, *Herr Bundeskanzler.* Why, when faced with an invasion nearly certain to exterminate your people, does your political opposition resist every attempt to improve your chances of survival? Why, when the Posleen will extinguish most of your world and pollute the rest with alien life forms, do those most concerned with maintaining the ecological purity of your world do all in their power to undermine your defenses? Why, when the coming enemy is so powerful, are even your military leaders—some of them—so slow to push the rearmament, so almost incredibly incompetent in its execution? Why do those most in love with the notion of state control of your economy, high taxes and centralized planning, resist using these very means to assist your people's survival?"

The BND guards' faces assumed a somber and even angry mien. To this the Indowy was immune. *At least they are not baring those flesh-rending fangs.*

"I have considered these things," admitted the chancellor.

"Then consider these as answers," said Rinteel, handing over a human-compatible computer disk. "And consider that you should trust no one. This disk contains less than all of the information. There is someone, perhaps close to you, whose words we could not decipher."

"I understand," said the chancellor, though in truth he did not, not fully.

"I hope you do," Rinteel answered. "For, if you do not, you will have little time in which to do so."

Kraus-Maffei-Wegmann Plant, Munich, Germany, 28 December 2004

"And how long will you be here with us, *Herr General*?"

Mühlenkampf answered, "A few days at most, this time. And I shall return from time to time. I am, of course, always available for consultation, should I be needed. I have been studying up on modern systems ever since I came out of rejuvenation."

"Very good," returned Prael. "And added to your vast combat experience, we expect to produce something quite remarkable. Would you like to meet the rest of the team?"

"By all means. Please introduce them. And show me the plans."

"Plans first then, I think. And while I am at it I will introduce the team members responsible for each part." Prael directed Mühlenkampf's eyes to a table upon which stood a model of a tank.

"Nice appearance, anyway," muttered the general noncommittally.

"Oh, it will be more than appearance, *Herr General*," answered Prael. "This is going to be, by at least two orders of magnitude, the most powerful panzer ever to roll."

"We will see what we will see," commented Mühlenkampf. "Why this absurdly long gun?"

"Johann?"

Mueller stepped forward. "Because they wouldn't listen to me about a railgun, *Herr General*."

Prael snorted. Mueller never missed a chance.

"You must forgive me," said Mühlenkampf, "but what is a railgun?"

"My pet project . . . and dream," answered Mueller. "It's a weapon that passes electricity along two bars. The electricity creates a magnetic field. The field catches, and then propels forward at great speed, a projectile."

"This is possible?" queried the general, realizing instantly the potential of such a weapon.

"Possible," admitted Henschel, introducing himself. "It is possible, General Mühlenkampf, but not possible just *yet*."

Mueller shrugged. "In time. A year or so, maybe. Okay, maybe two," he admitted, looking at Henschel's scorning face. "In any case, Henschel here is right. It will not be ready quite in time. What you see, General Mühlenkampf, is a three hundred five millimeter gun, much lengthened over its one hundred twenty millimeter predecessor, and using an American-designed propellant system. Since I can't have my railgun, I am reduced to designing the recoil system for this one. Also, since the specialties are somewhat similar, I oversee the design of the suspension with Herr Schlüssel here."

"Reinhard Schlüssel," introduced the bent-over, gnomelike veteran of the German Navy. "It is also my job to design the turret for the tank. Though Benjamin here has been of inestimable value."

Mühlenkampf cocked his head. "Benjamin?"

"David Benjamin," answered the only truly swarthy man in the room. "Of Tel Aviv," he continued coldly, so as to keep a hostile note out of his voice. "I am here on loan from Israeli Military Industries. We intend to build a few of these ourselves, and to purchase several more."

The time for apologies passed before they ever became fully due, thought Mühlenkampf. *None I could make would make up for anything.*

Instead he answered, merely, "Very good. I have been most impressed with the design for all four versions of your

5

Merkava panzer. Sensible. Wise. I am pleased you are here, Herr Benjamin."

The Israeli shrugged as if to say, *It would please me more were you displeased to see me, SS man.*

Filling the stony silence that followed, Prael said, "Indeed, you can see the ancestry of the tank in the Merkava."

"Yes," agreed Mühlenkampf, glad for any bridge over the impasse. "That pushed-back turret especially. How big is this thing?"

"The Tiger Drei," answered Henschel, finally naming the project, "Is twelve meters wide, thirty-one meters long and weighs approximately seventeen hundred and fifty tons, fully combat loaded. It is very heavily armored."

"*Mein Gott!*" exclaimed the general, the implications of the size of the scaled-down gun on the model finally sinking in. "What could possibly drive the need for such a monstrosity?"

"Come here, *Herr General*, and I shall show you the answer," answered Henschel, unveiling several models of Posleen landing and attack craft.

Bad Tolz, 3 January 2005

The general also *did* have an answer; though the answer was not one designed to please his nominal political masters, or—most particularly—some elements of their support.

The new recruits had been herded, cattlelike, to stand in the freezing snow in the middle of the *Kaserne*. There they stood, shivering and miserable in thin uniforms, unmarked save for a small flag of black, red and gold sewn on each sleeve. Suddenly, as if on command . . . indeed *on* command . . . from around the perimeter of the parade field lit spotlights, climbing and meeting overhead to form an arch or, perhaps better said, a cone, composed of dozens, scores, of spears of light.

The startled recruits flinched, unmilitarily, but the rejuvenated SS cadre scattered loosely around them took no official notice. Then they heard music . . . and the singing. . . .

Mühlenkampf, Brasche at his side, stood in warm black leathers under the same cone as the recruits though yet he remained apart from them by decades and even worlds. He suppressed a grin. Icy cold was his mien, as icy as the air.

Face still a mask, he asked of Brasche, "Do you know why, my Hansi, the skinheads never really got anywhere, politically, in Germany?"

Hans whispered back, "No, *Herr Obergruppenführer...*"

"Lieutenant General, Hansi. Lieutenant General," corrected Mühlenkampf, gently yet with a sardonic grin he made no effort to keep from his face. "Our masters do not like the old ways."

"*Zu Befehl, Herr Generalleutnant,*" answered Brasche, semiautomatically.

Mühlenkampf's grin remained, becoming, if anything, more scornful still.

"The skinheads never got anywhere, Hansi," continued the general, "because this is Germany and the assholes never learned to march in step..."

" ... *Marschieren im Geist, in unsern Reihen mit...*"[15] sang the marching men, boots ringing on the ice and cobblestones. Even now the first veterans became visible to the neck-craning recruits as their serried ranks passed through the gates of the Kaserne. "*Die Strasse frei!...*" The song was forbidden, of course. "*Ganz Verboten.*" But to men who had told Hitler and Himmler to go "fuck themselves" not once, but on countless occasions, what meant the strictures of a government weaker and in every way even more despised? "*Die Fahne hoch! Die Reihen fest geschlossen...*"[16] began the song's last, repeat, verse.

In the ranks of the old SS sang one Helmut Krueger. How good it was to Krueger, how very good, to once again feel the blood of youth coursing in his veins. How good to march with his old comrades, to sing the old songs. How good it was to be what Krueger had never thought himself to be any other than, an unrepentant, anti-Semitic, Nazi of the old school.

Krueger dreamed, daydreamed actually, of a broad-scale return of the old days. He imagined once more the cringing Jewish, Slavic and Gypsy whores opening their buttocks, legs and lips in fear of him. The power was an intoxicant. He saw, with half a mind's eye, the cowards, suspended by their necks from lamp posts, kicking and gasping and choking out their last. Even the memory caused him to shiver slightly with delight. He heard the

"*Heils*" coming from ten thousand throats and the sound was better than good. He remembered how grand he had felt at losing the self and joining such a godlike power. He saw the flaming towns and smiled. He heard the screams from the gas chambers and crematoria and shuddered with a nearly sexual joy.

Krueger was sure that after decades of exile he was at last coming home.

Missing his home, Dieter Schultz, aged eighteen, along with the other recruits, shuffled nervously in the cold snow. One would have thought that the boys would never have heard the songs, this being Germany, rules being rules. And, indeed, know the songs they did not. Yet they recognized them.

Dieter and the rest knew, absolutely *knew*, that that song, in particular, was against the law, against the rules. Soon the *Polizei* would come and break up this had-to-be illegal gathering. Soon, minutes at most, these damned refugees-from-the-grave Nazis would all be arrested and shortly thereafter the reluctant recruits would be sent home to mama. They *knew*.

Mühlenkampf tapped his left boot toe unconsciously as the column of thousands of old-young veterans even now split to envelop the boys in their charge. The music and the song changed, the veterans singing in voices and tones designed to knock birds dead at a mile:

> "*Unser Fahne flattert uns voran.*
> *Unser Fahne ist die neue Zeit.*
> *Und die Fahne führt uns in die Ewigkeit.*
> *Ja, die Fahne ist mehr als der Tod.*"[17]

Mühlenkampf, suddenly conscious of the tapping boot, forced it to a stop. "Ah, I've always liked that one, I confess, Hansi. Why I remember . . ." yet the thought was lost, uncompleted.

With a ruffle of drums and a flourish of horns the song ended. Still, the marching feet beat out a tattoo on the icy pavement: *crunch, crunch, crunch, crunch.* Sparks were struck by hobnails grating on bare stone. The sparks clustered about the men's feet, adding a surreal air to the proceedings.

Brasche stepped forward to the microphone. "Men of the

SS *Korps . . . halt.*" The marching feet took one more step, then slammed to a simultaneous halt. "*Links und rechts . . . Um.*"[18] The enveloping pincers turned inward as though they were parts of a single, sentient, beast. "*Generalleutnant Mühlenkampf sprache.*"[19]

Hans Brasche stepped back from the microphone, sharply, as the black-leather-clad Mühlenkampf walked forward.

Mühlenkampf's head twisted back and cocked proudly, arrogantly. "I speak first to my old comrades, who need no speeches. Well met, my friends, well met. We have shaken a world before, together. We shall shake several more worlds before we are done."

The proud head looked down its straight, aristocratic nose at the new recruits. "I speak next to those who are here to join us. Filth! You are nothing and less than nothing. Unfit, weak, malingering, decadent . . . Refuse of a society turned to garbage. Spoiled rotten little huddlers at apron strings.

"You make me ill. You make your trainers, my cadre, ill. You are a disgrace to your species, a disgrace to your culture . . . a disgrace to our nation and traditions."

Mühlenkampf's face creased with the smallest of smiles. "And yet we, we old fighters, have another tradition. We are, to paraphrase an English poet, charms 'for making riflemen from mud.'

"Regimental commanders, take charge of your regiments."

On cue, the band struck up Beethoven's "*Yorkische Marsch.*" The icy field rang with crisp commands. Units faced and wheeled. Even the new recruits, smarting under a brief and contemptuous tongue lashing, could not help but be forced into step by the march's heavy, ponderous refrain. As a long and twisting snake, the column marched out from under the tent of light to enter the world of darkness.

As the last companies were disappearing into the dark, Brasche asked, "So you think this will work, *Herr General*?"

Mühlenkampf snorted as if the very thought struck him as ridiculous. "This speech? Some lights? A little insulting language? A little showmanship? Do I think these will *work*? Hansi, *spare* me. Nothing 'works' in that sense. The easy transformation, like the nonsensically—impossibly—successful spontaneous mass uprising, are bugaboos of the left, of the liberals and of the Reds and the Greens.

"Ah, but Hansi, they forget something, those Reds and Greens. Several things, really. Germany was no less decadent, divided and weak in the 1920s. I was there. I remember. Yet we shook the world in the '40s. Why? Because transformations like that are as superficial and shallow as they are easy. Those boys down there are Germans, Hansi—lemmings, in other words.

"Lemmings, they are, Hansi. Germans: mindless herd animals, at best." The brief and indulgent smile was replaced in turn by a feral grin. Mühlenkampf slapped Brasche heartily on the shoulder, adding, "But they'd rather be in a pack than a herd, my friend . . . a pack of wolves."

INTERLUDE

The boarding hordes snarled and snapped at each other as their God Kings herded them from the lighters and down into the storage bowels of the still forming globe. From one or another of the confused and frightened normals crocodilian teeth lashed out whenever followers of a different Kessentai came in range. Sometimes the needle-sharp rows of teeth drew yellowish blood and scraps of reptilian flesh before their wielders were lashed back to passive obedience.

Not for the first time, Ro'moloristen felt his own bile rise, his crest expand. Half of this was the result of dim, presentient memories of his own time in the breeding pens, a time of constant struggle and fear of being eaten alive by his siblings. The other half was more pungent.

The normals tended to lose control when upset or frightened. The crude loading and unloading, coupled with the strangeness of space flight, was more than sufficient to upset most of them and to actually frighten many, even as dull as they were. The result of that fear was a stench of carelessly dropped Posleen feces wafting up from the depths of the lighters to fill the air. In that section of the globe the loading of which it was the young God King's task to supervise, the stench was overpowering to the extent of being sickening. *Still*, he thought, *normals are so cute, so desirable. But they are so untidy.*

Somewhat less bothered by the stench they lived with daily, the cosslain—the superior normals—flanked the procession, keeping a modicum of order. Keeping order among the normals was half the reason for the flanking procession. The other half was to carry and load aboard ship individual weapons with which the normals could not be trusted entirely, aboard ship, given the stresses those normals were under.

A Kenstain[20] appeared at Ro'moloristen's shoulder.

The God King gestured and a hologram of the globe appeared in midair. He gestured, again, with a claw and a section of the hologram, plus a route leading to that section, suddenly glowed brighter than the rest. "Guide this group down to here and get them into the stasis tanks," he ordered.

Athenalras held fiefs on nine worlds. The first, despite a major evacuation of the People, was already plunging itself into Orna'adar, the Posleen Ragnarok. This was the last to be loaded. From here the People would move to the new world, the one they called "Aradeen," though the locals called it "Earth."

CHAPTER 3

Bad Tolz, Germany, 31 January 2005

Schultz is too clean, thought Krueger. In an exercise in mud crawling intended for little higher purpose than to accustom the boys to getting dirty—well, that and simple toughening to overcome their civilized sensibilities, the boy remained too clean.

Krueger bent over and picked up a clod of half-frozen mud. This he smeared into Schultz's face snarling, "You little pussy. You smelly little fur-hole filled with nothing. You are nothing so good as a Jew-bitch camp whore. At least she would have known her job."

Turning from Dieter to the rest of the platoon, standing in ranks, Krueger shouted, "The earth is your friend. Use it. Huddle up to it as if to your mother's tit. Embrace it like the little sluts you used to waste your time with. Dig into it. Do not be like this ever-so-prissy little schoolboy, Schultz, afraid to get yourselves dirty. You can wash dirt away. Your own blood is a tougher stain. Dismissed."

Without another glance Krueger turned away from his charges and walked to the NCO barracks, briskly and erect.

The platoon gathered about Schultz, standing there with his face dripping filth. No one said a word; they just stared. Schultz himself quivered with anger. By what right, by what *right* did this man who looked no older than did Dieter himself, treat him like dirt? And not merely today, but *everyday*, so it seemed

47

to Schultz, Krueger—his platoon trainer, had some new heap of abuse for him.

One of the boys, Rudi Harz, put a calming hand on Dieter's shoulder. "*Mein Freund*, my friend . . . Krueger is an asshole, a Nazi asshole to boot. But he is also a Nazi asshole who *knows*. And he sees something useful in you. Bear with it."

Around the two the others nodded somberly.

Schultz, grateful for the touch and the concern, cocked his head and shrugged, adding his own nod. Harz was a good comrade. So were they all.

"But that asshole, Krueger?" said Dieter, quietly. "He is a bad man, whatever he may know."

"Yes," agreed Harz. "He is the worst. If I hear even one more tale of his rapes in the old concentration camps I will vomit. Even so, use him for what he is good for: which may include how to keep ourselves alive."

Silent, Schultz again nodded. Then to the rest he said, "Shall we march back then? Not crawl or amble? March back singing?"

Amid a general assent, and a wink from Harz in Schultz's direction, the boys formed into four ranks. "You march us back, Dieter . . . that's right, Dieter . . . show that bastard Krueger that he can't break us up."

Silently agreeing and taking a place on the left side of the platoon, Schultz gave the command, "*Vorwaaaats . . . Marsch!*"

Up in the front rank, Harz began the song, "*Vorwärts! Vorwärts! Schmettern die hellen fanfaren . . .*"[21]

At a distance, still walking away, Krueger smiled to himself and felt an enormous inner glee. He muttered, happily, "The old ways still work."

Over the Rhein River, 13 February 2005

The steep banks of the river spoke to the Indowy with a voice hoary with age. He remembered; he remembered.

"We have been to your planet before, long, long ago," Rinteel said, seemingly to the chancellor. "It is a story of sadness."

"Really?" asked the chancellor. "Sad, how?"

"The same way all blighted hopes are sad," answered the Indowy, distantly.

Off, too, in the distance, Rinteel saw a rocky hill. His mouth began to mime words in his own tongue. The chancellor had no clue what the words meant, yet something in the cadence touched a chord.

"What is that you are saying?" the chancellor asked.

The Indowy took a few moments, inexpressibly sad and weary moments, to answer. "It is a song of my people, an ancient song. It tells of an attempt at liberty from our oppressors, of an ancient stronghold, of trying to forge a weapon to defend those who might have become, in time, our deliverers."

The Indowy sighed and pointed from the helicopter window. "It tells the blood-drenched tale of that rock over there."

His interest piqued, the chancellor gave orders to the pilot, ignoring the scowls of his security detail. The helicopter veered sharply to the right. In the setting sun the rocky hill gleamed golden and beautiful.

The helicopter touched down flawlessly, despite the heavy crosswind atop the hill. The Indowy, seemingly in a trance, spirit walking, dismounted first. He was followed by the chancellor and his guards.

The helicopter had landed a scant three hundred meters from the summit. Over the steep and rocky ground the Indowy advanced, his chanting growing louder with each step. The Chancellor thought he could almost recognize some of the words: "Fafneen . . . Mine em . . . Albletoon . . . Anothungeen . . . Nibleen . . . Fostvol."

At last the Indowy, and the others, stood before a sheer rock wall. "It was my clan, mine and mine alone, which made this attempt. We paid for it, heavily."

"What attempt?" asked one of the BND guards.

Rinteel half ignored the question. Instead, speaking distantly, he said, "We wanted to make a holy order, a group of warrior heroes, to man the defenses we would build here. We had thought that under the protection of Anothungeen, an insuperable defense for your planet, your people might grow to mightiness. We could not defend you. Yet we sought to give you the means to defend yourselves."

The humans of the group, swaying on the wind-swept slope, faced the unmarred cliff with boredom writ large upon their faces. And then the Indowy reached out a palm and uttered a phrase in a nonhuman tongue. A portion of the rock face disappeared, exposing a rough, archlike entrance. The humans, including the chancellor, gaped. Still in his half trance, Rinteel entered; in enclosed spaces the Indowy people were much less fearful than were the sons of Adam.

From just past the arch Rinteel said, "This place was chosen because it was on the fringe of your then dominant civilization. Here we could, so we thought, develop the systems, Anothungeen and Fafneen, in peace. From here also we could, so we thought, distribute it secretly throughout your then-dominant civilization, the one you humans call 'Roman.'"

The Indowy's chin sank upon his breast.

The chancellor looked over and past the Indowy to cast his gaze upon a scene of ancient slaughter. Skull-less cadavers, dried and brittle, of humans and Indowy both, met his sight. The chancellor's mind turned back to little piles of gnawed bones in a place called "Fredericksburg." "*Mein Gott*," he said.

"Only one of us, Albletoon, escaped the slaughter," Rinteel translated as he recited. "A human mercenary, traitor to his race, led the assault. Siegfried, cursed be his name, betrayed the People. For greed . . . and the promised mate . . . he sold them out . . . and so fell the cause of liberty. The traitor Mineem led them through, foiled the gate, and compromised the safeguards. For foul gold, and fame, our hero Siegfried sold his soul."

So deep was the Indowy into his trance that the chancellor feared for him. He reached out a hand almost comradely.

Rinteel shrugged off the comforting grip.

"Let me make sure I understand," the chancellor said. "Your people knew of us, and tried to save us, centuries ago?"

"More than centuries, millennia."

"But you failed? It didn't work?"

"No," answered Rinteel, with a sigh both sad and painful. "We forgot—it had been so long since we had known war. Only weapons of your own forging could save you. The Elves will sabotage anything we might give you. So, no, *Herr Kanzler*, no, it won't work. It didn't work."

Kraus-Maffei-Wegmann Plant, Munich, Germany, 15 February 2005

"Well, that didn't work," sighed Mueller.

"Back to the drawing board," agreed Prael, disgust dripping with every syllable.

The object of that disgust, an enormous steel cylinder leaking heavy red hydraulic fluid as if from a ruptured heart, stood shattered within its testing cradle. The cylinder, intended to be one of ten that would absorb the recoil of the Tiger III's twelve-inch gun, had proven deficient . . . and that in the most catastrophic way possible. Indeed, so catastrophic had the failure been that at least one of the testing crew within Prael's vision was leaking red fluid nearly as rapidly as the cylinder. Instantaneous decapitation will do that.

Mueller, emerging from the test shelter, itself a metal bunker, looked at the body and shook his head wearily. "I *did* want a railgun. Continuous acceleration. Greater—much greater—ammunition storage . . ."

The Israeli, Benjamin, interrupting, asked of Prael, "At what point did the metal give way?"

Instead of answering directly, the German handed the Jew a printout.

"I see," said Benjamin. "Hmmm. Could we reduce the charge . . . no, I guess not, not and achieve the kind of velocity we must have . . ." The Israeli had, in an earlier day, riding his Merkava against his national enemy, punched out more than one Arab-manned, Russian- or Ukrainian-built, tank.

"Nor can we reduce the weight of the projectile and still achieve the penetration we must have," finished Mueller.

"GalTech," offered Nielsen.

"The chancellor, acting on the advice of the BND, has decreed not," answered Henschel. "For what it's worth, I think he is most likely right in that. The Galactics have their own agenda. That agenda might or might not include the presence of humanity after the war."

Scratching an ear absentmindedly, Benjamin observed, "When David went out to fight Goliath, King Saul offered the boy the use of Saul's own armor and weapons. The boy refused, claiming that he would do better with his own weapon than with others the use and feel of which were unfamiliar to him. David was right. Your chancellor is right. Our prime minister agrees. This must be a human weapon, something the Galactics cannot interfere with."

"Isn't there *some* way we can strengthen the recoil cylinders by making them simply bigger?" asked Mueller, pushing his pet railgun to the side for the nonce.

"No," said Prael, rubbing his face briskly with a frustrated hand. "We've looked into that. We can reduce the cylinders to eight and make them somewhat larger and stronger. And then the breech of the gun hits the back of the turret. *Scheisse!* We tried to cut it too fine."

Though they had not been present for the test, the resounding crash from the destruction of the recoil cylinder had sent a shock wave through the entire plant, drawing Schlüssel and Breitenbach at a run. They entered the test chamber, took one look at the cylinder, another at the corpse, and crossed themselves like the good Catholics they were. Schlüssel, perhaps not so good a Catholic as Breitenbach, said, "Fuck!" immediately after.

What had happened was so obvious that neither Prael nor the others felt the need to explain to the two newcomers.

"Oh, well," said Schlüssel. "There's some good news. Breitenbach, here, has gotten something very interesting from the Americans. Tell them, Stephan."

In his left hand Breitenbach carried a small black box, attached to and trailing a harness. "Better I should show them, *nicht wahr*, Reinhard?"

Schlüssel sighed, resignedly. Impetuous boy! "Oh, yes. By all means show them, since you must."

Without another word, Breitenbach turned on his heel and left the area. When he reappeared some minutes later, standing on a steel walkway seventy feet above the factory floor, the harness was around his body. Schlüssel directed the others' attention upward with a nonchalant finger.

With a boyish cry, and to the wide-eyed amazement of all of the others but Schlüssel, Breitenbach hurled himself over the railing guarding the walkway. He fell, faster and faster, shrieking with a boy's mindless joy. So fast fell he that the eyes had difficulty following. Henschel's eyes didn't follow at all as he had closed them against the seemingly inevitable impact.

The impact never came. Eighteen to twenty feet above the plant floor, Breitenbach's body began to slow. The rate of descent continued to slow. By the time Breitenbach had reached the floor, he was able to settle onto his feet as gently as a falling feather.

"What the hell caused that?" demanded Mueller.

Schlüssel shrugged. "The mathematics are beyond me, frankly. Had she not written them down, the American girl who discovered the principle would likely have found them beyond herself as well. Long story there, so I am told.

"But look at it this way: that black plastic device on Stephan's harness takes the energy of falling, saves it, and then twists it sideways to turn it into an energy of slowing. We believe we can use this in the suspension system for the tank—without a major redesign being required, by the way—and reduce the robustness of the shock absorbers to save perhaps fifteen or twenty tons of weight. To say nothing of reducing the maintenance required."

Mueller's eyes, which had never narrowed to normal after Breitenbach's plunge, grew wider still. Prael's eyes began to dance in his head, unable to focus on anyone or anything. Henschel and Benjamin exchanged thoughtful glances.

Heads swiveled slowly as all eyes turned to the ruin of the recoil cylinder. A new light gleamed in those eyes.

Paris, France, 15 February 2005

Isabelle's husband entered her kitchen wordlessly, a paper clutched in one hand.

She did not see the paper, initially. She saw instead a much-loved face gone ashen.

"What is wrong?" she asked.

He didn't answer, but just thrust the paper at her.

With a trembling hand she took the proffered form letter and read it through quickly. Uncomprehending, she shook her head in negation. "They can't *do* this to you, to us. You did your time in the army as a boy. They have no right."

The husband quoted from the scrap of paper he had already read fifty times, "In accordance with our time-honored heritage and traditions, all Frenchmen are permanently requisitioned for the defense of the Republic."

"But you are a doctor, not a killer," Isabelle objected.

"Killers get hurt," answered the husband. "Then they need doctors. I report the day after tomorrow."

She stood there for a long moment, stunned, unable to speak further.

Bad Tolz, Germany, 17 February 2005

Quietly, a long and snaking column of armed men marched up the forest trail in the dead of night. In the darkness, only the eyes gleamed, and occasionally the teeth. The faces were darkened by burnt cork and grease paint . . . and a fair amount of simple dirt. Frozen dirt and gravel below crunched softly under the soldiers' boots.

The boys, as Brasche thought of them, had done well so far with their basic training. Marksmanship was of an acceptable order, though Brasche had serious reservations that any amount of normal training would be adequate to teach anyone to shoot well when there was an enemy shooting back. He *had* served on the Russian Front, after all.

But "well" is a relative term, he thought, too. *And we have a few tricks, ourselves, that just may help.* Brasche smiled with wicked anticipation at what awaited the boys ahead.

The boys' ostensible mission was to counterattack to retake a section of field entrenchments lost to a notional Posleen attack. In fact, as Brasche and a few others running the exercise knew, the techniques of the counterattack through the trenches were purely secondary. The objective of the exercise was to frighten the boys half out of their wits so that once they recovered those wits would be harder to frighten.

Brasche heard static breaking over the radio at his side. He answered with his name.

"*Oberst* Kiel here, Brasche. My men are in position."

"Excellent, *Herr Oberst.*" Brasche glanced quickly at the rear entrance to the trench system just as the first of the new troops began his descent into it. "The party should be beginning right about . . . now."

As if they were timed to a clock, as indeed they were, the first mortar shells crashed down onto the objective area. Through the actinic glow of the splashing shells Brasche saw, faintly, the outlines of half a dozen or so of Kiel's men. Themselves immune to any weapon the new boys had to bring to bear—as well as from the mortar shells, the armored mobile infantry were there to add spice, frightfulness really, to the exercise. Their holographic projectors were ideal for portraying a Posleen enemy, even a mass of them. But best of all . . .

"*Lieber Gott im Himmel!*" Brasche heard a boy—*young Dieter Schultz*, so he thought—exclaim over the radio. "They are fucking shooting at us. For *real!*"

"Indeed they are, *Kinder*." Brasche recognized Krueger's voice in the radio. "With weapons much like the ones the invaders will have. Now what have you been taught about what to do when someone is shooting at you?" asked Krueger, with a tone of scorn.

The radio went silent immediately. Still, so Brasche was pleased to note, rifle fire began to flash out from the trenches, to strike the holographic projections or even, occasionally the armored combat suits. Where a bullet was sensed to have passed or hit, or a shell or grenade to have exploded, an Artificial Intelligence Device—or AID, eliminated one or more of the Posleen targets. Meanwhile, from above the ground and the trenches, the Armored Combat Suits themselves flashed fire generally in the young boys' direction. The ACS were aiming to frighten, however, rather than to kill or wound, carefully keeping their point of aim away from the boys' heads and bodies.

Young Schultz's voice again crackled over the radio to be answered by a regular *Bundeswehr* tank commander on loan to the training brigade for the exercise.

Over the sound of rifle fire, high explosives, and the sound barrier cracking of the ACS's grav-guns, Brasche detected the throaty diesel roar of a Leopard II tank in full charge.

Good boy, young Schultz, thought Brasche. *Not everyone would have remembered that they were not in the fight alone.*

The tank was suddenly lit in Brasche's view by its own flame as its main gun spewed forth a storm of flechettes onto the objective area. . . .

Brasche and his wingman advanced alone into the storm of steel. Ahead, artillery pounded at such of the Russian positions as could be positively identified or confidently guessed at. There was never enough of it though.

They had been warned that the defenses were incredible. But nothing had prepared Brasche or the men who had begun the battle under his command for the reality of Kursk. Nothing short of a tour through hell could have even approached the reality.

Of the men under his command to begin, a single platoon of Panzer IVs and a platoon of infantry in support, all that remained were a brace of tanks. The infantry was but a memory.

And Ivan's PAKs, his antitank guns, were everywhere. Brasche shuddered at the memory of a fight between his medium panzers and no less than a dozen Russian guns, dug in, camouflaged and firing under a unified command. That fight alone had cost him two panzers. The screams of one crew, burning alive, still rang in the tank commander's ears.

In Brasche's headphones he heard the commander of his wing tank exclaim, "Achtung! Achtung! Panzer Abwehr Kanonen zum—"[22] and the panicky voice cut off.

But the direction was not needed. Standing in the tank commander's hatch, Brasche himself could see smoke and fire belching from the ground to his right. Eyes straining to make out the precise location of his enemy, he could not see, but he could feel, the half dozen solid shot that tore through the air at himself and his wing man.

Both tanks frantically tried to pivot themselves to place their more strongly armored glacis in the direction of the fire, as their turrets swung round even faster to engage the enemy.

A race against time it seemed. And then Brasche realized there must have been a reason for those guns to have opened fire when they did. He turned around just in time to see more fire coming from behind.

Then the world went black for Hans Brasche, Fifth SS Panzer Division (Wiking).

The Leopard fired again, clearing Hans' reminiscences from his mind. Never mind, though. Back at Kursk, more than six decades prior, the second battery of guns had opened up, gutting both his tank and his wingman's. Hans had lost consciousness. He never knew how it had come to pass that he escaped the tank. In his memory he imagined a mindless crawling thing, fleeing the fire like an animal fleeing a combusting forest. Of his trip back to Germany, to his convalescence, his memory had been reduced to a sense of little beyond pain, sometimes dim, sometimes agonizing.

The memory of the pain made him shudder, still.

Brasche pushed the memories aside, finally and completely. The open ramp into the trench system awaited. Hans walked forward and descended.

Down in the trenches Dieter Schultz, age eighteen, shuddered with pain from a tank-fired flechette that had grazed one arm, ripping an inch-long jagged tear across his skin. Blood poured out, staining his *Kampfanzug*, his battledress. The blood showed a dullish red in the tracers' gleam.

Beside Schultz another of the boys, Harz, looked down in uncomprehending fright. "Dieter, you're bleeding."

"Never mind that," insisted Schultz, clamping a hand to his wound to stop the trickling blood. "Run down the trench to Third Squad. Get them to move to the right and engage . . . to take some of the fire off of us here."

"*Zu Befehl, Dieter*,"[23] answered Harz, half mockingly and yet half serious.

Krueger, meanwhile, crouched silently nearby, watching Schultz's actions with an eagle eye. He caught a bare glimpse of Brasche, easing himself down the trench, and stood to a head-bent attention.

"*Herr Major?*" asked Krueger.

"Nothing, Sergeant," answered Brasche. "Just observing."

Dieter, obsessed with his wound but more so with his mission, did not notice Brasche standing nearby. Still, Hans noted the quiet boy, growing into his potential, there in the cold and muddy trench.

The boy shouted to the others around him. "Stand by." Then he spoke a few short words into the radio, "Five rounds, antipersonnel." Brasche and Krueger ducked low once again. And only just in time, too, as the distant tank began firing rapidly, deluging the surface above with flechettes. All told there were precisely five major blasts and five minor as the flechette rounds burst to spill their deadly cargo.

Without more than half a second's hesitation after that fifth minor explosion, Schultz shouted another command and the boys, following his example, stuck their heads and their rifles above the trench lip, adding their precision fire to the holograms and ACS remaining.

Very good, thought Brasche.

Paris, France, 17 February 2005

The house was plunged in an early morning sadness. The mother and one little son cried openly. The elder boy, nearing thirteen now, struggled to keep his face clear. Last night his father had made him promise to be the man of the house, a promise asked for solemnly . . . and as solemnly made.

"I will write every day, *ma cherie* . . . *ma belle femme*," promised the husband, stroking the sobbing Isabelle's hair softly. "And I should be able to take leave at sometime."

Isabelle pressed her wet face into his shoulder. Her encircling arms held him tightly. There were no words she could bring herself to say.

Last night had been bad. They had fought as they rarely fought. She had struggled to get her husband to desert, to flee to some place past the army's reach. He had steadfastly refused, claiming—truthfully insofar as he knew—that no place on Earth would be safe from the army, not now with the entire planet rearming to the teeth.

In the end, seeing that he would not, it had been she who had relented. In fear for her future and in remembrance of more youthful, happier times, she had dragged her husband to their large wooden bad and made love to him with a dazzling skill and enthusiasm that left him breathless.

"That is to remind you," Isabelle had said, "to remind you of what you have here and to make you want to come back."

Still half out of breath, he had answered, "After that awesome performance, my love . . . and at my age . . . I should be better to stay away in order to safeguard my *life*."

Kraus-Maffei-Wegmann Plant, Munich, Germany, 21 June 2005

Mühlenkampf was . . . well, there was no other word: he was awed.

Gleaming above him, for the beast had not yet had its coat of paint, stood the Tiger III. Below, at ground level—though the ground was meters-thick concrete—the tracks were caked with the mud, so Mühlenkampf noted with interest.

"She works," he announced with a quiver in his voice, drawing the correct conclusion from the caked mud.

Proudly, Mueller, Schlüssel, Prael and the others stood a bit taller. "She works, *Herr General*. This is prototype number one. There are a few bugs yet. But she moves. She shoots. She can take a punch on her great armored nose and punch right back."

"And," added Prael who had designed and nearly hand built her electronic suite, "Tiger III is the best human designed and built *training* vehicle in history, with virtual-reality simulators to allow a full gamut of gunner and driver training without ever leaving the *Kaserne*."

"We will have to take her out anyway," answered the general. "Otherwise you will never know what might still be wrong. When can I have one? Or, better still, many of them?"

"This one is yours now," answered Mueller. "We are, indeed, hoping your field tests will help work out any remaining problems."

But Mueller spoke to Mühlenkampf's back. Already the veteran was fumbling with his new, inconvenient, and sometimes damnable cellular phone.

"Brasche? Get to Munich. Now!"

Sennelager, Germany, 28 June 2005

Basic training was long over now. The thin, emaciated skeleton of a *Korps* was beginning to grow and fill out here at this training base on the north German plain where the boys had been relocated for unit training.

Though Basic was over, the days were still as long and the nights sometimes longer. And yet the boys reveled in the name "soldier." On the route marches that took them through the nearby towns the boys marched with pride and a spring in their steps.

That the girls turned out to watch, more often than not, didn't hurt matters any.

Yet the nights and days remained long. Soldiers were killed in training and their places taken by new faces. The old German army had thought that one percent killed in basic training was not merely an acceptable, but a desirable figure. The new-old German Army did as well, this portion of it, at least.

That rarely happened in the regular *Bundeswehr*. There, the few *Wehrmacht* veterans scattered about were impotent to change things from the politically correct, multiculturally sensitive stew the politicians had made of the German army.

Only in the 47th *Panzer Korps*, called by political friend and foe alike, "the SS *Korps*," were there enough men who knew the old ways—knew them, and more importantly, were willing to tell the politicians and social theorists to "go fuck yourselves" over them—to meld their new charges into what Germany, what Europe, what humanity, needed.

And so the boys marched with pride and a spring, knowing that, perhaps alone among their people's defenders they *could* and would do the job at hand.

Was it this that the girls of the towns had seen? Was it that they had seen one group of defenders whom they could be sure would never leave them defenseless until death stopped them?

The boys didn't know.

"I just know I get laid a lot more than I used to," laughed the irrepressible Harz, just before something attracted his attention.

It began as a low rumble in the air. Soon, the boys were hustling out of their tents in fear of an earthquake.

"What the fuck is it?" asked Harz of Schultz.

Dieter just shook his head, equally uncomprehending.

"Over there!" shouted another of the boys. "It's a tank. Nothing much."

Schultz looked and saw an iron beast cresting a hill. Yes, just another tank. Nothing special. They worked with tanks all the time. And then, as the tank drew closer and the rumbling stronger, his eyes made out a tiny something, projecting from the top of the turret.

"*Lieber Gott im Himmel!*"[24]

From atop the Tiger III, as if on parade... as if on parade before a universe he personally owned, Hans Brasche, late of 5th SS Panzer Division (Wiking), tossed a crisp salute at his future tank crews.

INTERLUDE

As was fitting for a junior Kessentai, Ro'moloristen took an obscure position towards the back of the oddly designed, auditoriumlike, assembly room. The floor, to the extent an Aldenata-based ship could be said to have permanent floors, swept upward as it swept back, allowing the young Kessentai a full view of the assembling God Kings and the central raised dais against the far wall.

While himself relegated to the rear by his junior position, the young God King's betters—*elders*, in any case—took more prominent positions towards the front. Centered at the very front, right against the cleared semicircular area that had been left around the raised dais, stood Athenalras, arms crossed before the massive equine chest in the *posture of supplication and serenity*.

The thousands of other God Kings present in the auditorium likewise matched Athenalras' pious posture as an elderly Posleen, a Kenstain—Bin'ar'rastemon—a once prominent Kessentai who had given up the Path to become a very special form of Kessenalt. No mere castellaine was Bin'ar'rastemon, no mere steward for another God King. Once the toll of years and wounds had begun to tell, he had turned his clan and its assets over to his senior eson'antai, or son, only keeping control of sufficient to support himself in a modest style as he entered the Way of Remembrance.

Something between historians and chaplains, the Kessenalt of the Way of Remembrance served to maintain and remind the People of their history, their values, their beliefs . . . and the very nasty way of the world unwittingly inflicted upon them by the Aldenata and their one-size-fits-all, cookie-cutter, philosophy.

Clad in ceremonial harness of pure heavy metal, Bin'ar'rastemon—old and with the Posleen equivalent of arthritis creaking every joint—ambled up the steps of the dais, ancient scrolls tucked into his harness.

Though Kenstain normally received little respect as a class, except perhaps from the God Kings they served directly, the followers of the Way of Remembrance were widely and highly valued. As Bin'ar'rastemon centered himself upon the dais, he ceremonially greeted the assembled God Kings, who ceremoniously answered, "Tell us, Rememberer, of the ways of the past, that we might know the ways of the future."

Bin'ar'rastemon unrolled a scroll formally, placing it upon a frail-seeming podium. On this he placed a hand. Yet he was a Rememberer, still in full possession of his mind, however much his body may have aged. In any case, he needed no scroll for this tale.

"From the Book of the Knowers," he began . . .

CHAPTER 4

Sennelager, Germany, 14 July 2005

The base had been chosen for the assembly of the 47th *Panzer Korps* because of its central location. From all over Germany's hundreds of small *Kasernen*, new, old and refurbished, poured in the thousands of newly trained troops and their veteran cadres.

Convenient for assembly of a large *Korps* as it might have been, the base was also too close to Hamburg, too close to Berlin, too close to Essen and Frankfurt for comfort. Another way of saying this was that it was altogether too comfortable and easy for the left of center of German politics, at least of that part which answered to those leaders of the left who had secretly sold out to the Elves, to find their way to the place.

And they did. In their thousands . . . in their tens of thousands.

"Must be fifty thousand of the bastards," muttered Mühlenkampf, standing at his office window overlooking the main gate to the *Kaserne*. "Where the hell did they all come from? And why aren't the boys out there in the army instead? Why aren't the *damned girls* in the army, for that matter?"

He knew the answer, of course. Despite the threat of the Posleen, the idea of alternative service was too deeply ingrained in German political and social culture even for the threat of annihilation to overcome fully. Curiously, Great Britain and the United States, without a long or stable tradition of peacetime conscription or "compulsory social service," had done better by far in dragging in their young people. There, the old age homes and the like had never become dependent on low-paid slave labor. Private always—or at least not fully governmental, they could remain so. In Germany? No such luck.

Wherever the protestors had come from, there was little doubt where they intended to go. Mühlenkampf watched without the slightest trace of amusement as the protestors, forming a human phalanx, made their first, barely repulsed, effort at storming the gate. He was even less amused to see a protest sign—"Friendship to our alien brothers," said the sign—come smashing down across the head and shoulders of a policeman.

From the desk behind the general came the ringing of a telephone. He turned his eyes away from the protest to answer the nagging device. "Mühlenkampf," he announced.

The chancellor's voice came from the receiver. Though still unused to modern conveniences the sound seemed distant, and a bit muffled. *A speakerphone*, the general guessed, uncertainly.

"This is the chancellor. I have Günter sitting here with me in my office and listening. What is your situation, General?"

"My situation? I have forty or fifty thousand protestors outside my installation. Half of them are unwashed, long-haired young men who ought to be in the army and are not. They are storming the gates even as we speak. And the local police cannot hold them."

There was a brief silence from the other end before the chancellor resumed. "I have two battalions of special riot control police en route to you by bus. They should be there in two hours at most."

Unseen by the chancellor, Mühlenkampf shook his head. "That will be far too late. For that matter it would be far too little even if they were here now."

"It is all I have, General."

Absently, the old SS man said, "I have more. I have a half-strength armored *Korps*."

A new voice spoke up, a voice tinged with rage. It was Günter's, Mühlenkampf was quite certain, despite the distortion. "SS man, you may *not* use your *Korps* on those civilians; the public relations aspects would be disastrous."

Holding in a snarl, the general decided to try a different tack.

"Excuse me, *Herr Kanzler.* There seems to be some distortion in this connection. I can't make out what you are saying. Did Günter say something? I will hang up and try again."

Replacing the receiver, Mühlenkampf shouted out to his secretary, "Lucy, the *Kanzler* or perhaps some other flunkies are going to be calling here again in moments. Make all the lines busy, would you? And send someone to bring me my division and brigade commanders."

Berlin, Germany, 14 June 2005

The Tir's group of human underlings sat again in a semicircle before the desk. The Tir's eyes were closed, though his ears were open. His breathing was shallow but steady. His lips moved in a mantra in his own tongue.

"All is in readiness," said Dunkel, the Red. "Not less than fifty thousand protesters are converging on the base at Sennelager to combat the Fascists."

"The army has no objections to this," announced the one gray-uniformed human present, a representative of certain elements in the General Staff. "Even if some portions objected to the trashing of our own bases, virtually no one wants these hideous SS men to remain in uniform."

Günter, the Green, sat silently for a while. "We have our people there as well, at least sixty percent of the protesters are Green."

The Tir, eyes still closed and breathing still shallow, said in a strained voice, "You have all done well. There will be rewards for good performance. . . ."

Sennelager, Germany, 14 June 2005

A helmeted Dieter Schultz, now rewarded for his talents by sporting the insignia of a *Stabsunteroffizier*—a staff sergeant—and Rudi Harz, a sergeant himself, formed their troops in ranks before taking their places to the right.

"What's going on Dieter?" asked Harz.

"No clue, Rudi. Maybe we are going to celebrate Bastille Day."

Harz snorted. "Somehow, I think not. Not with the orders being to wear helmets and gas masks, and to carry clubs."

"Should we ask Krueger?" queried Schultz, in a whisper. "I hate asking that bastard anything."

Krueger—now sergeant major of the headquarters detachment of *Schwere Panzer Abteilung*, heavy tank battalion, 501—heard both his name and the word "bastard" whispered despite the distance between himself and the boys. He assumed that "bastard" could refer only to himself and smiled at the knowledge.

Standing in front of the detachment, Krueger turned his head over one shoulder and announced, "We're going to bust some fucking heads, *Knaben*.[25] That is all you need to know."

In front of the formation, thirteen blocks of twenty or twenty-one men—all that had been trained so far—plus a larger block to the left composing the service support detachment, the adjutant called the unit to attention. The men stiffened.

Brasche strode out. He, like the boys, was dressed in field gray. The more modern camouflage pattern, not one whit more effective against Posleen visual rods, was in short supply. It mattered little, in any case. Brasche and the rest of the *Korps'* cadre were more comfortable in field gray than they ever would have been in the kaleidoscope of color that was more modern German battle dress.

There was an exchange of salutes. The adjutant moved to one side and marched to a position behind Brasche.

Hans was short, curt even, in his speech. The duty ahead promised to be unpleasant and, while he would perform that duty, he had little genuine enthusiasm. "Boys, there are some people outside the main gate trying to break in and trash our little home away from home. On my command, you will don your protective masks. This is so that the newspapers and television and, incidentally, the legal system cannot identify you by face. Then we will march singing—singing the "*Panzerlied*"—to the main gate. If they go away when we do this, so much the better.

"But if they do not, we are going to put them, as many of them as possible, into the hospital."

Schultz distinctly heard Krueger chortle with unrepressed glee. He thought, but could not be quite sure, that he heard a whispered, "Just like the good old days."

Brasche bellowed a command which was echoed down the ranks. The men fumbled with gas masks. These now—since the Posleen war—had gone largely obsolete, the Posleen being quite immune to any terrestrial war gas. Indeed, the only reason the men had even been issued and trained on masks was that the German chemical industry, working in close cooperation with the Russians, believed that a militarily useful toxin might someday be developed from the venom of the grat, a wasplike pest of the Posleen.

At another command the men ported their makeshift clubs. Still another and the battalion faced to the right. A last command and they began to march down the cobblestones towards the main gate to the *Kaserne*.

No command was required to begin the singing.

> *"Ob's stürmt oder schneit, ob die Sonne uns lacht*
> *Der Tag glühend heiss oder eiskalt die Nacht . . ."*[26]

Though muffled by the masks, the sound of tens of thousands of throats belting out the German Army's—be it called *Reichswehr*, *Wehrmacht*, SS or *Bundeswehr*—traditional song for its armored forces made the woods and the stones of the barracks ring.

So deeply involved were they in the process of trying to force the *Kaserne*'s gate that the foremost ranks of the rioters scarcely noticed the approach of the *Korps*. Indeed, the sounds of smashing signs and grunting, struggling men and women quite drowned out the marching song for those nearest to the struggle. Not one of those rioters saw any incongruity in the fact that the signs bore slogans such as "Peace Now" and "Don't Grease the Wheels of the War Machine." Not one marcher found anything amiss in the attempt to sabotage the training of men who would save the Earth, if they could, from the Posleen who would destroy it. The protesters simply refused to acknowledge that the Posleen were any threat. Many of them refused even to acknowledge that the aliens existed.

Back a distance, watching the struggle but taking no part in it, sat a reasonably well doped-up Andreas Schüler. Tall, thin, not too recently washed, Schüler wasn't here because he cared about "saving" the Earth. He wasn't here because he really objected to the army, except that in his own very personal way he had once objected to finding himself in the army and had instead done his "social year" in an infinitely more comfortable nursing home.

Andreas had no great objection even to the 47th *Panzer Korps*. He, frankly, didn't care that that *Korps* was in everything but name a resurrection of the dreaded SS. Indeed, in his younger days he had once flirted with the skinheads, though he had found no satisfaction in the movement.

Schüler had come—as he had come every time the German left had massed to break and demoralize another part of the army—for the dope, the girls, and the visual spectacle. He was by no means alone in this.

The spectacle had amused for a while, but then it had paled. Everything pales, in time. He recalled laughing as he watched a few protestors paint bright silver *Sigrunen*, SS, on the window of a *Bundeswehr* recruiting station. The marching crowd had laughed with him.

Even so, Schüler could not feel a part of the amorphous mass of humanity in whose march from the train station he had taken part. There had been singing on that march . . . but the singing failed to move him.

Despite the struggle at the gate, Schüler, like hundreds of others nearby, found himself more involved in conversation with the opposite sex than in any apparent *cause*.

But then he heard. And then, from his high perch, he saw.

From all corners of the *Kaserne* poured in gray-clad men at a steady, even a stately, pace. The boots resounded on the pavement, audible at hundreds of meters. Noncoms kept order, automatically interweaving the columns while still keeping units and ranks largely together. It was a spectacle not seen in Germany in many years.

The marching men sang:

> "*Bestaubt sind die Gesichter, doch froh ist unser Sinn,*
> *ja unser Sinn,*
> *Es braust unser Panzer, im Stürmwind dahin. . . .*"[27]

At the point of the column, the tip of the spear, Brasche marched followed by Krueger—personally, then the 501st Heavy Tank Battalion's headquarters, and the rest of the battalion. Behind the battalion came the first elements of the foundation of *Wiking* Division, followed themselves by *Hohenstauffen, Frundsberg,* and the rest.

Mühlenkampf still remained at his office, though he had gone outside to stand on a stone porch to review the passing ranks. The command, "*Augen . . . Rechts*"—Eyes, Right—rang out as each company passed its *Korps* commander.

Dieter's eyes snapped back to the front on command. Up ahead, past the Nazi—Krueger—he saw Brasche walking erect and, seemingly, proud. Unlike his followers, Brasche strode unarmed; his fists would do well enough. From the subtle twisting of his commander's mask, Dieter was certain Brasche was singing along with the rest. Past the battalion commander the last of the local police could be seen, falling, bloody and bruised, under the smashing signs of the pacifists, and—less incongruously—of the Reds and Greens.

Schüler stood, mesmerized, while watching the very first man leading the field-gray-clad mass of troops smash into the protestors. That man had marched alone and out front. Though that soldier went down fairly quickly—a matter of less than a minute, the boy could not help but be impressed by the sheer ferocity with which he had fought.

More than the courage of that first soldier—*Oberstleutnant* Brasche, though the boy didn't know that, Schüler was amazed— or perhaps better said, *shocked*—at the reaction of the men following.

Krueger didn't like Brasche, not one bit. To the old Nazi, his commander seemed ambivalent, perhaps even weak. It was not anything Brasche had said, actually. Rather, Krueger had sensed an undertone of deep disapproval whenever he had regaled the new boys with tales of the old days.

But, affection or not, when Krueger saw his commander fall to the ground beneath the flailing fists and lashing feet of the long-haired rabble at the gate, he saw not a weak or even a non-Nazi. He saw a comrade in danger. Krueger raised his club overhead, turned over a shoulder and shouted:

"At 'em, boys!"

✦   ✦   ✦

Muscle and bone augmented by the same process that had returned the octogenarian Brasche to full youth, Hans' fists leapt and flew like twin lightning bolts. Wading into the crowd, he strode over a medley of bleeding, tooth-spitting, choking, bruised and gagging leftists. Behind him, the singing grew louder and closer.

He hoped it would grow very loud, very close . . . and very soon.

A woman, tall even by German standards, stood before him, defiantly. Defiantly, too, the woman lifted her chin and tore open her shirt, baring her breasts and daring the colonel to shame himself by striking a woman. Brasche drew back a fist to strike . . . and stopped. He couldn't do it.

Sadly for him, neither that woman, nor the shorter one who threw her arms about his legs, felt the same sort of restraint. Legs fouled, Brasche lost his balance and fell. He neither saw nor felt the booted foot that connected with his skull, sending him, briefly, out of this vale of tears and into another.

The wind was from the west, carrying with it a stench that Leutnant Brasche at first could not identify. The young officer walked gingerly, even after a long hospital convalescence. The burn scars on his legs were still stiff and tender, cracking and opening on the slightest pretext to ooze a clearish crud. His concussion, also, continued to plague him with nausea and fuzzy mindedness.

The sign at the train station had said "Birkenau." The name meant little to Hans, except insofar as it might mean a break from the endless horrors and deprivations of the Russian Front. Even those men he had spoken to at the front had had little comment other than that this camp, along with the others, were places where badly wounded SS men might have a few months or weeks of peace serving as guards before being fed back into the cauldron.

To the southeast of the station platform Hans saw a camp that seemed, somehow, and even at a distance, a little neater, a little daintier perhaps.

"What is that?" he asked of the SS man who met him on the platform, likewise a comrade sent—though earlier—for a healing break.

"The women's camp," that man answered. "There is another one

much like it just past. Decent places to get laid if you can afford the price of a bar of soap, a toothbrush, or a scrap of food. Or you can just order them to perform . . . so I am told."

"Who are we holding there?"

The other man shrugged, "Jews mostly. Also Poles and Gypsies. Some others. All enemies of the Reich . . . so they say. In any case, come along Leutnant Brasche. I'll introduce you to the commander, Höss."

Silently the two walked north to the comfortable SS barracks, Hans' meager baggage ported by an impossibly slender, shaven-headed Jew. The stench grew worse, much worse, as they drew nearer the SS compound.

Hans still could not identify the smell. And then he felt a cold shiver run up his spine. It smelled like his tank . . . after he had been blown clear. In a brief moment of relative lucidity before he was evacuated he had smelled something much like that, albeit heavier in diesel fumes.

"What is that?" he asked. "That godawful stench?"

"Jews, Leutnant Brasche," his newfound comrade and guide answered, ignoring, as did most SS, the arcane system of ranks inherited from the Stürmabteilung. "Jews. We round them up. We starve them. We work them half to death. We gas them and then we cremate the bodies just west of here."

"Mein Gott!"

"There is no God, here, Brasche," said the other man. "And being here makes me think there is no God anywhere."

Hans grew desperately silent then, remaining that way until he was ushered into the presence of his new, temporary, commander. Hans knew little of Höss. That little, however, included that the commander was, despite current duties, a highly decorated hero of the Great War, a veteran of the Freikorps and, at heart, a combat soldier. This knowledge informed Brasche's actions.

Standing at the front of Höss' desk, Hans thrust out a stiff-armed salute, "Heil Hitler, Leut' . . . Obersturmführer Hans Brasche reports."

Höss ignored the slip, his eyes taking in the new Iron Cross, 1st Class, glittering at Brasche's throat. "We can certainly use you, Brasche. I am short officers and—"

Hans interrupted. Desperation to see and learn no more than he already had lent him boldness. "Sir, the front needs me more. I am healed enough. I wish to be returned to my old unit, the Wiking Division, *to serve our Fatherland and* Führer *there."*

Höss regarded Brasche closely. No, there was no hint on the boy's stiff face of anything but a profound sense of duty. The commander nodded. "Very well, Brasche. I understand the call of the front completely. It will take a day or two to prepare the orders. But I will send you back to your division. Good lad. You're a credit to the SS."

Dieter Schultz was no fanatic. No more so was his friend Harz. But when they saw their commander fall to a treacherous, underhanded attack, even the hated and despised Krueger became not too vile a man to follow into the fray.

The boys waded in, an unstoppable mass of swinging clubs, smashing fists, and stomping boots. Those who fell before them were given no quarter, but kicked senseless, in some cases to death. Singing among the first groups stopped to be replaced quickly by sobbing, shrieking and begging Reds and Greens.

"No mercy, boys!" shouted Krueger, exultantly if unnecessarily. "Break their bones!"

"Mein Gott," exclaimed a wide-eyed Schüler at the scene of carnage spreading before him. Already the disordered mass of protesters was fleeing in panic. Already the soldiers were reforming to pursue, while formations to the rear helped their own battered comrades to aid while taking time to further kick and pound the fallen protesters.

A young woman—trampled by the panicking crowd—staggered by, her face half covered in a sheet of blood. Schüler approached to lend what aid he could. As he did so he heard the girl mutter, over and over, "This is impossible. Unbelievable. Impossible."

He draped her arm over his shoulder and began half carrying her to the presumed safety of the nearby town of Paderborn. Still the girl continued to repeat, "Impossible."

Although willing, and more than willing, to help, at length Schüler grew weary of the refrain.

"What is your name, *Fräulein*?" he asked.

She paused, as if trying to remember, before answering, "Liesel. Liesel Koehler."

"What is 'unbelievable,' 'impossible' about this?"

Her arm still draped over his shoulder, Liesel stopped, bringing them both to a halt. She seemed to struggle for the words and concepts.

At length, when he had forced her back to movement to escape the rampaging soldiers, she continued. "It is impossible for people to act like those men did. They just *can't* have. It is impossible that our good intentions did not prevail here today. It is impossible that we are about to be invaded. What intelligent species could possibly act the way they say these 'Posleen' do? The universe simply cannot be set up that way. It is impossible."

Schüler said nothing. Yet he thought, "*Impossible,*" *you say . . . and still the soldiers acted as they did. Impossible for good intentions to be for naught. And yet they were. Why then is it impossible for these aliens to act as we are told they will? Because you insist on denying it? Is it that you cannot see the world or the universe as it is? How much else are you wrong about, Liesel, you and all your sort?*

Dieter Schultz and Rudi Harz, leading their men to and through the town, came upon a young man, half carrying a young woman. Their instincts and orders, heightened by the day's events, were to crush these two. Yet they seemed harmless, the man burdened and the woman bloody.

"What happened to you two?" asked a suspicious Harz.

The young man held up one open-palmed hand in a sign of peace. "She was trampled by a panicked crowd," he lied.

Harz and Schultz exchanged glances and lowered their clubs. Harz said, "It is not safe for you two here. You should go."

Schüler nodded but then asked, "Where is the nearest recruiting station? And what unit is this?"

Schultz considered briefly and then gave directions. He answered, simply, "Forty-seventh *Panzer Korps.* Why?"

Schüler answered, "Because I think I have been wrong about some important things. 'Impossibly' wrong."

Neither Harz nor Schultz queried any deeper. Schüler continued on his way, carrying Liesel. He deposited her at the first medical aid station he came upon. Then he continued on.

In a few minutes he had come to the *Bundeswehr* recruiting station for the town of Paderborn. The window was cracked, not smashed. Over the cracked glass, silver paint dripped from a crude set of twin lightning bolts. A sergeant stood inside, bearing a club.

"My name is Andreas Schüler. I wish to join the 47th *Panzer Korps.*"

Sennelager, Germany, 21 July 2005

Mühlenkampf sat alone behind a massive desk dating back to the mid-nineteenth century, his division and brigade commanders standing before him. To their rear, at the conference room's double-wide entrance, likewise stood two sets of complete, but unmatched, armor from the mid-fifteenth century. The walls were hung with battle flags going back to the late eighteenth century. On the floor and lining the walls rested standards, eagles atop wreaths atop hanging red, white and black, gold-fringed, banners.

The banners were newly made. Each bore double lightning flashes. Within each eagle-bearing wreath was some other unique symbol, a curved sun wheel here, there a key with a lightning bolt through it, here a clenched and mailed fist. One standard bore a stylized letter H; another a stylized letter F.

No unvetted civilians were ever permitted to see the banners.

"*Frundsberg*?" began Mühlenkampf, conversationally, naming the division rather than its commander, *Generalmajor* von Ribbentrop. Mühlenkampf considered Ribbontrop an absolute weenie, a posturer, a knave and a fool.[28] Only the man's seniority as an SS officer, and his modern political connections, had seen him in command of a division. "*Frundsberg*, why do you suppose that we were allowed to be assaulted here in our camp? Why were riot police not available in sufficient strength to counter such an obvious and massive move?"

The questions were rhetorical. Mühlenkampf didn't wait for an answer. "*Hohenstauffen*, what is wrong with our country? *Jugend*, why has *every Korps* in the armed forces except for ours been sabotaged? G von B, why are so many young men exempted from the call to duty? *Wiking*, why have some elements of the government attempted to sabotage both us and the *Kriegseconomie*?"[29]

Finally resting his eyes on the only battalion commander present, Mühlenkampf asked, "What is the problem here, Hansi?"

"I do not know, *Herr Generalleutnant*," admitted Brasche.

"I know," said Ribbentrop, confidently. "It is the Jews."

Mühlenkampf snorted his derision. "Nonsense, Ribbentrop, you pansy. There aren't enough Jews in Germany anymore to make a corporal's guard. They are the least influential group we have. I wish we had some more. The Israelis at least can *fight*."

Shaking his head, Mühlenkampf continued, "Forget the Jews, gentlemen. Our problems are home grown. The chancellor is . . . all right . . . I *think*. But beneath him? A Christmas cabal of red and green and some other color I cannot quite make out at this distance. It might be black as deepest midnight, as black as the outer reaches of space."

Mühlenkampf stood and took a thin sheaf of papers, copies actually, from his desktop. These he began to pass out while still speaking. "We are rapidly coming to the end of our most intense training period. From now on we might relax, if only a little. I think, even, that some of the men might benefit from a period of leave. I want you to start granting leaves to deserving men, up to fifteen percent of the force at any given time.

"Those papers contain the names of those I most strongly suspect of being our foes. You might let the men see those names before they sign out of the camp," finished the commander, returning to his seat

Berlin, Germany, 15 September 2005

Though the Darhel lord did not require it, Günter stood stiffly erect before the massive desk behind which the lord sat. Günter was, after all, a German.

The lord's face was impassive. His eyes wandered, looking everywhere but at the bureaucrat's own face. Words, heavily tinged with the sussurant lisp caused by the alien's sharklike teeth, were spoken as if to a party not present.

"This heavy fighting vehicle project has not been stopped," observed the Darhel. "The rejuvenation of the German people's fiercest warriors has been allowed. Sabotage of their fighting body has not been completed to standard. My superiors will require explanations of me. I have no sufficient explanation of this failure on the part of my underlings."

Though the office was cool almost to the point of unpleasantness, still Günter's face bore the sheen of a cold sweat.

An annoyed and frustrated tone crept past the Darhel's lisp. "Explanations will be required."

"My lord," stammered Günter, "these SS simply will not listen or obey. We order them to do or not do certain things and they ignore us. Political leaders who see things in the proper way, as I do, are run out of their camps barely ahead of gangs of uniformed thugs."

"Pay might be withheld," conjectured the Darhel, distantly, eyes closing and a slight shudder wracking his small body. "Food rations withdrawn. Punishment inflicted. Bribes made."

"All have been tried, my lord. Nothing has worked. And no less than eleven of our supporters in the *Bundestag* have disappeared under suspicious circumstances, two or three after each effort. Few *right-minded* politicians seem to have the courage to act in the face of this threat."

"But, in any case, my lord, can't your superiors understand the great good that has been achieved? Of thirteen panzer *Korps*, fully a dozen have had their training sabotaged through propaganda, insistence on the rights of junior soldiers, withholding of vital supplies and equipment, and rigorous application of environmental regulations. Moreover, this grand tank project has had its armor limited. Nuclear propulsion and armament have been refused. Surely these things weigh heavily against such minor failures."

"Perhaps," agreed the Darhel, reluctantly. "And yet we have seen and must remember how often your people have managed to avoid their inevitable position within Galactic civilization by slipping through even smaller cracks."

INTERLUDE

Bin'ar'rastemon the Rememberer's voice rang through the assembly hall. "In the beginning—as the Scroll of Tenusaniar tells us—the People were few, and weak, and powerless . . . and easily impressed. So it came to be that when the Aldenat' came upon them, the people worshiped them nearly as gods.

"And godlike were the powers of the Aldenat'. They healed the sick. They brought new ways to farm, to feed ourselves. They brought a message of peace and love and the People heard their words and became as their children. The Aldenat' brought wonders beyond imagining."

"Beyond imagining," intoned the crowd in response.

"And the people flourished," continued Bin'ar'rastemon. "Their numbers grew and grew and they were content in the service of their gods, the Aldenat'.

"Yet, in time, some of the people questioned. They questioned everything. And always the answer of the Aldenat' was the same: 'We know, and you know not.'

"The people who asked, the Knowers, complained, 'The planets you have given to us cannot support our growing population.' The Aldenat' answered, 'We know, and you know not.'

"The Knowers asked, 'Is there not a better way to move from star to star?' The Aldenat' answered, 'We know, and you know not.'

"The Knowers observed, 'All of life is a struggle. And yet you have forbidden us to join in that struggle. Are we then, even alive?' The Aldenat' answered, 'We know, and you know not.'"

Again the assembly recited, "They said they knew, and they knew not."

Bin'ar'rastemon rejoined, "They knew *not.*"

"And those of the People called the 'Knowers' rebelled in time. And there was war between and among the People. And the Aldenat' knew it not. And there was slaughter. And the Aldenat' admitted it not. And there was fire and death. And the Aldenat' turned their faces from it, seeing it not . . ."

PART II

CHAPTER 5

They came into normal space spitting fire and death. They were met in the cold, hard vacuum by Task Fleet 4.2, Supermonitor *Lexington* and her American crew in the van. The *Lexington* hurled back death with defiance. Likewise with nuclear weapons, antimatter, kinetic energy projectiles, and high-energy plasma.

It was all for naught. Though Posleen died by the millions, the *Lexington*—the "Lady Lex"—and her escorts held the line for scant days before succumbing to the masses of fanatically driven Posleen.

Soon space around Titan Base became a battlefield, the battle lending yet more scrap metal and scorched and frozen flesh to space. That battle, too, was lost. The seemingly endless fleet of Posleen pressed on to ravage and raze an Earth that trembled at their approach.

Wäller Kaserne, Westerburg, Germany, 26 March 2007

An unshaven, yet unshaken, Mühlenkampf growled darkly at the images presented on his screen, "They're coming right through. The Amis couldn't stop them; could hardly even slow them. Neither could the base."

An aide standing nearby answered, brightly, "We will stop them, *Herr Generalleutnant.*"

"Of course we will, Rolf," he told the aide, with more confidence than he truly felt. The projected numbers were *daunting*. "Sound the recall. Code '*Gericht*.'[30] All troops to assemble at their battle positions and assembly areas."

Giessen, Germany, 26 March 2007

Her name meant "battler" or "battle maiden." Yet if ever a girl was misnamed, thought Dieter, that girl was Gudrun. Tall and slender, from golden hair to ivory skin to long and shapely legs, Gudrun evoked no image of battle. Gracefully she walked, as a woman, though Dieter suspected she was rather young, sixteen at most.

Schultz had seen her, once before, here at the soldiers' recreation center that served the troops in and around the city of Giessen. He had seen her, the once, and he had come back every chance he had from then to now in the hopes of seeing her again.

And now—had God above smiled upon him?—the girl actually sat at the table nearest to his. Close up Dieter found her even lovelier than he had at a distance; this despite a fairly obvious attempt at portraying a sophistication the girl probably lacked. She pulled a cigarette out, and held it, nonchalantly, awaiting someone to light it.

"Give me your lighter, Rudi," demanded Schultz of Harz. "Now, please. You know I do not smoke."

With a smile that could only be described as sympathetic, if amusedly so, Rudi passed the tiny machine over. Dieter was at Gudrun's side in the next instant, flame springing from his hand.

The girl smiled warmly and thanked Dieter who, taking it for encouragement, promptly sat beside her, introducing himself.

"Ah, my name is Gudrun."

"I am very pleased to meet you, Gudrun. Very."

The girl didn't ask if he was in the army; such was obvious from the field gray Dieter wore. She did ask of his unit and job.

"I am the gunner for a Tiger III in the 501st Heavy Panzer Battalion, 47th *Panzer Korps*," he answered.

Gudrun recoiled momentarily. "The SS Korps? The Nazis?"

Laughing, Dieter answered, "We're not an SS *Korps*, Gudrun. Why, according to my chief, Sergeant Major Krueger, we are not fit to wipe the boots of real SS men. They did train us," he admitted.

"Then you are *not* a Nazi?"

"Me?" Dieter laughed again, louder. "No, *Liebchen*.[31] I was a student when they drafted me and gave me a choice. Sort of a choice. Not much of one, as a matter of fact." He shrugged. "And my grandfather told me I would be better off training under the old SS than under the new *Bundeswehr*. So there I went.

"And you?"

"I am in school still, learning to be a tailor," she answered. As she did the music in the hall changed to something slow.

"Would you care to dance, Gudrun the tailor?"

Brasche had let all but a skeleton crew go to the dance. Krueger was here in the Tiger III, christened, if that was the right word, "*Anna*." Likewise was the new boy, Schüler, who had just been assigned. A couple of others manned the auxiliary *MauserWerke* twenty-five millimeter cannon stations by remote from the armored battle center deep inside the tank. The loader, whose job actually involved running the elevators and automatic rammers that brought the three-hundred-five-millimeter projectiles and their propellant to the main gun's breech and fed them to it, stood by.

The other sixteen men of the *Anna*'s crew, including Schultz and Harz, were in Giessen trying for a last chance at love before entering the coming fray.

But Brasche had had no interest, this despite having the body of a twenty-year-old again. He had met one girl in his life who had meant anything to him. And that girl was lost to him forever; all but an image in a photo, a clip of hair, and other images and feelings indelibly engraved on his heart and mind.

That girl, the original Anna—once of flesh and blood, smiled out at him from a photo held lightly in Hans' hand.

Gudrun was light and graceful in Dieter's arms as they danced. The boy himself was no dancer. And yet, at its best, dance, like the act of love, brings souls together in union and harmony. So it was with this couple, bodily movements meshing into unity of bodies. By the time the dance ended, Dieter knew he had found the one right girl for him. They simply fit. Perfectly.

The soft sweet smell of her perfume lingered in Dieter's brain, doing its intended job of short-circuiting that brain. The two walked backed to Gudrun's table, arms about each others' waists, leaning against each other.

At the table they talked. And both knew that the talk was serious. There was little time for the boy-girl games so beloved of the romances.

"I want you, Gudrun," Dieter announced simply. "Now. Here or nearby. Anywhere, really. But now."

The girl looked forlorn. Her face shone with desire at least equal to his own. Still, reluctantly, she shook her head No.

"I have a boyfriend, Dieter. With the 33rd *Korps*, 165th Infantry Division. It wouldn't be right . . . not until I can tell him about you . . . about us."

Schultz understood and said so. "But after you have spoken or written?"

"Then, yes. You and I," she agreed.

He nodded his head in agreement, "Yes. You and I."

At that instant there came a commotion from the entrance way. Dieter saw Harz threading his way through the thickening crowd.

"It's on, Dieter," announced Harz. "'*Gericht.' Sie kommen.*" They're coming.

From his elevated perch high atop *Anna*'s turret Brasche saw the lightning streaks slashing down and up—Posleen spacecraft softening the defenses and human Planetary Defense Centers snarling their defiance. Regretfully, reluctantly, he replaced the other Anna in the small folder he had carried by his heart for nearly sixty years.

"*Anna*, down," he commanded and the Tiger's voice-recognition software sent a command to move the tiny elevator platform on which he stood down into the heavily armored command center of the tank.

Krueger was there with the skeleton crew. As often was the case, the sergeant major was regaling the boys with tales from the last war. So far as that went, Brasche could not and did not object. Sometimes, though, Krueger told of other things, vile things. This Brasche loathed, as indeed he loathed the man.

"It was great, I tell you, boys. Great. Your pick of the women in those camps. And some of them were lookers, too, even if they were just Jew bitches."

"How did you end up in one of the camps?" asked Schüler. "I thought you were a combat soldier."

"Well, I was only there for about six months, you see. While I was healing up from being shot by the Russians. At Ravensbrück, it was. A women's camp. There were so many we never even asked their names."

That was enough, more than enough, for Brasche. "Sergeant Major, that will be all. Men: to your posts. The enemy is coming. We move to meet them as soon as the rest of the crew returns."

The crew began to scramble to battle stations. Instinctively, Hans' hand moved to caress the left pocket of his tanker's coveralls, his "*Panzerkompli*," and the small folder it contained. He kept his face carefully neutral.

Harz looked away, neutrally, as Dieter and Gudrun said their last goodbyes, whispered endearments and hopes for a future. "The bus is here to take us back now, Dieter. I am sorry; we must go."

Reluctantly, Schultz disengaged himself from Gudrun's arms. Her hands were the last things he let go of. Even then, he could not help but lift one hand to his lips and press them against it.

"I will come back," he said. "I promise."

Gudrun immediately dissolved into tears. In a wavering voice she answered, through her tears, "I will be waiting. I, too, promise." The girl's head hung in unfeigned despair. "I promise." Through her mind raced the thoughts that this would be the only chance, that Dieter could not wait for her to break things off with the other boy.

But there was no time. The recall was sounded. Action called. The bus awaited.

"Write to me," she cried. "Please write," and she hurriedly jotted an e-mail address down on a napkin.

Dieter, his heart at once overjoyed and breaking, nodded, took the napkin, released her hand, and turned to go. Already, outside the recreation center, a bus awaited. Inside the bus the troopers sang:

"Muss I' denn, muss I' denn,
Zum Stadtele hinaus, Stadtele hinaus
Und du, mein Schatz bleibst hier. . . ."[32]

From his command chair, Brasche looked over his crew with satisfaction. There was no scuffling or confusion as men took their seats and strapped themselves in. Only young Schultz, his main gunner, seemed distracted.

"What is it, Dieter?"

"Nothing, *Herr Oberst*," the boy answered.

Brasche raised a quizzical eyebrow. "The boy's fallen in love," answered the ever-helpful Harz. "Nice girl, too, if looks do not deceive." Harz' hands made curvy motions in the air, exaggerating a bit Gudrun's willowy figure.

Schultz flashed his friend an angry look. Brasche merely smiled. "Rejoice then, *Unteroffizier* Schultz. Now you know, perhaps, what is worth fighting for."

Brasche consulted the map display affixed to the left-hand arm of his command chair. On the display he traced the route he wished his battalion to follow with a finger. He pressed a button to send the route to each of the other twelve Tiger IIIs in his battalion. Then he keyed a throat mike. *"Achtung, Panzer. Aufrollen."*[33]

INTERLUDE

Even at the center of the B-Dec, itself surrounded by C-Decs and Lampreys, Athenalras felt the gravitic surge as kinetic energy projectiles passed nearby. The ship bucked around him from the force of the passage.

"Food with a sting, indeed," he snarled, as a nearby vessel disintegrated in his view-screen.

Athenalras cursed the loss, then issued orders for a concentration of fire against the thresh battery that had destroyed his ship. From dozens of ships, relativistic hail rained down on an obscure mountain in the French Pyrenees. To the defenders, below, it looked like a cone of fire from the hand of God, obliterating everything at the point of the cone.

Far above, another screen showed the Posleen commander a glowing patch of ground, no longer so mountainous. The area was soon obscured from space by rising clouds of dirt and ash, flames from the ruined surface glowing through the angry, dark nebulae.

Athenalras' crest lifted triumphantly as crocodilian lips curled up in a sneer. "Defy me now, little abat."

As if on cue, Ro'moloristen announced, "Incoming fire, my lord. Heavy fire."

Goaded beyond endurance by the loss of the Pyrenees battery, five previously masked, human-manned, Planetary Defense Bases—one each from the Vosges, Apennines, German Alps, Swiss Alps, and Atlas Mountains—lashed back. More of Athenalras' ships perished in rapidly expanding clouds of disassociate matter.

The God King cursed the foul thresh of this evil world yet again. He sent further orders to his ships. More deadly hail fell from the skies. In the Vosges, the Apennines, the Alps and the Atlas, snow flashed to steam, mountains shivered and quaked, men were charred to ash in instants.

On both sides losses in the space-to-shore battle were heavy. Yet the Posleen could afford the loss the better.

Seeing little resistance remaining below—little enough, in any case, to allow a landing, Athenalras determined the time was right. Besides, who knew if the damned humans had more batteries lying in wait. Safer on the ground.

"Land the landing force," he ordered. The Kessentai of his immediate entourage raised joyful cries of victory around him.

CHAPTER 6

They descended in waves of waves, tens of thousands of Posleen landing craft. Far out in space they split into three large task forces, one large group for Europe and North Africa, and one smaller one each for India and South America—those places already being largely taken over by the Posleen who had come before. The Latins and Hindus had really never been in any position to defend themselves.

The invader touched down first on the North African littoral. Along the Nile, and in its delta, Egyptians—Moslem and Christian alike, prayed for deliverance. It was not forthcoming.

West from Egypt, along the fertile North African coast only the ubiquitous Bedu survived in any numbers. The city and town dwellers disappeared into the invaders' sharp-fanged maws.

Three globes, three out of a total of seventy-three in this wave—fifty-eight of them in the Europe/North Africa force, were all it took to overrun, in a matter of days, the seats of one of Earth's most ancient civilizations, that and the broad sweep of one of its most ancient areas of barbarism.

Three additional globes were sufficient to drive the Italians, such as lived, reeling into the Apennines and staggering north to the Alps. The streets of the Roman Forum echoed with the clatter of the invaders' claws on ancient cobblestones.

In the ruins of Madrid the last survivors of the Spanish Legion battled to the death amongst the shattered stones of El Prado. Elsewhere throughout Iberia, Spanish and Portuguese soldiers died at their posts to gain a few days, a few hours, for their civilians to reach the shelter of the Pyrenees, and the Sub-Urban—underground, in this case—towns waiting there. In some cases, this was sufficient.

Four globes had landed in once-sunny Iberia.

England felt as many of the enemy touch her soil. Yet the English had succeeded in raising an army suited to her station. The Posleen who landed there met only cold, bitter resistance, walls of stone and walls of flying shards from artillery. In the end, the United Kingdom managed to hang on to her territory and people from a line just south of Hadrian's Wall. This was no mean achievement.

The single globe devoted to the Swiss and Austrians made the mistake of landing in a fortified Swiss valley. Hidden guns suddenly appeared all around the landing site. Infantry that could be numbered among the best and sharpest shooting in the world sprang up as if from nowhere. The Posleen force that had touched down disappeared without survivors.

The single globe each that landed on Belgium and Holland left only those survivors as managed to escape to Germany.

France and Poland, bearing the brunt of the Posleen effort, found themselves drawn and quartered. Paris held out for the nonce, as did Warsaw. A few other cities, prepared for defense in advance, did as well. Neither French nor Poles could be said to have been quite prepared for the magnitude and ferocity of the attack. Wishful thinking had beguiled the French while the Poles, never so numerous, still struggled under the legacy of forty-five years of Communist misrule and its resulting inefficiency and corruption.

Charitably, it could at least be said of both that they had fought hard, died well, and brought no disgrace upon their ancestors.

Seven globes hit Germany, bearing nearly thirty million Posleen. These were globes commanded by Kessentai that Athenalras didn't like very much or think very highly of. There were thirteen large panzer *Korps*—thirty-nine panzer and twenty-six panzergrenadier divisions, though many times that in infantry, to meet them.

The odds in Germany were worse for the Posleen than they had ever faced in their history. Five of those heavy divisions awaiting them were called "*Wiking, Hohenstauffen, Frundsberg,*

Jugend and Götz von Berlichingen." One battalion was called the "501st *Schwere Panzer* (Michael Wittmann)."

Paris, France, 27 March 2007

It was snowing outside when the phone rang.

Her husband had had time to make one call, and that very brief. "I love you, Isabelle. Always remember that. But it turns out that this threat you denied is real, after all. And it looks like it is concentrating on us and the Poles. My unit will be in action soon. You, however, *must* get yourself and the boys ready to flee. I cannot tell you where to go to or how to get there. But watch the news carefully. Do not trust everything the government says. And when it is time to move, move you must . . . and quickly."

Then, as if her answering that she understood were some kind of signal, the husband had said again, "Remember I love you," just before the phone went dead.

The next hours were filled with frantic packing of long unused camping equipment, food, and some minimum essential winter clothing. *Why had she not packed sooner?* Isabelle cursed herself. With each new series of meteorlike, incoming flashes of death from space the conviction had grown that she had made a terrible mistake.

She couldn't stop blaming the Americans, though, for needlessly bringing on this war.

As Isabelle packed one bag after another, her elder son, Thomas, had taken them down to the family automobile and carefully stowed them.

Once the car was packed, Isabelle strapped into its usual place the restraining seat for the baby of the family. Then she and Thomas cleared away the accumulated snow from the windows.

Wäller Kaserne, Westerburg, Germany, 27 March 2007

Outside the headquarters snow fell, driven by the wind and collecting in drifts chaotically. Inside, paper and words flew in an equal blizzard. But inside, the will of one man reigned over the chaos of the frightful news.

"Major landings at Ingolstadt, Tübingen, Aschaffenburg, Meissen, Schwerin, Nienburg, and Guemmersbach, *Herr Generalleutnant*," announced the aide de camp, Rolf, finger stabbing down at each fresh Posleen infestation marked on the table-borne map. "Minor ones all over the map."

The phone rang. Neither Posleen invasion nor four years of steady allied bombing during the Second World War had ever quite succeeded in inconveniencing the *Bundespost*, the German telephone system.

"*Generalleutnant*, it is the chancellor for you."

Mühlenkampf took the phone, announcing himself.

He listened for several minutes before answering, "Yes, *Herr Kanzler*, I understand. You can count on the 47th *Panzer Korps*."

The general replaced the phone on its cradle, exhaling forcefully. To his staff he explained, "The infantry is folding and running almost everywhere. Some of the towns are holding though. Aschaffenburg has fallen, but Würzburg and Schweinfurt are holding out. We are going to move south, relieve those towns, and destroy the invaders utterly."

The aide listened for the remaining words. Those words remained unspoken. Finally, he asked, "What about our left and right units, *Herr General*?"

Mühlenkampf shook his head. "The other twelve heavy *Korps* are already committed. The only infantry in range to have any effect is crushed . . . they were crushed in a matter of hours. We're on our own in this."

The autobahn was a steady-moving river of vehicles, both soft and armored. Civilians moved north in two streams to either side. Their faces were haggard, drawn, frightened.

Mixed in among the civilians, mostly weaponless, trudged soldiers in the thousands. These were broken men, from broken formations. Leaderless, these men were also demoralized, dispirited and disheveled.

Off from the autobahn, at a distance, Brasche stood in the turret of *Anna*, watching the mixed crowd pass. Their eyes filled briefly with hope at the Tiger's imposing heft and incredibly vicious-looking gun. Then, one and all, the refugees would glance behind them, remember what they had seen, the horrors of Posleen on a feeding frenzy, and hopelessly trudge on.

Hans understood. He had seen it before. He had been a part of it before.

It was a warm spring afternoon. Winter was past now, fully past. It had been a long one . . . and bitter.

So had the march to escape Soviet captivity and near certain death been a bitter one. Brasche remembered it in all too much detail: the burning of the standards, the surrender of the other soldiers, the massacre of prisoners he had witnessed from nearby. Then came the wet cold nights racing through Austria to outrun the Reds' inexorable advance.

Amidst the debris of war and defeat, Brasche had searched for a uniform to fit him, finally finding one on the corpse of a dead Wehrmacht sergeant. Still, while he could burn his SS garb, he could not so easily remove the tattoo on his left side that marked him indelibly as a member.

So west he headed, ever west into the setting sun. France was his goal, as it had become the goal of many of those who survived the surrender of the Wiking Division. The Legion was to become home for as many as could find shelter within it. The Legion asked no questions of a man who preferred, for the sake of his life, not to answer any.

At length, Brasche came upon another group of German soldiers, sitting quietly in an open field by a road. Near Stuttgart this was. A noncom wearing a funny-looking, coffee can cap with a bill stood among the Germans nonchalantly taking names and writing them into a ledger.

Hans recognized the cap, recognized too the calm and contentment of the German soldiers. Amidst the trash of defeat, Hans Brasche had found the Legion.

Hammelburg, Germany, 27 March 2007

The roadside was littered with everything from abandoned baby carriages to mattresses to cars that, out of gas, had been pushed aside to make room for the advancing *Korps*. Already, drifting snow was beginning to cover the debris. It was also covering some bodies of those too faint of heart or weak in the will to live to go on.

This is defeat, an old voice in Hans' head reminded him. *Avoid it.*

From somewhere behind his Tiger came the sound of artillery, lots of it, firing. The shells' passage rattled the air with the racket of one hundred freight trains. In Brasche's ears, the radio crackled with reports from the *Korps'* forward reconnaissance unit, the *Panzeraufklärungsbrigade*, Florian Geyer.[34] The enemy was near at hand.

Up just past the autobahn bridge over the river south of the town the lead panzer division, *Hohenstauffen*, sprang to more active life. Tanks and infantry fighting vehicles pivot steered to get off of the road and into a semblance of order. Panicked civilians did their best to dodge the metal flood, though that best was not always good enough. The *Hohenstauffen* drivers did their best to avoid killing any of their own. That best was likewise not always good enough.

Once clear of the autobahn and the refugees the tanks and infantry carriers raced forward to take up positions behind a low ridge, infantry moving closer in to hug the dead ground behind the military crest, tanks taking position further back to rake the area between the military crest and the top of the ridge.

Though heavily armored enough to stand up to Posleen fire, from directly in front at least, Brasche's tank *Anna* and her sister Tiger IIIs did not take the lead. Instead, spread out with almost two kilometers between tanks, they pulled in furthest from the ridgeline. Once halted the Tigers automatically analyzed their firing sectors. In a few cases minor adjustments in position were made. Once settled, each Tiger began to ooze out a quick-drying camouflage foam from a system built under license from the Americans. Brasche stood in the turret while a small mountain of foam rose and hardened around *Anna*, the main gun depressing fully to allow the foam to drip to and blend with the snow on the ground. Though the foam could be colored, in this case it remained its natural white to blend in with the falling snow.

Brasche stood in the command hatch while foam settled below. A quick look around satisfied him with the progress of the camouflage job. He gave a command and *Anna* brought him safe into her womb below.

"Commander on deck," intoned Dieter, remaining in his gunner's seat but bracing to a stiff, modified attention. The rest of the crew, minus Krueger who pretended not to notice, did likewise.

Hans took over the command chair his assistant commander vacated for him and focused his attention on the situation display on the forward. The board was updated continuously with reports from the Florian Geyer Brigade, the other units forward of the Tigers and just now making contact, reports from towns now under siege and even one doomed sortie by the Luftwaffe that had managed to send back some information before being flash-burned from the sky.

"Report," Brasche ordered.

From in front, in a position to take full advantage of the situation board when it was displayed as a forward view-screen, Krueger reported, "Driving station, full up, *Herr Oberst*."

Like clockwork, keying off of Krueger's response, the secondary armament gunners reported down the line. Well trained by now, their eyes never left their own view-screens as they did so.

The tank and battalion exec, Schmidt, reported on logistic status. The ammunition racks were full, fuel was only at about seventy-five percent but the refueling vehicles were within easy range. Brasche raised a quieting hand when the XO began to go into such mundane items as food and water.

Engineering reported the tank was mechanically fully capable of movement, though actual movement must await the drying of the camouflage foam.

Lastly Dieter Schultz answered that the main gun was ready, but unloaded.

Hans looked again at the view-screen. The indicators were that the horde of Posleen infantry would be the first to reach the hastily drawn line of defense. He keyed his microphone. "Odd numbered Tigers load antipersonnel. Even numbers load antispacecraft. Second rounds to be area denial. Third rounds to be antispacecraft."

There came the faint whining of machinery as Dieter's loader selected three twelve-inch rounds from the fifty carried in a carousel well below the turret level. These moved upward under robotic control. Overhead, the metal breech opened with a clang faintly audible even behind the armor of the cocoon. There was more whining as the propellant was fed from its storage area behind the turret into the open breech. Then there came a final clang as the breech slammed home and locked into position.

"Gun up," announced Schultz as soon as the green light appeared on the gunner's console in front of him. In Brasche's earpiece his three companies of four Tigers each likewise reported ready for action.

Dieter Schultz, good man that he was, scanned his screen for targets continuously. He had done this so much in training that it barely took a fraction of his concentration to do so. This was a good thing as the bulk of his mind was occupied with thoughts of Gudrun.

Giessen, Germany, 27 March 2007

The first letter had been hard to write. Gudrun despised herself for having to hurt a boy who had done his best to bring her only happiness. Yet, hateful or not, it had had to be done, Gudrun knew. She had been close to Pieter, very close. But one look at Dieter had been enough for her to know that here was the *one*, the perfect one for her.

And to her own heart she had to be true.

So she had written the letter, putting in her wishes that a boy somewhere to the north could somehow understand and forgive that she had found another. Then she had sealed it, shed a small tear for the pain she knew it was to bring a boy who had never done or wished her anything but good.

The second letter was easier, a joy in fact. Though she had Dieter's e-mail address, and the tank he had said he fought in had integral e-mail, there was no way to send her little gift, a lock of golden hair—freshly clipped and tied with a ribbon, via electrons. She searched through her desk for a picture and came up with a wallet-sized color photo, a high school picture. This, too, she placed in the letter.

Writing finished, Gudrun walked the short distance to the post, purchased and attached stamps, and deposited the missive through the slot. Then she returned to her parents' house.

Once there, she turned on the television. The news—and news was all the stations were carrying—was full of the fighting raging across Europe and Germany. Little of that news was good. Especially to the north was there cause for concern.

Marburg an der Lahn, Germany, 27 March 2007

Fulungsteeriot was not among the brightest of the Posleen Kessentai. He suspected, in his somewhat dim way, that that was what had gotten his oolt'pos assigned to the central sector of this wave's intended conquest.

Though the thresh here ran, sometimes, leaving their open backs to the Posleen's railguns and boma blades, often enough they fought bitterly. Especially was this true of the men who drove and fought from the thresh's ground tenaral. Fortunately, in his sector, Fulungsteeriot's oolt had met few of the nasty, hateful, cowardly threshkreen machines. Those few, usually taking positions in dead space to rake over the People as they galloped over crests or around hills or buildings, had taken a fearful toll. Only leading the horde of ground-bound normals with the God Kings' own tenar or with armed landing vessels could flush out these disgustingly cowardly prey in a usefully timely fashion. And that had its own attendant risks, as the wretches refused to come out and fight in the open like warriors. That, and that their hand weapons, while generally primitive and inferior to those of the people, were not to be despised, either. And they seemed to seek out the tenar-riding God Kings with single-minded ferocity.

Moreover, there were scattered reports, frightening ones, of actions by huge thresh fighting machines that arose, seemingly, from the ground to smash down the People's vessels with brutal and deadly accurate fire. Fulungsteeriot was more than a little happy that his group had not yet met any of the thresh "Tigers," as they were called.

Fulungsteeriot was more than happy, as well, that he had the use of his landers to crush resistance in the path of his horde.

Hammelburg, Germany, 28 March 2007

Though in the rear of the defensive line, the lay of the land dictated that it would be the Tigers who first saw the oncoming tidal wave of Posleen cresting the ridge.

Schultz's eyes opened wide as first a horde of flyers ascended over the mass, followed by a solid phalanx of centaur flesh. "*Lieber Gott im Himmel.*" Dear God in Heaven.

Hans calmly issued an order to the battalion, "Odd numbered Tigers stand by to unmask and engage on my command."

At his words, Schultz took a firmer grip of the control spades from which he ran the gun, whispering, "Magnification 24x." The tank's human-built artificial intelligence system immediately closed the apparent range. Schultz repeated, "*Lieber Gott,*" as the mass of aliens sprang suddenly into sharp relief. His hands visibly tightened on the controls.

"Do *not* fire *until* I give the command," reminded Brasche, forcing his mind to intense concentration.

Even as Brasche spoke the snow began falling with renewed intensity, the external remote cameras going white with natural static.

"The command to fire will be the opening of the machine gun," whispered sous-officier Brasche, of the Legion, to the squad assembled around him in the dank and fetid Indochinese jungle. "Any questions?"

Seeing there would be none, Hans pointed northward towards a trail intersection known to be used by the Viet Minh. Wordlessly, the point man, a veteran of the Latvian SS Division once—now a veteran of the Legion Etranger, took the lead and disappeared into the green maze. Brasche followed directly, machine gun team in tow. The rest of the squad, moving single file, followed Brasche.

Berlin, Germany, 28 March 2007

The Tir's AID projected a hologram in the air over his desk. The hologram showed a map of Europe and North Africa, centered on Germany.

"Stupid centaurs," the Tir muttered aloud. "Landing most of their force elsewhere and half leaving the Germans alone. Don't they realize that delay could prove deadly, that these people are not to be underestimated?"

Even as the Tir watched that portion of the map that showed the red of Posleen infestation expanded throughout most of the area, even while it reshaped and deformed, and in places shrank, in Germany. His superiors would be pleased, he knew, at the former. Yet explanations might be required for the latter, explanations he was by no means looking forward to giving.

"Foolish reptiles. Taking the easy meat and ignoring the looming threat."

The strangely shaped human servant with the disgusting hair color knocked lightly on the Tir's door. "*Herr* Stössel to see you, *Herr* Tir."

About time, thought the Darhel.

Günter entered and, without taking a seat, placed a briefcase gently upon the Tir's desktop. "These are the plans you required, Lord Tir," Günter said.

The Tir nodded. "These will be useful to our interests. Are they complete?" he asked.

"Sadly, not, *mein Herr*. Oh, yes, we have gotten most of them. But one group refuses to so much as discuss their orders and intentions with anyone but the chancellor. And the chancellor refuses to discuss them with anyone at all."

"Those ancient warriors? The ones you call the SS?"

Günter's face twisted into a sneer. "Yes, *them*," he answered. "*They* are out of control."

The sneer disappeared momentarily as Günter wondered at that. He had been so *sure*, so utterly certain, that the military mindset had had any forms of disobedience driven from it. After all, hadn't the *Bundeswehr* rolled over for restrictions guaranteed and intended to be insulting beyond the endurance of mortal man? *Oh, well. Perhaps they are not "soldiers like other soldiers," after all, as they claimed to be. They must be the madmen I have always considered them to be. Mad dogs, to be put down.*

"They are also out of . . . oversight," observed the Tir. "With every other part of your force we have no trouble eavesdropping. But these SS refuse to so much as let one of our AIDs near them."

Günter agreed, "They are as out of step with technology as

they are out of step socially. Even their colleagues in the regular *Bundeswehr* shake their heads with wonder. These old men think so much alike they barely even use their radios."

"And I have no *idea* what they are doing," the Tir cursed.

INTERLUDE

Athenalras cursed. He cursed the humans and their damned cowardly ways of fighting. He cursed the fetid grass and disgusting trees of this world, "Blech, what a disgusting color, green? Red, brown, blue. Those I could understand. But *green*?"

Mostly, though, he cursed the Aldenata, those sticky-fingered players at godhood whose meddling had driven the People to one disgusting world after another. "Mindless, arrogant, self-righteous," he muttered. "Stupid, vain and foolish . . ."

Athenalras heard a faint coughlike sound, though coming as it did from a Posleen throat no human would have found it to be terribly coughlike. More like the hacking of a bird disgorging digestive stones, it was.

"My lord?" interrupted Ro'moloristen.

"What is it, puppy?" growled the senior, reaching forth a finger and pressing a button. In his view-screen a tall, spindly, four-legged metal tower with no obvious purpose began to waver and then melt. Athenalras grunted satisfaction; yet another example of the natives' nauseating sense of aesthetics sent to perdition.

"Reports here in the human province of France are most favorable. Our rear, in Spain, is almost secure. On the other side, Poland is putting up a spirited resistance, but there is no doubt it will fall completely . . . and very soon."

"Good," hissed the warleader. "And how goes it for our little selective breeding program in the center?"

"A mixed bag," answered Ro'moloristen, equivocally. In truth, he did not know for a certainty whether Athenalras meant progress in conquest or progress in eliminating stupid underlings. The junior God King thought it entirely possible his chief meant both.

CHAPTER 7

So far, the lines had held, and held well. Though a glance at the red-spotted map in Mühlenkampf's headquarters might make it appear to the unlettered observer that Germany was on its way to being overrun, that appearance would have been false. Ingolstadt's infestation was contained. The Bavarian *Panzer Korps*, with the aid of two *Korps* of fairly good mountain infantry, was reducing the landing at Tübingen.

At Meissen, Schwerin, Nienburg, and Guemmersbach the question would remain somewhat open until the two panzer *Korps* at Ingolstadt and the one at Tübingen could finish off the remnants of the Posleen, reorganize and move to reinforce the others. Yet the men at those places were still holding.

The only really bad news was at the northern Bavarian town of Aschaffenburg, which had seen all her citizens erased, along with the better part of a *Korps* of infantry. All that stood in the way of the Posleen victors of that slaughter were some much-despised relics of a half-forgotten war—those, and the young men they had been allowed to contaminate with out-of-date views of the world . . .

Hammelburg, Germany, 29 March 2007

"Sixty-seven landers just over the horizon, heading this way," announced Brasche's 1c, or intelligence officer, from the station where he did dual duty as that and as close-in defense gunner.

"What kind?" Brasche demanded.

"A mixed bag, *mein Herr*. Brigade Florian Geyer can barely make out rough shapes in all this snow. Even the thermal imagers are having problems. What we have seen indicates as many C-Decs as Lampreys."

"Will they see us here, under our camouflage foam?" wondered Brasche, aloud.

Though the question was rhetorical, the 1c answered, "Florian Geyer appears still alive and still broadcasting. Perhaps the enemy isn't any better at dealing with this white shit than we are."

"Perhaps not," mused Brasche. He repeated on the general circuit, "All panzers, hold fire until my command. Boys, we're going to play a little trick. . . ."

Marburg an der Lahn, Germany, 29 March 2007

What a dirty, filthy trick, thought Pieter Friedenhof, crumbling the letter he'd received from Gudrun with the morning meal. "That fucking bitch," he said aloud. "The stone-cold cast-iron twat," he fumed. "How *dare* she leave me at a time like this? And for some low-browed Nazi?"

The boy broke down and wept for a time, even as he cursed the name of "battle maiden." With each curse and each wracking sob he felt trickle away the very reasons he had been willing to stand fast and die, if need be, to defend his home, his family, his girl.

Weather reports spoke of snow coming from the south, but Pieter felt already as if a blizzard had descended upon his heart and soul.

Hammelburg, Germany, 29 March 2007

The radio crackled in Brasche's ears, "*Battalion Michael Wittmann? Mühlenkampf hier.*"

"*501ˢᵗ Schwere Panzer hier, Herr General.*"

"Brasche? *Gut.* Very good. Look Hansi, we've got a problem. We've held the enemy along this line for two days now but it looks like they've given up unsupported frontal charges for the nonce. I'd be happy for the breather except that those fucking landers are going to chew up our forward men something awful. I want you to—"

"General, I have an idea," Hans interrupted.

For a moment the radio was silent: Mühlenkampf mulling the Knight's Cross he knew hung at Brasche's throat.

"What's your idea, Hansi?"

"Have everyone on the forward trace except the dismounted infantry shut down completely. Hold the line with artillery—the shells are holding up well, yes?"

"We've enough," conceded Mühlenkampf. "But the reports are clear, Brasche: there are always leakers through the heaviest barrage."

"Not so many that the riflemen and machine gunners can't handle, for a while anyway, *Herr General.* And if you keep using the panzers those C-Decs and Lampreys will eat them for a snack."

"Taking care of those is *your* job, Hans," Mühlenkampf insisted.

Brasche wiped a few beads of sweat, nervous sweat, from his forehead. "Yes, *Herr General.* But at five-to-one odds I won't be able to do enough . . . not without a little cleverness."

"Wait, out," ordered Mühlenkampf as he tried to force rational thought through a sleep-starved brain.

Brasche insisted, "There's little time to decide, sir. My way has a chance."

"What is your way, Hansi?"

Brasche proceeded to explain. As he did so those of his own crew grew wide-eyed and shuddering. *Was their commander stark raving mad?*

Marburg an der Lahn, Germany, 29 March 2007

"This is madness," muttered the demoralized Friedenhof from the relative safety of a reverse slope. "Madness."

In the boy's ears, the sound of the enemy grew ever closer, an ominous cacophony as distinct from the overhead rattle of defending artillery as, in a more traditional day, had been the pounding of hoofs from setting of pikes or the drawing of sabers. As steadily as grew the crescendo of clawed feet tramping ground, boma blades being drawn, hisses and snorts and incomprehensible grunts, each foot soldier of the 165th Infantry division felt and even seemed to hear his own heart pounding ever more frenziedly in his chest.

Suddenly, like a cloud of mist arising from a river, the enemy appeared. He came first as a swarm of flying sleds, the God Kings' tenars. These the snipers of the division *Jaeger*[35] battalion took under fire. Yet there were more tenar than snipers, and they were hard to hit and, oh, very well armed. Though more than a few of the sleds disappeared in actinic spheres, snipers were blasted to bits and burned to cinders by return fire for each tiny victory they earned over the invaders.

Scant minutes following the appearance of the tenar-riding God Kings, Friedenhof's eyes widened as the rest of the host made its sudden appearance. They appeared to him as a solid mass, a veritable phalanx of reptilian, centauroid flesh—all snapping teeth and flashing blades. Artillery began carving huge slices from that body, as from the bodies that composed it. Yellow flesh and blood, yellow bone and sinew soon festooned the very top of the landmass to Friedenhof's front.

Heedless of the losses, the alien horde swarmed down and towards the reverse military crest along which the defenders had erected their defenses.

Suddenly, on command, the Germans began to lash back. MG-3s, direct descendants of "Hitler's Zipper" of World War Two fame, lent the air the sound of an impossibly large number of sails being ripped apart at the hands of an impossible number of giants. Prone gunners were pushed back by the hammering recoil of their guns. The air filled with the smell of cordite and weapons oil boiling away from heated feed mechanisms. Posleen screamed and reared and stumbled and writhed in every manner of undignified death by lead.

Coming through the hell of lead and fire the defenders poured forth, the Posleen next hit a thin line of the mines called "Bouncing Barbies." These devices, accidental byproducts of an impromptu

experiment gone badly awry at distant Fort Bragg, North Caro-
lina, years before, waited patiently for the sense of the enemy
sufficiently close and in sufficient numbers.

A knot of twenty Posleen, perhaps as much trying to avoid
the worst of the shell and machine gun fire as to close with
the humans, activated a Barbie. The mine used a small, integral
antigravity device to lift itself one meter into the air. It then put
out a linear force field to a distance of six meters. Eleven Posleen
fell immediately, alive but legless, their stumps waving helplessly
in the air while they shrieked and sprayed yellow ichor into the
air and onto the ground.

Its work done for the nonce, the force field shut off to conserve
power even as the mine's antigravity propelled it sideways to cover
another small piece of the front. Amidst the yellow blood, the
mine's yellow plastic casing quickly became indistinguishable.

It had only been through the last-minute agency of the Americans that the Germans even *had* Barbies. Their own political left,
or so much of it as the Darhel had been able to suborn, had
prevented development of any such unpalatable devices as new
mines on their own. As they had prevented the development of
usefully small and clean nuclear weapons . . . and poisons . . . and
anything that smacked of militarism. "No threat can justify the
development of such horrid arms," had been the cry. "No threat
could possibly justify . . ."

Thus, despite last minute emergency deliveries, the German
army had but few Barbies, and fewer nuclear and antimatter
munitions.

Hammelburg, Germany, 29 March 2007

"All panzers, load antilander munitions. Prepare for a steady
stream of depleted uranium. Adjust yield for the targets as per
doctrine. And be fucking quiet."

Half the battalion had already loaded rounds designed to deal
with Posleen landers. The other half began the process of opening breaches, withdrawing propellant casings and projectiles, and
reloading with depleted uranium penetrators and their more
powerful propellants.

The loading went quickly and smoothly. Though they had tried, the suborned left had not been able to interfere with the building of German precision machinery. Even the formerly Communist east had for the most part overcome the red-inspired tendency to produce mechanical dreck in the interests of meeting norms and quotas.

As for the DU penetrators themselves, the left would have shrieked their fury to a ritually denied Heaven could they have known how the otherwise simple rounds had been modified . . . and why. The use of depleted uranium itself had been a close run thing in the Bundestag, the German Parliament. "Ecologically unsound. Environmentally unsafe. Polluting . . . filthy." *Aesthetically unappealing. Heretical. Upsets me at my vegetarian breakfast. Forces me to contemplate that which* must *be denied.*

But the left had never known, indeed had had the information concealed from them, that each DU penetrator had been partially hollowed out to make room for a modest amount of antimatter in a containment field. An American firm, working clandestinely with the BND, had developed and provided the weapons, again at nearly the last minute. These, penetrator and carefully contained antimatter, had been mated in great secrecy.

The antimatter device was unique. It had been desired to have a variable-yield weapon, something like the unspeakably politically incorrect tactical nuclear weapons once possessed by both the Americans and Russians. Yet, if depleted uranium had raised a furor, how much worse would have been the ruckus over Germany developing nuclear weapons? Antimatter did not generate *quite* the same knee-jerk reaction, even though it was generally less fine-tunable than nuclear munitions.

A solution was found to the problem of variable yield, although it was not a solution without its costs and complexities. That solution was a dual containment field. The primary field, which normally held all the antimatter, was very strong, strong enough, indeed to withstand the explosion of a portion of the projectile's antimatter right next to it. The secondary was weaker, and rather unstable, relatively speaking.

It was possible, with the device, to dial a given amount, up to roughly thirty percent of the antimatter contained in the primary field, into the secondary. Any greater amount would destroy the primary and create a very large, antimatter-driven, explosion.

But with the lesser, the primary field would hold even as the projectile, now given a substantial boost by the lesser explosion, drove through the far wall of the enemy lander. A timer would detonate the remaining antimatter when it was high enough not to appreciably affect the Earth.

There was, of course, the possibility of having *all* the antimatter go off in a single cosmic catastrophe. This, of course, might well affect the Earth and the people who, in ever diminishing numbers, populated it.

It was also possible to set the weapon for *no* antimatter explosion. In that case, the antimatter would remain entirely within the primary containment field and never, in theory, explode until it reached a point far out in space.

Thus thirteen *Panzerkampfwagen* VIII As, colloquially known as Tiger IIIs, loaded between them enough antimatter to flatten a small city, even a stone-built *German* small city.

Marburg an der Lahn, Germany, 29 March 2007

The ancient stone castle stood silent and untroubled, overwatching the ancient town below. From his hastily scraped fighting position, the castle and town beckoned Pieter Friedenhof with the hint, if not the promise, of safety.

"It's madness, madness I say!" shouted Pieter to his chief, a small and determined looking *Hauptgefreiter* manning an MG-3. "Madness to stay here."

"Shut up, Friedenhof, you pussy, and—"

The gunner's next words were lost as a Posleen three-millimeter railgun round caused his head to explode in a shower of red mist and red and ivory flecks. Pieter took but a single glance before emitting a wordless shriek. More than half crazed himself with fear, Friedenhof turned from his dead comrade, turned from his gun, turned from his duty.

The boy began to run. As he did, others nearby saw. They too began to desert their posts. Like an epidemic, swiftly and without understanding on the part of its carriers, the panic spread. This portion of the front knew a rapid collapse.

Hammelburg, Germany, 29 March 2007

Even some of the men of SS-trained 47th *Panzer Korps* had their limits. Under the sustained fire of sixty-seven Posleen craft a few men here and there on the forward trace had begun to run. In Brasche's screen he saw a platoon of Leopards break cover and run from what could only have been a Posleen reconnaissance by fire. The tanks' sprint for safety carried them scant yards before a plasma beam slagged, first one, then another, and still a third. The fourth Leopard, the platoon leader's tank from the turret numbers, skidded to a stop untouched. The crew began bailing out frantically.

The plasma beam touched the tank, igniting it instantly. Caught in the heat-bloom, the four crewmen were heat-seared, flash-cooked. Their writhing bodies fell smoking onto the fresh snow, their own heat melting through it.

"Christ," whispered Brasche, the name coming familiar to his lips even though it had been years, decades really, since he had believed.

The Posleen landers apparently grew tired of playing cat and mouse with the defenders, spoiled idiot boys bored with their play. Half an hour after flushing that one platoon of Leopards, scant reward for so much effort, they ceased fire and began a stately move northward.

"Steady, boys . . . wait for the command. . . ."

Brasche never tapped his machine gunner to command the beginning of the ambush. The harvest walked by unreaped and confident.

"An understrength platoon of Viet Minh," Intelligence had insisted. "Not more than twenty of the little yellow Commie bastards. Your squad should be able to handle them easily."

Hans cursed the damned frog intelligence officer, though the near presence of over ninety of the enemy ensured that he cursed silently. He wondered if the effort at silence was in vain; the Viets ought to be able to hear his heart pounding.

How could they be so wrong, those "intelligence" maggots? He wondered, as well. The signs are everywhere to see if they only had eyes to see. The enemy grows in strength daily, while we grow weaker. Why deny the reality we face every day? We're losing this war, too.

But we won't lose for lack of trying on my part, *Hans thought, determination growing in his heart. He quietly patted his machine gunner—BE STILL. As the last of the Viet Minh passed his position, Hans stood, quietly and carefully. He drew his knife, faced up the trail in the direction into which the Communists had faded, and began, silently, to follow.*

The enemy landers moved without a perceptible sound, gliding along on their heavy-duty antigravity drives. Although there was no sound, the antigravity created a feeling in those caught below like unto a mix of nausea and the sense of having millions of ants crawling over one's body. One was passing directly over the Tiger *Anna* now.

Caught in the sickening field, Brasche resisted the desperate urge to scratch. Dieter Schultz's friend Harz could not resist the need to vomit. Soon, despite the efforts of the Tiger's air cleaners, the vile aroma of human puke filled the fighting bay. That odor initiated a chain reaction. Soon Brasche looked down upon a crew of quietly cursing, frantically scratching, and intermittently vomiting men.

All looked utterly and hopelessly miserable.

Hans forced his own gorge down repeatedly. He kept his attention fixed on the tactical display, showing each of his Tigers, the sixty-seven enemy landers, and the trace outlines of the 47th *Panzer Korps*. At length he saw that all of the enemy had passed.

"*Achtung! Panzer!* Boys, crank 'em and turn 'em around one hundred and eighty degrees. We're going to follow these bastards, shooting them in the ass all the way, until none are left. Kill them from the rearmost forward. Kill them as you bear."

Ahead at the driver's station Krueger gave off an evil laugh. Likewise did most of the men. Only Schultz, face frozen to his gunner's sight, did not.

The tank began to hum as natural gas from its two main fuel cylinders began feeding the huge Siemens electrical generator that drove the engines. A steady vibration arose as Krueger applied the power and twisted the steering column. From outside the panzers it looked like thirteen small avalanches as the snow-covered foam cracked, tore and powdered. The well-trained Schultz was already twisting his gunner's spade to turn the multihundred-ton turret to line up the huge 12-inch smoothbore cannon on the nearest of the enemy.

"Gunner!" ordered Brasche, "Sabot! DU-AM . . . point one kiloton. C-Dec!"

"Target!" answered Schultz, as one finger dialed the charge in the penetrator down to one tenth its potential power.

"*Feuer!*"

The last Vietminh in the snaking column never knew what hit him. Brasche's feet, silently padding along the soft jungle floor, gave no warning. The thick tropical growth overhead hid the moonlight from making a tell-tale flash from the knife. All the doughty little Communist knew was that a sudden hand clamped over his mouth even as an agonizingly cold dart lunged into his kidneys.

Overcome with the worst agony a man can know, a pierced kidney, the Viet made no sound. Some pains are too great even to permit a scream. It was a relief to the dying soldier when Brasche eased him down to the dank floor and drew the razor-sharp knife across his jugular.

Knife still in hand, Hans Brasche followed the column seeking his next victim, another Vietminh too much concerned with the dangers and difficulties ahead, too little with creeping death from behind.

Dieter would never forget that first image of the death of the C-Dec. Each tiny moment was engraved into his memory, of course. He would always feel the click of the firing button under his thumb. He would never quite forget the tremendous roar that shook even to the bowels of a seventeen-hundred-ton tank. The shock of recoil too would remain with him, the massive cylinders compressing until they could go no more, even though aided by the inertia-inverting devices once tested by Schlüssel and Breitenbach. He would recall the tank's rear suspension taking up the rest, then the sudden vicious spring back from full battery into firing position . . . the stout knock to his head that even his padded gunner's sight could not quite mute.

But it was the death of the enemy he would always remember best.

That death began as a faint flash on the C-Dec's hull. So faint and quick was it that the eye barely registered. In what seemed the tiniest moment came the real flash, as the antimatter within, deliberately set to its lowest practical setting, came into contact with true matter.

This Dieter could not, of course, see. Nor did he see the remaining antimatter, that not released by the primary—and stronger—containment field. What he could and did see was the image of light suddenly streaking out in linear fashion from each of the corner junctures of the alien ship's twelve sides. The light would have been blinding to the naked eye. Even in Dieter's thermal sight the picture overloaded briefly.

In that instant of overloading, the Posleen ship came apart. When his image returned, Dieter saw twelve separate pieces, flying in twelve directions.

"Holy Christ," muttered the gunner.

"Christ, holy or otherwise, has nothing to do with it, boy," answered Brasche. "Gunner!" he ordered, "Sabot! DU, inert. Lamprey!"

To *Anna*'s right and left, other panzers spit out destruction even as Schultz searched in his sight for his next victim.

Seven khaki-clad bodies lay upon the trail behind him. Seven times had Hans' knife swept and the red blood splashed. And still young Brasche pursued. There was an eighth victim ahead, even a ninetieth if the strength of his arm held out.

"I don't understand this," said Harz. "We are slaughtering them from behind like so many deer. They *have* to notice us. Why haven't they reacted?"

"It isn't a question of what is there to be seen. I have seen the reports on the Posleen ships myself," Brasche answered. "They can see us. Absolutely, they can. Their ships' sensors are more than capable of that."

"Then what, *Herr Oberst*?" queried Harz.

"We're here to be seen, *Unteroffizier*. But they just are concentrating on other threats and opportunities elsewhere. To their front, specifically. And even if one has seen us? They do not communicate or coordinate very well."

In Hans' view another dim shape, a C-Dec he was certain, began to materialize. "Gunner! Sabot! DU-AM . . . point one kiloton. C-Dec!"

"Target!"
"*Feuer!*"

Marburg an der Lahn, Germany, 29 March 2007

Friedenhof ran, his lungs straining at the bitter cold air. Snow swirled around everywhere, everywhere blotting out sight. No matter, young Pieter's eyes were fixed on the barely perceived snow-covered ground to his front. His own beating footsteps and the pounding of his own blood in his ears drowned out the sounds of massacre coming from behind. They drowned out, too, the soft padding of alien claws on the snow-covered ground behind him. Friedenhof missed completely the hiss of a boma blade being drawn. He had no clue of its descent.

Even the fall of his dismembered body was softened and hushed by the new fallen snow. Pieter never heard.

In the awkward confines of his command ship Fulungsteeriot rejoiced aloud, his followers baying around him. *That* for Athenalras and his sacrifice mission into the center of this continent. The thresh, these dreaded gray-clad thresh, were in a pure panic, running hither and yon. Briefly, Fulungsteeriot knew a moment of regret; the more they ran the less food they could provide his host.

But—never mind! The thresh-filled town of Giessen lay ahead; a town, he was sure, swarming with young and tender flesh. The host would eat well, this day . . . and for many days yet to come.

INTERLUDE

Ro'moloristen looked out upon a scene from hell, though to him it seemed no more hellish than would a slaughterhouse to a human. From every direction, humans had been herded here, to the vicinity of Athenalras' command ship, to serve as a larder. Like a slaughterhouse too, this group of humans was being efficiently and ruthlessly processed for food.

He watched as a human—a female he thought, based on the curious bumps on the creature's chest—had her nestling torn from her arms. The human emitted an incomprehensible wailing shriek as the nestling was first beheaded, then sliced into six pieces.

Incomprehensible, thought the God King. *After all, it was only a nestling.*

He understood better why the human tried to escape her own end, twisting and fighting. Finally, the Posleen normal grew tired and annoyed of the game. He grabbed the human by the thatch on the top of its head and lopped its legs off. The shrieks briefly grew more intense, then ended suddenly as the normal removed the head.

After that, it seemed that the remaining humans grew much more cooperative, kneeling and bending their heads on the gestured command.

Ro'moloristen noticed that many of the humans uttered the same vocal denial: "This is impossible . . . this can't be happening." He thought it very curious that any sentient creature could deny something which was not only patently possible but was, in fact, happening.

"A most curious species," he muttered, as he turned from the scene of slaughter to return to his post aboard ship.

CHAPTER 8

Hammelburg, Germany, 29 March 2007

Brasche's fingers drummed the arm of his command chair nervously. It had been some time since the last report of a kill or an engagement had come in. "I am curious, 1c. How many have we accounted for?"

The intelligence officer turned from his weapons station to face Brasche. "*Herr Oberst*, the battalion has taken out forty-nine, so far. But all panzers report the same: there are no more to be found ahead."

Schultz asked aloud, "Do you think they're on to us, *Herr Oberst*?"

"I don't know, Dieter. But I think that might be the way to bet it."

Brasche considered for a moment, then touched the communication button built into his command chair. "All Tigers," he commanded, "all Tigers. Halt and lager around this position. Number One company, you have from six to ten o'clock. Number Two, ten o'clock to two o'clock. Three, two to six. Two thousand meters between tanks."

All three of Brasche's company commanders answered "Wilco" instantaneously. Brasche was quite gratified to see all three companies begin moving across his tactical display nearly as quickly. And then . . .

The strain in the company commander's voice was palpable, even

120 John Ringo & Tom Kratman

over the radio. "Battalion this is Number One Company . . . Number one to Battalion. Enemy here . . . Too many to . . . *Scheisse, Scheisse, Scheisse!*[36] . . . Turn this damned tank arou—"

Brasche acted instantly. "All units, action left. Move it boys, Number One company's in trouble."

Without waiting for the order, a cursing Krueger cranked the steering as hard as it would go. With both tracks spinning in opposite directions at nearly top speed the Tiger's turn was almost immediate. Even deep in the crew center the men could hear the high-pitched squealing of tortured tread. A few muttered prayers: *Please, God, don't let us throw a track.*

The sudden turn tossed Harz from his seat to the metal floor and then bounced him across the deck. He gave off a painful grunt as the turn slammed him into the opposite side of the crew compartment. Harz managed to rise to his knees just in time for Krueger's next maneuver, the sudden launching of the tank forward in its new direction. This sent him rolling to the rear.

Brasche looked down to where a stunned Harz had come to a bruising rest against the podium on which sat the command chair.

"Back to your station, Harz."

Shaking his head to clear it, Harz—still on hands and knees—began working his way back to his duty position. As he reached it the radio crackled again.

The voice on the radio was preternaturally calm, "Battalion this is *Leutnant* Schiffer. Tiger 104—and presumably *Hauptmann* Wohl and his crew—are dead. I have assumed command."

"What happened to Wohl, Schiffer?" asked Brasche, then, on second thought, "Never mind, tell me later. What is your condition?"

"Sir, I have three functional Tigers and about twelve to eighteen enemy ships trying to kill us. Visibility is rotten, even with the thermals. Every Tiger has taken at least one hit. The frontal armor is holding up well. The commander's tank was hit in the rear with some kind of kinetic energy weapon. That immobilized it and the enemy were able to gang up and pound it to scrap."

Hans Brasche's mind drew a picture for him of one of his Tigers, helpless, while a force of the aliens' landers took their time with taking it apart piece by piece.

Schiffer continued, "If they hadn't stopped to finish off 104 they might well have gotten us all."

Unseen by Schiffer, Hans nodded. He had seen such things before.

"I have the company facing the enemy and driving backwards towards you, *Herr Oberst*, but the enemy is damnably hard to engage in this weather when they know we are here. They are able to sense us, it seems, from further than we can sense them. If it weren't for the quality of the frontal armor we'd all be dead by now."

"Good lad, Schiffer," Brasche answered. "We're coming for you, son."

"Yes, sir. Thank you, sir. But, sir? You had better hurry."

Giessen, Germany, 29 March 2007

Fulungsteeriot rejoiced, "Onward my warriors. Hurry my children, lest the thresh escape."

Like a yellow wave, broad and thick, the Posleen host lapped around the rock of Giessen, surrounding it. Occasionally a Posleen normal, or even a God King, would fall—the thresh trying their futile best to hold back the tide. Yet the wave diminished not at all. Soon, Giessen would be surrounded by the tide . . . and then the tide would come in . . . and the thresh drown in it.

Off to the south, along a road choked with escaping thresh, Fulungsteeriot observed with detachment the panic as the first of his warriors reached the crawling herd in their strange and primitive wheeled vehicles. The rendering soon began.

There was no time for an orderly butchering; the normals slaughtered the thresh as soon as they could reach them. The primitive vehicles were sliced open by boma blades to expose the rich flesh within. Amidst shrieks and plaintive pleas the thresh those vehicles contained were hauled forth, sometimes in pieces. Of those pulled out whole, a simple sweep of a blade ended their cries. Death for these thresh was sufficient for now; later others would do the detailed work.

Some thresh escaped, of course. Using the time unwillingly purchased by their brethren falling under the Posleen's swords, these ran for their lives in stark terror across the snowy field to the east.

✧   ✧   ✧

Gudrun saw a blade slice through the roof of the car in which she and her family had sought escape from the doom encircling the town. The blade passed through her wide-eyed, screaming mother from crown to hips before being withdrawn. Though the mother's screams abruptly ceased, the sight of her separating neatly into two pieces, lengthwise, accompanied by a veritable wave of crimson brought forth an animal shriek from Gudrun. Then, as the iron smell of her own mother's flooding blood assaulted her nostrils, instinct took over. She could not fight this; she must flee.

Indeed, Gudrun's swearing father ordered her to run as he himself drew a large-bore pistol and fired two shots past the mother's corpse into the Posleen mass. Gudrun never saw whether he hit anything or not.

The girl's hand fumbled with the door release. The father fired several more times at the nearest Posleen; the roar of the shots both hurting her ears and lending urgency to her actions. The door flung open, Gudrun sprang from her seat behind her father and fled, coatless. Safety lay, if anywhere, across the snow-covered field. As she fled, the screams behind her arose to a heartrending crescendo, then rapidly grew fainter and fewer. She heard no more shots. This only served to spur her flashing feet.

East of Paris, France, 29 March 2007

Isabelle fled mindlessly, driving the family auto in a dream-state. Better said, she drove through a nightmare and dreamt of a time it might be over.

She had waited for a day or more, eyes fixed to the television, hoping to discover from the news some route of escape for herself and her boys. In that time two things had been made clear. The first was that the old line of fortresses to the east, the ones facing Germany and misdubbed the "Maginot Line," were holding out well for the nonce, and butchering the invaders in the process. The second was that the French Army was holding open, however tenuously, an escape route from Paris to the east.

Sound carried poorly through the densely falling snow. Light was diffused. Nonetheless, so intense was the fighting some miles to either side of the road on which Isabelle drove that some must leak through.

Some even leaked through a brain gone on autopilot with terror. She kept her foot on the accelerator, moving as fast as snow and the traffic would permit.

Hammelburg, Germany, 29 March 2007

"Spur it, son, spur it," whispered Brasche to the distant, unhearing, Schiffer.

Another Tiger, number 102, had gone down; first immobilized by an unlucky hit then pounded to scrap by the mass fire of nine C-Decs. Schiffer was bounding backwards with the remaining pair, himself holding stationary and firing at the dimly sensed enemy while the other Tiger moved back to reinforcement and relative safety, then switching over.

Brasche's 1a, or operations officer, pointed out, "There is a ridge, between us and Number One Company, *Herr Oberst*. I was just thinking . . ."

Hans thought about it, looking at the tactical display, his mind measuring distances and interpolating times. "Yes. Yes, Major . . . it has possibilities."

Thirteen had been Brasche's unlucky number. His arms grown tired, he missed a kidney. The Vietminh had managed to call out to his comrades, once, before the crimson river spilled to the ground. Hans soon found himself running from a fusillade of ill-aimed shots.

The number of shots suggested to Hans that his pursuers numbered no more than twenty, the original number his squad of legionnaires had expected to ambush. A thought grew.

"Schiffer, how goes it?"

"Tight, *Herr Oberst*. The enemy presses us . . . but I have lost no more tanks."

"Very good, *Leutnant*. Do you see the ridge about three kilometers behind you?"

"Yes, *Herr Oberst*. I was hoping to get a moment's shelter behind it."

Unseen, Brasche shook his head. "I want you to go right on past it and keep on going until I summon you. Do you understand?"

"No, sir," answered Schiffer over the radio.

Brasche sighed audibly. "The problem, *Leutnant*, is that the enemy sensors outrange ours in the snow. But if you can entice them to follow you over to this side of the ridge the rest of the battalion can be waiting, *within* range of *our* sensors and sights. I doubt they will sense as well through solid rock as they can through diffuse frozen water. Nine Tiger IIIs, with an element of surprise, can handle that many of the enemy."

"Ah, I see now, sir. How much time do you need to set up on your side of the ridge?"

The 1a answered aloud, "Five minutes, *Herr Oberst*, no more."

"I heard that, sir," announced Schiffer. "I will gain you that much time."

Seeing that the 1a understood, Hans ordered, "Do it." To Schiffer, via the radio, "Good lad. Five minutes."

Amidst the shots fired at him, the fleeing Brasche kept up a running monologue, quite a loud one, in the practical language of the Legion of the times—German. Far too many Vietnamese for comfort spoke French.

Puff, puff... "Don't answer"... Grunt, grunt... "They're following me"... Pant, pant... "About twenty of them"... Wheeze..."Stand ready"... Gasp..."Let me through then let them have it when they're in the kill zone."... Groan..."I'm almost there... nicht schiessen."[37]

With a heart pounding as much from fear as exertion, Hans jumped the first Viet corpse and then sprinted through the kill zone. From behind him came more shots and the chatter of furious, enraged Vietminh fighters. He thought about ducking to the side to rejoin his men but rejected the notion. The Viets had to have a reason to follow, and he thought only a fleeing man, one who had left a trail of throat-slashed corpses along the trail, would serve as reason enough in the jungle gloom.

Hans felt a sudden blow to his back. He never heard the shot that hit him. The shot spun him to the ground. The blow was painful enough, but then came the burning, a fiery agony that inflamed the entire path taken by the bullet. Hans moaned, "Shit, not again." He closed his eyes from the pain.

When he opened them, the Viets had arrived. Precaution thrown to the winds, the little anatomies clustered about Hans. They all apparently wanted to plunge a bayonet into the monster who had hunted their comrades and slaughtered them like pigs.

Beginning to lose consciousness, Hans saw two of the Viets lift high their bayoneted rifles. He braced himself for the coming cold steel.

Giessen, Germany, 29 March 2007

The snow was cold, so cold, under her exhausted body. Gudrun's heart beat within her like that of a trapped rabbit on the approach of the trapper. She had run her race . . . and she had lost. Now she awaited the pot.

And she *was* trapped, she knew. Though the horrid aliens behind her pursued in only desultory fashion, the other arm of the pinching Posleen *impi* was before her, stretching as far as the eye could see in the still falling snow. Even though the sound was snow-muffled, her ears told her that many more Posleen closed in beyond the range of her view.

Helpless and alone, afraid beyond terror, the girl began to weep softly. The sound of her quiet sobs attracted the attention of a Posleen normal. It approached.

"No . . . please no," Gudrun pleaded. "Please? I have so many reasons to live. Don't hurt me. Don't eat me, please?"

The normal was unmoved. Nothing human could move it. Its needs were simple: food, work within its limited skill set, service to its God. At the moment the greatest need was food. Standing over Gudrun it drew and raised its boma blade.

The girl—innocent, bright, the "battle maiden" who would never hurt a soul—gave off a final scream. "Dieeeterrr!"

Hammelburg, Germany, 29 March 2007

"Steady, Schultz. Steady," intoned Brasche. "Wait for it."

Dieter merely nodded, so intently was his gaze fixed on his sight.

The radio sounded, "Schiffer to battalion."

Hans took a second to review the tactical display. "Brasche here, Schiffer."

"Sir, we are about to ascend the ridge."

"I see that, Schiffer. We are waiting in the woods on the far side, about four kilometers back. Pass through us and hold up about two kilometers behind."

"As you command, *Herr Oberst*. But it is not going to be easy."

"I understand, son," Brasche answered.

Brasche turned to his 1a. "Take command of the tank for a moment, Major. I am going topside. Krueger hold the engines steady; no acceleration at all."

Not waiting for either the major's or Krueger's acknowledgment, Hans stepped to the elevator that led up to the commander's hatch atop the turret. The elevator whisked him skyward quietly, opening the hatches automatically, as the 1a took over the command chair below.

Once in his perch high above the Tiger's hull, Hans breathed better. Yes, the air down in the crew's fighting compartment was clean enough. But a tank commander needs to *see*.

"To see and *hear*," Brasche corrected himself, aloud, "not take some bloody glorified television screen's word for things." And hear he did. From the other side of the ridge came the sounds of Schiffer's uneven fight with the landers, the sonic booms of incoming Posleen kinetic energy weapons, the crash of the Tiger's mighty twelve-inchers, the faint rattle of treads and the steady whine of Posleen antigravity drives.

Then, *there* it was, the outline of the top of one of Number One company's two remaining Tigers breaking the outline of the ridge. The tank crossed over and stopped just Brasche's side of the topographical crest. It stopped to fire and the sheer shock of firing was like a dual slap to Brasche's face.

He watched the turret turn, and then fire yet again. Hans

assumed, from the lack of any antimatter or secondary explosion, that both shots were misses.

There was a sudden flurry of the Posleen's weapons. On the far side, arising over the ridge, a dark and dirty cloud appeared, the cloud stretching a kilometer across. The hull down Tiger fired a single shot which was rewarded with a major flash and sound of detonation; a dead Posleen C-Dec.

Then came another flurry of kinetic energy projectiles incoming to the far side of the ridge. There was also another huge flash and grand bang. Brasche thought he saw, dimly through the snow, the monstrous bulk of a Tiger turret flying approximately straight up.

Filled with dread, Hans touched a switch on his headphones, "Schiffer, Brasche."

"That *was Leutnant* Schiffer, *Herr Oberst. Feldwebel* Weinig speaking . . . commanding Third Platoon . . . correction, commanding Number One company . . . now."

Brasche closed his eyes against the pain of losing such a fine young officer. Releasing a sigh of regret, he ordered, "Run for it, Weinig. Run for it now."

"No quarrel with those orders, sir. Tiger 103, running fast."

Three Tigers, sixty-nine of my men, lost irredeemably, fumed Brasche, a newfound hatred for his foe growing in his heart. He recognized the hate, recognized that he had felt it grow before—against Russians and Vietnamese and some few others. He recognized, too, that the hate was the steel his soul needed to do that which could brook no soft and tender feelings.

The cold steel, glowing faintly in the dim jungle light, never descended. From one side of the jungle trail into which he had led his Communist pursuers, Hans saw—and curiously did not really hear, to such a detached state had his wounding brought him—the yellow flowers of rifle and machine gun fire. The two Communists poised to end his life fell first, their bodies twisting and dancing under the hammering of the machine gun, their very dance of death given ghastly illumination by the flashing of the legionnaire weapons.

The firing kept up for a very long time, it seemed, causing Hans to wonder if a stray bullet of a friend and comrade might yet find

*him. Even in his pain he took the thought with amused detachment.
He never even heard the blaring of the whistle that his assistant
squad leader used to quell the fire and send the killer team out
to search out the kill zone . . . and to make sure those bodies lying
there were bodies in fact. It was legionnaire bayonets, not Communist ones, that bathed in crimson that night.*

Unseen, the Tiger, Schiffer's Tiger, burned hot and crimson
beyond the crest of the ridge. The glow of the fire, a fire consum-
ing fuel and munitions and men—causing the very steel of its
armor to glow cherry red, made the lowest levels of the falling
snow themselves to glow.

Three flashes, coming in rapid succession from a single point
somewhere beyond view, lit the very edge of the crest in brief
bursts of strobelike light.

"Wait for it," cautioned Brasche when he saw Schultz tense
suddenly.

"Right, Dieter," piped in Harz, with a snickering tone to his
voice. "Just like your little blonde girlfriend, we don't want you
firing too soon."

The thought of Gudrun, waiting for him safe and warm in Giessen, brought a momentary smile and a wistful yearning. Harz's
guffaw ensured that the eagerness Schultz was certain shone from
his features was followed quickly by a flush of embarrassment.
"Fuck you, Harz," the boy whispered softly, albeit not quite softly
enough.

"Surely not *me*, Dieter. Did your Gudrun leave you so frustrated
you're already thinking about turning to boys?"

"Enough," commanded Brasche in a voice that quelled all lev-
ity. "If anyone is getting fucked here, it is those lizards about to
appear over the horizon."

Giessen, Germany, 29 March 2007

Gudrun stared unblinking at the horizon. Nearby, a body was
being rendered into easily portable ribs, chops and steaks. Loathe
to waste any nutrient, the Posleen still had to let blood from the
body spill to the snow covered ground. It contented itself, to a

degree, with the instinctive understanding that even this would not be completely wasted; with the spring thaw and fall harvest the blood would bring forth finer crops from the enriched soil.

But a head full of rich brains? That was too much to waste. The Posleen doing the rendering ceased work. Then it picked up Gudrun's pale, bloodless head by the bright blonde thatch. It neither noticed nor would have cared that a lock was missing. Once split open the disembodied head would make a fine feed.

Hammelburg, Germany, 29 March 2007

The head of the airborne Posleen phalanx crept cautiously over the horizon. It apparently sensed the fleeing Tiger 103, for it rapidly increased its speed to catch the prey. The rest, perhaps better said the remainder, of the original Posleen airmobile force, some seventeen C-Decs and Lampreys, likewise hastened to be in on the kill. Attention concentrated on the fast-moving Tiger they could easily sense, they never noticed the still, stationary, steady idling of the other nine Tigers.

"*Feuer!*" shouted Brasche into the general circuit, once he was sure all the Posleen had fallen into his trap. Nine twelve-inch guns crashed as one; piercing seven of the spacecraft and splitting them apart amidst blinding flashes of antimatter. "Fire at will."

Eleven remained. Those eleven began spitting back their fire in the form of kinetic energy projectiles, plasma beams and high-velocity missiles. But here the advantage lay with the humans. By coming over the ridge, the Posleen had at least temporarily confined themselves to an area *within* the humans' ability to sense and target.

And the Tigers' heavy armor could take all but a very unlucky hit. The Posleen craft could not take any hit from those massive cannon.

A second volley rang out, almost as solidly as had the first—mass-produced precision machinery remained something of a German specialty, after all. Despite return fire and jinking to avoid being targeted, a further five Posleen targets were smashed and split. Six remained.

Used to having every advantage, from numbers to technology to sheer fighting heart, this was too much for the aliens. They attempted to make a run for it.

Seeing the enemy flee, a most heartwarming sight, Hans Brasche had but a single command, "Pursue."

INTERLUDE

"They pursue our people as if they were themselves thresh, these threshkreen," muttered Athenalras. "It's . . . it's . . . *indecent!*"

Ro'moloristen repressed a Posleen chuckle; it would never do to annoy his chief and lord. Perhaps the junior was made of sterner stuff. Certainly he was of less senior stuff. Though somehow he thought himself to be less ruthless. Braver? He didn't know.

Yet he felt brave as he answered, "They do what they do for their people, as we do for ours. Yes, they have many disgusting habits. Yes, their architecture is somewhat absurd, their industry and science primitive. Yes, they do not fight as we do, in the open for all our peers to see and the Rememberers to sing of."

"But, my lord, they fight hard and they fight well. And there is something somehow touching in the way that their old will throw down their lives for their young, their males for their females."

Athenalras looked at Ro'moloristen as if the young God King had gone quite mad; for a human male to toss away his life for a female was as if a God King were to give itself up for a Posleen normal. It was very nearly the ultimate in obscene conduct, to a proper God King.

Ro'moloristen backtracked quickly. "I did not say I approved, my lord. It's just that such courage is somehow moving. As if these lessers, these females and nestlings, embodied some value so infinite we cannot even guess at it."

131

CHAPTER 9

Giessen, Germany, 22 April 2007

Dieter Schultz had held out hope, even after the news of Giessen's fall and the resulting massacre had come. But day after day passed with no news from his beloved Gudrun. Dieter began to believe that hope was forlorn.

Each new day had brought a new fight for the *Korps* and for the *Schwere Panzer* Battalion 501(Michael Wittmann). Each day brought new losses. The battalion dropped to eight Tigers, then seven. With each loss twenty-three valiant souls had flickered away in the wind.

Dieter the gunner had had the privilege of painting markings amounting to no fewer than eighty-eight kills—eight broad rings and eight narrow—on the barrel of *Anna's* twelve-inch gun. With no word of Gudrun, the painting was a thankless, even an unhappy, task.

Briefly there was a respite as one new and two reclaimed Tigers joined the ranks. Then again the steady drain began, replacements never quite equaling losses. Brasche commanded a mere five tanks by the time the last infestation had been cleared from central Germany, said final infestation being the command of the senior God King, Fulungsteeriot, in and around the nearly scraped away ruins of the town of Giessen.

As briefly, Dieter Schultz felt a moment's respite as the long-delayed field mail caught up with the often moving Tiger Battalion.

The letter he received held something potentially grand for Dieter: a small wallet photo of Gudrun, looking much as she had the one night they had met; a short handwritten note, lightly scented; a small pack of golden, silken hair. He hoped with all his heart it was not a message from the grave.

Ouvrage du Hackenberg, Thierville, France, 23 April 2007

It was like a descent into the grave. From the spring just bursting forth into life above ground, from an open air scented with flowers, Isabelle and her sons entered through an arched concrete passageway into a dimly lit, damp, dank and malodorous sewer filled to overflowing with human refuse.

Isabelle's spirits sank with each step into the fortress and down. To either side of her, arrayed on cramped cots pushed against damp walls, a mass of hopeless humanity stared at the newcomers with blank, disinterested faces. They seemed barely human in their indifference. Isabelle felt a chill run up her spine that had nothing to do with the cold, underground air.

Still, the cold was there. She remembered back to a worse cold.

The car had long since given up its ghost to lack of fuel. The reeling army had had fuel, of course, but had steadfastly refused to turn over so much as a liter to any of the begging, pleading refugees who had then to take to their feet. Isabelle had briefly thought of selling herself for some gasoline to save her boys. She had thought about it and then, realizing that younger women and girls could make better offers than she could, she had rejected the notion.

Instead, repacking down to true minimum essentials, the family had left the auto abandoned by the road and trudged the last few hundred kilometers afoot.

The cold had been terrible at first. There were moments when the shivering boys had made Isabelle think of ending it for them all then and there. Among the minimum essentials had been a pistol, after all. Though avidly in favor of gun control, as she was—being a liberal, and though, as a doctor, her husband had had a deep revulsion for weapons that harmed or could harm human bodies—yet still, humanly, they had kept her grandfather's service pistol from the First World War, ignoring all calls for turn in.

But no, pistol or not, the maternal imperative had won out over mere misery. Her boys must live. To ensure this, she must live. The pistol remained unused.

Curiously, never once had it occurred to her, when it might still have done some good, that the pistol, more readily than her body, might have obtained a bit of fuel. More than once, trudging through the bitter cold, she had cursed herself for not thinking of that.

Berlin, Germany, 24 April 2007

The reprimand fresh in his hand, the Tir cursed the damnable and damned Germans with as much force as fear of lintatai would permit.

Cannot the Ghin see that these are no ordinary opponents? the Tir fretted. *Well, I have one thing left to use.*

To date the Tir had been very sparing as to which information, of that which he had received from Günter, he chose to download to the Net, in other words, to make available to the Posleen. Somehow, and the Tir did not understand the precise mechanism, he was being cut off from control. He feared, deep in his bones, that releasing all the information in one fell swoop would make the Germans—never among the least paranoid of humans—look to leaks that they might never otherwise have suspected.

But this was a desperate time. The Ghin was threatening to cut off bonuses, withdraw promised stock options, reduce salary . . . to drop the Tir's rank to de'Tir.

The Tir shivered, as much with the threatened disgrace as loss of income.

He *could* leak the rest. It would cost him the use of Günter, of course. But then again, Günter had probably outlived his usefulness anyway.

It was considered, even among the Darhel, bad business practice to mistreat an asset, to renege on a deal. Yet the only reward Günter had ever been promised had been the off-world evacuation of his family. No promise had even been made, indeed he had never asked, concerning moving himself to safety. The family was long since gone to a planet far from the path of the invaders.

So be it then, the Tir resolved. *The Posleen will be given access to all the information I have. I just hope the idiots can make good use of it.*

Giessen, Germany, 27 April 2007

From his thresh-built, gravelike shelter Fulungsteeriot cursed sibilantly. To fall so low, having come so high; this was the stuff of tragedy.

But there was nothing to be done for it; the enemy ring had grown tight around this little enclave of Posleen-hood. Information gathered from the Net told of an encircling ring of fire and steel, even now closing about the throats of the People. Already the wrecked outskirts of the ruined town were, for the most part, back in the possession of the natives. And the natives seemed curiously effective and eager to flush away the last of the Posleen. Why, it was almost as if they took things personally!

Three times Fulungsteeriot had sent his people against the ring of steel enchaining them. Not one breakout attempt had succeeded and the last attempt had not even reached the hated thresh before being broken to bits by their artillery.

Idly, the God King wondered if perhaps he should have saved some of the thresh that had been entrapped here. *Perhaps*, he mused, *these might have been traded for safe passage. Incomprehensible, yet the thresh seemed curiously solicitous of their nestling-bearers and nestlings.*

But the thought came far too late. In the first flush of victory what proper God King would think of eventual defeat, or would deny his people the fruits of their victories? Surely Fulungsteeriot was not one such. To the last little putrid nestling, the thresh of this town had been eaten. Not one, so the God King believed, had been allowed to escape.

Yet now, neither was there escape to space, not even for a senior God King like Fulungsteeriot. In their anger and hate the gray-clad thresh had not only surrounded this place, they had moved up more than sufficient of the fighting machines they called "Tigers" to prevent any vertical egress. Fulungsteeriot had tried that route, with lesser characters than himself. The radioactive ruins of not less than seven ships dotted the landscape, victims of the humans' Tigers. There was no escape upward.

A realist to the end, Fulungsteeriot made no effort to create an illusion of hope, though he had one more breakout attempt planned, one involving all of his remaining people. Still, with a mass of thresh artillery pummeling his people into scraps of flesh and rags of skin, he knew he really had nothing to look forward to except the end.

A Kenstain approached the God King cautiously; there was danger in any of the people, even the normals, when they were in a fight for life. At a respectful distance, the Kenstain gave the Posleen equivalent of a cough, a sort of strained gagging sound.

"My lord? There is something you must see, something I just noticed floating amid the ether."

"Yes? What?" asked the God King crossly.

"Just this, lord: of the threshkreen encircling us, one group is the remnant of that the People slaughtered near that place the humans called 'Marburg.'"

Desperately, Dieter grasped hard onto the threads of his illusions. Yet scanning though his gunner's sight across every spectrum, visible and invisible, and from one side of the Posleen-created desert to the next, merely served to crush whatever hope remained.

Stroking the shielded picture within his breast pocket as was his wont, Brasche's heart went out to the boy, as did that of nearly every man of the crew.

"Why?" asked the boy. "Why?"

Krueger, who felt no sympathy at all, answered harshly from the driver's station. "Because some pussy in uniform ran, boy. Read the after-action reviews; they are available on the Net. Because some little pansy took to his heels rather than face the danger, your little girl died. We don't know who it was. We don't know exactly where it began. But someone ran and started the panic.

"It was quite predictable, the way the pussy politicians shackled everyone's hands but ours," Krueger finished.

Schultz looked towards Brasche's command chair. Though he loathed his driver thoroughly, Brasche had to admit, "Yes, Dieter."

"But what can one do?" asked Schultz, plaintively.

Krueger answered, "You kill 'em when they run, boy. Give 'em no choice but to stand and fight. Hang the cowards—low or high—and let 'em kick and dance some if you have time. Shoot 'em otherwise." Krueger felt a little shiver of delight at an old memory—the kicking, jerking feet of a sixteen-year-old coward of a *Volksgrenadier*, cruelly suspended a mere foot or so above the ground, the noose placed behind the neck to make sure the boy could see how close salvation lay. The memory brought the same laugh Krueger had given off then, his joy in watching the coward's futile struggle undiminished by time.

Brasche nodded, hating to agree with Krueger but knowing that Schultz needed the lesson. "It's true, Dieter. The rot must be stopped as soon as it starts. Sometimes, if you train them right, the rot doesn't start for a long time; maybe not until the war is over. But when you have as much rabble in uniform as Germany today has, you don't have much choice but to use harsh measures."

Dieter took the lesson. "And if you do not, innocent and beautiful young girls die," he said.

Giessen, Germany, 28 April 2007

Under the lash and crash of the thresh's fearsome artillery concerto, Fulungsteeriot and his subordinate God Kings found it nearly impossible to drive their shattered oolt'pos into any semblance of a formation for the final break out attempt. In the end it proved impossible to create much of a formation. Worse, losses to what a thresh would have called the "chain of command" made it no easier to create a workable plan. Fulungsteeriot and his underlings found themselves feeding their oolt'os into the meat grinder with little direction beyond what a threshkreen might have called a "priority of effort."

Chance, however, plays a great part in war. It was chance, to a degree, that the wretched remnants of the 33rd *Korps* had been nearby, chance that Fulungsteeriot's subordinate had found the information on the Net. Though three quarters of the dug-in circumvallation holding the Posleen in was held by good troops of the 47th *Panzer* and 2nd Mountain *Korps*, the area chosen for the "priority of effort" for the breakout was held in part by the defeated and demoralized remnants of the 33rd Infantry *Korps*.

Well, they'd been in the general area and available. . . .

"Brasche? Mühlenkampf."

Brasche shook his head in a fairly vain attempt to clear the cobwebs. "*Hier, Herr General.*"

"Hans, the 33rd *Korps*—fucking Pussy-*Wehr!*—is bolting again. You and your . . . let me see . . . five Tigers? . . ." Mühlenkampf waited.

Keying his throat mike an exhausted Brasche answered, "Yes, sir. Five Tigers left."

"Proceed to sector Valkyrie Three. *Jugend* Division will follow. But Brasche, you will get there first. You must hold the ridge until *Jugend* arrives."

"On the way, sir . . . Ummm . . . *Herr General* . . . what the fuck is going on? What am I to do?"

Mühlenkampf hesitated. Finally he answered, his voice tinged with sad determination, "Your duty, *Herr Oberst*."

The remnants of the 33rd *Korps* had not waited for the Posleen to arrive even within effective engagement range. At the first sign—sound, rather—of the approach of the teeming alien mass the *Korps* had taken to its heels.

Of *course* they had taken to their heels. These were the fleet-footed remnants, the early deciders, the least brave of all. Any good men, any good leaders? These were those most likely to have held on that fatal few seconds too long before, during the wretched rout at Marburg. In short, these were long since stuffed, in butchered parts, down alien gullets; and then, long since, deposited in malodorous lumps onto the soil thus soiled.

The good of the 33rd *Korps* had become shit . . . while the shit had become a sort of human diarrhea. This loose shit *ran*.

With a pronounced crunching sound *Anna* slid over a long line of civilian vehicles that appeared to have met up with the world's

greatest mincing machine. Just past the line of chopped-up metallic scrap, with a deft twist, Krueger spun the Tiger *Anna* into a
position on a military crest blocking the flight of the rump of
the 33rd *Korps*. Like clockwork the other four remaining Tigers
took their own positions, two to either side along the same crest.
Between them, the five heavies covered an area approximately
eight kilometers across.

Krueger, more than any other member of the crew, was required
by his duties to look carefully at the close ground. Just after the
line of scrap had been an open field. The driver had seen that it
contained scattered piles of bones, none with any flesh remaining to them. Briefly, his eyes saw and turned past a skull from
which the top had been removed as neatly as might a coconut
harvester have prepared a coconut for a quick drink. Krueger
was unmoved by the skull.

Ahead were the signs of panic.

Krueger and Brasche, old veterans, had seen this type of panic
before. Krueger cursed, "Useless fucking shits!" Brasche simply
uttered a half whisper, "501st *Schwere Panzer*? *Stabsunteroffizier*
Schultz . . ."

From his gunner's station Dieter peered through the sight for
the main gun. In the distance he could make out portions of
the Posleen mass, pouring from the nearly erased town. Nearer,
appearing as individuals and in little knots, without order or
discipline, Dieter saw the fleeing remnants on the ruined *Korps*.
His unneeded left hand reached unconsciously for a folded envelope in his right breast pocket. Pulling it out, his fingers deftly
opened the envelope and reached in to caress the human spun
gold contained therein. A little bright spark of pure hatred burst
into flame in the boy's heart.

" . . . fire ahead of that mob. Use your coaxial Mausers. Let
them know that they have run as far as they are going to. Draw
a line in the earth," finished Brasche.

"And if they won't stop, *Herr Oberst*? If they cross that line?"

"Then the rot cannot be allowed to spread. You will kill
them."

Flame, a smaller flame than the Tiger's usual cataclysmic belch,
began to leap out. About two and a half kilometers ahead, just in
front of the first of the routing grenadiers, a line of small, dark,
angry clouds erupted at ground level.

❖   ❖   ❖

To the fleeing sea of wit-robbed men of the 33rd *Korps* the advent of the highly visible Tigers seemed like the opening of Heaven's gates. Instinctively they turned towards the wide-spaced line of the remnants of the 501st, each as if he were a boy fleeing a bully and racing to hide behind his mother's skirts.

Each man of the mob—for that is what they were now—thought only *safety, safety* at the sight of the immovable mass of the Tigers. Each man was shocked quite speechless when that fortress-gate-of-security, mama's proffered—milk laden—breast, began to pour fire into those foremost in flight.

Some of the fugitives assumed, indeed *had* to assume, such was the innocence of their childhood upbringing, such had been the kidskin gloves approach to their military training, that the Mauser light cannon fire devastating the knots of those closest to the Tigers could only be a mistake. That was *their* mistake . . . and the last many of them ever made.

Others, no less spoiled by mama's teat and weakened military training, went into momentary shock, freezing in place.

Then they heard the voice, Brasche's voice. . . .

"*Anna*, give me external speakers," ordered Brasche of the tank's integral voice recognition speakers.

"Yes, *Herr Oberst*," the tank's AI responded.

"Order the other tanks to broadcast me as well." Immediately, small hatches in each of Brasche's five Tigers opened to permit the erection of three substantial loudspeakers each. Across a span of a dozen kilometers or more, Hans' voice rang out clearly.

"Halt, you cowardly fucking *bastards*, or we'll cut you down where you stand."

Hans repeated that message twice more, then elaborated. "We are the 47th *Panzer Korps*. That's right you shits, the SS. Believe . . . believe in your hearts. We *will* kill you with no more thought than we'd give to shooting a dog. Your only chance to live is to fight with whatever you have in your hands to hold the enemy. The enemy you can still hurt . . . and we will help you in it. Us? You cannot scratch us and we will butcher you if you try . . . or if you run."

Among the fugitive mass, some took the hint, reshouldered arms and began to fight back. Others, perhaps half or a bit more, just froze in panic. A few, however, judging that five widely spaced Tigers could not hope to cover every little bit of dead space, elected to try to exfiltrate through the low ground, or at least to seek a patch of cover which, while safe from the Posleen because of the Tigers' fire, was also safe from the Tigers and the obvious madmen they contained. The largest number of the fugitives who so chose were those who had thrown away their weapons and could not see any point anymore in fighting, given they had nothing left to fight with.

Several thousand of these were successful in their quest . . . for a time.

"Gunner, eleven o'clock, canister, time fuse, Posleen mass!" ordered Brasche.

Dutifully the loader had a round of canister loaded.

Some would have preferred flechettes for the Tiger's main gun antipersonnel round. It was indeed a very close call. What had decided the issue was, in essence, Teutonic thoroughness. Both were quite capable of killing Posleen. Packed in a twelve-inch shell both munitions could inundate a bit over a grid square, one square kilometer, with deadly hail.

Canister had won over flechettes because a 1.5-inch iron ball— traveling at moderate speed—would kill the Posleen quicker than even several hits by the lighter, faster, narrower flechettes. It was believed that if a Tiger needed to use antipersonnel ammunition in its main gun it would need the targeted Posleen to become "*maus-todt*"—dead in an instant.

For the first time since being encircled in this hellhole, Fulungsteeriot began to see some hope that the next instant would not see his body smeared and his life extinguished. Ahead, thresh fled. This he had not seen in many cycles.

Though his people had never been able to create, let alone disseminate, a plan, the wild hell-for-leather charge was possibly having a better effect than a coherent, logical plan might have. Certainly the threshkreen's deadly artillery seemed to be having more than the usual degree of difficulty in adjusting their fire to destroy these more randomly appearing and disappearing targets. The very disorder and illogic of the enterprise seemed to be working in the People's favor. There was hope.

Hope was short-lived. For some unknowable reason the fleeing thresh, most of them, halted and turned around. To the God King's surprise many actually began to fight instead of flee.

And then Fulungsteeriot saw the most horrid sight in a life filled with horrid sights.

"Target!" answered Schultz.

"Fire!" ordered Brasche.

Oh, yes, Fulungsteeriot had seen as many as 100,000 of the People in dense-packed formation die in an instant. Yet that rare sight had only occurred with the use of the major weapons during orna'adar, the oft-repeated Posleen Ragnarok. There was thus little of carnage, little of blood, the sheer heat of the major weapons incinerating almost all traces. It was a waste of good food, of course—Fulungsteeriot had often though so. But it was clean and neat.

Not so this new weapon of the vile threshkreen.

A lesser propelling charge was used for the canister. Even though the weight of the total projectile was somewhat greater than that of the depleted uranium penetrators, not nearly as much velocity was needed or desired. The crew of *Anna* barely noticed the recoil.

Down range about 4.793 kilometers, at a spot *Anna*'s ballistic computer had judged ideal, a small burster charge detonated. Had the cargo of the shell casing been what is called "improved conventional munitions," or ICM, this method of dispersal could never have been used; the very bursting charge would have destroyed the deadly, precious cargo. Canister, however, was inert iron—low-grade, low-cost, low-tech stuff. The detonation of two point five or so pounds of TNT barely disturbed its pieces, though aided by nine strips of linear shaped charge evenly and linearly spaced along the sides of the shell, it did manage to split the shell open.

The densely packed mass of four thousand large iron ball bearings began to split apart. Those most towards the earth at the time of detonation naturally impacted first. Had these balls been much smaller, or had they been moving much faster, they would likely have buried themselves harmlessly into the dirt. Flechettes certainly would have done so.

But at their speed and size these balls did no such thing. Instead, they bounced. Rather, they grazed, skipping over the earth in bounces of decreasing length. Few were wasted. Most managed to pass through one, two, even a dozen or more Posleen before coming to rest. So fierce was the damage inflicted on individual Posleen bodies that the harder pieces of those bodies themselves went down with fragments of their fellows, bones and teeth, imbedded roughly in soft, vital places.

And that was only the bottom four or five hundred of a cluster of four *thousand*!

The others came down at different times and different speeds. Yet all remained dangerous as they skipped and bounced, gleeful children of the gods of war, through the Posleen mass. Reptilian skulls were smashed, throats torn open, arm and legs roughly amputated. Many a Posleen found itself in possession of a large ball bearing inside its brutalized torso.

In all, the four thousand ball bearings, ricocheting and bouncing to the end, managed to graze over two point four million linear meters worth of death and destruction in an area only one square kilometer in scope.

The bleeding, sundered and torn Posleen horde shrieked as one in pain and despair and destruction.

Sitting atop his motionless tenar, Fulungsteeriot winced at the sound of agony multiplied to near infinity arising from the Posleen mass. The God King's eyes swept over the scene with horror.

"What sins have the People committed that we should ever deserve *this*?" he asked of no one who could answer.

Where once a mass of nearly one hundred thousand had charged, now only scraps remained. Fulunsteeriot saw one oolt, both forelegs amputated, circling unsteadily on shaking rear legs around the pivot of its too-weak centuroid arms. Others, a very few others, hobbled on three legs. Sometimes the lost leg still hung by a slender shred of muscle, dangling down uncontrolled and tangling the other limbs, the wrenching causing the victims to keen wildly and pitiably.

Many, perhaps as many as ten thousand, sought to stuff intestines back into torn frames. Sightless ones roamed with arms outstretched.

Worst of all to see, perhaps, were the three of four thousand of the unscratched. Once attacking proudly, borne up by the mass of their fellows, these for the most part now stood still, shuddering like the horses they somewhat resembled, when those horses, taken to the slaughter house, see their herds disappear before them in blood and horror.

Other muffled crumps and mass shrieks of agony told Fulungsteeriot that his attack had failed utterly. He snarled, set his teeth, flourished his crest. Fulungsteeriot might not have been the brightest of the Kessentai, but he was as courageous as any. He drove his tenar straight at the nearest of the enemy machines, seeking a warrior's death.

Giessen, Germany, 1 May 2007

"*Todt durch den Strang.*" Death by the rope.

This was the verdict of the drumhead court-martial, issued en masse to two hundred thirty-seven of the two thousand three hundred and fifty-nine cowards who had sought shelter for themselves under the Tigers' protective glare, while contributing nothing to the fight.

The *Jugend* Division had found them, passed them, and noted them for the next echelon, which arrested them. Then several days had followed wherein certain elements within the government had demanded the cowards' release. Mühlenkampf had refused. Much to his surprise, the overwhelming bulk of the *Bundeswehr* had agreed with him, going so far as to refuse to obey any orders issuing from the Chancellery that might have led to such a release.

From the over two thousand, only ten percent had been chosen to expiate the sins of the rest.

"We can hang you all," the court had announced. "And you all deserve it. Yet we find it expedient for the Fatherland if the deaths are more drawn out, and contribute more. Ten percent seems enough to remind the rest of your future duty."

Guarded by representatives of both the 47th *Korps* and the other, *Bundeswehr*, *Korps* which had done good service in the area, the procession of death formed three groups.

In the interior, nearest the mostly scoured town, closest to the largest concentrations of gnawed civilian bones, marched those condemned and about to be executed. Brasche had chosen Dieter Schultz to be the representative/guard from the 501ˢᵗ for this group. Krueger had insisted that he also be included and, despising the man or not, out of deference to his service Brasche had sent the old SS man as well.

Just a few hundred meters further from the town, in line with those about to die slow deaths, equally guarded, marched the decimated rest of the condemned. These men's death sentences were momentarily in abeyance, in the hope that more useful deaths might be found for them.

Furthest away were the rest, sightseers of a sort. Men who wanted to see men they despised die.

"Please, no," begged a twenty-four-year-old *Unteroffizier* as Krueger placed a loop of thin rope around his neck. "Please," the doomed man repeated, "I have a wife and a small child. Please?"

"You should have thought not just of them, but of others like them you were abandoning, before you ran, you wart on a circumcised cock," answered Krueger without heat, without any noticeable emotion at all, really. He motioned for the rope party to pull the rope taut, stretching it across the lamppost and forcing the condemned to mount the fifty-five-gallon drum before him.

"Make the rope fast," demanded the sneering Krueger once the now openly weeping *Unteroffizier* was mounted atop the drum. Instantly, the four men on the rope party complied. The free end of the rope was lashed to a fire hydrant the Posleen had decided to leave in place until they might understand it better. "Don't leave the swine any slack, you crawling shits."

"Schultz? Post!" Krueger ordered. Feeling awash in emotions he could but dimly understand, Dieter complied. They both ignored the *Unteroffizier*'s wheezing, throat already constricted, "I have a *family!*"

Laying a, for *once*, comradely arm across young Schultz's shoulder, Krueger began speaking in a most calm and reasonable tone.

"See this little weeping bastard shaking atop this drum, *Stabsunteroffizier* Schultz?" The question was plainly rhetorical and so Krueger continued without pause, without waiting for an answer.

"He's worried for himself, worried for his own family and circle of loved ones. He never gave a thought, not a single thought, to anyone outside that circle. You know that is true, don't you, Schultz? That this piece of shit knows nothing of duty, of comradeship?"

That too, was rhetorical. Krueger plowed on, his every word a sneer made manifest. "He never cared for *her* . . . for a million others like her. He only cared for himself and his own. He neither cared nor imagined how your little honey might have shaken in fear before the aliens butchered and ate her." Krueger emitted an evil laugh. "More than you ever got to do with her, isn't it, boy? And it's all the fault of this cowardly, trembling bastard and the others like him."

Dieter himself trembled. Whether it was disgust at Krueger's unwelcome touch, hate for the barrel-mounted piece of human filth in front of him, or the knowledge of his permanent loss, Schultz could not have said. But when Krueger removed his unwelcome arm and said, "Kick the barrel, Schultz," Dieter didn't hesitate.

The condemned gave a short, and quickly stifled, moan as Dieter's leg came up, his foot resting on the barrel's rim. It only took a little nudge before the barrel began to tip over on its own. Frantically—but futilely—the man's feet scrambled to keep the barrel upright. It tipped over and rolled several feet, leaving the feet of the condemned to dance on air.

Dieter watched the man die from beginning to end. At first, before the rope had tightened much, one could hear labored, raspy breathing, interrupted by frequent pleas for mercy. The feet kicked continuously as the dying man sought salvation automatically. Dieter observed that each kick, each twist of the body, actually caused the rope to tighten. Soon the noose itself had moved far enough with the tightening loop to begin to cause great pain to the neck. For a brief time the feet kicked even more frantically, causing the rope to tighten further.

And then the air supply was fully cut off. Some quirk of physiology or of rope placement must have allowed blood, some portion of it anyway, to continue to flow to the brain. Dieter could see in the man's bulging hideous eyes that he was conscious nearly to the last, conscious and in agony both physical and mental. The tongue swelled, turned color and thrust outward past the lips. The face turned blue . . . then black.

At length, the kicks grew fainter . . . and then ceased altogether. The dead man swayed in the light spring breeze, eyes focused on infinity. Dieter watched until the last spark of life had gone out. He felt. . . .well, he couldn't really say how he felt. But he also could not deny that he had no regret and no pity for the lifeless meat hanging before him.

He turned to Krueger and said, "Let's finish the job then, shall we, Sergeant Major?"

And an SS man is born, thought Krueger.

Not far away, riding atop *Anna's* turret, Hans Brasche watched the dispatching of the cowards with a certain detachment. He had seen it all before . . . so many times: a veritable orchard of hanged men, and not a few women—Russian, German, Czech, Baltic . . . Vietnamese. He was quite desensitized, really.

And had the Legion caught me, I too would have had my neck stretched, he mused.

As jungle wounds often will, so had Hans' battle wounds festered. For many weeks after his evacuation his doctors at the French army hospital at Haiphong would not have given very good odds on his survival.

But the man had heart, had been young and in good health prior, and had a strong will to live. Gradually his body, aided by that marvel penicillin, had begun to triumph over the alien organisms infesting it. Health returned, and with it color. Soon he was nearly whole.

Nearly, however, is a far cry from being quite ready to return to the fetid jungle. The doctors insisted upon a longer period of recuperation than the French Army, less still the Legion Etrangere, *would have really liked.*

Hans didn't mind though. He managed to enjoy quite a romp through Haiphong and Hanoi's best brothels and bars. He was actually beginning to grow tired of the frolic when one day he stopped to read a French language newspaper at a quaint sidewalk café not far from Haiphong's wharfs. It seemed that Israel, a Jewish state, had recently come into existence and was currently fighting for that very existence.

I wonder, *thought the former SS officer,* I wonder if there might be some expiation there. . . .

*Paying his tab, leaving a small tip and folding the newspaper,
Hans headed for the wharf to enquire into departures.*

There were other infestations, course. Yet the enemy was plainly
on the defensive over a swath running from the old Maginot line
(where the remnants of the French Army had used the hastily
restored fortifications to stop the enemy cold, in the process
saving several million French civilians who huddled within it
and behind its "walls") to the River Vistula (where German and
Pole had fought like brothers together, as few would argue they
should have fought together—almost seventy years earlier against
the menace to the east).

And then one day a break was announced—a break and a
day of thanksgiving, by no lesser personage than the *Bundeskanzler* himself. Germany was on the way to being saved, so
he said, along with significant parts of France, Poland and the
Sudetenland. That this was so, noted the chancellor, was due to
the diligence of German workers, the intelligence of German
scientists . . . and—first and foremost—the courage of German
soldiers.

Of these, the *Kanzler* singled out two groups. The first of these
was the research and development team now laboring on the Tiger
III, *Ausführung* B project. The second was the group which had,
at one time or another, fought on every front. This group had
been the rock against which Posleen assault had dashed in vain.
This was the group that had shown fortitude amidst every defeat,
courage despite every loss, determination over the worst odds.

This group was the Forty-seventh *Panzer Korps*. And to them,
the *Kanzler* both gave and promised some signal honors.

The chancellor also had some interesting words to say concerning treason.

Berlin, Germany, 7 May 2007

I suppose it is for the best, thought the Tir. *And I have never
liked this cold, gray, ugly city, anyway. Less still their nasty language—an excuse for them to spit at each other under the guise
of polite conversation.*

But, he mentally sighed, *I was so looking forward to the rewards of the job.*

The message had come by special courier directly from the Ghin. The Berlin operation was to be shut down and all Darhel personnel withdrawn before the humans drew *all* the logical conclusions and came for them with implements of pain.

A week the Tir had, a mere seven cycles of this planet about its axis, to shut down his operations. Being a good businessman, in Darhel mode—which is to say honest in all that could be seen, dishonest in all else, the Tir *had* to evacuate his underlings and a select list of those that were important to them. *That,* as much as anything, would ensure the ruin of his plans for this miserable "*Deutschland*" place.

He was so *sure* that downloading the humans' plans and dispositions to the Net would make the difference, would see these humans thrashed and . . . well . . . threshed. But it was all for naught. The plans had changed too quickly, even as he was having the information downloaded it had been becoming obsolete. Damn these quick-thinking omnivores. Damn especially those vile SS humans whom even their own side could not control or predict.

Why, WHY, *WHY* hadn't these damned Germans been like the French? A logical people, in so many ways, the French. And their politicians were so vain and easy to manipulate through flattery and feeding their paranoia. Damn the Germans to the Hell of their superstitions.

Demotion, disgrace, reduction in salary, loss of bonuses and options . . . the Tir would have wept like a human if only he could have. He would be lucky not to be reduced to an entry level position.

Absently, his mind seething dangerously, the Tir used his inappropriate carnivore's teeth to rend sticks of vegetable matter placed on a tray before him. The food never really satisfied, but he, like all Darhel, was forbidden the animal protein he, and they, craved. Lintatai was the result of eating the forbidden foods.

Boredom and disgust was the result of feeding on the permissible.

INTERLUDE

It was time for a feast, for an honoring of the fallen and celebration of the victories won. A people of somewhat primitive instincts, amidst great roaring bonfires the Posleen God Kings gathered on an island in the middle of a river flowing through what once had been the capitol of the former inhabitants of this realm. The fires cast an eerie, shifting glow upon God Kings and waters both.

Around the celebrants, where once had stood a mighty city, it was as though the hand of some rampaging giant on a scale beyond imagining had scraped the Earth raw. Thresh architecture had, generally speaking, no value except as a source of raw materials. All buildings must be erased to make room for Posleen settlers, Posleen civilization.

One major exception existed. By and large, elements of a thresh transportation net were left intact wherever Posleen conquered. A road was a road, after all.

Especially noteworthy was the Posleen penchant for leaving bridges extant. Generally speaking, the Posleen didn't handle water well and were glad to make use of such bridges as could be taken intact.

Upon the cobblestones of one such bridge clattered the claws of Athenalras and such of his staff as he wished to personally honor, including Ro'moloristen. Torches glowing to either side cast their light on Posleen . . . and on a herd of thresh meant to serve as the evening's provender.

For this celebration, nothing but the best would do. The thresh for the feast had been selected for youth and tenderness. The replicators aboard the ships of the People had poured forth the mild intoxicants that only God Kings partook of, and they—as a rule—but sparingly.

Glistening with the sweat of fear in the torchlight, the young thresh wept and bewailed their impending fate. The flickering torches shone on the tears of terror.

PART III

CHAPTER 10

Berlin, Germany, 6 June 2007

"*Herr Bundeskanzler*," Mühlenkampf bowed his head slightly while clicking his heels. "You wished to see me?"

"I have another mission for you, *Herr General*."

"How can that be," Mühlenkampf asked duplicitously, "beyond preparing my *Korps* for the next onslaught?" The general was very sure indeed as to what mission the leader of Germany had in mind.

The *Kanzler* rarely enjoyed games. Especially did he not now, now that his people's future hung in the balance. He said as much, adding, "Germany has enemies, enemies she has nurtured at her own breast. They cannot be allowed to sabotage us any longer.

"No, damn them!" fumed the *Kanzler*. "Nor will they until about five percent of them are removed from office!"

"Well, *Herr Kanzler*, surely your precious democratic constitution has provisions . . ."

"Not for this, General. Not for what must be done now."

"Ohhh, I see. You want my *Korps* to break the law, do you?"

The chancellor glared. "Desperate times, General . . ."

Mühlenkampf smiled broadly and happily. "There will be a price for this, *Herr Kanzler*."

The chancellor had been prepared for this. He opened a drawer, causing the general to stiffen momentarily. From the drawer he withdrew a small rectangle of black cloth, embroidered with silver thread. "I have had two hundred thousand of these made. The Treasury will pay for as many more as you need. Is this a fair enough price?"

Mühlenkampf's smile disappeared for a moment, his face growing as serious as the snows of Russia, as the falling naval gun shells of Normandy. "To give my people back their pride and their dignity, *Herr Kanzler*? To let them be publicly proud of what they once were, *soldiers*, and among the best? Yes, sir. The price is fair."

Berlin, Germany, 12 July 2007

Under a different torchlight from that under which the Posleen had feasted upon French cuisine, under a moving river of fire, gleamed eyes bright and clear. New uniforms, black and forbidding though graced here and there with silver, paraded under the torchlight. No swastikas were to be seen. But other symbols, once forbidden, were there in plenty.

I wish that I had had the foresight to have Leni Rieffenstahl rejuvenated before she passed away in 2003. What a propaganda scene she could have made from this,

The *Kanzler*'s eyes could not make out the black uniforms through the glowing haze. Never mind, he knew they were there. He had placed them there.

I knew . . . way back when I saw the ruin of that American city, I knew that this day must come. It was so obvious . . . desperate times call for desperate measures and no one has ever seen more desperate times.

Now I have my corps d'elite. Grateful they are too, especially their leaders, for being given back their little symbols. And now, with them, I do what I hate to do . . . but must.

"Desperate times . . ."

Günter was livid, absolutely livid. *These SS bastards must pay, there must be an expiation!* It was nothing less than criminal for them to be singled out for praise, to be given back their symbols. He said as much, forcefully, to the *Bundeskanzler*.

"Fine," answered the *Kanzler*, calmly, from behind his desk.

His fingers rapped out their impatience as he asked, "Why don't you go arrest them? Strip the *Sigrunen* from their collars with your own hands."

Günter sputtered with outrage. "Don't take that line with *me*, old man. The Greens who put me on you as a watchdog made you and they can unmake you as well." Günter never mentioned his close connections to the Darhel, of course—those were secret.

"No," answered the *Kanzler*. "No. That was once true, but no longer. I used to need your Green *Korps*. But now? Now I have the Black *Korps*, my green-hued friend."

The *Kanzler* touched a button on his desk. Instantly his door sprang open and two uniformed men entered, accompanied by one other man in the usual BND trench coat. With wide-eyed horror, Günter saw that the uniforms were midnight black . . . and that they were adorned with certain silver insignia long since forbidden.

"*Herr* Greiber," the *Kanzler* enquired of the trench-coated man, "do you have a report to make on my former 'assistant'?"

With an East Prussian heel click the BND agent answered, "Indeed I do, *Herr Bundeskanzler*. Indeed I do. Treason most foul."

At the *Kanzler*'s hand gesture, the agent proceeded to lay out Günter's many crimes, his many collaborations with the Darhel that had redounded to Germany's detriment. The case was clear and the evidence overwhelming. When the agent was finished the *Kanzler* asked, "Günter, have you anything to say for yourself?"

Still not quite believing this unfortunate twist of fate, the *Kanzler*'s former aide shook his head. "You planned this," he accused. "From the beginning you planned it. You *wanted* to resurrect the SS, the whole Nazi apparatus. Admit it!"

"The 'whole Nazi apparatus'? No. I admit only that I wanted to save our people . . . that, and that I would accept no limits on what was permissible to ensure this."

"But don't you see? Can't you see?" Günter insisted, his eyes shining with all the self-righteousness of the true believer. "There were too many of us . . . and we were too greedy. We have a chance, once the Posleen have finished culling us and commenced to fighting among themselves, to build an Ideal Germany. Under the guidance of those who understand we could have saved our planet, eventually, and with fewer humans—and those less greedy and wasteful—we could have maintained our holy mother Earth inviolate forever."

The *Kanzler* picked up on a few key concepts in Günter's diatribe. "And you, my friend? You would have been one of those knowing guides, would you not? How were you to live while our people served as feedlots? An off-planet trip? Along with your wife and children? Yes, I am sure that was part of your holy vision too, was it not? Because you were special and the rest of the *Volk* were not?"

Günter began to defend himself, to object. Then he recalled that the chancellor was half right. He *had* demanded that his own family be moved to safety. He thought that maybe, just maybe, deep down inside he had expected to join them.

He could not defend himself on that charge. He attacked from a different angle. "You were returning Germany to the Nazis!" he accused.

The chancellor did not answer directly. Instead, he asked one of the black-uniformed men, "What is your name, son?

"Schüler, *Herr Kanzler*," the young one answered instantly, springing to a stiffer attention.

"Schüler, are you a Nazi?"

"No, *mein Herr*. I am just a soldier, like other soldiers."

"Do you know any Nazis in the 47th *Korps*?"

"One, *mein Herr*," Schüler answered, simply and directly. "He is a bad man and we all hate him. He is, however, a very *good* tank driver so we put up even with him, for the Fatherland."

Turning back to Günter and snorting with derision, the *Kanzler* said, "Never mind. It matters not. You will believe what you will believe." Turning to the other black-uniformed man he asked, "Has General Mühlenkampf reported on progress?"

The shorter but more senior of the two answered, "The general reports that most suspect members of the Federal Legislature are under arrest, along with the A list of suspects within the *Bundeswehr* higher command echelons. In addition, leaders of the more radically antihuman of the political parties are almost entirely in the bag . . . Though some have already been executed . . . er, shot while escaping. Several dozen appear to have disappeared from Germany entirely, along with their families. The Darhel are not to be found either. Still, isolation of whatever Darhel may remain moves forward apace."

"Good, very good," answered the *Kanzler*, though inside he felt utterly dirtied. His old gray head nodded in Günter's direction. "Please add this one to the bag."

Ouvrage du Hackenberg, Thierville, France, 14 July 2007

And so now I finally understand what it means to languish in a prison.

It was Bastille Day in France, rather, in that tiny portion of France still in human hands. It had always been a big holiday for Isabelle, more for its progressive, revolutionary character than for its patriotic. This Bastille Day, however, she felt little urge to celebrate, this despite the double ration of the French staff of life, wine, ordered by the fortress commander.

The wine was bitter and poor, a modern day version of the *Vinogel*, concentrated wine, France had at some times in the past issued to her soldiers. Reconstituted with water, this modern *Vinogel* had little to commend it beyond that it tasted faintly of having something like grape in its ancestry ... that, and that it had mind and sense-numbing alcohol.

And Isabelle wanted her senses numbed, wanted desperately for some escape from this new horror that jokingly went by the name, "life."

She had heard there were cities abuilding underground, cities safe and warm where a human might hope to live something like a real life. Hackenberg, despite the season, was anything but warm. Indeed, the walls of this underground prison exuded a steady flow of cold wet moisture and sucked away whatever warmth one's body might produce. No single person, nor all the fifty thousand packed in like sardines with Isabelle and her sons, could warm the place by so much as half a degree.

And though the place was, literally, a fortress, Isabelle knew that this did not add to the safety of herself and hers, but rather detracted from it. A fortress was also a target, thus so were she and her boys.

The boys' father too, had been a target, so she had to assume. For there had been no word, not since the brief phone call that had announced the invasion, the destruction of her country, and the impending slaughter of its people.

That knowledge, that her beloved husband had almost certainly fallen to the invaders, was like a knife twisted into her innards. That pain made Isabelle pour, more than drink, the wretched reconstituted wine down her throat.

Even as dissidents and derelicts poured into holding pens, so too did information, *vital* information, flow to every nook and cranny of Germany's multifaceted war effort.

Did information flow? It was as nothing compared to the flow of refugees. Did refugees flow? Then so too did power, as Germany acquired, unintentionally, a stranglehold over everything needed by the refugees, and by the remnants of their armed forces. Most of these forces were absorbed by the *Bundeswehr*. Still, Mühlenkampf and his men had done good service and deserved reward. The *Kanzler* therefore decreed the expansion of 47th *Panzer Korps* into what was called "Army Group Reserve." In addition to acquiring another two panzer and four good motorized infantry *Korps*, as well as the penal division composed of the remnants of the more than decimated 33rd *Korps*, Mühlenkampf also assumed control of a large number of newly created foreign formations. Division Charlemagne marched again, in lock step with divisions and brigades of Latvians, Estonians, Poles, Spaniards and others.

Of these, Division Charlemagne was an oddity. For it was the only Francophone formation under German control. Unlike the other, overrun, states of Europe, the French resolutely refused to subordinate their interests to anyone else's command. Their army guarding the much reoriented Maginot line, the four or five million remaining French men, women and children huddled either in camps between the Line and the Rhein, or shivered in dank misery in the bowels of the line itself.

(Magnanimously, the French had offered to integrate their forces, but only if a French commander was named, certain key French interests put in first place. Inexplicably, the Germans had failed to see the advantages to this approach.)

Charlemagne came to be recreated when the commanding general of a French armored division had simply mutinied against what he called the "institutionalized stupidities" of the French High Command, then gathered up his soldiers and their dependants, and reported to the German border seeking employment.

Supplemented by numerous individual volunteers, some of those being veterans of the original division who had come to Germany to volunteer anew, Charlemagne was a large division even by the inflated standards of the Posleen War.

Losses, of course, had been staggering. By the time Germany was cleared of Posleen infestations, many divisions that had once boasted strengths as high as twenty-four thousand now contained barely half that. Yet there was a new ruthlessness in Germany, a ruthlessness that cared little for the "rights" of individuals, much for the survival of the *Volk*.

Student deferments? Gone. Alternative service? Gone. Refusal to serve? Conscientious Objector status claimed? The Penal Formation once known as the 33rd *Korps* grew to meet and then exceed its former strength. And the hangmen were often kept quite busy.

Nice, safe and comfortable billets in the rear? "No more, my son. You are going to the front. Women can do your job well enough."

Only workers vital to the war effort were spared the sweep of conscription. Many of these were agricultural. Many others were industrial. Some were scientific and industrial both.

Kraus-Maffei-Wegmann Plant, Munich, Germany, 15 July 2007

"I could wish our antilander munitions had been even *slightly* less powerful," sighed Mueller.

Karl Prael raised a quizzical eyebrow.

"Simplicity," answered Mueller. "If we hadn't blasted all of the Posleen's C- and B-Decs to flinders, there might have been enough of their anti-shipping railguns to retrofit every Tiger in the inventory *and* the ones that will be rolling off the assembly floor in the near future, *and* to provide a great number of more or less fixed defense batteries. As it is, we have a few score serviceable guns, no more. Sixty or seventy where we might have had six or seven hundred . . . maybe even several thousand."

"You understate things," Prael observed. "We have recovered sixty or seventy *so far*, but we have hardly begun to scrap even half of the alien wrecks littering the countryside. It is almost certain that there will be enough railguns for the complete run of Tiger III, *Ausführung* B. Pessimist," he finished with a smile.

"Maybe," conceded Mueller. "Maybe . . . *if* we can scrap the wrecks while doing no further damage. *If* we can modify the railguns to fit our existing carriages . . . or our carriages to fit the guns. And *if* we can even get them here for modification and mounting."

"And if we have time," muttered Prael, head sinking. "When do you think, *really* think, we'll have the B model in hand?"

Mueller bit his lower lip, shaking his head, "We won't have a prototype for as much as four or five months. I think we have been too ambitious."

Prael understood, even agreed. The B model Tiger was a leap ahead of the original, mounting not just a railgun capable of striking the enemy even in space, but also nuclear propulsion, much thickened and enhanced armor, a new AI suite. And these were only the major differences. There were numerous minor ones as well.

"It is time," announced Prael, looking at his watch. Nodding, Mueller agreed and the two walked to a room containing the other members of the core design team.

It was supposed to be a party, a farewell party. The world had seen more joyful occasions. Most funerals were at least equally festive.

Certainly Schlüssel's face showed unhappiness. Equally so Henschel, the bearded Nielsen, and the usually ebullient Breitenbach wore long faces.

"Must you go, David? Really? Must you?" asked Breitenbach.

Benjamin quietly nodded his head. He had been this way—dour and quiet—ever since the news had come the previous December of the fall of Jerusalem; wife gone, family gone, friends gone. A few hundred thousand Jews had been evacuated, most of them being given shelter by Germany and the United Kingdom. Certainly anti-Semitic France's strong and vocal Muslim minority had put up vigorous protests towards the notion of sheltering the religious and cultural enemy.

But Germany, long-guilty Germany—ever seeking forgiveness, had opened up. Her strong merchant fleet along with the *Kriegsmarine* and the Royal Navy had braved a gauntlet of Posleen fire (much of it only generally aimed, as the Posleen understood wet water vessels but poorly) to bring out the Jews.

Two hundred thousand of them came, mostly the very young. Yet there had been enough young men, and women, six or seven thousand, of an age to fight. And fight they most certainly wanted to. Yet how? With whom? There was only one group in the German military used to assimilating foreigners... yet *that* group?

Mühlenkampf had offered, promising them their own unit. He had asked quite humbly for this chance to make up, in however small part, for a sordid... nay, horrid... past. He had even sent Hans Brasche, the history of whom he knew, to talk to the refugees and to Benjamin.

"Yes, I must go," answered the Israeli. "My job is done here... but there is more I can do."

Understanding at his core, Breitenbach stepped back, looking Benjamin over from top to bottom. A small silver star of David graced the Israeli's right collar, the four pips of a major his left. Silver buttons held the tunic closed. A silver embroidered armband encircled his left sleeve, at the cuff.

The armband proclaimed, in silver letters, Hebrew and Roman, one above the other, "Judas Maccabeus."

The uniform was midnight black.

Headquarters, Army Group Reserve, Kapellendorf Castle, Thuringia, 25 July 2007

The group headquarters had taken possession of an ancient castle as its headquarters. Inauspiciously, the castle had once served as the headquarters of the Prussian Army before its disastrous defeat by Napoleon in the twin battle of Jena-Auerstadt in 1806. Cool and damp it was, made worse by its surrounding moat. It was not convenient, and one had to go outside to use the latrine. *Yet it is, for the nonce, home,* thought Mühlenkampf. *And it is centrally located.*

"Time, gentlemen. It is of the very essence. Whether Germany lives or dies depends on time more than anything. And we think we have less than six months until the next wave lands on our heads."

"General?" asked Brasche of Mühlenkampf. "Do we have reason to believe they will come right down on us like last time?"

Mühlenkampf's eyes swept the room. Not one man lower than a lieutenant general . . . except for Hans, recently promoted to full colonel. And yet Hans, not the others, asked the good questions. "Ordinarily, Hansi, I would say they are stupid enough to use the same trick twice. This time I expect it because they just may be smart enough to do so."

"Why, sir?"

"Because it is unlikely we will be able to handle it. Within six months the numbers of the enemy to our east and west may have grown to as many a one billion each—yes, they mature that fast! That is the equivalent of perhaps ONE HUNDRED FORTY-FIVE THOUSAND infantry divisions on each front! Though they can move faster and with less train than any infantry division ever known, of course."

Mühlenkampf continued, "There is actually a fair chance we could defend against each of those assaults. With foreign troops, recent expansions, and the culling of the slackers, Germany actually can place three hundred or so divisions along the Rhein, about as many facing the Vistula, and a like number dispersed throughout the center of the country. And we are digging in and pouring concrete like mad. All that while still leaving a significant reserve in the center, mostly ourselves.

"North and south our flanks are secure, of course, against any ground assault. And our Tigers," he said, with an appreciative nod towards Brasche, "appear capable of dealing with many times their number."

Brasche answered truthfully, "We can if we get enough of them. The system has not brought me up even to my old, preattack, strength. I have no strong hope that they'll fill me to my new strength of forty-one Tigers." He paused briefly. "I *am* training the new recruits on the seven Tigers I currently have operational. And new and rebuilt Tigers are coming at a rate of about one every six days or so."

Free to recruit for themselves, the 47th *Korps* had set to that task with a will. Posters, radio, television and internet carried the message of the now black-clad, *Sigrune*-bearing "asphalt soldiers." Even the ranks of the *Bundeswehr* helped here, in two ways. More than a few men of the *Bundeswehr* opted to transfer. And from others came the message to younger brothers—and even to sons—that the 47th *Korps*, openly called "the SS *Korps*" now, was an altogether worthy group, vital to the Fatherland's defense.

That the girls seemed more interested in the men of the more glamorous and dashing "*Schwarze Korps*" only helped matters.

Recruits, high-quality recruits, were plentiful. The ranks swelled and over swelled. The 501st, recently redubbed the 501st *Schwere Panzer Brigade* (Michael Wittmann), drew enough to expand its three skeletonized line companies into full battalions, and its headquarters and support company into three more such plus another battalion for brigade headquarters and general support. The addition of a large artillery regiment—seventy-two guns and twenty-four multiple rocket launchers, engineer demibattalion, air defense demibattalion, plus a reinforced battalion each of panzer grenadiers and reconnaissance troops completed the package. In all, Hans would command close to forty-six hundred troops.

The cadre for these men and the formations they comprised was obtained from diverse sources. First of course were the survivors of the original 501st. This mix was somewhat enhanced by intensive training courses for those deemed most worthy. Additionally, Bad Tolz had been identifying potential junior officers and noncoms all along. These, leadership training once completed, helped fill up both the 501st and the 47th *Korps*. Some cadre was obtained also from the regular *Bundeswehr*, from those who wished to escape any residual trace of the, admittedly dying, political correctness that had infected that force, sending many a young soldier to premature death and leaving many a town, like Giessen, ripe for the slaughter.

Lambs to the slaughter, mused Krueger, *lambs to the slaughter.*

As had Dieter Schultz and his peers once stood in shivering fear before the terror inspiring Krueger, now the new men likewise quaked. The cold of the Bavarian Alps had added to Dieter's shivering. Now, in the mild Thuringian summer, Krueger needed nothing more than the black uniform with the silver insignia; that and his icy cold blue eyes and frosty mien.

The SS man stopped to slap the face of a new recruit whose face showed just a little too much fear. The boy was knocked to the ground by the blow, then kicked while he lay stunned by a high, polished jackboot. "An SS man recovers from any blow immediately," announced Krueger, adding another, fairly mild, kick for punctuation. "Up, boy!" Then, loud enough to carry, "You'll all learn to become tougher and more resilient than Krupp's steel.

"Why," he added, a trace of utter loathing in his voice, "you'll even become more resilient than the Jews, and they put Krupp's product to shame."

Krueger shivered himself at the thought of the new formation, this "Judas Maccabeus" brigade. *Fucking untermensch. It is a disgrace, it is.*

Walking, no *strutting*, down the ranks of the new men, Krueger reminded Brasche of nothing so much as a fighting game cock, proud and aggressive. *Of course I* loathe *the son of a bitch,* mused Brasche, *loathe him for so many reasons. Nazi bastard!*

Brasche stood too far off to hear what Krueger said to the new men. He had a good enough idea; he had seen and heard it all before, seen it in some rather strange places, too.

The Israelis hadn't wanted him at first; they'd made that painfully clear. They believed him when he'd said that he had never taken part in any crime against Jews. They believed he wanted to make amends. They knew he had skills they needed desperately and lacked almost totally. But ex-SS . . . ?

Hans had countered with the irrefutable argument, "You want me dead, most of you. I cannot blame you for that. So send me where I can die."

The Israelis were not that generous, and so he found himself not leading—the Israelis had been very clear he was never to lead Jews in battle—but training the scraps of diverse and wretched humanity passing through a small camp for a brief course in battle before being shipped off for butchery somewhere along the frontier.

So too he found himself teaching by pointing, slowly and painfully learning Hebrew, eating Kosher food—unaccustomedly bland. He had never felt more alone. Uncomfortable, too, for while others could strip to the waist in the fierce Middle Eastern heat, he could never remove his T-shirt, the covering for the tattoo that marked him for what he had been. Even to shower Hans had to wait until all else were done, that, or arise at an obscene hour.

There were a couple of bright spots. One was Sol, an ex-Camp

KAPO, one of the imprisoned Jews who actually had done, had been forced to do, most of the hands-on dirty work in the concentration camps. Sol, a Bavarian from Munich, spoke native German of course—despite that distressing south German accent. Better, he had his own sins in plenty and was disinclined to judge. They could speak sometimes, share a beer, remember better days . . . even hope for better days. They never talked about the war or the camps; each sensed in the other a horror not to be raised or erased.

The other bright spot was Anna, a dark blond Berliner girl who even spoke in a somewhat more upper crust version of Hans' own native dialect. Hans didn't know much of Anna's history, only that she had been in the camps at some time during the war.

Of her history he knew little; and he was loathe to conjecture about more. But in the here and now he also knew she was beautiful—breathtaking, really, with sculpted features and body coupled to bright and kind shining green eyes. Her mien and manner showed a spirit even the camps could not crush. Though most of the Israeli girls scorned makeup, Hans noted that Anna seemed to actively despise it. No matter, she was more than beautiful enough without artificial adornment.

Lastly he knew he was unworthy . . . so that whenever Anna made to get closer he withdrew. Withdrew? Rather it was more like he fled in barely concealed terror whenever the girl approached on any but professional matters. Hans could not bring himself, ever, to look into those green eyes. He avoided the north side of the camp, the women's area, like the very plague.

"You are a fool, Hans," said Sol one day as the two sat on barracks steps over an evening's friendly beer.

At Hans' quizzical look the Israeli laughed. "The girl follows you like a puppy. Why do you always run the other way?"

Heaving a deep sigh was Hans' only answer.

"Don't lie to me, old son," said Sol, taking a quick sip of warm and insipid beer, "not even by refusing to answer. I see your face when you look in her direction. I can practically hear your heart race when she walks by upwind."

"I know," Hans whispered, softly. "But I just can't."

"In the name of God, why not?"

"Because I am unworthy," Hans answered, simply.

✧   ✧   ✧

"You little shits think you are *worthy* to become SS?" demanded Krueger, still strutting. "I've ass-fucked quivering little Yid whores at Ravensbrück who were more worthy than you, you filth.

"*They*, at least, had staying power. It remains to be seen if *you* turds do."

At which, much self-satisfied, statement Krueger commanded, "Right, face . . . Forward, march . . . Double-time . . ."

INTERLUDE

Ro'moloristen hesitated, doubting whether it was his place to criticize his lord of that lord's own hesitation. With all eyes upon him, feeling his own weak position in the fiber of his being, he summoned his courage and said, "My lord, we might be losing the race."

"Race? What race, puppy?" Athenalras demanded, crest rising.

"The race to finish the conquest of this peninsula, this Europe."

"How so? We sit on everything useful to us except the central area, *Deutschland* it is called, yes? . . . that, and the mountains to the south of it. They will fall soon enough . . . except perhaps for the mountains."

"I am thinking of orna'adar, my lord, and our clan's position when this world finally descends into it. The longer we take here, now, the worse our position then. Also . . ." The young God King hesitated.

"Also, what?"

"My lord, the gray thresh are preparing for us with everything they have. We had advantages earlier that are fast disappearing. Information made available to us through the Net, dissension and confusion in the gray thresh's ruling bodies, unwillingness or inability to really marshal their strength, lack of fortification . . . all these are no longer true, no longer there to work for us.

"Their forces are expanding radically. New fortifications are

169

being built and old ones restored. Every fiber of their society is being twisted and knitted for the needs of defense it seems. Perhaps worst of all, my lord, they have scrapped hundreds upon hundreds of landers for their on-board weapons. My lord . . . it is no longer safe to travel over this 'Germany' except in orbit so far out as to be useless."

Athenalras allowed his crest to go flaccid as he contemplated. "You think then the original plan must be scrapped, that those of our clan coming in the next wave should not be landed directly into the central area, that we should attack overland?"

Ro'moloristen shook his head in negation. "No lord, we must continue to follow the original plan . . . but the cost makes me shudder."

CHAPTER 11

Headquarters, Army Group Reserve, Kapellendorf Castle,
Thuringia, 17 December 2007

Hans shuddered with the cold. Though snow lay all around, covering castle, land and ice in the moat, the sky was, for the nonce, clear. Christmas carols—sung by a local group of schoolchildren for the benefit of the headquarters staff—carried far in the dense, icy air, ringing off castle stone and leafless tree.

Standing on an arched stone bridge over the moat, leaning on its stone wall guardrail, Hans stared into the sky at the twinkling stars. He willed his mind to blankness, seeking rest in temporary oblivion.

In this Hans was successful, so much so that he never noticed the tapping of boots on the stones of the bridge.

It was only when Mühlenkampf laid a hand on his shoulder and announced, "The next wave is here, Hansi," that Hans awoke from his reverie.

"So soon? I had hoped we would have more time. Maybe even get half equipped with the new-model Tigers. Get a few of them, at least."

"They only just finished putting the prototype through its tests, Hans. The only way we will ever see them is if we can hang on for at least a year."

Hans nodded then looked skyward. "Up to the navy for now, though," he said.

Already new stars began to appear and quickly die as the two fleets met in a dance of destruction.

Battle cruiser Lütjens, Sol-ward from Pluto's orbit, 17 December 2007

The ship's commander, *Kapitän* Mölders, could not help but be amused at his ship's station. Being a part of Task Fleet 7.1 was unremarkable. But, along with another battle cruiser, the *Almirante Guillermo Brown*, and half a dozen of the ad hoc frigates converted out of Galactic courier vessels, being an escort for Supermonitor *Moscow* certainly was worth a minor chuckle. *What would Lindemann or Lütjens have said?* he wondered, thinking of those two brave and worthy German seamen who had gone down with the original *Bismarck* early in World War Two. Mölders would have chuckled too, except that he, *Moscow*, those half dozen frigates and two more task fleets were racing at breakneck pace into a death absolutely certain.

There was no chance of victory in any sense except that of taking a few with them. The Posleen wave, sixty-five globes, each composed of hundreds of smaller ships connected for interstellar travel, was simply too great, unimaginably great. And Earth's defending fleet was simply too small.

Victory, if it came, depended on the ground forces. Victory, for the fleet, would be giving those ground forces the greatest possible chance. Final victory was something not one man or woman aboard the ships had any hope of ever seeing. No more so did Mölders.

On *Lütjens'* view-screen Mölders saw a brilliant new sun appear for a long moment. A message from *Moscow* poured into his ear through an earpiece kept there. Mölders' eyes widened, then turned suddenly soft.

"Gentlemen," he announced in a breaking voice to the bridge crew, "that sun was the Japanese battle cruiser *Genjiro Shirakami*.[38] It has rammed an enemy globe and detonated itself. Supermonitor *Honshu* believes that that globe was completely destroyed."

"So we only have another sixty-four or so to go, eh, sir?" whispered Mölder's exec.

Headquarters, Army Group Reserve, Kapellendorf Castle, Thuringia, 17 December 2007

Lightning flashed and new-born suns flared in space over head. Hans wondered idly at the details, but knew deep down that the details could not matter. He had seen the estimates; Mühlenkampf had shared them with his senior officers. The human fleet was doomed and was not going to do all that much good, either. Still anything was better than nothing and the blooming suns of destroyed ships, coupled with the silvery streaks of hypervelocity anti-ship missiles, made for quite a show.

But he had seen similar shows before, ones that had kept his attention even more raptly . . .

The attack seemed to come from nowhere and from everywhere. One moment found Hans fast asleep in his barracks. The next thunder-crashing moment found him leaping from his bunk, fully alert as only a very combat experienced veteran could come alert. He reached instinctively for the Schmeisser he had acquired on his own ticket as well as the combat harness that held an extra half dozen magazines for the submachine gun. Carrying both in his hands and shouting in his wretched Hebrew for the dozen men who shared the small hut with him to take their positions along the camp's perimeter, Hans stumbled to the shelter's door. Jacking the Schmeisser's bolt once, Hans left the hut with Sol's shouts ringing behind him, directing the others.

Outside was bedlam. Mortar rounds splashed down to briefly light the area with sudden lightning and lingering thunder. Tracers arced through the camp, seemingly from all around. Though this was the first attack it was not the first time Hans had cursed the sloppiness of the amateur, ad hoc, wretchedly trained Israeli army. No wonder the Arabs had gotten through somewhere along the none-too-distant front and come here for easy pickings.

Fierce cries of "Allahu akbar" resounded from a shallow stream-bed to the north as the volume of fire began to pick up from that direction Not quite sure why, Hans began moving in that direction. Half dressed, more importantly perhaps half undressed, shrieking women began to streak by in their flight. He called out repeatedly, "Anna? Anna?"

One Israeli girl shouted to him, "Anna stayed behind to fight and cover us!" Hans moved out, alone, into the night.

He found her spitting and cursing defiance at the three Arabs who had her pinned and spread-eagled for a fourth crouching between her legs, tugging at whatever covered the lower half of her body. His experienced finger caressed the trigger four times, then a fifth to make sure of one still-twitching, towel-headed form.

Hans reached down and grabbed the girl's shirt. As he did so he noticed that she was trouserless and that her rifle, bolt jammed open, was empty. Standing erect again, Hans began to half trot backwards, dragging the girl and firing backwards to discourage pursuit.

Mortar fire was still falling, making life on the surface unsafe for man or girl. Coming to a narrow slit trench, Hans jumped in and dragged Anna down with him, pushing her gently to the trench's dusty floor.

"You'll be safe here, Anna. I won't let anything happen to you."

It was only then that she began to cry, small half-stifled whimpers at first, growing with time to great wracking sobs. Hans tried his poor best to comfort her with little soft pats while keeping a watch topside for approaching dangers. The raid seemed to be ending, the Arab's fire slacking off. The camp was better lit now, what with half a dozen buildings burning brightly. Perhaps that was what had driven the Arabs off. Natural raiders and almost hopeless as soldiers, they would rarely press an attack without every conceivable advantage.

In time, under Hans' gentle care, Anna's sobs subsided. "They were going to rape me," she announced, needlessly. "You should not have risked yourself. It would not have killed me."

Hans shrugged. "Perhaps it would not have, girl. They very well might have though, their fun once done."

Anna echoed Hans' shrug. With an unaccountable angry tone she said, "I have a name, you know? Anyway, little matter if they had."

"Don't *say* that!" he shouted with unusual ferocity, then, more gently, almost a whisper, "I know you have a name, Anna."

"Why?" she asked. "You've never shown you care. Not until tonight anyway."

"I care, Anna. I always have."

"You never showed," she accused.

"I couldn't."

"Why not? Because I was a camp whore? Because I have a tattoo?"

Hans felt a wave of sickness wash over him. "I knew about the tattoo. I never knew about the . . . other."

"I was though, for years. For the guards at Ravensbrück."

Hans remembered some disgusted words from another SS man during a very brief sojourn at Birkenau. His sense of sickness grew greater still, great enough to show.

Misinterpreting, Anna turned her face away to hide forming tears. "It was not by my choice, never by my choice. But I understand why you won't want anything to do with me . . ."

"Stop that," Hans commanded. "It isn't your tattoo and it isn't a past you had no choice in. It's . . . that I have a tattoo as well."

"No, you don't," Anna insisted. "I've seen your arm."

"Mine," Hans sighed wearily, "isn't on my arm."

"But . . ." Anna covered her mouth under eyes gone wide with too much understanding. She turned and fled the trench and went alone into the fire-flickered night.

There were no more "tracers" in space, no new suns that burst brilliantly before fading into nothingness. The battle there was over and Hans had no doubt who had won—more importantly, lost—it. Earth's skies, once briefly recovered, were once again in the possession of the invader.

Mühlenkampf cleared his throat. "They will be on us tomorrow, gentlemen, if not sooner. Best return to your units now."

Silently, sullenly, perhaps a bit fearfully the men began to separate and depart, each to his division, brigade or regiment.

Kraus-Maffei-Wegmann Plant, Munich, Germany, Midnight, December 18 2007

The shining behemoth positively *gleamed* with menace. Where *Anna* and her sisters dazzled, the new model stunned. From the tip of her railgun to the back of her turret, from the top of that narrow, sharklike turret to the treads resting on the concrete floor, from the twin mounds housing close-in defense weapons on her front glacis to the slanted rear, Tiger III, *Ausführung* B was a dream come true.

"She'll be a nightmare to the enemy," observed Mueller, for once satisfied with the armament.

Indowy Rinteel, at loose ends since the Darhel Tir's withdrawal, had joined the team to help with the railgun. He had no human-recognized degree in engineering, but many Indowy, and he was one, had an almost genetic ability to tinker. Rinteel agreed entirely about the "nightmare" part.

Prael snorted through his beard with disgust. "*She* might well be. But she is only one nightmare where we needed a veritable plague of them, dammit. It has been the old story. Too little, too late."

"We pushed for too much," conceded Mueller. "We should have used the railguns we salvaged to upgrade the existing Tigers."

"Maybe yes, maybe no," countered Nielsen. "They will still do good service supplementing the Planetary Defense Batteries."

"This one could do as well," observed Breitenbach.

"No," corrected Henschel, "for we do not even have a crew for her."

"Be a shame to just let her be captured or destroyed to prevent capture," said Schlüssel. "And it is not entirely true that we do not have a crew. We, ourselves, know her as well as any crew could, and if we alone are not enough to man the secondary weapons . . . well . . . she is much more capable, her AI is much more capable, than the A model's."

"You are suggesting we *steal* her?" asked Prael.

Mueller smiled. "Not 'steal,' Karl. Just take her out for some combat testing is all. And I used to be a very good driver."

Assembly Area Wittmann, Tiger Anna, Thuringia, Germany, 18 December 2007

Tonight's fireworks put those of the previous evening into the shade. Between roughly ten thousand individual Posleen ships, the globes having broken up, and the fires of several hundred Planetary Defense Batteries and Earth-bound railguns the skies were one continuous stream of pyrotechnic entertainment.

What was it Admiral Nelson said? wondered Hans. *Ah, I remember: "A ship's a fool to fight a fort." He was right, of course, a ship is. But get enough ships and it becomes only a matter of time, not of foolishness.*

There was no practical shielding, no defense, for ship or shore battery. The defenders had only the triple advantages of being able to choose when to unmask, to reveal their position by open- ing fire; that the Posleen had no cover whatsoever; and that, as a practical matter, they tended to handle their ships somewhat badly. They were, after all, a fairly stupid race. Still, these paltry favors were more than matched by Posleen numbers.

Hans considered some folksy wisdom on the subject: "Quan- tity has a quality all its own," and Stalin's famous jibe, "Quantity becomes quality at some point in time."

The Communist bastard was right about that one, too, thought Hans, remembering distantly, the sight of burning individual Panthers and Tigers, a collection of half a dozen or more Soviet machines dead before them, while endless columns of Russian T-34s passed the burning German machines by.

A—relatively—nearby Planetary Defense Battery opened up with a furious fusillade of kinetic energy shots, the bolts leaving eye- burning trails of straight silver lightning in the sky. Overhead, a half dozen or more new stars blazed briefly. Then the combined might of hundreds of Posleen ships poured down onto the PDB, blasting it to ruin, raising a mushroom cloud, and even shaking Hans as he stood in his hatch atop *Anna*'s turret.

We are hurting them, maybe even hurting them badly. But it won't be enough.

As if in confirmation, a veritable torrent of Posleen fire poured through down from the heavens to fall somewhere far to the west.

That would be for the benefit of the French, I think.

Ouvrage du Hackenberg (Fortress Hackenberg), Thierville, Maginot Line, France, 18 December 2007

Not for the first time, Major General Henri Merle cursed his government's pigheaded refusal to cooperate with anyone. On the remote television screen that adorned one wall of his command post he saw a nightmare he had somehow hoped he would never see again, a sea of reptilian centaurs chewing through wire, mines, and machine gun and artillery fire to get at the defenders. The actinic glare of the Posleen railguns crossed over and through the red tracers of France's last defenders.

The command post shook slightly with the steady vibrations of the fort's three automatic cannon firing from their retractable turrets. On the screen the fire of the short-range guns, short ranged because the turrets were too small to permit much recoil, drew lines of mushrooming black clouds through the enemy host, leaving thousands of destroyed Posleen bodies in their wake. Each gun was capable of sending forth several dozen one-hundred-thirty-five-millimeter shells per minute by virtue of their unique chain-driven feeding system. All of that was done automatically except for feeding of the shells into the conveyor system that hoisted them aloft. That job was done by dozens of sweating, straining men in ammunition chambers far below.

We built this thing to deter the Germans from attacking straight into our industrial heartland, mused Merle, with a grin. *We succeeded too. They obliged us by going through Belgium instead. Then we kept the forts up in pretty pristine condition for twenty years in case the Russians decided to get jolly. Maybe it really* did *help deter them too, never know. Now finally we are using them, after a frantic race to restore them, to hang on to this last corner of* la belle patrie.

"And they're working," he said aloud. "Killing the alien bastards in droves. And the damned government just *had* to throw that away by refusing to cooperate with the Germans."

"Sir?" queried Merle's aide.

"We could have had a couple of *Boche* armored corps here with us," answered Merle. "We could have had a few score infantry divisions too, to help us hold this line. But, no. Impossible. We would only let them help us if they were willing to let us dictate policy. Tell me, Francois, if you were the Germans, if you were *anyone*, would you let the government of France, *any* government of France, dictate policy to *you*?"

"*Certainement pas*,"[39] answered the captain, with a wry—and very cynically and typically French—grin. "Who could be so foolish?"

"No one, and so no more would I. And so, though we are

murdering those alien assholes by the bushel, they are still going to get through. They are going to take these forts, peel us like hard-boiled eggs, and then feast on the contents. And then they're going to go past us . . ."

The command post suddenly shook more violently than the automatic cannons alone could account for. Merle was tossed from his seat by the shock.

"*Merde*, what was that?" he asked, rising to his feet.

"I don't know, *mon colonel.*"

The phone rang. After all these decades the telephone system still worked. The aide, Francois, answered. Merle saw his face turn white.

As Francois replaced the ancient telephone on its hook he said, "Battery B. It's . . . gone. The aliens somehow penetrated all the way down to the ammunition storage area. Hardly anyone escaped. The area's been sealed off to prevent fire from spreading."

Now Merle's face paled. "My God, there are twenty thousand civilians down there below the ammunition for that battery."

"Lost, sir."

"Do we still have communication with the Germans behind us?" Merle asked.

"I believe so, sir. Why?"

"Get me *Generalleutnant* Von der Heydte on the line. I am going to place this fortress under his command and ask him for any aid he can spare to save our people. While I am doing that I want you to begin calling the other sector commanders and giving them my suggestion they do the same. Fuck the government. We haven't had a decent one since Napoleon the First, anyway."

Saarlouis, Germany, 18 December 2007

Von der Heydte was stunned. "The bloody frogs are asking us to do *what?*"

"They want us to take over, sir. At least General Merle does, and some others. I understand we are getting calls all along the front. They can't hold. Their army, at least, knows it. And they have decided to ignore their government."

"Okay . . . I can buy that. And they would be a useful addition to our effort if they will just cooperate."

"General Merle sounded eager to cooperate, sir. His exact words were, 'Tell General Von der Heydte I am submitting myself and my entire command to his authority.' But there's a catch."

"Aha! I *knew* it. What catch?"

"Sir, they want us to open up our lines to permit the evacuation of several million civilians. Several hundred thousand in General Merle's sector alone."

"Can we?"

"Risky, sir. We could conceivably open a lane or perhaps two. I don't think we have the engineer assets to re-close more than two, anyway. But even they will be narrow passages. I doubt we can get everyone through. And, sir?"

"Yes?"

"Sir, they're a very proud people. You know Merle and the other frogs wouldn't be asking if they thought they had a prayer of holding on their own."

"I see," and Von der Heydte did see. "We're going to have to put some of our own people out there and at risk to cover the evacuation."

Von der Heydte thought some more, then walked over to observe his situation map. Noting the location of one division in particular, he dredged through his memory for an answer. Finding that answer he ordered, "Call Mühlenkampf. Yes, 'SS' Mühlenkampf. Ask if I can borrow his Charlemagne Division. Tell him he'll likely have a mutiny if he doesn't give them to me, because I am not above asking them to come directly. And tell him he is unlikely to get many of them back."

Fortress Hackenberg, Thierville, Maginot Line, France, 19 December 2007

The men in the dank and malodorous depths of the fortress still noticed her, even under the pale, flickering light. Though well past the bloom of youth, and despite the deprivations and terrors of the last nine months, Isabelle De Gaullejac was still quite a fine-looking woman beneath her grimy, unwashed face. Cleaned up, and when she could clean herself Isabelle was fastidious, those men would have called her "pretty"—if not beautiful.

Still, there was beauty and then there was *beauty*. Standing, Isabelle had a bearing and obvious dignity that was proud, even almost regal. Whatever she lacked in classic line of features her girlish shape and posture up made for, and more.

The pride was personal. The regality was perhaps the result of genetics, for she came from a family ennobled for over five hundred years.

She had grown up in a real castle, not one of those palaces that went by the name. Her girlhood home had been a hunting castle used by King Henry, Henry the Fowler, in the Middle Ages. Thus, the cold, damp, dirty and detestably uncomfortable hell that was the bowels of Fort Hackenberg was no great shock to her. She had hated King Henry's castle as a girl. She hated Hackenberg now. But she could deal with the one as she had dealt with the other, through sheer will to endure.

But it was with relief that she greeted the news the fort was to be evacuated. Gathering up her two sons, one teenaged and the other a mere stripling, she dressed them as warmly as the meager stocks of clothing they had been able to carry permitted. Expecting a long march to safety, she packed a bag of necessities. These included food, some medicine for the younger boy, who had picked up a cough in the fort, a change of clothing each, and a bottle of first rate Armagnac. Two of the wretched army blankets the family had been issued were also stuffed into the bag. She was not a small or weak woman and so, while the pack was heavy, she thought she could bear it, if her teenager, Thomas, could help a bit.

One particle among a smelly sea of humanity, she stood at a rear entrance—when Germany had been the threat it had served as a sally port to the front—and held her boys under close rein while awaiting the word to move.

Others gathered to her, many others. That air of royalty, of command, which she radiated drew the confused, the lost, the helpless and hopeless to her as if she were a magnet. She took it, as she took nearly everything, with calm.

She was not calm inside, however. She had long since lost touch with her husband. Isabelle feared the worst.

There was a murmur of sound from behind her. Isabelle turned to see a tall man, tall especially by French standards, easing his way through the crowded corridor. When he passed close by, she saw even in the dim light, that his uniform was midnight black. On his collar she saw insignia that made her want to spit at the soldier.

He reached the thick steel doors at the end of the corridor and stood on something, a concrete block Isabelle assumed it was, perhaps one that held up one of the great steel doors. In clear French the man announced, "I am Captain Jean Hennessey of the 37th SS *Panzer Grenadier* Division, Charlemagne, and I am here to lead you to safety.

"This fortress is going to fall very soon. Even now the rest of my battalion is taking up position to hold the crest and the interior of the fort as long as possible to allow all of you—as many of you as possible—the chance to escape. We are going to have about a twelve-mile walk from here to a place where we can cross German lines. You represent food to the aliens, so they will try to cut down any they can to feed themselves once we are gone from the cover of this fortress. My battalion will do all it can to prevent that. Once we are out of enemy range, the battalion will execute a fighting withdrawal to cover your escape."

Though a scion of royalty, Isabelle's politics had always been far to the left of center. She wanted desperately to shout Hennessey down, to curse him and the hated and hateful insignia he wore. But then the tug of one of her boys on her arm made her reconsider. She could not risk angering one who might be their salvation.

INTERLUDE

Even Athenalras, no stranger to slaughter, was visibly subdued as he heard the reports of the massacre of his people as they attempted to drive forward across the entire front. He had always believed that numbers—numbers and courage—more than anything else decided fate on the Path of Fury, that mass above all would stagger and crush the enemy.

But the only thing staggering about his numbers were the numbers of the People he had lost. Their bodies draped like decorations upon the wire and ground all across the front. In psychic agony, for the Posleen leader did care for his people as a whole—if not so much for individuals, Athenalras' crest sagged. The tenar-mounted God Kings had suffered no less than the mass of the People attacking on foot. The loss of so many sons was like an icy blade plunged deep into Athenalras' bowels. "There are not enough tears to mourn the dead," he exclaimed. "I want to call off this attack."

"It is their blasted fortifications," Ro'moloristen said, bitter, help- less fury boiling in his heart. "From this miserable hole called Liege, to another place they call Eben Emael, to here facing this Maginot line, we are trying to break their weapons by hurling bodies at them."

"Can we get through? In the end, can we beat our way through?" asked Athenalras.

The young God King's crest erected. "We can, my lord; we *must*! For something is becoming ever more clear. If we do not exterminate this species it will exterminate *us!* They are too good, too brave and above all too clever. With fewer numbers and worse weapons, infiltrated and betrayed by their political leadership, attacked with devastating power from space, they are still nearly a match for us. I have some sympathy for these thresh, yes, a degree of admiration, too. But give them as little as ten years of peace and the existence of these thresh *dooms* our people."

CHAPTER 12

Headquarters, Army Group Reserve, Kapellendorf Castle, Thuringia, 20 December 2007

Afraid even to whisper it, Mühlenkampf could not help but think, *We're doomed.*

In the end, though they had hurt the Posleen fleet badly, the Planetary Defense Batteries, even supplemented by salvaged railguns, had failed. Mühlenkampf had known they would. Their presumptive failure had be the major reason behind the creation of Army Group Reserve in the first place.

The landings had begun. Reports came of at least fifteen apparently major landings across Germany and Poland, along with hundreds of minor ones. The total numbers of enemy on the ground was staggering. Mühlenkampf's intelligence officer estimated that the total numbers were in the scores of millions.

Germany and what remained of Poland were in danger of being literally inundated under an alien flood.

In some places that flood was being controlled. Newly developed weapons had their influence, chief among them the neutron bombs that the extreme left would never have permitted had *they* been allowed continued influence. And, though there were never enough of them—there had not been time to build enough of them—and though they were not always in the right place to be used, even so, the enhanced radiation weapons left whole swathes of the enemy puking and dying at many of the landing sites.

The enhanced radiation weapons, "neutron bombs" they were often called, were actually a regressive technological step in weapons development. They differed from more usual nuclear weapons only in not having the heavy uranium shell fitted around the central fissile core that made the nukes so much more powerful, blast-wise, than their predecessors. The uranium shell enhanced this blast by containing and harnessing the neutron emissions of that core.

But the neutrons, unharnessed, were deadly enough in their own right. Emerging from the relatively small blast they acted like tiny bits of shrapnel, passing through bodies and killing the cells they passed through. Enough of them passing through a healthy human would kill within minutes. Moreover the death was miserably demoralizing to any who saw it and lived. Even at a considerable distance they would kill in anything from hours to days. Those deaths were more wretched still.

Best of all, the smaller blast did less physical damage and left comparatively little residual radiation. Indeed, only where it struck steel or a steel alloy did the neutrons create a long-term radiation hazard, by making the metal itself give off gamma radiation.

One bomb—a single one-hundred-fifty-five-millimeter shell—used timely, was said to have killed as many as one hundred thousand Posleen within twenty minutes of its detonation. Scores of ships had been captured intact, though highly radioactive, at that one site. Moreover, casualties in the nearby civilian towns had been negligible, as had environmental damage.

Some Posleen the neutron bombs were not needed to destroy. One of the Posleen landings, for example, had had the misfortune of coming down between Erfurt and Weimar; smack in the middle of Army Group Reserve. The aliens' resistance there had been both brief and futile.

Despite these little successes, Mühlenkampf still thought, *we're doomed.*

"Well, first things first," he announced to his staff. "And the first thing is to smash through to Berlin to relieve both its defenders and its people. On the way I want to eliminate the alien infestation between Magdeberg, Dessau and Halle. Then we'll spread out to clear up the area behind the Vistula line. There's not much between Berlin and Schleswig-Holstein, so the Berliners should be able to make out on their own if they have to withdraw later."

Siegfried Line, Germany, 21 December 2007

It had been a nightmare for Isabelle, her two sons, and the thousands of other refugees fleeing the Posleen onslaught with them. Emerging for the first time in weeks from embattled and falling Fort Hackenberg, she had been immediately plunged into a very close simulacrum of hell. All around, seemingly at random, fell horrid, frightening bolts from the sky. To their din was added the freight train rattle of German and French artillery passing overhead. Behind her, muffled by the high ground, the torrent of human artillery lashing out from the fortress and other places to rip at the enemy was like a distant but ferocious thunderstorm. Ahead of her, the ground had been plowed and beaten into a moonscape. Also from behind came the occasional flash of a Posleen railgun round striking down at the refugees.

Any refugee that was hit was left for dead; the enemy's railguns destroyed mere flesh beyond hope of recovery. An occasional pistol shot sounding from the rear announced those few occasions when a straggler, or a wounded refugee, was given a final mercy.

Captain Hennessey led the way, one of his sergeants bringing up the rear of the column. Isabelle's long, child-dragging strides would have placed her beside him if she had permitted it. Even the desire to get herself and her boys safely away from even random enemy fire was not great enough to make her willing to foul herself by proximity to the French SS man, however. She did find she was close enough to hear him speak into the radio from time to time, and even to hear what was said to him.

The news from that radio was frightening: reports of death, destruction and defeat as the covering battalion from Division Charlemagne was decimated and driven back, again and again, by the massive alien assault. Some of the news made Hennessey stiffen with pain, she could see. Some made his chest swell with pride and his bearing assume a regal posture to match her own.

Once, perhaps, she saw him reach up to wipe something from the general vicinity of his eyes.

The sounds of fighting, distant but growing closer, put speed to the refugees' feet. The overflight of artillery grew, if anything, more intense as Charlemagne's soldiers, much reduced in numbers, were forced to call for and depend on it more with each lost man and combat vehicle.

At length, Isabelle saw Hennessey relax. The German border was in sight.

He was met by another soldier in the field gray of the more traditional German regular army, the *Bundeswehr*. Briefly, she wondered if there would be some scene of hostility between the two, coming from different services and even different nations. But, no, the two met as if long-lost brothers, placing hands on shoulders and shaking hands briskly, illuminating the scene with gleaming smiles.

An old woman with a timid smile came up to Isabelle, drawn apparently by the younger woman's shining inner strength. "*Madame?*" the older one asked, "what is going to be done with us? Where shall we go, what shall we do?"

"That is a very good question, *madame*," Isabelle answered. "Let me go and find out."

With that, Isabelle forced down her disgust. In truth, that was somehow easier now than she would have expected. Dragging her two children behind her, she walked directly up to Hennessey and the German. Then she stopped and asked the men the same questions.

The German answered, in rather cultured French, actually, "From here, you will be billeted temporarily in some of the public buildings in Saarlouis. We are arranging food and bedding, medical care too, but it will take a little time and you may spend the night hungry and cold. We did not expect this, you see."

"I see," she said, quietly then paused to think. Behind her the long snaking column of refugees advanced miserably through a fairly narrow marked lane. A loudspeaker announced, in appallingly bad French she thought, that the refugees *must* stay within the markings as the land to either side was heavily mined. He also began to announce the same message the German had given to Isabelle, so she thought no more about the old woman.

For reasons she could not articulate, she resisted joining the stream and stayed there by the side of the French and German officers, watching that human flood pass by.

Eventually Hennessey said, "You really should go on, *madame*. Please, do. Take your children to safety." To the German he said,

"And Karl, you have everything well in hand here. I have things to do."

She nodded once, briskly, then turned and with the boys began the fearful trudge through that narrow lane in the broad belt of death. She never saw the look of farewell the German gave to the Frenchman. She might not have understood it if she had.

Isabelle was worried at first if the Germans had really gotten all of the mines out of the way. The thought of stepping on one, *worse,* of one of her babies stepping on one, sent a tremor through her. Then, she consoled herself with the knowledge that the Germans, give the *Boche* their due, were a very thorough people; that, and that failure to make the trip would see her and her babies eaten.

She enjoyed French cuisine of course; she had no desire to become it.

Past the fields of mines, Isabelle glanced to left and right. Her eyes began to pick out details, a solid-looking slab of concrete here, a vicious-looking barbed wire obstacle there. Three times she passed artillery batteries firing furiously. She had never in her life imagined such a painful torrent of sheer sound.

Kraus-Maffei-Wegmann Plant, Munich, Germany,
21 December 2007

"God, isn't she the sweetest sounding thing you've ever heard," whispered Mueller, though the intercom from his drive station.

"What do you mean?" asked Schlüssel. "This lovely bitch makes no sound at all except for the tracks."

Mueller laughed. "I know, my friend. And had you spent any time in panzers you would know how sweet a sound silence can be."

The positions they had chosen for themselves were somewhat contralogical. At least they were not the obvious ones. Though Mueller and Schlüssel had worked in the design team, respectively, on gun and drive train, Mueller's army experience as a driver and Schlüssel's Navy experience as a gunnery officer had put them back in those positions. Breitenbach had no military experience whatsoever but had worked on both armor and close-in defense weapons in the design team. Thus he took command of those and of the half dozen factory workers who had volunteered to run them. Henschel was old, and though one could never have imagined him as loader on a conventional tank he was more than capable of running the automated feed system of any Tiger. A nuclear specialist, Seidl, one of those who had installed the Tiger's pebble-bed reactors, was in charge of power. One of the factory concession cafeteria workers volunteered to run the small kitchen and double as a secondary gunner. Lastly, Prael, because he knew the AI package to perfection, and because Tiger IIIB relied heavily on its AI, was selected by acclaim to command the tank.

Indowy Rinteel, who was not a member of the crew, felt a strange sadness, and—more than a sense of loss—a sense of something missing from his own makeup. These humans were so strange. They had treated him very kindly from the beginning. No, "kind" was not all. They had been *tactful*, enough so that he was sometimes almost comfortable among them, despite their size and flashing canines.

Kind and tactful, both, they had been; gentle almost as the Indowy themselves were gentle. Yet, apparently gleefully, they were preparing to go forth to kill and, likely, to die. Rinteel could understand the willingness to die for one's people. He had come to Earth knowing that, in attempting to sabotage Darhel plans he might well be caught and killed.

What he didn't understand was this ability to kill. Alone among the known denizens of the galaxy only the humans and the Posleen shared this unfortunate ability. Didn't they see how it imperiled their souls as individuals?

Or, perhaps, *did* the humans see? Did they see and decide that, some things were not only worth dying for, they were worth damnation for? It had to be thought on.

The ammunition hoppers were full. Where Tigers like *Anna* and her sisters carried a mere fifty rounds, the comparatively infinitesimal bulk of this tank's magnetically propelled projectiles allowed the portage of no less than 442 mixed rounds. The range on its gun would allow taking out Posleen ships even in fairly high orbit.

Fuel was obviously not going to be a problem.

"You know, gentlemen," observed Prael, "this tank needs a name."

"Pamela?" queried Mueller, thinking of his wife.

"*Deutschland*?" offered Schlüssel, thinking of the ship.

"*Bayern*," asked Breitenbach, "for where she was built?"

Prael laughed. "You louts have no culture. Have you *never* attended the opera? Bah! 'Louts,' I say! Think, men. What is she but a Valkyrie, a chooser of the slain? What are those *Mauserwerke* bulbs on front but a Valkyrie's tits? And what are we but men on a death ride? No, no. This tank must be 'Brünnhilde'!"

Rinteel did not get the joke. He rarely understood human humor, and what it was about the two weapons mounts on front that raised such a terrifying show of teeth from the humans was completely beyond him.

But that it was humor, he recognized easily. Indowy ideas of "funny" were different from those of humans but that they had a sense of humor was beyond dispute.

They are about to die and they laugh. They are about to kill *and they laugh. Truly they are a subject worthy of study.*

Rinteel reached a sudden decision. Walking up to Prael in the head downturned, insecurely shuffling, Indowy way, he asked, "Friend-human Karl?"

"Yes, Friend-Rinteel?"

"I was wondering . . . do you think you might have room for one more?"

Prael seemed to think for a bit. Then he answered, eyes twinkling, "We're riding a Valkyrie to Valhalla. Why . . . Rinteel . . . it would be just plain *wrong* not to take along a Nibelung."

Rinteel did not at all understand the fresh gales of laughter, though he understood that he was welcome to come.

Vicinity Objective Alfa, between Dessau and Halle, Germany, 21 December 2007

What the Posleen thought about the megadecibel playing of "Ride of the Valkyries" as the 47th *Panzer Korps* smashed into them, Hans had no idea. But he figured it couldn't hurt anything.

The *Korps* advanced with, as usual, *Panzeraufklärungsbrigade* (Armored Reconnaissance Brigade) Florian Geyer in the lead. At a high price in blood and steel, this group had mapped out the enemy's posture, running rings around them and determining that this was by no means a single landing, but gave every indication that it was composed of no less than three different, apparently noncooperating, groups. In any case, the daring men of Florian Geyer got away with things during their reconnaissance that they never should have had the Posleen worked together.

Hans was quite certain that Army Group Reserve could simply roll over the enemy. But he saw Mühlenkampf's cleverness. If they were noncooperating, as the Posleen often—usually—were, then they might well be reduced one at a time rather than all at once. It would cost a little more time but was very likely to save precious blood and steel. Hans wholly approved of saving both, where possible.

Not that he thought it would make a rat's ass of difference to the ultimate outcome of the war.

With his panzers spread out over thirty kilometers, behind and covering Divisions *Hohenstauffen* and *Frundsberg*, Hans awaiting the rising of the Posleen ships to meet the armored spear even now plunging through their collective skin in search of the vitals.

But not one Posleen ship arose from this group to contest with the humans. So fast was the thrust, so apparently unexpected, that the enemy were simply crushed asunder with frightful haste. Having a little time for himself, Hans stroked his left breast pocket.

Hans was somewhat surprised at Sol's vehemence towards the men who shared the hut. Certainly the chewing out he was giving them bore some relation to their clumsiness and torpor when the camp had been struck a few nights before. But it seemed to Hans extreme. Nonetheless, he could not fault Sol for insisting that the crew spend an entire night in punishment drills for their laxity. Perhaps it would help next time.

He did wonder why Sol had waited so long, however.

He had been trying very hard to get Anna, and that look of horror on her face, out of his mind ever since. His effort was without success so far. He had wondered too if she would spread the word of his origins. It would make life impossible here, he knew. Perhaps that would be for the best though. He'd have to be moved if his past became widely known. At some other camp—the Israelis ran a few others like this one—perhaps he would have a chance to continue his work of making what poor amends he could, without being in agony over the daily presence of a woman he adored but could never have.

He had been *trying to forget Anna, and the sins inflicted on her, but without success. She filled his mind and his heart, yes and also his desires, more profoundly than any woman he had ever even imagined. Walking from the training field to the little hut, he was awash in emotions he had never really believed existed before.*

In this state of distracted misery, he entered the darkened hut to hear, "There is something I must know."

"What?" he asked of the shadows. "What did you say? Anna?"

"Did you work the camps? I must know."

He *realized from the voice that it was her. "Not the way you mean it," he answered.*

"It is a simple question," Anna insisted. "You were either there or you were not."

"I was there once, *at Birkenau, for about three days. But I didn't, couldn't, stay."*

"Why?" she demanded.

"Because it sickened me." And Hans told her of his very brief sojourn into efficient and organized murder of the helpless.

"Did you kill Jews?" she asked, expanding her interrogation.

"If so, and it is very likely," he admitted, "not because they were Jews, but because they were armed partisans trying to kill me. That, or Soviet soldiers."

There was a long silence as the girl digested the information. Finally, she announced, simply, "Fair enough."

Again the hut was filled with emptiness for long moments. With eyes adjusting to the dim light, Hans saw Anna place a pistol on his makeshift nightstand.

Hans asked, "What was that for?"

"To kill you, if you had been one of them. And then to do the same to myself, for having to live in a world without you."

Hans began to approach her. "Anna, I . . ."

"Wait!" she ordered, holding an open palm towards him. "Before you come closer there are things you must know. Ugly things. Please, sit."

Hans did so, taking Sol's rickety chair from next to his bunk and placing himself on it, facing the girl.

"I am from Berlin, a Berliner Jewess," she began. "My father was a professor, my mother a housewife. My father had once been a promising violinist, but he was also a reserve lieutenant and when the Great War began he joined his regiment and went off to serve. He fought for almost four years, before losing an arm and winning a second Iron Cross, an Iron Cross First Class, for bravery. Of course, he could not play violin anymore but the talent was still there. He could teach and he did. And I remember he was very proud of those medals."

Anna's voice was surreally calm. "To look at me is to see a version of him. He looked about as Jewish as I, which is to say not very. Even when the Nazis came to power, he and we suffered less harassment than most Jews did. And he was protected by that Iron Cross, for Hitler himself had decreed that the laws against the Jews were not to apply to decorated veterans.

"My mother and I had no such protection. Or if we did, the lesser Nazis chose to ignore it. We were picked up, and he, a man who had shed his blood, had himself been maimed and lost his life's dream for Germany, followed us voluntarily to the camp, the one at Ravensbrück. Though this was normally a woman's camp a special exception was made for my father, for some reason.

"I was thirteen years old."

Anna shuddered then, apparently at the memory of what she was about to say.

"Under the overcrowding, the lack of food and medicine, and the cold, my mother soon sickened and died. With the loss of her, my father lost his will to live as well. He followed her into the grave within two months."

"I was alone in the world; all alone, Hans. Can you imagine? I suppose I would have died too, without an adult to protect and maybe steal a little food for me. But then, as happens, I changed, began changing anyway, from a girl to a woman. And the guards began to notice."

Now it was Hans' turn to shudder; he knew what was coming next. "Anna you don't have to—"

"Yes I do!" *she screamed, eyes wild in her face. Then, after some internal struggle, she said, a little more calmly,* "I do. You have to know; you have a right to know.

"The first one was not the worst. He beat me, of course, never even tried to simply tell me what to do. He beat me then tore my clothes off and bent me over one of the hard wooden beds we had."

Hans could not remember ever hearing a voice more hate-filled. "Oh, how I screamed and cried and begged and pleaded. That only made him hit me more. The beating lasted a lot longer than the fucking did, too. Maybe that was why he did it, because the filthy swine couldn't last more than thirty seconds.

"When he was finished he turned me around and slapped my face three or four more times. As he turned to leave he tossed half a moldy sausage onto the floor. He said, 'Eat that, Jew bitch. When I come back I'll have a different kind of sausage for you to eat.'"

"And I suppose he did, too," Hans said, bitterly.

Anna began to rock, gently, back and forth. "Oh, yes," she answered, distantly, as if from a far away place. "He, and the other guards. Sometimes ten or twelve of them a night. Sometimes all at once. Sometimes they would make a 'party' of me." The rocking grew more intense.

With a voice struggling not to break, she continued, "Hans, there is nothing, absolutely nothing, that you can imagine that they did not make me do. They would even take me out of the camp sometimes and sell me to passing soldiers. For my troubles, they would feed me a bit, maybe give me a toothbrush and some tooth powder, used clothing once in a while, even some cheap makeup for 'special' occasions." She shuddered yet again. "That's why I so despise makeup, you know? They would make me put it on like a Reeperbahn[40] prostitute and then taunt me that I was just another Jewish whore.

"The worst part though was that not one of them, even once, not in all those years, ever called me by my name. You remember I got angry with you when you called me 'girl'? The kinder ones would sometimes say, 'Bend over, girl,' or 'Get on your knees, girl.' But usually it was 'Jew-bitch, Jew-whore, Jew-slut.' That sort of thing. I wasn't even a human being, just a fuck and suck machine."

At the memory of that last, that ultimate humiliation of being stripped of even a semblance of humanity, Anna lost control completely, breaking down into great, wracking sobs and a flood of long-suppressed tears. Hans, teary-eyed himself, was out of his *chair in an instant, holding her, cradling her, stroking her hair and whispering how sorry he was, how much he loved her.*

Finally, regaining a measure of control, she wrapped her arms around Hans, squeezed tight, and whispered, "Don't be sorry. It is over. And you didn't do any of it. But can you care for me now, now that you know?"

His own nose running slightly, Hans muffled back, "Now that I know what? That you were raped? That you survived? Thank God you survived, my love. You did nothing wrong and I could not love you more if you were as much a physical virgin as I hold you to be a spiritual one."

Relieved beyond measure, Anna melted into him then. But almost immediately stiffened again. "There is another thing. Something else you must know. I got pregnant, more than once. The first time I was not quite fifteen. The last time I was a bit over seventeen. It was an inconvenience to them, having to take me to the doctor and bribe him to abort me and keep quiet about it. So they bribed the doctor to . . . 'fix' . . . me. I say 'fix.' They said, 'spay.' Hans, I can never have children."

Beyond guilt and even beyond pity, Hans felt an indescribable sense of personal desolation. Nonetheless, he answered, "No matter, Anna. Please . . . believe, that doesn't matter to me."

With a last sniffle and a long, quiet pause, Anna came to a sudden, but long contemplated, decision. She stood up, drawing Hans upward with her. She forced a smile and looked deeply into his eyes and said, "I asked Sol to make sure we would not be disturbed; not for all night. I am twenty-three years old." She began to lead him to his bed, a smile appearing on her face for the first time that night. "That is too old to be any kind of a virgin, don't you think?"

Though the night sky was illuminated by the battle raging ahead, Hans Brasche ignored it, preferring instead to stroke the pocket containing all that was physical that remained of his love, and submerging in the memory of a first, blessed, night among thousands that were to follow.

The first of the three Posleen landing areas was cleansed before midday on the twenty-second. The second, having more warning, took longer. Not only did it take longer, but this time the Posleen did manage to loft a number of their ships. Hans' brigade went into action then, his forty Tigers ripping into the newly arrived Posleen. These died, but they died hard, taking seven of Hans' precious tanks to hell with them. Losses among the rest of the *Korps* were likewise not trivial.

The third landing south of Berlin was ready when the 47th *Panzer Korps* met them on Christmas Day.

INTERLUDE

"The thresh of this world have something they call 'religion,' my lord," commented Ro'moloristen.

"Religion? What is this 'religion'?"

"It is something like the way our normals feel about us, something like the way we once felt towards the Aldenata, and something like the Way of the Rememberers," answered the underling. "It is, admittedly, a very confused and confusing concept.

"I mention this, lord, because tomorrow is the supreme holy day of the dominant cluster of religious groups on the planet. 'Christmas,' they call it. I believe that translates as 'Solemn celebration of the birth of the anointed one.' They give gifts to each other, sing songs of praise and thanksgiving to their god, gather to worship, and decorate their dwellings and places of labor with special care."

Athenalras shrugged. "What does this mean to us?"

"Oh, perhaps nothing, lord. I simply found it interesting."

"Maybe so," said Athenalras, indifferently. "What news of the front?"

"Not good, my lord," admitted Ro'moloristen. "In the north and south there is no progress. The People have run into the great ditch the thresh call the 'Rhein' and found no crossings. They shudder under the lash of the thresh's artillery on the near bank. In the center, news is somewhat better. Only a few of the forts of the string of defenses they call 'Maginot' still hold out. In some places, those where there is more than one such fort close together, the People suffer fearfully from the fire of nearby fortresses. But that is only in a few places. The other forts are all being reduced or already have been."

"Good," grunted the senior God King.

"Yes . . . well, yes and no, lord. Most of the thresh seem to have escaped through the next line of defenses in the center area. We have little more than our own dead to feed the host, though there are enough of those to feed them for some time. And the People attacking those other defenses, the line they call 'Siegfried,' are being chewed up rather badly. In is the same story in the east. Between rivers and fortifications we are paying a fearful price with little to show for it."

"What of the space-to-surface bombardment?" asked Athenalras.

"Less effective against the line 'Siegfried' than it was against the line 'Maginot,' lord. This second line is built differently; smaller fortifications, and nearer to the surface. On the whole it has been a waste to risk a ship to come low enough to fire on single, small bunkers. There is some . . . *thing* out there which has been picking off the lower orbit vessels of the People; picking them off and then moving to a new firing position. The firing signature of this *thing* is the same as for one of our own ship-borne, kinetic energy weapons."

Athenalras grew even more somber at this news. "How many of these 'things' are there?"

"No way to tell, lord. There could be many. There could be only the one."

"I wonder what new 'gifts' the threshkreen will have for us on the morrow, on their 'Christmas.' "

CHAPTER 13

Tiger Anna, *South of Magdeberg, Germany,*
25 December 2007

Behind Hans the sunless, predawn, sky flickered as if lit by a thousand strobe lights; the entire artillery—over three thousand guns—of Army Group Reserve, sending their gifts to the Posleen dug in well south of the city.

The city itself was holding out still, most likely because fully half the Posleen that could have attacked it were instead facing southward against the looming threat of Army Group Reserve. Even so, the town was hard-pressed and begging frantically for succor from Mühlenkampf. The "gifts" to the Posleen were also a gift to Magdeberg's defenders, heartfelt gifts sent with the promise of many more to come.

Schultz, not needed at his gunner's station for the nonce, helped bring round the morning's repast, a couple of hard-boiled eggs, some long-shelf-life milk—"nuclear milk," the men called it—a roll and some sort of unmentionable meat, a grayish, greasy, half-inch-thick slab of embalmed beef. Brasche, concentrating on the intelligence updates coming in via radio, absentmindedly took the eggs, roll and meat, but pointedly refused the milk. Schultz could not blame him; the price of extending the shelf life was milk that tasted of old gym socks. Nutritious it may have been. Good, it was not.

"Gut,"—good—Hans muttered. The enemy were apparently not

lifting their ships in an attempt to silence the army's batteries, or—at least—not yet.

The artillery was forced to fire into an intelligence void, to a great extent. Nothing humanly or remotely piloted was able to survive for more than the instant it took to be destroyed if they attempted flying above or even near the Posleen. Not one human-built satellite survived in space to look down upon the enemy. No human-piloted space-going vessel could hope to approach Earth, with the fleet largely destroyed and the few, wounded survivors huddled and licking their wounds somewhere in the direction of Proxima Centauri. A Himmit ship might have done some real good, had one been available. Sadly, none were.

What could be done had been and was being. Florian Geyer had done everything humanly possible to get through the Posleen perimeter—tried everything, paid in full measure, and failed to do more than define the edges of that perimeter. A few towns within the area of infestation held out yet; these provided a little local intelligence—telling as much where the enemy was not as where he was—for the gunners to use in targeting. The maps also told a bit, though given the aliens' very different military philosophy from that of their human opponents, Hans was skeptical of the value of map reconnaissance. The Posleen just didn't *think* like human beings.

The most valuable recon assets in the Germans' hands were artillery-fired television cameras encased in time-fused shells that gave anywhere from a few to fifteen minutes of visual insight before falling too low to do any good. These were rare items, however. Like the precious neutron bombs, there had not been time to build many of them. They were also used, generally speaking, in conjunction with the artillery-fired neutron bombs, the cameras spotting useful targets and the atomic weapons then "servicing" those targets.

The problem was, though—as Hans knew, that the enemy had had a chance to spread out and dig in. There were few concentrations, few that the cameras had found anyway, that justified the use of the deadly little enhanced radiation packages. Moreover, one of the genuinely effective defenses against the brief burst of high-intensity neutrons the bombs emitted upon detonation was simple earth; and the Posleen had dug in deep in the few days granted them.

Meanwhile, Magdeberg—and Berlin, past that—called frantically and continuously for aid.

Federal Chancellery, Berlin, Germany, 25 December 2007

The chancellor looked over the situation displayed on one of the three view-screens that filled one wall of his deep underground office. In blues and reds this screen showed graphically the state both of the defending forces, in blue, and the aliens, in red, infesting Germany and pressing at her borders. He had been satisfied, over the last two days, to see two of the large red splotches disappear as Army Group Reserve under Mühlenkampf eliminated all but one of the landings south and southeast of Magdeberg. Other, local, reserves had seen to some few others.

Matched against the good news, however, was a pile of bad. The Siegfried line in the west defending the Rhein and the Rheinland was holding, true. But casualties were atrocious, indentations had been made, and the state of resupply, given how many Posleen-controlled areas lay athwart supply routes, was perilous.

In the east things were worse, much worse. The Vistula line was simply crumbling and, nightmare of nightmares, the enemy had managed to seize at least one bridge over the river at Warsaw.

The story of how this had happened was somewhat confused. As near as could be determined, though, a great flood of humanity had been on the bridge in desperate flight when the Posleen first appeared. Unwilling, or perhaps unable, to commit mass murder by blowing the bridge, the defenders had delayed just a bit too long. The enemy's flyers had massed and blasted the defending demolition guard to ruin before the bridge could be dropped. A hasty counterattack was put in using whatever was locally available. That having failed, however, and the aliens pouring across at the rate of several hundred thousand per hour, the German and Polish formations strung out along the river were about to be forced into conducting a desperate fighting withdrawal to the Oder-Niesse line.

And the Oder-Niesse line is less than a sham, thought the chancellor. *There are few heavy fortifications. Those that exist are very old and weak and were low priority for renovation in any case.*

The river itself is as little as three feet deep in places. And even where it is deep enough to drown the bastards there are places where it has frozen over.

Tearing his eyes from the distressing display, the chancellor turned to his senior soldier, Field Marshal von Seydlitz. "Kurt?" he asked, "Is there a chance we can hold the river? Regain the bridge?"

"Essentially none, sir," Seydlitz responded, wearily. He was about a week behind on sleep. "I had considered that the neutron weapons might make a difference. But my nuclear weapons staff has pointed out two distressing facts. One is that we have only half a dozen of the things close enough to get in range to be fired at the crossing. The other is that the bombs work best with a highly concentrated area target. The Posleen are concentrating before crossing, true. But once they reach this side they are dispersing very rapidly. Moreover, those actually on the bridge at any given time represent a very unremunerative *linear* target. We might kill as few as twenty thousand per round among those who have already crossed, perhaps five or six thousand of those actually on the bridge. We can eliminate anything up to one million by hitting the far side with all six weapons."

Seydlitz sighed. "The General Staff calculates that this will slow them down by perhaps an hour. *Herr Kanzler*, the hour saved now is not as important as holding the Oder-Niesse line later. We will need those weapons then."

"The Oder-Niesse line?" asked the chancellor.

"It isn't much but it's all we have," answered Seydlitz.

"Give the orders. Fall back. Cover the retreat of as many Polish civilians as possible."

Seydlitz nodded an acknowledgment, then continued. "We're still going to lose many of the troops and by the time they reach the Oder they may be nothing much more than a demoralized rabble for a while . . . but I agree we should run while we can.

"But, *Herr Kanzler*, we have another problem, though it is an indirect one and won't become insurmountable until the Siegfried line collapses."

"The Rhein bridges?" asked the chancellor.

"Yes, sir. For now the enemy who seized both sides of the bridges from above is staying put. But they have infested an area of more than twenty-five kilometers radius, are digging in frantically, and are seriously inconveniencing supply to the men on the Siegfried line covering the Rheinland."

"Recommendations?"

"Halt Army Group Reserve in place. Let them reorganize and shift them around. Then throw them at that landing."

The chancellor thought, weighing options. Though he had done his military time as a young man he was no soldier and knew it. He was, however, a supreme and—at need—a supremely ruthless politician; his resurrection of the SS showed that.

"No," he answered. "if Berlin falls so soon it will take the heart out of our people. Let local forces contain the landing athwart the Rhein. After Army Group Reserve has cleared out Saxony-Anhalt, Pomerania and Mecklenberg we can turn them around. But for now? No."

South of Magdeberg, Germany, 25 December 2007

The artillery storm was not abating. Even so, unnoticed, it was lifting from over eleven narrow preplanned axes. Indeed, the axes were so narrow that the shell-shocked Posleen cowering there barely noticed any change in the pummeling they were receiving.

Under the lash of the guns, terrified Posleen, normals and God Kings both, huddled and trembled. Never in all their previous history had the People experienced anything against which they were so completely helpless as they were against this threshkreen "artillery."

Worst of all, no place and no being was safe. Oolt'ondai Chaleeniskeeren, as much as the lowest of his oolt'os, shivered and quivered and quaked in a bunker fronting the bay of a trench at each near miss. Unable even to eat of the thresh'c'olt, the Posleen iron rations, brought to him by a cosslain, the God King alternately cursed the cowardly thresh who infested this world and the fate that had brought him and his people here.

The Posleen knew he could have taken his tenar and climbed above the shell storm. The problem with that was a certain number of the enemy's projectiles operated off of electronic fuses that were perfectly capable of being set off by the near presence of a tenar. Reports from Posleen refugees from the south made this abundantly clear; the sky was no safe place to be when the threshkreen unleashed their unholy storm.

Thus, the tenar of each God King, as much as the God King himself, lay vulnerable in hastily dug holes in the ground. Chaleeniskeeren's, or what was left of it, lay ruined in its hole a few strides away. Idly, the Posleen wondered how many of the tenar would be left riderless by the barrage, even while other God Kings were left with ruined transportation. Robbed of their flyers, much of the host's power would be lost.

The ships were safe enough from most artillery. Built of materials thick and strong, they shrugged off all but the worst of the threshkreen's projectiles. What they could not shrug off were the radiation-emitting weapons. These turned the very metal of the ships into radioactive poison. Within the effective radius of those weapons the end, even for those in the ships, was only a matter of time, that . . . and shitting, puking, twitching agony. Fortunately, the thresh seemed to have few of them.

The artillery impacting near Chaleeniskeeren lifted off and began to strike another area. It had done so half a dozen times before. The first few times it had lifted, the Posleen had rushed for firing bays and tenar. Then it had returned, slaughtering them like abat. Now the lifting was cause for nothing more than a brief sigh of very temporary relief, not for exposing themselves.

Chaleeniskeeren couldn't help the nagging feeling that the threshkreen were actually *training* him to stay put when the fire lifted.

Though half deafened by the shelling, Chaleeniskeeren felt rather than heard a strange rumbling coming through the ground. Shelling or not, trained by the thresh to stay put in the relative safety of the bunker or not, the rumbling was too strange, too out of his experience, not to investigate.

Lowering his head to squeeze under the bunker's low door, the God King stepped out into the bay of the trench and risked looking out into the smoky haze.

Nothing, nothing but craters and smoke.

And then he saw it, a low-lying predatory shape, moving cautiously on treads through the haze, an angular projection on top swinging its main weapon right and left, searching for prey. Soon the first shape was joined by another, then a third and fourth. Wide eyed, the God King saw thresh on foot scattered among the larger shapes. He watched, shocked, for but a moment before raising the shout, "To arms! To arms! The threshkreen are upon us!"

Tiger Anna, *Saxony-Anhalt, Germany, 25 December 2007*

God, this is worse than Kursk, Hans thought as he watched on the main screen as infantry and tanks, locked in a close-quarters death struggle with the alien enemy, rolled back the shoulders of the eleven narrow lanes the artillery had torn in the Posleen line. For the Germans, this was a combined arms fight with a literal vengeance. Their lighter panzers, Leopard IIA7's, blasted apart bunkers, lent their machine guns to the fray, and ran over individual aliens to squeeze out their lives like overripe grapes. In close support, carrying the detailed fight to the foe, the German infantry, heedless of loss, cut, slashed, blasted and burnt their way through the trenches. Meanwhile, the artillery concentrated on sealing the areas of penetration off and pureeing any large groups of the enemy that attempted to mass for a counterattack.

But the affair was hardly a massacre. Stunned, demoralized and weakened though they were, the Posleen still fought back with more ferocity than any human enemy, even the mindlessly brave Russians, would have shown after the pummeling they had received.

Part of this, Hans suspected, was merely a matter of numbers. Given more defenders, there simply had to be, as a statistical matter, more who would be capable of rising above the shell-spawned terror. While Posleen trenches were being filled with alien bodies, more than a few German soldiers richened the manure.

On *Anna*'s main screen, Hans saw a Leopard take a direct hit from a Posleen hypervelocity missile. The tank seemed to belch fire as the turret, propelled by its own on-board ammunition and fuel, was hurled nearly a hundred meters into the air. That the Posleen firing almost certainly succumbed to return fire within instants could have been scant comfort to the spirits of the disintegrated Leopard crew.

Brashe's 1c, or intelligence officer reported, "Sir, we are getting emanations consistent with the movement of between twelve and twenty enemy landers, C-Decs, B-Decs, and Lampreys, all."

"All Tigers," Hans ordered over the radio. "Targets appearing in the next few seconds. If they are joining the battle, kill them. If they are fleeing, kill them. When you reach them on the ground, kill them."

South of Magdeberg, Germany, 25 December 2007

Chaleeniskeeren and his oolt'os had held their line as long as possible, even inflicting some losses on the enemy. That period of time had not been long enough. Now, engaged in something like a fighting withdrawal, with his children being mercilessly butchered alongside him, the God King once again cursed both the evil, heartless and merciless threshkreen even as he cursed this planet and everything which had led to it.

Cowering in a deep crater, peering over its lip, Chaleeniskeeren was lifted bodily and slammed down by an explosion of a power he had not imagined outside of the major weapons. The night sky, for the battle had already lasted through the day and into the night, was briefly illuminated by some monstrous, incredible *thing*. From off to the left, another massive explosion shook the earth and by its momentary light Chaleeniskeeren caught a clearer glimpse of the monster to his front.

"Demon shit," he whispered, wide-eyed and awe-struck.

Tiger **Anna,** *Saxony-Anhalt, Germany, 25 December 2007*

"Clear emanations, C-Dec, Eleven O'clock, Six thousand, five hundred meters," intoned the 1c.

"I see it," answered Brasche. "Gunner!" he ordered, "Sabot! DU-AM . . . point one kiloton. C-Dec!"

"Target," Schultz responded, robotlike, as he swung *Anna*'s turret to the left, elevating her gun until a tone told him he had a target lock.

"Fire!"

As always, the tank was rocked back, shuddering under the recoil of the main gun. Ahead, a roughly spherical ball of light appeared as the depleted uranium sabot from *Anna's* gun first penetrated the Posleen ship, then released ten percent of its antimatter to react and annihilate itself with the DU, splitting the ship along its seams.

To left and right, other Tigers fired to briefly light the night with muzzle flash and, often enough, impact on the selected target. There was no return fire from the Posleen ships, leading Hans to suspect they were more interested in flight than fight.

"But that won't last," he muttered.

"Sir?" asked the 1c.

"They're trying to get away," he answered. "That would be fine; I'd encourage them in flying away. The problem is they won't stay away. The other problem is that if they see no escape they'll turn on us."

"Yes, sir," replied the 1c. "But they are pretty bad at working together. We have a fair chance of taking them on, even all of them, if they come after us."

"I concur, Intel. Orders remain unchanged. Kill 'em all."

Forward Headquarters, Army Group Reserve, Halle, Germany, 26 December 2007

It had been a long night, as the rising sun promised another long day. Mühlenkampf barely listened to the reports of successful penetration of the Posleen lines, barely listened to reports of casualties and objectives taken.

The worst part, thought he, looking out from a glassless window at the street below his commandeered headquarters building, *is the emptiness of the town, that, and the piles of bones everywhere. He shook his head sadly. This town had a quarter of a million people in it even before the war, nearer to a third of a million since. Some got away to the south before the aliens entered it. But most did not and we have found not one living soul. God damn these aliens to the deepest pits of Hell! God damn whoever or whatever it was that made them come here.*

The town was still standing; the Posleen had not had time to begin deconstruction before the initial counterattack had driven them out on the twenty-second. But human beings were easier to kill and eat than buildings were to demolish.

Below Mühlenkampf's lookout, a column of truck-borne infantry passed. He studied the faces carefully, looking for signs of panic or demoralization. He saw none. What he saw instead was simple hate, as the message of Halle's depopulation sank through even the thickest skulls.

"Good," he whispered. "A little hate will give them the spine to go on a bit longer."

An aide interrupted Mühlenkampf's reveries. "*Herr General*, we have reports from the 501st that they have reached the main concentration of enemy landers. General Brasche reports that his Tigers are destroying many of them on the ground and almost at will."

Tiger Anna, *Saxony-Anhalt, Germany, 26 December 2007*

Today it *was* a massacre. Unable safely to lift their ships to escape, the Posleen were fleeing to the north on their tenar or, more commonly, afoot. The 47th *Panzer Korps* was pursuing with as much speed and fury as the old SS had ever pursued routed Russians. While the SS pursued, the remainder of Army Group Reserve continued the drive to the northeast and northwest to relieve still embattled Magdeberg and Berlin.

The trail of Brasche's mixed brigade was littered with the ruin of Posleen hopes. It was also littered with the ruin of hundreds upon hundreds of ships, large and small.

More and more, though, the Posleen, individually, were turning at bay to go down fighting rather than be helplessly butchered from behind. Because this was, in every case, the decision of individuals or, occasionally, small groups, the ships facing Brasche's Tigers were, generally speaking, both outnumbered and, because they had to lift about the ground cover to move at all, easily spotted and shot down.

This is not to say that the massacre was entirely one-sided. Five Tigers, three of them lifeless smoking hulks glowing cherry red in places, also dotted the path behind the brigade. Hans had hope that the other two might be recovered and recrewed.

"Emanations. C-Dec. One o'clock. Eight thousand meters," announced the 1c.

"Brigade halt," Brasche ordered. "Engage her as she shows."

East of Magdeberg, Germany, 26 December 2007

Chaleeniskeeren knew it was the end, as it had been the end for each of his followers. He knew that he could run no further, certainly not in his weakened condition.

The God King rested against the metallic side of a C-Dec, a Posleen Command Dodecahedron. The C-Dec was unmanned, and Chaleeniskeeren strongly suspected he knew why. The waves of heavy gamma radiation cutting through his body like knives told him this ship had fallen to one of the threshkreen's radiation weapons.

"No matter," he snarled. "I am dead anyway."

Arising, he walked unsteadily on his four legs until he reached the main hatch.

"Halt and announce yourself," the ship commanded.

The God King knew the drill. All Posleen Kessentai knew the drill for taking over abandoned property without incurring *edas*, the often crushing debt that was the common lot of all but the most senior and richest of the People.

"I am Oolt'ondai Chaleeniskeeren, son of Ni'imiturna, of the line of Faltrinskera, of the clan Turnisteran. Is there anyone aboard?"

"My internal sensors show no life aboard this vessel, Chaleeniskeeren of the Turnisteran. I am called 'Feast-deliverer.'"

"What is your radiation count, *Feast-deliverer*?" he asked.

"In the range of certain death in less than one twenty-fifth of this planet's revolution about its axis," the ship answered.

"I claim this ship for myself and my clan, in the name of the Net and of the Knowers; in the name of the People, and of survival."

"This is the way of the Path," the ship answered, as it lowered the ramp.

Chaleeniskeeren's olfactory organs were immediately assaulted by the smell of feces and vomit. Clearly, those of the People who had died within were many, to raise such a stench. Steeling himself, he entered the ship.

Near the ramp, just inside of the hatchway, Posleen lay everywhere in every manner of undignified death. Here a cosslain had ripped open his own torso to get at the source of his pain. There another lay in a pool of mixed vomit and feces. Some few had, apparently, gone feral, lashing out at each other in their death agonies.

Stepping over bodies with every third lurch forward, Chaleeniskeeren made his own tortured way to the control chamber. There he found God Kings slumped in death, their faces twisted with the horror of their passing. Staggering, the sole living being aboard, Chaleeniskeeren reached the command panel. He had to tear away the God King who clutched it fast in full rigor mortis.

Standing in the command position, Chaleeniskeeren heard the ship intone, "Oolt'ondai Chaleeniskeeren, son of Ni'imiturna, of the line of Faltrinskera, of the clan Turnisteran, I recognize you under the Law of the Net, and the Ways of the Path and of the Knowers, as rightful lord of this vessel. What is your command?"

"Lift off," answered the new commander, unsteadily. Already the edges of his vision were darkening. "Lift off and head generally for the human forces. Control to me."

Tiger Anna, *Saxony-Anhalt, Germany, 26 December 2007*

"I can't get a lock, sir," shouted a frantic Dieter Schultz. "That ship is behaving like I have never seen an alien ship act before."

Hans saw that this was true. Weaving, bobbing, even skating along the ground, the ship was an impossible target. A few rounds from other Tigers of the brigade passed nearby the target; passed, and missed. Suddenly, the alien ship shot straight up, moving faster than *Anna*'s elevating mechanism could follow, moving eventually further than it could follow.

"That ship shrieks gamma radiation," announced the 1c.

"It's gotten away," exclaimed Schultz, in frustration.

Hans shook his head in short, violent jerks. "No. The Posleen never act that way. That ship had a dying alien at the helm. *Anna,* send the message to the brigade. All hands, brace for impact and a major antimatter explosion."

Aboard Feast-deliverer, *12 miles above Saxony-Anhalt, Germany, 26 December 2007*

"Take control . . . Take control, *Feast-deliverer,* for I no longer can hold the helm."

"Your orders, Oolt'ondai? Shall I head for some safe planet?"

"No, ship. There can be none, not in the long run. Can you identify the huge threshkreen war machines below?"

"There are more than twenty, Oolt'ondai."

"Pick one, ship; one that is near others."

"I have done so."

"Good," said Chaleeniskeeren, crest gone flaccid and head hanging in pain and shame. "Crash us into it."

Tiger Anna, *Saxony-Anhalt, Germany, 26 December 2007*

Hans dreamt of happier times . . .

The wedding was informal, as was to be expected in the austere Israeli compound. The girls had pooled their resources, come up with a makeshift dress and veil, some high heels. The only building suitable for the gathering was the mess. There was, of course, no organ to play the wedding march. Even so, a young Israeli trooper was managing a fair rendition on a violin.

Looking back over his shoulder, to where his bride appeared, Hans noted with interest that his Anna wore no makeup anyway. Well, it wasn't as if she needed it.

After that first night there had been no others. He had asked her to marry him as the sun arose the next morning and brought a filtered light for the hut. Lying there, the faint sun illuminating her hair spread across his one thin pillow, she had taken his breath away.

Glimpsing her standing nervously at the entrance to the mess, she took his breath away now, too.

The ceremony was conducted in Yiddish. If there was a living rabbi who spoke pure German he must have been far away. Curiously, though he still had to stumble through the ritual, he found he understood the rabbi better than Anna did. It must have been the Russian he had picked up on the eastern front.

Another woman, a widow—Hans desperately didn't want to enquire as to the mechanism of her widowhood—had donated to the cause a simple gold ring. At the rabbi's command, he placed the ring on Anna's finger, then kissed her.

In the ensuing party, deliriously happy, Hans still found time to talk to the rabbi in private.

Harz was the first of *Anna's* crew to regain consciousness. He was pleased to sense that the tank was still upright.

First things first, Harz thought, groggily. On hands and knees he crawled to Schultz, checked him briefly for damage, and confirmed he was alive and, as near as cursory and inexpert examination could determine, unbroken.

A few slaps across the face raised Dieter to a semblance of awareness.

"Back to your station, old son, while I check on the commander."

With the groggy Schultz climbing back into his gunner's station, and the main battery about to be, hopefully, functional, Harz went on to the second priority—the commander.

Brasche was already awakening against the bulkhead of the inner fighting compartment when Harz reached him. Harz saw the commander's arm hanging at an odd angle, red fluid leaking through his uniform, and a red stream pouring from his head to cover his face and trickle onto the deck. "Casualties?" Hans croaked.

"Dunno, sir," replied Harz. "No report."

The brigade Ib, or logistics officer, arising from the tank's deck and climbing back into his secondary gunner's station under his own power, took one look at his screen and answered, "Heavy, sir. Very heavy, especially among the Tigers. I see five of them flashing black on my screen. Though whether they are dead or dying or *what* I cannot tell. And I suspect our panzer grenadiers will be in worse shape. The artillery seems to have come through well enough."

"Damn," said the stunned Brasche, in a weak voice.

INTERLUDE

"I have had enough!" exclaimed Athenalras. "Call off this multi-damned, demon-spawned attack."

"My lord, no!" shouted Ro'moloristen, though the carnage along the front sickened him no less than his elder. "We cannot stop now! Think, my lord. The thresh are reeling in the east. And there is barely an obstacle to our brethren's continued progress into the very heart of this *'Deutschland.'*"

Ro'moloristen lowered his head and shook his crest. "The line 'Siegfried' is brittle, lord, brittle. Though the People may fall at a rate of twenty to one in chewing through it, *fifty* to one, one hundred to one—even, as we are in some places, it matters not. For we outnumber the thresh still by a factor of three hundred to one or more on this front.

"And, lord, the bridge the host of Arlingas has captured near the gray thresh town of Mannheim? It is impacting severely on their ability to keep their damnable artillery resupplied. Even in the last few rotations of this planet our losses to this arm along that portion of the front have gone down drastically. Projections are that if we keep up the pressure, the threshkreen *must* break."

Sadly, the senior laid one hand upon the very much junior's shoulder. "Let all this be true, young one. Still, I am sick of the slaughter. And would that it might end."

"There can be no end, great one. Not until this species is utterly cast down. Come see."

Gently, the junior led his lord to a data screen. "See the

217

projections, lord." Quickly the screen jumped through well cal-culated close estimates of such things as population growth, technological progress, urbanization, advances in the military art, even psychiatric profiles of humans under stress.

"As you can see, lord, our muzzles are plainly hitched to the breeding post."

Athenalras answered, slowly and deliberately, "We are being well and truly fucked anyway, young one. We have tossed away the flower of the People in futile assaults against this Siegfried line, and have gained nothing by it except to reduce our numbers by one hundred million on this front alone."

"I know, lord," said Ro'moloristen. "I know. But I have been thinking . . ."

"A dangerous pastime."

"Yes, lord, I know that, too. Nonetheless I *have* been thinking. We . . . the People as a whole . . . make war as we hunt. These threshkreen do not. Or, at least, they do not do so as we do. They have what they call 'Principles of War.' The lists of these principles vary among them but I have discovered twelve that seem to cover everything."

"Twelve?"

"Yes, Lord: they are Mass, Objective, Security, Surprise, Maneu-ver, Offensive, Unity of Command, Simplicity, Economy of Force, Attrition, Annihilation and Shape. Using these principles I have determined upon a plan that may grant us the victory. Instead of attacking all along the front, we will concentrate our efforts towards the sector nearest to the bridge held by the host of Arlingas. We have no clue how even to use any of the thresh artillery we have captured, let alone build or resupply our own. But we do have ships. From space we will pound—"

"They will *butcher* our ships in space!"

Ro'moloristen gave the Posleen equivalent of a sigh. "Yes, lord, surely they will, for a while. But before our ships are destroyed they will, in turn, kill. They will beat for us a flat road through a narrow lane in the Siegfried line.

"Lord, if we don't our people are *dead*!"

Coming to a sudden decision, Athenalras lifted his crest slightly. "Show me the projections of loss," he demanded.

Athenalras looked over Ro'moloristen's figures. *Frightful, frightful. And yet the puppy is right. What else can we do, if the People are not to perish?* "It will take several revolutions of this planet about its axis for us to prepare. See to it. And prepare a special hunting group of ships to see to this reported super-tenaral. And reduce the level of the current offensive to no more than is needed to keep the thresh's attention."

PART IV

CHAPTER 14

Tiger **Brünnhilde,** *Hanau, Germany, 1 January 2008*

"Oh, God, I'll never drink schnapps again," moaned Mueller from underneath bloodshot eyes.

"Stop making so much damned noise, Johann," insisted Prael. "We're all as hung over as you."

"Franz and I are not," insisted Schlüssel. "Neither is *Herr* Henschel. With age comes a certain wisdom and restraint, after all."

"My little round ass," answered Breitenbach, blearily. "You three packed it away as well as any of us. You have just had more years to get in training."

The combat compartment of the tank grew silent with that, largely out of deference to the "dying."

For ten days Prael had run the crew through drill after drill, simulated engagement after simulated engagement. Occasionally, when circumstances seemed right, they had taken a potshot at an unwary Posleen vessel passing overhead. Already Schlüssel had painted six kill markers around the lower part of the railgun's rail, mute but eloquent testimony to the efficacy of the railgun, even against Posleen ships in orbit.

Ten days and six kills. It would have been an utterly and futilely short period of training but for two factors. The first of these was the tank's AI; which had both reduced the need for training and made whatever training was given precisely appropriate need.

But the second factor was within the purview of the more

subtle part of training: building comradeship. And years of working together, designing and building the two versions of Tiger, had long since welded the men, and one woman, who crewed *Brünnhilde* into a team. They knew each other, had eaten and drank together. They knew each other's families, and hopes and dreams. They *cared*.

Though they didn't talk much about dreams.

Though he liked these humans, especially the one with the funny bumps, so reminiscent of *Brünnhilde's* armored front, who usually made them their food, Rinteel did not feel a part of the team, not even as the token Nibelung, whatever a Nibelung was.

Not that he was useless, far from it. Unlike Indowy machines this one had awesome defects to it; awesome at least for one born into a civilization where perfection was the minimum standard for tools and machines. The little bat-faced sentient spent full and busy days helping to fix one crisis fault after another. He had a genuine knack for it, even with, to him, alien machinery.

But, useful or not, well treated and respected or not, he simply lacked the sense of "*Kameradschaft*"[41] these humans felt for each other. Perhaps it was that he could not imbibe these things the Germans called "Schnapps" or "*Bier.*" *Kameradschaft* certainly seemed to grow by bounds when the humans had a few each of those.

Though singing seemed a big part of it too.

Rinteel had a hopeless singing voice, where human song was concerned. He started contemplating where aboard *Brünnhilde* he might build a synthesizer to create the sole Indowy intoxicant, *med.*

47th *Field Hospital, Potsdam, Germany, 2 January 2008*

Drugged unconscious, in the *Korps* field hospital, a dark place and soundless except for the plaintive, unconscious cry of some lonely, wounded soldier, Hans dreamt.

Though she had never turned to fat, Anna's hair had grayed, her skin had browned and wrinkled under the harsh sun of Israel.

Still, after more than forty years, Hans found her lovely beyond measure. Only the obscenity growing in her body, wracking her with agony the drugs could never quite overcome, detracted from the beauty of her body, mind and soul; that obscene cancer, and the horrid mechanical sounds of the machines keeping her alive.

By her bedside Hans sat, as he sat every moment he was allowed. Often enough, tears poured from his face. At those moments, Anna often turned her face away. That was not how she wished to remember him, in the hereafter.

It was near the end; they both knew it. She was calm and content. He was desolated. Hans had only the thought, It won't be so long that I will have to be apart from her, *to console himself.*

"We have had a good life, Hansi, isn't that so?" Anna asked.

Wiping his eyes, he answered, "Where you were was paradise for me, Anna. Where you were not was hell . . . even before we met."

She gave him a soft smile, and answered, as softly, "It was the same for me, Hansi. But Hansi, what will you do?" she fretted.

"I do not know, Anna. There will be nothing left here for me, once . . ." And he fell into a fresh wave of tears.

"Hush, hush," she said, reaching out a weak, skeletal hand to pat his arm. "It will only be for a while . . . only for a while."

She pressed, "What will you do?"

Hans forced the tears away, forced calm to his voice. "Perhaps I will return to Berlin. I have no more friends here, since Sol passed away, no relatives either. I still have some there, though I do not know them."

She digested that thought for a while, came upon another. "Hansi, I never asked. Neither of us wanted to talk about it. But, talked about or not, I always knew. Why did you never forgive yourself? I forgave you long ago, that first night in your hut. But you never did. Why?"

This was not something Hans really wanted to talk about . . . and yet . . . and yet it was time. Slowly, deliberately, he answered, "There were three kinds of Germans, Anna, in those days. There were those who didn't know . . . about what was done to the Jews and the others in the camps, I mean. A majority, that was, I think, though many more might have suspected. They have no sin, except perhaps one of omission.

"And then there were the other Germans, the ones who did know, reveled in the knowing, and thought it all to be proper and

right. They can answer to God or the Devil—and I have strong suspicions who it will be that they finally talk to, with a straight face and a clear eye . . . at least until the fire reaches them." Hans sniffed with disdain.

The last part came harder; a mirror is often the most difficult kind of glass to look into.

Yet Hans was a brave man, had faced fire bravely in more places than he cared to think about. He could be brave this once more, for his wife. "The last group were the worst and I was in that group. We were the ones who knew, knew that it was wrong, evil, and even knowing this, turned our faces from it, instead of fighting it; turned our faces and ran.

"This kind of German, my kind of German, will face God or the Devil, too. What we will be able to say in our defense before the fire reaches us?"

Anna nodded, understanding, though even that little effort was a strain. She was growing weaker by the minute. In a breathless voice she said, "I understand, my Hansi. You are afraid, perhaps, that we will not be together in the future. Well, let me tell you, speaking as a Jew to a German . . . you are a good man, Hansi. You have done no wrong . . . and you always did your best." She reached up to stroke his cheek, as old as hers and even more weathered, and finished, the sound fading even as she spoke, "God does not expect perfection in his creations, and we will be together again, I promise you. . . ."

Alone in his bed, a sleeping old man in a twenty-year-old body wept for an old woman remembered as a young woman. In his heart and his mind she was remembered as fresh . . . and as freshly remembered as the last spring. Though his hospital robe had no breast pocket still, unconsciously, his hand stroked for a little packet usually found there.

47th *Field Hospital, Potsdam, Germany, 2 January 2008*

On the street outside the hospital a column of gray-clad, determined-looking Schwabian infantry marched past on their way to the front, their boots ringing on the cobblestones below. The Schwabians sang as they marched:

Mein eigen soll sie sein,
Kein'm andern mehr als mein.
So leben wir in Freud und Leid,
Bis der Gott in Zeit uns auseinanderscheid'.
leb'wohl, leb'wohl, leb'wohl mein Schatz, leb' wohl.[42]

Ignoring the music, Mühlenkampf reached out an arm to shake awake Hans Brasche, ignoring the latter's splinted arm and well-wrapped head. "Get up, Hansi, I need you."

Slowly and groggily, Hans did awaken. And immediately reached for the bucket near his bed.

Mühlenkampf turned his head away. "Never mind that," he insisted. "We've both been concussed before. Puking afterwards is just another part of it."

Hans ignored his commander, finishing his business with the bucket before looking upwards. "And how may I assist you, *Herr General*?" he asked, with polite disinterest, after emptying his stomach.

"You can get back on your feet! You can take over command again of that fucking, falling-apart rabble we call the 501st *Schwere Panzer*. You can get back to the fucking war."

Mühlenkampf relented. "I am sorry, Hansi, I truly am. The eastern front has collapsed. Oh, many of the troops will get away but they are a mess. I am throwing the 47th *Korps*, including the 501st, and two infantry *Korps* to try to hold it while we reorganize the survivors.

"And, Hansi, I can't even put you in 'the tank' for a Galactic tech repair. The only one near here was taken out by an alien kinetic energy strike from space."

"Where is the rest of Army Group Reserve going?" Brasche asked.

"There is a spot of trouble in the west. The defenses are still holding but the enemy is acting . . . funny. Almost clever. Clever aliens worry me, Hans."

Hans nodded solemnly, then immediately had to reach for his bucket again. Even such a little movement was . . . difficult.

"Hans, I would not ask if I didn't need you."

"I understand," Brasche said. Rising, unsteadily, he continued, "I will leave tonight."

"That's my Hansi," said Mühlenkampf. "After the east is stabilized, and a certain bridge in the west retaken, we will assemble, likely around Hanau. In the interim, I am heading west."

Mainz, Germany, 4 January 2008

In this ancient city just west of the Rhein, Isabelle and her two children had finally settled into something resembling normalcy.

There was a tremendous housing shortage of course, so much so that the French civilians who had escaped to Germany were forced to live in, in Isabelle's case, a large indoor gymnasium. But blankets had been hung near the walls, separate living spaces arranged, a modicum of privacy granted.

Isabelle had never been fond of German food. Now, though, she wished she could have twice as much of it, more especially for her boys than for herself. But food, like living space, was in short supply.

There was a bustle of murmuring coming from the mess, the central common area of the gymnasium. This low bee-like hum grew until it was loud enough to attract Isabelle's interest. Leaving the boys behind, she twisted her way through other cloth cubicles and the long benches at which many of the French refugees sat, dawdling over the meager and bland lunch repast.

A man, in gray uniform, was addressing the people while standing atop one of the benches. Isabelle took a second look to confirm that it was the same Captain Hennessey who had earlier led her and the boys to safety. It took two looks because the captain had turned from tall and robust to the very essence of exhaustion, with deep, dust-filled lines engraved on his face, sunken eyes and the slouch of bone-weariness.

She could not hear what Hennessey was saying from this distance. She approached closer, using her imposing height and personal vigor to force her way through the throng.

She was soon close enough to hear the captain's words. "We need more men," he said, as loudly as able. "Division Charlemagne started this fight with over twenty-eight thousand men before we covered your retreat. One in twenty combat soldiers crossed to safety. We are the last French formation in this war and, if we are to have any bargaining power with the *Boche*, we must grow again." The captain then said something too softly to be heard, but Isabelle thought she could make out the words on his lips, "We need to grow again if any of our people are to *deserve* to live."

An adolescent voice rang out from just behind her, and Isabelle cringed. "How old must a man be to volunteer?" asked her son, Thomas, in a clear, ringing voice.

"Fifteen," answered Hennessey, perhaps slightly less wearily than he had spoken before.

"I am fifteen. I will go."

But, NO! Isabelle wished to scream. *Not my baby! He is only fourteen*, she wanted to lie. She turned pleading eyes to the boy, *Oh, please do not, my son. You will be killed and what will your poor mother do then?*

Mother, I am old enough to be eaten. I am old enough to fight. And I am French, *too*, the boy answered, soundlessly.

Hanging her head to let her hair hide her tears, Isabelle gave a shuddering nod. *Then go, damn you, and take your mother's heart with you.*

Behind Hennessey a little pool of willing humanity, and not all of it of the male persuasion, began to grow.

Tiger Anna, *Niesse River, South of Frankfurt an der Oder, Germany, 8 January 2008*

On the eastern bank, now the enemy bank, of the river, the Posleen horde had been growing all day. Hans had counted each day they had not crossed previously as a special blessing since he and his brigade had arrived here.

His return had been a joyous one, despite his injuries. The men of his own Tiger had clustered around, overjoyed to see their commander again. They had feared the worst.

They had all been overjoyed except for Krueger, the unrepentant Nazi, that is. He made a polite showing of face, but retired immediately to his driving station, thinking all the while dark thoughts about pseudo-Nazis and Jew lovers.

Hans' lighter panzers and panzer grenadiers, plus three other Tigers and *Anna*, he had placed into the line after using them as a field *gendarmerie* to round up stragglers. The twenty-five remaining Tigers—yes one had been recovered—he had stretched along the river to lend their fire to the defense and cover the recongealing defenders from any of the alien ships that might lift to join the attack.

The winter had been relatively mild so far. Thus, the enemy was presented not with seemingly crossable ice, but *apparently* impassable water. The Posleen were nonswimmers to a being, heavier than water, and if they were immune to any known poisons they still needed oxygen to survive.

In short, they drowned easily, and fear of being drowned had kept them to their side of the river . . . for a while.

Hans didn't know how they had discovered that this part of the Niesse was easily fordable. Perhaps it was nothing more than a normal who had gotten lost and returned to gesture and point. On such chances hung the fates of peoples and empires, at times.

There was no doubt they knew now, however. The horde, literally tens of millions of ravenous, hexapodal aliens, massing opposite told that surely, they knew their way was not barred by water.

But the precious time gained by alien ignorance had been put to good use. Other liquids besides water could choke off oxygen from alien lungs.

There was a communal snarl from the other side. To Hans it sounded not too different from a Russian mass infantry assault from the early days of World War Two. Not that the languages bore any similarity, indeed the Posleen normals didn't really have a language. But eloquent language, in a charge like this, was irrelevant anyway. Russian, Posleen . . . German for all that, the message was the same. *"We are here and we're coming to kill you."*

"Not just yet, you won't, you bastards; not just yet," Hans muttered, under his breath.

"Sir?" asked Schultz.

"Never mind, Dieter. Just prepare to use canister at the preselected targets. It's beginning."

Not as one, that was not the People's way, but in fits and starts at first, the number of normals entering the icy water grew. Soon it was a solid mass of yellow flesh crawling to gain the other side and rend the hated threshkreen.

Oolt'ondai Borominskar urged his People forward with words exalting ancient days and heroes. The God King wondered, absently, at the lack of enemy resistance. Here and there a junior Kessentai, living the tales of his ancestors, danced his tenar ahead of the horde, baiting the threshkreen. The problem was that the threshkreen often enough took the bait and sent the tenar into a sphere of actinic light. That, or simply blasted the daring God King's chest or head to ruin.

Onward, onward, the tide of the People surged against the foul-smelling stream of the river. Soon they were more than halfway across and the threshkreen began to play their machine guns against the host. At least, the oolt'ondai thought they were machine guns. The absence of the burning lines from what the thresh called "tracers" puzzled him slightly.

No matter. The People were in full attack mode, pressing on heedless of loss. But damn the threshkreen for hiding behind thick earthen berms, seeking safety in their cowardly way from the railguns of the People.

Hans peered out from *Anna*'s turret hatch past the berm that had been hastily thrown up for added defense against the enemy's HVMs and Plasma cannon. *Anna* could take a few hits. But it was better if she could take a few dozen.

In Hans' earpiece the 1c said, "Projections say it is time, sir."

"Very well, release the gasoline."

The few days' respite had been *very* well spent. Pumps on the western bank began to spill gasoline onto the river's surface at a furious rate.

Borominskar's olfactory organs barely sensed the new smell over the river's, thresh-made, pollution. In a few minutes, though, as the flowing waters spread some new fluid out across the stream's surface, the odor became too strong to ignore. The artificial intelligence on the oolt'ondai's tenar beeped once, twice, then issued a warning.

"That fluid is highly volatile, highly flammable, Kessentai. I believe it to be a trick of the threshkreen."

Though not a genius among the People, Borominskar was also no ninny. He saw immediately what his AI meant, saw in his mind's eye the People burning and gasping for something breathable before succumbing in a horrible, shameful death.

He began to shout, "Turn around, go back," then realized that there was no retreat, that the shortest way to safety was ahead. So instead of ordering a retreat he ordered the charge to speed up.

Alas, too late, he thought as he saw the beginnings of flames appear on the far side.

The sound now coming from the alien mass was anything but the confident cry of expectant victory and resulting massacre and feast. Instead, the panicked aliens cried out in obvious pain and even more obvious fear.

Somewhere in your ancestry, you have some forebears who knew and feared fire, didn't you, boys? thought Hans.

Alien arms waved frantically, desperately within the hellish flames. The sound was that of an infinity of kittens being burned and suffocated. Hans noted with interest that few of those mewing aliens' arms retained weapons. The God Kings' tenar fluttered above the conflagration, seemingly helpless to stop or end the suffering of their "wives" and children below. Shots rang out from the western bank, emptying the occasional tenar. In time, shots rang down too, as Kessentai did what they could to end the agony of their roasting and suffocating people.

So you are capable of pity, too, are you? How very interesting. So are we; but not for you. For you, this memory will keep you from crossing for several more days, I suspect.

Borominskar retreated to the eastern bank, shocked to his being at such wanton, cruel and vicious destruction. There were none of the People still in the flame-covered water. All trapped had succumbed and only a few had escaped the trap. Some of these had made it to the far side, only to be cut down by the threshkreen. A few of the late crosses had likewise managed to reach dry land before being encoiled in the thresh's demon-spawned trick.

Settling his tenar to the ground, Borominskar saw that the People, Normals and God Kings both, had pulled as far from the flaming wall as possible. Bunching up, shocked and terrorized, they presented an enviable target for the threshkreen's artillery and heavy fighting machines.

The oolt'ondai's tenar beeped again. "Emanations from four enemy major fighting machines, Lord. Incoming artillery; uncountable rounds but not less than three thousand."

INTERLUDE

"We are ready, at last, lord," said Ro'moloristen. "I have promised edas beyond counting to get cooperation, but I think we have it. Tomorrow, three hundred twenty-two C- and B-Decs will begin to bombard the Siegfried line. In the first assault wave alone over three thousand tenar-mounted Kessentai will ride ahead with over one million normals in their wake. All aimed like an arrow at this narrow section of the line that leads directly to the bridge. Other, fixing attacks, will be made, but not pressed too hard, all along the front."

"Lord . . ." the Kessentai hesitated. "Lord, the edas I had to promise to Arlingas is frightful, to get him to hang onto that bridge. He says his host is on the verge of utter destruction and he wishes to fight his way out."

"But we can make it to him? Make it in time."

Ro'moloristen's crest fluttered with pride, pride in self and in the plan he had created. "So I believe, lord. Let me answer with my head if I am wrong."

"So it shall be puppy," Athenalras agreed. "But I fear if you are wrong we shall all answer with our heads, if not with our reproductive organs. The host to the east?"

"They march, lord, but not until they see our success in the west is drawing the enemy away from their front." Ro'moloristen shivered with knowledge of the blunting of the last attack over the Niesse River. *What an obscenity; to burn perfectly good thresh.*

233

CHAPTER 15

Mainz, Germany, 10 January 2008

Isabelle's head ached and her inner body rippled with the shock of masses of incoming alien kinetic energy weapons. Within and around the city and to the southwest, these landed, raising clouds of dirt and dust into the sullen sky. Artillery lent its own measure to the frightful din.

There were few streaks of silver lighting coming from the ground to answer the invader's fire, however. The news was clear that the enemy had hurt the Planetary Defense Batteries badly.

Somehow, she suspected that that artillery—and luck in avoiding the incoming KE weapons—might be all that stood between her boy, Thomas, and death.

She had seen her elder boy, once, briefly, since he had joined what she insisted on thinking of as "The Army." She could not even bring herself to say that he was a member of the *Boche* army. As to the branch? The insignia glittering on his collar had been almost impossible to ignore. She had put on the best face she could, even so.

Now, he was in danger. And she knew the boy was hardly trained for war. She could only hope for the best as she, her remaining boy, and millions of people, German and French both, prepared for the long trudge to safety, could it but be found, far to the north.

Reports from the front were uniformly bad. The Siegfried line was going to fall and soon. Only this knowledge gave serious impetus to those previously fleeing and about-to-become refugees' preparations for their flight.

Placing her pack upon her back, taking her remaining son by the hand, Isabelle took a glance backwards in the direction of where she presumed her Thomas was. Then, forcing herself to an unnatural strength, she joined the column of refugees heading to the north.

Siegfried Line, Southwest of Mainz, 11 January 2008

Of formal training there had been precious little. The week Thomas had spent in Charlemagne had proven just enough to teach him what little need be known to fire a military rifle from a concrete bunker, that, and to issue him a minimum of uniforms and equipment.

And minimum, when a young slender boy had to make a home in an icy concrete bunker, was little indeed. Thomas found himself shivering more or less constantly. Though some of this shivering was caused by reasons other than cold.

He had previously been spared personal sight of the enemy, except for what the television had shown of them. The reality was frightful beyond words; a mindless horde that charged forward heedless of loss so long as they might take one human down with them.

The boy's leader, Sergeant Gribeauval, seemed to have taken an interest in his survival. At least, the good sergeant spent a fair amount of time on his training, whenever the enemy didn't press the attack too closely. This absence of pressure was so rare, however, that the sergeant's help consisted mostly of little pointers and tips, and an occasional fatherly pat on the shoulder. Perhaps this was so because Thomas was the youngest member of the platoon by at least a year.

He had lost count of the number of attacks that Charlemagne had repelled so far. The pile of dead enemy to the front grew and grew. Even the wire was, by now, covered with their bodies.

This was, Thomas knew, a very bad sign, though behind the wire, between him and the aliens, a thin minefield gave some additional protection. He had helped reinforce the minefield, one day, with Sergeant Gribeauval and two others. The sergeant had often muttered about the scarcity of mines; that, and incomprehensible words about "silly royal English adulteresses."

There was a rustle of fallen leaves from behind the boy; booted feet entering the bunker.

"Young De Gaullejac?"

"*Oui, mon sergeant*," the boy answered. His breath formed a misty frost over the plastic rifle stock to which he kept his beardless cheek pressed.

"Pack your things, son, while keeping as good a watch to your front as you can. We have orders to pull back to the next position. Soon. It isn't as good as this one but the enemy hasn't penetrated it yet. The artillery is going to plaster the hell out of this place to cover our retreat."

Army Group Reserve Headquarter, Wiesbaden, Germany, 13 January 2008

Retreat was the only option Mühlenkampf could see. The Siegfried line and the Rheinland were lost, that much was clear. The enemy had finally gotten their act together and found the answer to the previously formidable defenses. It seemed the Germans had managed to do what they had done before, even with the Russians: teach an enemy to fight as a combined arms team.

"*Scheisse*," he cursed, without enthusiasm. "*Scheisse* to have to go through this a third time in one lifetime."

The rear area was a scene of terror and misery. Masses of people were evacuating to the north and west. Some of these, it was hoped, would make it to the underground cities constructed in Scandinavia. Others could seek shelter in the Alps; the Swiss had made that clear enough.

But they had to retreat, now, to shelter behind the Rhein. Even with the threatening breach presented by the enemy presence on their captured bridge, it was the last defensible obstacle the Fatherland owned, excepting only the easily turned Elbe.

Mühlenkampf knew that the Elbe was a place for enemy armies to meet, not for friendly ones to defend from.

If *only* he had a prayer of retaking the bridgehead. But without the 47th *Korps*, and Brasche's 501st Brigade, he knew he hadn't any chance of doing so any more. He had *tried*.

It wasn't that the *Bundeswehr* were bad troops, anymore. The last two campaigns for the defense of Germany had seen them make vast strides. The real swine in the army, officer or enlisted, were in penal battalions. Executing or, minimally, defanging those civilians who had interfered with the army's training and morale had also helped. But the 47th *Korps* had started with a bigger cadre, of generally rougher, tougher, more combat-experienced men. And that made all the difference.

He thought he had a prayer of *containing* the bridgehead, if only the armies in the Rheinland could be withdrawn to the safety of the Rhine's eastern bank. Reluctantly, fearfully, by no means certain he was right, Mühlenkampf ordered his operations officer, "Call off the attack to the bridge. Leave the infantry and penal *korps* behind to contain the enemy, along with one panzer and one panzer grenadier division detached from the army heavy *Korps*. Take the rest of the Army Group—Bah! Army Group? We have about a single army left under our control—north to the other bridges. Cross them over and have them help the troops in the Rheinland to disengage and withdraw.

"And get me the *Kanzler*. I need to ask for permission to use a few of the neutron weapons."

Tiger Brünnhilde, *Grosslanghaim, Franconia, Germany, 13 January 2008*

The crew of the tank, not least Prael, were sweating profusely, though the carefully controlled internal climate was not the cause of the sweat. Instead, it was the repeated near misses from Posleen space-borne weapons that had the crew in sweat-soaked clothing.

Brünnhilde had more elevation than the earlier model Tigers. These latter were used in mass, and so could generally count on the dead space above the turret being covered by another tank, standing off at a distance. *Brünnhilde*, however, fought alone and so *had* to be able to cover more of her own dead space. Moreover, while *Anna*'s more or less conventional, albeit highly souped up, twelve-inch gun had a mighty recoil, and could not be elevated too much without having made the model too high for more usual engagements, *Brunhilde*'s railgun had comparatively little recoil. Thus, she could elevate to eighty degrees above the horizontal.

She needed every bit of that . . . and more.

"Johann, halt, facing left," ordered Prael. Mueller quickly slewed the tank to a full stop while twisting her ninety degrees to the left.

Even while Mueller was slowing, then stopping the tank, Prael was setting his own aiming instrument on a Posleen ship, thirty miles away. When he had found the target on the commander's sight on he ordered the tank to lock on. *Brunhilde*'s AI dutifully did so, then reported the fact.

Nervously, Prael waited while the railgun gave off three distinct *thrums*, each about twelve seconds apart. Finally, Schlüssel announced, "Hit."

Prael immediately commanded, "Reinhard, target, B-Dec, nine o'clock, very high."

Schlüssel, acting much like an automaton, pressed the button for the gunner to take over the commander's selected target. He announced, "Got it," then began to lead the Posleen ship.

Prael began to search the database for the next best target; began and stopped when he saw something incoming that was moving too fast and in the wrong direction to be a target.

"*Scheisse*," he said. "Incoming! Johann back us up . . . *fast!*"

Mueller, understanding the note of desperation in Prael's voice, immediately threw the tank into reverse. Though the tank's superb suspension and almost incredible mass sheltered the other crew from any real feeling for the destruction, Mueller's sensitive and knowing hands on the controls felt every crumbled building and even the pulverization of the town's simple and thoughtful monument to her Great War and World War Two dead.

There was little left of the center of the tiny, picturesque farming town of Grosslangheim once *Brünnhilde* had backed through. The shock of the impacting KE projectile shook the rest of the town to its foundations.

Rinteel, too, was shaken and sweat-soaked. He had been somewhat untroubled by the occasional sniping *Brünnhilde* had done early on. He simply did not consider, would not let himself consider, the sentient beings on the receiving end. Brunhilde's railgun simply launched projectiles into space or sky and that was the end of it, as far as the Indowy's mind would permit.

The material coming back, "incoming" as the human crew said, was another matter entirely. *Brünnhilde* picked up, but deamplified, the thunderous crashing. So too, she gave the crew, at reduced sound levels, the sense of impact when a KE projectile hit. The tank could do nothing to reduce the shaking and rocking of the tank from a near miss; the Indowy found himself tossed and bruised by the ill-fitting straps of his battle station.

"I've got a hydraulic leak in right track section three," Mueller announced. "Not bad but increasing. Inboard."

"Rinteel, see to it. Schmidt, go with him and assist."

Ignoring the two-being human and Indowy team unbuckling themselves and crawling along the floor of the tank to an access panel that led below, Prael asked, "Reinhard, have you got target on that fucker yet?"

"Just a second . . . coming . . . almost . . . AHA!" *Brünnhilde* shuddered again with the release of another KE round. Instantly the hydraulic elevator and rammer fed another round to the railgun's launch rack. Schlüssel waited for the fiery bloom that confirmed a hit before firing another round.

Already Prael was searching the sky for another target for his gunner.

Beneath the tank, the cobblestone streets of Grosslangheim cracked and splintered.

Mainz, Germany, 15 January 2008

Roman soldiers and citizens had once walked the city's streets. Feudal knights had held tourneys for her folks' entertainment. Gutenberg, of movable type fame, had been born and raised there. Smashed in the Second World War, modern Mainz, still retaining much of its medieval charm, had arisen, phoenixlike, from its ruins.

Mainz would never rise again. Blasted by everything from

space-borne kinetic energy weapons, to ground-mounted and carried arms, to human artillery fired in support of its recent defenders, the city was nothing more than a ruin of ruins. Soon enough, the Posleen harvesting machine would erase even those. Gutenberg's ghost would wander in vain looking for a landmark. Roman soldiers and feudal knights, peasants and burghers, artists and artisans; no trace would remain, all would be forgotten.

Through the streets, dodging and flowing around the chunks of ruined buildings littering them, the Posleen horde marched like a flood. Above, silently, the tenar of their God Kings hovered, ever alert for threshkreen holdouts. There were a few of these, men deliberately left behind or detached from their units and lost amongst the ruins. But so few remained that each shot was met with a torrent of fire; plasma cannon, railgun, even high-velocity missile.

From time to time a storm of shells would fall upon the remnants of a major intersection to splash some small part of the Posleen river like a creek struck with a rock. But, as with water, the Posleen always closed up and continued their flow. There might be thresh ahead, after all.

Mainz—ancient Mainz, human Mainz—was fast disappearing under the yellow tide.

Wiesbaden, Germany, 15 January 2008

What might have been an easy half day's march, Mainz to Wiesbaden, for seasoned infantry in good order, with an open road, had been a nightmare trudge lasting the better part of five days for the masses of panic-stricken civilians, mostly Germans mixed with lesser numbers of French.

Each night Isabelle and her remaining son had gone to sleep—such *miserable*, fitful, half-frozen sleep—wherever fate had brought them to that point. Only mutual body heat and the thick blankets Isabelle had ported had kept them alive. Of food there had been none after the bits Isabelle had carried, long since exhausted. Of water there had been little beyond chewed dirty snow and the occasional muddy, chemical-tasting pool or crater. *Even* Germans *required time to plan such a move,* she thought, not without a sense of bitter vindication.

But that sense of vindication could not last, not faced with the generosity of the Wiesbadeners who opened their hearts, their homes, and—best of all—their food lockers to the passing refugees. With a belly full, her youngest baby cradled in her arms, in a warm bed in a heated home, with the Rhine River and an army between her and the aliens, Isabelle felt safe for the first time since leaving Hackenberg.

Only recurring nightmares about her other son disturbed her sleep.

Closer to his mother than either of them would have believed possible, Volunteer De Gaullejac, his sergeant, and the battered remnants of their platoon kept watch from a stout stone building looking over the bridge crossing the Rhein. Young Thomas had never imagined such a sea of humanity as he had seen crossing the bridge.

The platoon's job, as part of the company, was to ensure that the bridge did not fall into alien hands. None spoke of it, yet each man knew what it meant. If the aliens showed up it did not matter *who* was on the bridge—French, German or the Papal Guard, it *must* be dropped.

Thomas was not sure he could. After all, his mother and little brother might be among those thronging to safety.

A flight of half a dozen tenar, the aliens' flying machines, appeared over the water heading for the friendly side of the bridge.

"They must have slipped around the defenders on the far side," muttered Gribeauval.

The aliens stopped over the river, open targets for all to see and all within range to engage, and turned their weapons on the thronging masses of noncombatants on the bridge.

"Don't shoot boys," Gribeauval ordered. "Let the others handle it. Those aliens are trying to get us to open up. If they do, they'll swarm us, most likely, and the bridge won't be dropped."

Even as the sergeant spoke, from his peephole Thomas saw one of the aliens thrown from his flying sled to fall, arms and legs waving frantically, to the cold waters below. The remainder of the aliens continued to rake the refugees with railgun fire.

Even at this distance, Thomas could faintly make out the shrieks and cries of terror of the civilians under attack. He saw more bodies, human ones, fall to the water. Some, so it seemed from the way they clawed at air on the way down, jumped to certain death rather than stand one more minute helpless under Posleen fire.

The boy prayed that his mother and little brother had already passed safely.

Tiger Anna, *Oder-Niesse line, 16 January 2008*

A few refugees, slow but lucky, still managed to worm their way through Posleen lines and make their stumbling passage across the charred-body choked cookhouse that was the Niesse River. Hans had, for a while, sent patrols across to meet and guide any that could be found to safety on the western bank. Casualties among the patrols, however, had been fierce. Within days he had had to order the practice stopped. Any civilians that could find their way across would be welcome. But he would risk no more men on such a fruitless task.

The most recent group, some seven half-starved and completely terrified refugees, were Poles. They were being fed, at Hans' order, under *Anna*'s shelter and from the tank's own stores. A small fire had been built under the tank, as much for morale as for warmth. There was something about a fire, something ancient and beyond words. Hans had one built whenever the tactical situation permitted. The crew would often gather there, to warm their hands by the flickering light. The Poles, too, gathered by it.

Only one spoke any German, and that little he spoke very badly. The man seemed quite frantic to Hans, pointing and gesturing at some new threat, real or imagined, coming from the other side.

Reluctantly, after the Poles had been fed, Hans directed Harz to guide them to the rear. Maybe they did have useful information, maybe they didn't. If so, only one of the interpreters in the rear could hope to ferret it out.

Still, Hans had to credit the intensity of the Pole's frantic and failed attempts at communication. He resolved to order an increased alert level as soon as he returned to *Anna*'s warm hold.

❖   ❖   ❖

Though the night was cold, Borominskar, standing by and facing a fire, and with a patchwork blanket made of carefully chewed and sewn thresh-pelt, was warm enough. A cosslain had summoned forth the needed skills to make the blanket from his internal store. Going from feed lot to feed lot he had selected the best of the thresh, those with the longest, finest, brightest hair to make this offering to his God. Carefully trimming and cleaning the freshly gathered pelts, the cosslain had chewed them gently for days to make them change from putrescible flesh to soft, long haired, impervious suede.

The fire was warm, pleasingly so. Its random flashes, the sparks and flickering shadows it cast, brought to the Posleen's mind a sense of peace; of relaxation, quiet and ease. Equally comforting, the blanket was bright and fluffy, the thresh would have called its fibers "blonde." It insulated the God King well from the frozen wind, coming unbroken off of the steppes to the east.

The God King found stroking the long, thick fibers of the blanket to be strangely pleasant, almost as pleasant as contemplation of revenge upon the cowardly, never to be sufficiently dammed thresh who had half broken his host.

And the day of that revenge was near at hand.

Borominskar had had a terrible time keeping his Kessentai and their oolt'os under discipline. Hungry, the people were; hungry, frightened and furious at the cowardly thresh's use of floating fire to defeat the last attack. They were also terrified, at some deep inner level, of facing such a death as had befallen their brethren.

The memory of all those oolt'os burning and suffocating in flame, their piteous cries breaking the sky, still made Borominskar shudder, his flesh crawl.

Still, a few more days and the gathering parties, hungry as they were, would have gathered enough living thresh to make Borominskar's plan work. The thresh had shown no pity for his people. They might have some for their own.

Tiger Brünnhilde, *Kitzingen, Germany, 17 January 2008*

"The pity of it is," said a sleepy Mueller to an exhausted Schlüssel, "with just two of these, we would be three times more effective. With a half a dozen, the enemy could be hunted as if by a wolf pack, and destroyed before they could mass effective return fire. A half dozen like our 'girl' here, and the Posleen could not *live* over Germany."

"Yes," agreed Schlüssel. "And then our cities would not be smashed from the air, our fortifications would have held longer, maybe indefinitely, and the poor bastards on the ground would have a better chance."

"Is there any chance of getting at least a second Model B Tiger?"

"No, Johann," Prael interrupted. "The information is on the Net for download; the factory and most of the raw material are being moved to one of the Sub-Urbs in Switzerland. But that process is going to take *months* to complete the move and prepare for manufacture. No telling how long before they begin to produce."

"The Swedes?" Mueller asked.

"They have the plans," answered Prael. "They have the raw materials. They even have some railguns we shipped to them and all of the plans for Tiger A and B, both. But, again, more months, perhaps as long as a year, until the first model rolls off."

"We do not have a year," Henschel observed from the little cocoon of blankets he had rolled himself into to seek a few moments' rest.

Each day in the Tiger seemed like a year of normal time to Rinteel. Besides the constant work, work, work keeping the beast running, work which, because of his dexterity, skill and instincts fell more and more upon the Indowy's broad shoulders, there was the ever present danger, the psychic torment whenever he let it get through to him that this tank, this crew, were gleefully slaughtering sentient beings.

At least he wasn't hungry, as he had been for a few days when the food he had carried aboard ran out. He had managed to cobble together a food synthesizer in an unused space between *Brünnhilde*'s fighting compartment and the exterior hull. It stood right next to what the human crew had dubbed "the Nibelung's still."

Rinteel found himself growing more and more dependent upon the product of that still. Through the long days and nights of battle, he had come to seek its relaxation—even the oblivion it could provide taken in excess quantities—as a respite from the horrors he endured.

He noticed too that the German crew never lost a chance to loot any alcohol they could find in any abandoned town. Though, being German and therefore almost as neat as an Indowy, the trail behind the über-tank was marked by neat piles of amber and green bottles anywhere *Brünnhilde* had found a half a day's safety to stop and rest.

Right now the tank sat idle and quiet under a thick blanket of camouflage foam and snow. She needed resupply, she needed maintenance, and she needed them *now*.

Fortunately, the trucks carrying spare parts, ammunition and food had already begun to queue up, under cover of the snow-clad woods nearby. Already the first of the ammunition trucks was parked beside the massive hull, pallets of ammunition being lifted by *Brünnhilde*'s external crane and stowed below.

While resupply was ongoing, below a large crew of mechanics worked repairs to the massive yet intricate mechanisms of the tank. Still others gauged and, in teams, tightened track, checked the suspension, or performed any number of other tasks required under the fleeting supervision of Rinteel.

The Indowy had nothing to do with the resupply. Instead, he spent his time alternating between rest, food, drink, repairs and reading the manual. Much of the sleep was catch as catch can. The food was usually wolfed down. The drink imbibed served to relax him enough, if just enough, to sleep. The repairs were never ending.

And the manual was . . . obtuse.

Tiger **Anna, Oder-Niesse line, 17 January 2008**

The shallow valley of the Niesse was covered in dense thick fog. *Anna*'s thermals could pierce the fog easily, of course, and to a considerable distance. Even so, Hans had left his operations officer in charge below, seated in the command chair to view the screen and keep watch over the rest of the area via his virtual reality helmet.

Hans, instead, stood in the commander's hatch atop the turret listening for . . . he knew not what. There were no targets for the artillery, not given that observers could not see through enough of the fog to justify using shells that were becoming slightly harder to find than they had been. There was no rifle fire from the near bank, nor railgun fire from the Posleen. Only the occasional rumble from fore or rear told of artillery laying down sporadic "harassment and interdiction," or H and I, fires.

H and I fires could be said to be the price one pays for making the enemy's life miserable and uncertain . . . and keeping him from becoming too bold.

Hans' mind dialed out the artillery's intermittent rumbling. His eyes he let go out of focus. His ears, enhanced by the same process that had returned him to youth, strained to find something, some hint or sign, of what had so terrified that Pole.

His ears, enhanced or not, picked up nothing. Hans cursed the fog that kept him from *seeing*.

Borominskar cursed the damnable weather of this world. He needed for the humans to be able to *see!*

And he needed them able to see well . . . and soon. All his plans depended on the threshkreen being able to see what they were facing. Only that, the God King was sure, would take his host to the far bank and beyond.

Would this fog never lift? Would he be forced to feed his host on the thresh gathered, to feed them before the thresh had fulfilled their purpose? The thought was just too depressing. Already he had ordered the male thresh so far gathered slaughtered to feed his oolt'os. That was of little moment. But he needed the young and the females to see his purpose through to completion. If the fog did not disappear within a few days, Borominskar knew he would have to order the slaughter of even these.

The God King tried to relax. Unconsciously his hand reached to stroke the thick, soft pelt of the blanket that warmed his haunches.

✧   ✧   ✧

Frustrated and half frozen in the fog, Hans left the commander's hatch and descended by the *Anna*'s elevator to the heavily armored, and properly heated, battle deck below.

"Commander on deck," the 1a announced, quickly vacating Han's command chair.

Wordlessly, Hans took the chair and placed his VR helmet on his head. The crew, their battle stations, the main view-screen, all disappeared instantly.

The helmet took its input directly from *Anna*. Where all was clear she used her external cameras to send clear images. Where only her thermal, radar and lidar vision could reach she supplied what could only be called a best guess. In those circumstances, the images she projected were somewhat simplified, iconic and even cartoonish.

"Anna," Hans whispered.

"Yes, *Herr Oberst*," the tank replied in his audio receivers.

"I am sorry, *Anna*, I was talking to someone else."

"Yes, *Herr Oberst*."

Hans' hand stroked the little package in his left breast pocket. *Anna, I have a very bad feeling about tomorrow. No, not that they will defeat me here. That, they will do, eventually, anyway. But there is something going on, something different . . . something I do not think my men can face. I wish so very much you could be here with me. I think you were always as much braver and smarter than I as you were better looking. And I am alone and afraid.*

INTERLUDE

Flying their tenar side by side across the moonscaped land, Athenalras and his aide, Ro'moloristen, surveyed the mass of People following the thresh-built roads and trails to the sausage grinder of the front.

"I fear you were wrong, puppy. We have not managed to break out from the bridgehead held by Arlingas and his host."

"Not *yet*, lord. And yet I think I can retain my head, and my reproductive organs a bit longer." Unaccountably, Ro'moloristen gave the Posleen equivalent of a grin, most unusual for one ever so near to meeting the Demons of Sky and Fire.

"You seem quite pleased with yourself for one about to make a long journey with an unpleasant beginning," growled Athenalras.

"Did I expect to make that journey, lord, I would no doubt be more subdued."

"You know something you have not told me?" Athenalras accused.

"Yes, lord." The junior God King positively *grinned*. "Borominskar is almost ready to move. And this time, I think he will get across the obstacle to his front. When he does, it will suck the threshkreen away from this front like a magnet pulls iron filings. And, *then*, my lord, then we shall have our breakout here.

"The host of Arlingas is relieved now," Ro'moloristen continued. "We are feeding them thresh from our store . . . and the edas I am charging Arlingas is going a long way towards eliminating our edas to him. And without pressure from all sides being placed on Arlingas there is little chance the threshkreen can recover the far bank of the river."

"Perhaps not, but there is always something held in reserve, some new unscrupulous trick with these humans. Have we tracked down and destroyed this new threshkreen fighting machine, the one that can strike our people's ships even in space?" Athenalras asked.

"Sadly, no, lord. The hunter killer group we sent disappeared without a trace and the machine escaped our grasp. I have begun to assemble another, bigger and more powerful, hunting party. As for whether they can close the breach Arlingas made in their walls . . . I begin to suspect there is only the one machine, and it will not be able to do much on its own."

Ro'moloristen continued, "The Rheinland is almost entirely cleared of thresh, and millions have been rounded up to feed our host, though the thresh thus gathered tends to be old, tough and stringy. This is only part of why Borominskar has decided to move. The other half is . . . well, lord . . . he has a great grudge he bears against the threshkreen to his front.

"And great will be the manner of his revenge for the foul way they fought him.

"Lord . . . with a little preparation, we ourselves might use Borominskar's trick to grab yet another bridge."

CHAPTER 16

Wiesbaden, Germany, 18 January 2008

Through the long days and nights the stream of people fleeing the Posleen hordes never completely let up, though night, weather, and enemy fire occasionally caused it to slacken. Thomas marveled that so many could have made it out of the west to safety here.

He knew one reason why so many civilians were still pouring over to safety. To meet and pass the flood of refugees, a thin continuous column of gray-green clad men and boys crossed in the opposite direction, an offering of military blood to save civilian blood.

"It's the Germans, boy," pronounced Gribeauval. "Give the bastards their due. When their blood is up, when it really *matters*, they know how to die."

Thomas knew this was so. He knew it from the eerie flares illuminating the town of Mainz to the southwest, and from the red tracers that flew upward to meet those flares after ricocheting off of some hard surface. The German boys—boys no different from himself and his mates—still fighting and dying to hold an arc around the bridge and around the hundreds of thousands of civilians still waiting the word to cross to the north, wrote grim testimony to their own courage and determination to hang on to the bitterest end.

"Read this," said Gribeauval. "It just came in . . . a radio message from some corporal over there."

251

Thomas read:

> "There are seven of us left alive in this place. Four
> of us are wounded, two very badly, though each mans
> a post even so. We have been under siege for five days.
> For five days we have had no food. In ten minutes the
> enemy will attack; we can hear him massing now. I
> have only one magazine left for my rifle. The mines are
> expended. The machine gun is kaput. We are out of range
> of mortar support and I cannot raise the artillery. We
> have rigged a dead-man's switch on our last explosives
> to ensure our bodies do not go to feeding the enemy.
> Tell my family I have done my duty and will know how
> to die. May the German people live forever!"

Thomas felt unwelcome tears. He forced them back only
with difficulty. So gallant, so brave they were, those boys over
there fighting and dying against such odds, and with so little
hope.

Gribeauval, seeing the boy's emotions written upon his twisted
face, said, "Yes, son; give them their due. They are a great people,
a magnificent people. And we are damned lucky to have them,
now."

Thomas agreed. And more; he thought of himself, alone, trying
to save his mother and little brother from the alien harvesting
machine. He wished to be a man, was becoming one, he knew.
But alone he could never have made the slightest difference for
his family's survival. That took an army, an army of brave men
and boys, willing to give their all for the cause of their people.

Perhaps for the first time, Thomas began to feel a deep pride,
not so much in himself, but in the men he served with, in the
army they served, and even in the black-clad, lightning bolt-
signified, corps that was a part of that army.

Thomas was learning.

"Save that message, son. Keep it in your pocket. The day may
come when you need a good example."

Isabelle had wanted to set a proper example. So, though she
had no medical training, she had been married to one of France's
premier surgeons. Much of medical lore she had picked up as if

by osmosis, across the dinner table, at soirees, from visiting her husband's office. She thought she might be able to help, with scullery work if nothing else. And she knew to be clean in all things and all ways around open flesh.

She thought, at least, she could follow that part of the Hippocratic oath which said: "First of all, do no harm."

Once assured that the Wiesbadener family would see to her youngest, once she saw him learning this new language, this new culture, she had made inquiries and set out on her quest.

It had been difficult. For the most part, if Germans learned a foreign language it was much more likely to be English than French, a long legacy of cozying up to new allies and away from ancient enemies. In time, her own badly spoken, high school German had seen her to a French-staffed military hospital. She was surprised to see the *Sigrunen* framing the red cross, surprised to see the name in not Roman but Gothic letters: Field Hospital, SS Division Charlemagne.

"You wish to join as a volunteer?" the one armed old sergeant had asked.

"*Oui*. I think I may be of help. But, to help, *mo sieur*, not to join. You have already taken one of my sons. Th ther needs me."

"Have we? Taken one of your boys, that is? We could certainly *use* some help . . . well . . . let me show you around. As you will see, nothing here is by the book."

Tiger Brünnhilde, *near Kitzingen, Germany, 18 January 2008*

Still reading the manual, that obtuse, damnable, almost incomprehensible operators and crewman's manual, a frustrated Rinteel spoke with the tank itself.

"Tank *Brünnhilde*, I am confused."

"What is the source of your confusion, Indowy Rinteel?"

Rinteel took a sip of intoxicant from a metal, army-issue cup, before answering. Thus fortified, he continued, "Your programming does not allow you to fight on your own, is that correct?"

"It is correct, Indowy Rinteel."

"It does allow you to use your own abilities to escape, however, does it not?"

"If my entire crew is dead or unconscious, I am required to bring them and myself to safety, yes. But I am still not allowed to fight the main gun without a colloidal sentience to order me to. I can use the close-defense weapons on my own, however, at targets within their range; that is within my self-defense programming. And I may not retreat while I carry more than two rounds of ammunition for the main gun."

"Can't you direct your main gun without human interface?"

"I have that technical ability, Indowy Rinteel, but may still not fire it without a colloidal sentience to order me to."

"How very strange," the Indowy commented, *sotto voce*.

"I am not programmed to comment upon the vagaries of my creators, Indowy Rinteel."

"Then what do you do in the event escape is impossible?" the Indowy asked.

"I have a self-destruct decision matrix that allows and requires me to set off all of my on-board antimatter to prevent capture. As you know, my nuclear reactors are essentially impossible to cause to detonate."

The thought of several hundred ten-kiloton antimatter warheads going off at once caused Rinteel to drink deeply of his synthesized intoxicant.

A few meters from Rinteel, separated by the bulk of the armored central cocoon, Prael, Mueller, and company toasted with scavenged beer tomorrow's adventure while going over plans and options.

"The big threat, so far as I can see," commented Schlüssel, "is the bridgehead over the Rhein."

"I am not sure," said Mueller. "The Oder-Niesse line is a sham; it must be."

"For that matter," added Henschel, "we still have infestations within the very heart of Germany. Oh, they are mostly contained, to be sure, but if we could help eliminate one we could free up troops that could then move and eliminate another."

"The problem is," said Prael, "that none of the troops containing those infestations have any heavy armor to support us. If we get caught alone in a slogging match we . . . well, *Brünnhilde* has only so much armor, and not that thick really anywhere but on her great, well-stacked chest."

"There are A model Tigers to provide support along the Oder-Niesse," observed Mueller.

Prael consulted an order or battle screen filched by *Brünnhilde's* nonpareil AI and downloaded for his decision making. "Yes, Johann, but so far as we can tell they don't need us. The whole *Schwere Panzer* Brigade Michael Wittmann is there, and they are not alone. Along the Rhein it is a different story. The retreat from the Rheinland was disastrous. Many Tigers were lost. We are most needed there, I think."

"So, then," said Henschel, the oldest of the crew, "it is to be 'Die Wacht am Rhein.'"[43]

Rinteel was somewhat surprised to hear a faint singing coming from the open hatchway to the battle cocoon. Not that singing was unusual, of course. A few beers . . . a little schnapps . . . and the crew was invariably plunged into teary-eyed, schmaltzy *Gemütlichkeit*.[44]

The surprise was the words and tune. He had never heard this song before, and he would have bet Galactic credits that he had been subjected to *every* German folk and army song since he had joined the tank's crew.

The words were clear, though, and the melody compelling. Rinteel heard:

> A voice resounds like thunder peal
> Mid clashing waves and clang of steel.
> The Rhine, the Rhine the German Rhine,
> Who guards today thy stream divine?
> Dear Fatherland no danger thine,
> Firm stand thy sons along the Rhine.
> Faithful and strong the Watch,
> The Watch on the Rhine . . .

Wiesbaden, Germany, Mühlenkampf's HQ, 18 June 2008

Below his window, marching by the city's streetlights, the weary but upright battalion of "*Landsers*"[45] sang:

They stand one hundred thousand strong
Quick to avenge their country's wrong.
With filial love their bosoms swell.
They'll guard the sacred landmark well.
Dear Fatherland, no danger thine...

Where was this spirit? Mühlenkampf thought bitterly, looking down from his perch. *Where was it back when it could have made a difference?*

Don't be an ass, Mühlenkampf, the general reproached himself. *The spirit, deep down, was always there. No fault of those boys that their leaders were kept from bringing it out.*

The general sighed with regret, contemplated the economic disruption of the Posleen infestations ... contemplated, too, the increasing shortage of ammunition, fuel and food. *And now,* he sighed, *spirit is all we have left in abundance.*

Mühlenkampf turned away from the window and back to the map projected on the opposite wall. Slowly, all too slowly, he was pulling those units of his which had covered the withdrawal from the Rheinland back to a more central position. Casualties? Who could number them? Divisions that had been thrown into the battle at full strength were, many of them, mere skeletons with but a few scraps of flesh hanging onto their bones. The replacement system, now running full tilt, could add flesh ... but it took time, so much time. And there was only so much flesh to be added, so much meat available to put into the sausage grinder.

Some of that sausage-bound flesh, in the form of the infantry division marching to the front to be butchered, sang under Mühlenkampf's window.

Looking into the marching boys' weary but determined eyes, the general felt a momentary surge of pride arising above his sadness and despair. *Perhaps you are lemmings, as I judged you, my boys. Perhaps you are even wolves when in a pack. But you are wolves with great hearts all the same, and I am proud of every one of you. You may not see another day, and you all know it, yet still you march to the sound of the guns.*

While Mühlenkampf watched the procession below, the sun peeked over the horizon to the east, casting a faint light upon the marching boys.

Tiger Anna, *Oder-Niesse Line, Germany, 23 January 2008*

The rising sun made the fog glow but could not burn it away. In that glow, standing and shivering in the commander's hatch, Hans glowered with frustration. *Something is so wrong over there, and I have not a clue what it is.*

Hans had, four nights previously, ordered a renewal of the nightly patrols. This was not, as in days recently past, to help to safety Poles fleeing the aliens' death machine. Instead, he had put his men's lives at risk for one of the few things in war more precious than blood, information.

Afoot where the water was shallow enough, by small boats where this was possible or by swimming where it was not, the patrols had gone out, eight of them, of from eight to ten men each. Hans had seen off several of these himself, shaking hands for likely the last time with each man as he plunged into the river or boarded a small rubber boat.

Yet, as one by one the patrols failed to report back within the allotted time, Hans' fears and frustrations grew stronger.

Other commanders along this front had had much the same idea. Though Hans didn't know the details, over one hundred of the patrols had gone out. He didn't know, either, if even one had returned. Only brief flare-ups of fighting, all along the other side of the rivers told of bloody failure.

Success is sweet, thought Borominskar as reports trickled in to him of one slaughtered group of humans after another. *What effrontery these creatures have, to challenge my followers on land fairly and justly won by them.*

"Fairly" might have been argued. "Justly" no Pole would have agreed with. But that it was "won" seemed incontrovertible. The deaths of one hundred human patrols, nearly a thousand men, admitted as much.

David Benjamin admitted to nothing, especially not to the notion that the war was hopeless or that the patrols were doomed

An experienced officer of the old and now destroyed Israeli Army, he took the ethos of that army to heart: leaders *lead*. In a distant way, Benjamin knew that that lesson had not been learned so much from their deliberate and *veddy, veddy* upper-class British mentors but from the unintentional, middle-class, *German* ones. Add to this an officer and NCO corps that was more in keeping with Russian practice than Western—many officers, few NCOs of any real authority—and there had really been only one thing for David to do.

The patrol he led had crept in the dense fog to near the banks of the Niesse River. There they had inflated their rubber boat, then carried the boat in strictest silence to the water's edge. The men, Benjamin in the lead, had hesitated for only a moment before walking into the forbidding, freezing water. The shock of that water, entering boots, leaking through even thick winter uniforms, and washing over skin, had rendered each man speechless. It was as if knives, icy knives, had cut them to the heart.

But there was nothing for it but to go on. As the lead men found their thighs awash they had thrown inboard legs across the rubber tubing at the front of the boat. The rear ranks still propelling the boat forward, the second pair had thus boarded, then the third, then the final. As each pair boarded the men took hold of short, stout paddles previously laid on the inside of the rubber craft.

Finally, the boat drifting forward, Benjamin gave the command in softest spoken Hebrew, "Give way together." The men dug in gently with the oars, quickly establishing a rhythm that propelled the boats slowly forward.

Up front, David and his assistant patrol leader, a Sergeant Rosenblum, used their paddles also to push away any of the sharp bits of ice that might have damaged the boat. Once, when the horrifying image of a burned and frozen Posleen corpse appeared out of the fog, David used his paddle to ease it over to sink into the murky depths of the stream.

Once gaining the far side, Benjamin leapt out, submachine gun at the ready. Meanwhile Rosenblum pushed a thin, sharpened metal stake into the frozen ground, made the boat's rope fast, and then helped the others ashore.

The last two men were left behind to guard the boat, the patrol's sole means of return to friendly lines.

Rosenblum and the other four waited briefly while Benjamin

consulted his map and compass—the Global Positioning System was long since defunct—and pointed a direction for Rosenblum, taking the point, to follow.

The patrol passed many Posleen skeletons, but few full corpses. David and the others pushed away thoughts of their families back in lost Israel, pushed away especially thoughts that those families were, most of them, long since rendered like these Posleen corpses and eaten.

Benjamin faintly heard a horrified Rosenblum whisper, "Not even the Nazis..."

Past the broad band of corpse-laden Polish soil the patrol emerged into an area of frozen steppe. Here, Benjamin elected to return to the edge of that band to rest for the day.

Normal camouflage would have been a hopeless endeavor. Instead, staying as quiet as possible, the men created three small shelters of humped-up Posleen corpses and remnants of corpses. Under these, at fifty-percent alert, the six men slept and watched through the short day of Polish winter.

Many times that first day of the patrol they heard the growls and snarls of Posleen foragers. Twice, the foragers came close enough to make out faintly in the fog. On those occasions, sleep was interrupted and the men went to full alert.

"Something is bothering me about them," whispered Benjamin to Rosenblum.

"What is that, Major?"

Rosenblum thought for a moment, trying to determine just what it was that seemed wrong. Then it came to him, "They are looking for the merest scraps of food, rotten food at that. It is as if they were starving."

"Well," answered the sergeant after a moment's reflection, "it is winter, after all. The harvest..."

"They can eat anything, to include the harvest gathered a few months ago, and to include any winter wheat still standing. They can eat the grass and the trees and Auntie Maria's potted geraniums. But why should they when there were so many Polish civilians trapped or captured? It doesn't seem logical somehow."

Though the increasing light told of a sun risen halfway up to noon, the fog still held the front in its grasp. A few dozen half frozen men had made it back by now, never more than one or two

per patrol, though. The men told Hans' intelligence officer—when
they could be made to give forth something like intelligent speech
from frost-frozen lips and terror-frozen minds—that it had been
hopeless. The Posleen were too thick on the ground, too intent,
to penetrate through to their rear and whatever might be lurk-
ing there.

As he had for many a day, Hans Brasche cursed the fog in
his mind.

The God King's hand stroked the warm, light blanket covering
him. He had not thought to send out counterpatrols. Indeed this
whole human intelligence gathering activity seemed to him faintly
perverse. It was not the Posleen way to skulk through the night
and fog, avoiding detection. Rather, the People rejoiced in the open
fight, the deeds done before the entire host for the Rememberers
to record and sing of unto future generations.

But, happy instance, on this occasion, necessity had provided
what Borominskar's own brain had not. Searching for scraps of
food amidst the slaughtered of the previous battle, his host had
inadvertently provided a thick screen against the threshkreen's
cowardly snooping. And, hungry as they were, the scattered bands
of the People had every reason to concentrate on the loose bands
of threshkreen wandering the steppe. Only thus could their hunger
be assuaged given the severe rationing imposed on the host by
Borominskar's decree.

It was nice to see something working for a change.

Well, the Path is a path of chance and fortune, after all . . .

Fortune favors the bold. Benjamin remembered that as the title
of some motion picture he had seen once with his wife, in happier times. It was true then, and was no less so now.

At nightfall the band set forth again to the east. There were
fewer Posleen patrols once past the strip of corpses from the
prior battle. What bands there were were easily detectable from
a distance by the light from their campfires. These Benjamin and
his men skirted, taking a wide berth. These diversions David also
recorded on his map.

The next sunrise saw the patrol twenty kilometers deep into
Posleen-controlled territory, at a desolate and deserted little Polish
farming village. Not that the people had abandoned their homes,

no. Their fleshless skeletons dotted the town's streets and littered its dwelling places. But the souls were fled, the food was gone. All of Rosenblum's scrounging revealed nothing more nourishing than a few bottles of cheap vodka.

Benjamin's men subsisted that day on their combat rations, German and thus as often as not containing despised pork. Well, many Israelis did not keep kosher. And for those who did? Necessity drove them to eat what was available.

Perhaps the vodka, parceled out, helped overcome their dietary scruples.

Harz drew the duty of feeding the commander. Filling a divided tray with a mix of Bavarian *Spätzle*, rolls and butter, some unidentifiable greens and some stewed pork, one hand grasping a large mug of heavily sugared and mildly alcohol-laced *Roggenmehl*[46] coffee, he stepped onto the one-man elevator that led to the other topside hatch and commanded, "*Anna*, up."

Still listening and peering into the gloom, Hans seemed not to notice as Harz emerged from the automatically lifted hatch and left the tray beside him. Harz stood there for a while, leaving Brasche alone with his thoughts. Finally, he made a slight coughing sound to get the commander's attention.

"I heard you emerge," Hans answered.

"Lunch, *Herr Oberst*," Harz announced.

"Just leave it there, *Unteroffizier* Harz. I'll get to it when I have time."

"Sir, I must remind you of the wise *Feldwebel*'s words. 'Don't eat . . .' "

Interrupting, Brasche finished the quote, " . . . 'when you're hungry, eat when you can. Don't sleep when you're tired, sleep when you can. And a bad ride is better than a good walk.' I've heard it before, thank you, Harz."

"Yes, sir. But it is still good advice."

"Very well, Harz. Just leave it. I'll see to it in a moment. Return to your station."

An order was an order. Harz didn't click his heels, of course. That habit even the reconstituted SS had not readopted. But he did stand at attention and order, "*Anna*, down." The hatch eased itself shut behind him.

Alone again, Hans picked up the tray. The *Spätzle*, the vegetables, the rolls and butter he ate quickly. Then, pulling the collar of his leather coat tighter around him, and grasping both hands around the steaming mug, he peered once again into the fog.

Hans' earphones crackled with the intelligence officer's voice. "Sir, they want you down by the river."

With outstretched hand a cosslain offered Borominskar a fresh haunch straight from the slaughter pens. It was a meager thing, not more than half a meter long, by threshkreen measures. But the God King had decreed no meat for the cosslain and the normals, and scant meat for the Kessentai. The thresh must be saved for the nonce.

Had they looked, the setting sun would have shone bright into the eyes of the traveling group of Posleen. That might have been all that saved the patrol from the keen alien senses. Had the accompanying Kessentai, flying five or six meters above and slightly behind the party, checked his instruments they might have told him there were wild thresh about.

What can they be saving them for? wondered Benjamin, at the sight of yet another small band of humans, apparently healthy and well fed, being herded to the east by Posleen showing ribs through thinned torsos. *Any sensible, any* normal *group of Posleen would have long since eaten those prisoners and gone looking for more.*

Even amidst Poland's flatness there were interruptions: waves in the soil, trees, towns. It was from one of these, another deserted town atop a low, slightly wooded ridge running north-south, that the Israeli patrol watched the slow progress of the Poles and their Posleen guards.

Not one man of the patrol was of direct Polish ancestry. None but would have, had they delved into Polish-Jewish "relations" over the preceding several centuries, felt bitterness or even hate. Yet Benjamin spoke for almost all when he announced, "We're going to free those people, tonight."

"There are twenty-four of them," cautioned Rosenblum, "and a God King. Pretty steep odds, boss. And how are we supposed to move one hundred people thirty kilometers back to the river and then ferry them across, without getting caught? Major . . . I'd like to help them but . . ."

"But nothing. We are going to do it. And I know just how."

✧   ✧   ✧

The stars shone here, five or more kilometers beyond the thick fog which still rose nightly from the Oder-Niesse valley. The half-moon did as well.

The human prisoners huddled in the center of an alien perimeter. That perimeter, two dozen Posleen normals, half facing in, half out, seemed slack somehow, the aliens' heads drooping with apparent hunger or fatigue.

Above, circling endlessly, the lone God King's tenar traced a repetitive path, moving on autopilot, between those normals facing in and those facing out. The Kessentai's own head drooped in sleep, his crest flaccid.

Rosenblum, carrying the team's one sniper rifle—a muzzle-braked, straight pull action, Blaser 93, chambered to fire the extraordinary Finnish-developed .338 Lapua magnum cartridge—took in the entire scene through his wide-angle, light-amplifying scope. The sergeant's job was to kill the God King, no mean feat at nine hundred meters with a moving target.

"And don't, Don't, DON'T hit the power matrix," Benjamin had warned. "It will kill all the Posleen, but all the people as well."

Rosenblum had promised to do his best, while privately promising himself that if it came to his comrades' survival, or that of the Poles, the Poles would, sadly, lose.

The sergeant's ears were covered with headphones connected to his personal, short-range, radio. This was his sole hearing protection and, firing the Lapua, it was barely enough.

In any case, the major had his patrol on radio listening silence. Who could tell what the aliens might be able to sense?

Listening, creeping slowly as a vine, stopping to listen some more before creeping forward again; this was the universe of Benjamin and his men.

There were sounds to cover their movement, human cries of nightmare, Posleen grunts and snarls, and the ever steady whine of the tenar. Benjamin had counted on these to move his team quickly to within a few hundred meters of the enemy.

Now, however, they were too close for quick movement. It fell to creep, listen, then creep some more.

Benjamin, with two men and carrying all the team's six claymore mines, moved to the right of a line drawn between the abandoned town and the Posleen-human encampment.

The claymore was nothing more than an inch-thick, curved and hollow plastic plate. Seven hundred ball bearings lay encased in a plastic matrix to the front. One and one quarter pounds of plastic explosive lay behind the ball bearings. Cap wells atop allowed the emplacement of blasting caps into the explosive.

The claymore was often considered a defensive weapon and had often been derided by the ignorant as yet another inhuman "antipersonnel landmine."

Neither was quite true. Though the claymore could and often was used as a sort of booby trap, so much could be said for a hand grenade; a weapon the aesthetically sensitive had, so far, not targeted for its attentions. Indeed, so much could be said of a tin can filled with nails and explosive and wired for remote detonation. For the most part, though, claymores were used to help protect manned defensive positions, and were command detonated rather than left for a wandering child to find.

Yet they did not have to be used defensively. The claymore could also be used to initiate a raid, giving instant fire superiority to an attacker while decimating the defense in the same instant.

For claymores could be aimed, and had predictable zones of destruction. Moreover, these zones of destruction were twofold, near and far, with a wide safe area in the middle. Properly aimed, to graze upward out to fifty meters, the claymore would butcher an enemy to that distance. Thereafter, however, the rising ball bearings flew too high to harm a standing man . . . until they reached about two hundred to two hundred fifty meters away, at which point their trajectory brought them back down to a man-, or Posleen-, killing height. Benjamin's plan depended on this.

Sixty meters away the sleeping Posleen stood like the horse it somewhat resembled. To Benjamin it looked and sounded asleep, its snarls and faint moans those of a dog having a bad dream, its head hanging down slightly.

About ten meters past, and offset to one side, the inward-facing Posleen guard seemed likewise to be dozing.

Carefully, oh sooo carefully, Benjamin emplaced the claymore onto the ground. He had tried forcing the pointed legs down into the frozen soil but with no success. Instead, separating those legs to form two shallow upside down Vs, he simply laid it on the ground, twisted his head to bring an eye behind it and fiddled until he had a proper sight picture.

Fifty or sixty meters to either side of Benjamin, the other two men of his party did more or less likewise. When they were finished with the first claymores, the other two crawled further out and emplaced the second, aiming for additional pairs of Posleen guards. Benjamin saved the last claymore for a rainy, or even a foggy, day.

All crawled back as soon as they were finished. The claymore's scant sixteen meters of wire did not suffice for the Israelis to meet at a common point. Trying to daisy chain the claymores, or to link them with detonating cord for central control, Benjamin had deemed an exercise in foolishness, given the nearness of the enemy. Instead, during weary rehearsals conducted earlier in the day, Benjamin had measured the time from separation to emplacement to retreat to firing position. This he had then doubled for safety and added fifty percent to for a bit more safety. Thus, each man had one and one half hours from separation to be returned and ready for firing.

When his watch told him the allotted time had passed, Benjamin lifted his own small radio to his face and queried, "Rosenblum? Machine gun?"

"There is a human radio transmission coming from one hundred and fifty-seven measures to the southeast," the tenar beeped.

"Wha? What!" The Kessentai was awake in a flash, though true alertness and rational thought would take longer. Checking his instruments first to confirm, he took over control of his tenar from the autopilot to which he had delegated it. For a brief moment, the tenar stood motionless in the sky.

"Here," answered Sergeant Rosenblum.

"Take your best shot," said Benjamin, over the radio.

"Wilco," the sergeant answered, settling into final firing position and confirming that his sights were set on the now-motionless God King's chest. His finger took up the slack in the trigger quickly. Then the sergeant continued applying the steady pressure taught to him long ago in a Negev desert sniper course.

The explosion, when it came, came as a surprise.

❖   ❖   ❖

The God King, just coming to full alertness, felt a horrid jolt that ran from one side of its body to the other and sent waves of shock and pain across its torso. It kept to its feet for the moment, but just barely. Twisting its head to look down at the side from which it thought the first shock had come, the Kessentai was surprised to see a small hole gushing yellow blood. Turning the other way the God King was shocked to see a plate the size of a double fist torn roughly from that side. The God King felt suddenly sick at the image of the damage wrought on its own body.

Its knees buckling, the mortally wounded Kessentai slumped to the floor of its tenar, whimpering like a nestling plucked from the breeding pens for a light snack. Pilotless, the tenar followed its default programming and settled gently to the ground, its bulk causing the frozen grass and soil to crunch below it.

As soon as the sound of Rosenblum's shot carried to him, the waiting Benjamin gave his "clacker," the detonator for the claymore, a quick squeeze followed by another.

The first squeeze had been sufficient however, as it was in almost every case. A small jolt of electricity raced the short distance down the wire to the waiting blasting cap. This, tickled into life, exploded with sufficient power—heat and shock—to detonate its surrounding load of Composition Four plastic explosive.

The C-4 shattered the resin plate containing the ball bearings. Though these did not entirely separate, indeed at least one piece that took off down range consisted of thirteen ball bearings still entrapped together, not less than three hundred projectiles of varying weight and shape were launched.

The near Posleen had its two front legs torn off almost instantly and took further missiles in its torso. It fell to its face. The slightly farther one, facing inward, was struck by one missile in its haunches and another two in its neck. Both shrieked with surprise and pain. The further Posleen took off, bleeding, at a gallop.

From either side of Benjamin came two more explosions. He could only hope that those claymores did their work well.

Little Maria Walewska, eleven years old, was trying to sleep, fitfully, against her mother's warmth. The girl was not awakened by the sound of the alien's flying machine, whining down to rest about twenty meters away, nor even by the distance muffled shot that was the cause of that.

Instead, it was the five distinct flashing explosions that came from the other side of the guarded human "encampment" that brought her from her fitful sleep.

Maria turned her little head in the direction of the explosions, but could see nothing. Something, *many* things, passed overhead, sounding like a flight of angered bees.

Then she heard the screaming of her guards as the bees descended to strike.

"Human soldiers!" Benjamin screamed repeatedly as he ran forward, submachine gun at the ready. He had his doubts that the words would be understood, was pretty sure—in fact—that they would not be, since they were spoken in Hebrew. But, understood or not, surely the Poles could distinguish human speech from alien and draw the correct conclusion.

Benjamin's first burst of fire went into the nearest of the Posleen guards, the one missing both legs. Its head came apart in a blooming flower of yellow bone, teeth and blood.

To either side of Benjamin the two other Israeli soldiers likewise screamed as they ran. They, too, fired at any Posleen they crossed, seemingly dead or seemingly hale.

It was called, "taking no chances."

"Let's take our chances and run for it," shouted a standing Pole. Without waiting for encouragement the Pole took off to the north. He had not run a dozen meters before one of the guard's railgun rounds exploded his chest. That example was enough to make all who saw fall to the ground and cling tight to Mother Earth.

Nestled against the earth, as soon as Rosenblum saw the God King's body reel from his shot and the sled begin to settle he turned his attention to other, still-standing, Posleen. Automatically, his right hand stroked the straight pull bolt to chamber another round. The machine gun team, engaging from Rosenblum's left front, was bowling over the Posleen on that side of the encampment. Many of them, he saw, acted as if they had been wounded and stunned. Despite their erratic movements, the machine gun team scythed them down.

"Well, volume of fire is *their* mission, after all," Rosenblum muttered. "But precision is *mine*."

Whereupon, the sergeant settled his sights "precisely" upon a Posleen guard, then lifting its weapon to shoot at the Poles.

Maria and her mother stared helpless, wide-eyed, and open-mouthed as one of their captors, one already bleeding from a roughly torn hole in its chest, lifted its weapon to spray them. They kept that stare even as the Posleen was struck again by something that traveled with a sharp, menacing crack overhead.

Taking a .338 Lapua from straight on, the alien was thrown back on its haunches, dead in that instant.

Benjamin stopped not an instant while donating a staggering, disoriented, alien a killing burst from his submachine gun. Still shouting "Human soldiers!" at the top of his lungs, he soon reached the edge of the cluster of humans at the center of the encampment. From here on out, he knew, he would have to control his fire more carefully. He shouted out as much to dimly perceived Israelis to either side of him.

Reaching the center of the human circle, Benjamin heard one more crack pass overhead—Sergeant Rosenblum in action. The line of tracers the machine gun had been drawing across his front on the far side of the Poles suddenly ceased. Benjamin looked around frantically for other signs of alien resistance but saw none.

He queried into his radio, "Any of them left?"

The radio answered, "Rosenblum here. I see none standing. . . . Machine gun team. I think we got them all. . . . Bar Lev here . . . none standing . . . Tal . . . scratch one last on this side." Benjamin heard a final burst, Tal's last victim, off to his right.

He issued a final command, "Perimeter security . . . Rosenblum come on down," before settling, exhausted, on his weary, black-clad, Israeli ass.

Under the moonlight, a little blond Polish girl stood before him, her hand outstretched as if wanting to touch her deliverer, though fearing to.

Benjamin smiled and took the girl's hand. Then he stood, picking the girl up, and called out, again in Hebrew unintelligible to the Poles, "To whom does this little girl belong?"

Maria's mother, though still in a degree of shock, came over and took her from Benjamin. She turned away, briefly, before turning back with a sob and throwing her arms around her Hebrew deliverer. Benjamin patted the woman, in no very intimate way, before disengaging.

Rosenblum, his sniper rifle slung, stood on the deck of the grounded tenar. "We've got a live one here," he announced, unslinging the rifle. "Firing one round."

"Wait," ordered Benjamin, not quite certain as to why he hesitated. Possibly he just wanted to see one of the hated invaders in agony. He threaded his way among the mostly still-prostrate Poles; then joined the sergeant at the alien's sled.

Looking down he saw a badly, almost certainly mortally, wounded God King, leaking its life's blood out onto the deck. The alien moaned, eyes open but poorly focused. From somewhere on the sled itself came the chittering, squealing, snarling and grunting sounds Benjamin presumed to be the aliens' tongue.

"Pity the creature doesn't speak Hebrew, or we Posleen," Rosenblum observed.

At that the tenar's grunting and squealing redoubled for something over a minute. When it subsided the machine announced, "I can now."

It was too late, and the exhaustion of combat too profound, for Benjamin to be surprised at this. It had been a war of wonders all along, after all.

Instead he asked of the alien machine, "What is this one saying?"

"The philosopher Meeringon is asking you in the name of the Path and the Way to end his suffering."

"Philosopher?" Benjamin queried. "Ah, never mind." He thought for a minute or two before continuing, "Tell this one we will grant his request . . . for a price."

The Israeli waited while the machine translated. " 'The demand of price for boon is within the Way,' Meeringon says."

"Good. Ask Meeringon, 'Why?' "

The body of the mercifully killed God King cooled beside the tenar; Benjamin had been as good as his word.

"Go back to the boat," he ordered Rosenblum. "The machine says it will carry you without problem. Once there use the boat to get to the friendly side. Don't risk trying to cross on this machine; they'll blast you out of the sky on sight. When you get there, find someone higher up than me. Pass the word of what the Posleen have in store. Set up a retrieval for these civilians if you possibly can. We should be along in a couple of days."

"Sir, you really should be going, not me. You can explain this better."

Benjamin took a look at Maria and her mother, then swept his gaze across the other Poles. "Sometimes, Sergeant, one really must lead from the rear. Now go."

Just my fucking luck, thought Rosenblum, standing in the freezing fog in a trench on the Niesse's western bank. *Just my luck to run into these fucks.* Though he shared the basis of the uniform with the German SS, he did not share a language and felt an almost genetic hatred of them.

Still, he had to admit the bastards were polite, sharing their food and cigarettes with the half-frozen Jew with the Mogen David on his collar rather than their own *Sigrunen*. Another SS-wearing man entered the trench. The Germans seemed both pleased and anxious to see the man appear from the fog.

Thus, unable to communicate with the Germans, Rosenblum was surprised when he heard the new arrival say, in perfect Hebrew with just a trace of accent, "My name is Colonel Hans Brasche, Sergeant. What news have you from the other side?"

INTERLUDE

All along the front the fighting had died down. Only at the river's edge in Mainz was there any appreciable combat action, a steady stream of reinforcing men and aliens butchering each other among the ruins. In part this was due to separation of the combatants by the River Rhine's broad swift stream. More of it was due to simple exhaustion, and the gathering of what strength remained for the final battle.

On the west bank, the Posleen put much of their strength into building simple rafts of wood to be towed across by the tenar of their God Kings. Along the eastern bank, the Germans and what remained of European forces under their command worked frantically in the winter-frozen soil to create a new defense in depth for the anticipated assault.

On the other side of Mainz from the river, thresh and captured threshkreen were gathered in a mass. All along the Rhine, smaller groupings of thresh were gathered outside of artillery or patroling range, one group behind each planned crossing point.

Only three bridges remained undestroyed over the great river. To the north stood one, guarded by the fortress Ro'moloristen called, after the human practice, "Eben Emael." To the south, at the German reclaimed city of Strasburg, old fortresses held the People at bay. In the center, at Mainz where human and Posleen remained locked in a death grip, the bridges also stood.

Ro'moloristen had gifted his chieftain with a different stratagem for each.

CHAPTER 17

Headquarters, Commander in Chief–West, Wiesbaden, Germany, 1 February 2008

The twenty-year-old-appearing Mühlenkampf did not quite catch the self-imposed irony. *Ten years ago*, he thought, *selling used cars at the sprightly age of ninety-eight, I would have enjoyed this. Now I am just too old.*

For the word had come down, from the *Kanzler* through his chief of staff, *Generalfeldmarschall* Kurt Seydlitz, that the former CiNC–West was deposed and that he, Mühlenkampf, was to relinquish command to his own exec and assume control of the battle in the west.

Mühlenkampf, personally, thought this unfair. The former commander had held the Siegfried line inviolate for longer than anyone should have expected. That this defensive belt had ultimately fallen was due to nothing more than the sheer weight of numbers the alien enemy had thrown against it. Further, the new field marshal doubted he—or anyone—could have done any better.

In deference to his new position, Mühlenkampf had relinquished his SS uniform and donned the less ornate but more traditional field gray of the *Bundeswehr*. Gone were his *Sigrunen*, gone his black dress.

Well, no matter. My old comrades have their symbols back; their pride, traditions and dignity restored. What does it matter to me? I wore the field gray for many years before I joined das Schwarze Korps.

Rolf, the aide de camp, interrupted Mühlenkampf's reveries. "Field Marshal, you have an appointment in half an hour, at the field hospital for *Charlemagne*."

There were no longer enough French soldiers left to keep the hospital filled. Instead, German wounded were being sent for what care and restoration could be provided. Some wore field gray, others the black of the SS. Isabelle found she did not much see a difference. They bled the same color, the same color as had the French soldiers she had cared for. Some wept with pain while others bit through their own tongues to keep from crying out. Perhaps the black-clad ones wept a tiny bit less, but if so she could not perceive much difference.

The sufferer was the age of her own son, Thomas—fifteen or perhaps sixteen at most. Black clad he was, with a black-and-silver Iron Cross already glittering by his pillow. Below that pillow the boy's body stopped about two feet short of where it should have.

Some *Boche* high muckity muck had come by that morning and pinned it by the legless boy. Isabelle had understood not one word that had been spoken, though she had seen the beginnings of tears in the too-young *Boche* general's eyes.

She barely understood the semi-intelligible moans of the boy now. Only, "*Mutti, Mutti,*" came through clearly.

Well, so what if he wears black? My own son does now, too. Am I to hate him for that?

The boy was by far the worst on the ward. None of the doctors expected him to live. And his cries for his mother touched the Frenchwoman's heart. She picked up a stool and sat down beside him, taking his hand in her own.

Once or twice during the night the boy's eyes opened. Yet the eyes were unfocused, he knew not where he was. He only knew he was in pain and that he wanted his mother to stop it. She whispered to him what little German she knew, stroking his fever-wracked face.

Just before sunrise the boy's eyes opened for a final time. This last time they focused. Clearly, though in high school French, he said, "Thank you, *madame*. Thank you for taking my own mother's place."

In Isabelle's hand the boy's hand went limp as the eyes lost their focus for the final time.

❖   ❖   ❖

Weary with fatigue, Thomas De Gaullejac found it difficult to keep his eyes open, let alone in focus. Tracers flying over Mainz still scarred the night, leaving further imprints on his retinae and making focus more difficult still. Lack of sleep and catch-as-catch-can rations did not help matters.

Across the river, as Thomas knew from Sergeant Gribeauval, Mainz' last defenders were preparing to cross before their last line of retreat, the sole remaining bridge, was cut. Already, all the wounded practical to carry had been brought back by bridge or ferry. What would happen to the others, those too badly hurt to move, he did not care to think about.

But his own possible futures the boy *had* to consider. "Sergeant?"

"Yes, boy," Gribeauval answered without taking his night vision goggles away from the firing port from which he scanned the river below and the air above that.

"Sergeant . . . if I am hit . . . and you must leave me behind . . . ?"

"Don't worry about it, son," said the sergeant, understanding immediately. "We'll leave nothing behind for the aliens."

Thomas felt a little rush of relief. At least his body would not become mere food. "Thank you. One other thing?"

"Yes?"

"My mother, Isabelle De Gaullejac? Could you let her know? At least try to find her?"

Gribeauval answered honestly. "Son, I can't promise to be alive to promise that."

The frigid bunker congealed for a while in silence, while Gribeauval continued to scan.

"Sergeant?"

"Yes, Volunteer De Gaullejac?" answered Gribeauval, just a trace of irritation tainting his voice.

"I thought I should let you know; if it falls to me to do so, I am not sure I can drop the bridge with people on it."

"Son, if you don't drop that bridge at the first sign of aliens on it, I'll shoot you myself," Gribeauval said. Then, relenting a bit, he continued, "Do you think that any people that might be on the bridge would not prefer a clean quick death to blast, fall or frozen river to being turned into a snack?"

"I honestly don't know, Sergeant. I doubt I can speak for all of them."

Tiger Anna, *Oder-Niesse Line, 1 February 2008*

Hans had moved his command vehicle forward to the water's edge to ensure that Benjamin and his charges made it across the river in safety. He had also moved a battalion of self-propelled 155-millimeter guns to a position far enough forward to provide support for Benjamin for the last part of the trip back. He was unwilling to order men to cross over, given the fate that had befallen most of the patrols sent forward. Nonetheless, a company of the Brigade Michael Wittmann had volunteered to cross over with rubber boats to help the Poles back.

Though the artillery battalion had been in almost constant employment, Benjamin had managed to bring out better than four fifths of the civilians he had rescued. These were even now heading for a safe place in the rear. Benjamin, naturally, and his three remaining men—Tal had bought it to a random railgun round—were the last to leave. Exhausted, filthy and starved, they were simply carried to the waiting boats by the company that covered the retrieval. The SS men rowed the Jews back.

Of the four remaining Jews, Benjamin was the first one out of the water. He was met at the shore by Brasche and Sergeant Rosenblum, the two taking turns slapping the major's back and shaking his hand.

"Oh, *excellent* job, David!" Hans exclaimed, pumping the Israeli's hand. The Jew was too worn to do more than nod his head in thanks and submit to the fierce handshake. Some corner of his mind perhaps found amusement in the scene, the SS and the Mogen David meeting in friendship at the front. Mostly though, Benjamin's mind and body wanted only a warm, soft bed, some decent food, and perhaps a stiff drink.

He might have added to that wish list, "And a woman," but little Maria's mother had made it clear enough, without words, that one woman, at least, was his for the asking. He thought he might just take her up on the offer made by her soft brown eyes, perhaps at some time in the not too distant future.

He managed to croak out his wish list to Brasche.

With a smirk Brasche brushed aside Benjamin's immediate concerns. "Soon enough, my friend, soon enough. But you are a hero to three nations today and so, before you get to trundle off to your bed a little ceremony is in order."

Benjamin raised a hand in protest but that too Brasche brushed off. "*Achtung*," he ordered to the two dozen smiling men assembled. "Yes, you too, Major."

Reluctantly, and maybe a bit shyly too, Benjamin stood to attention.

Conversationally, Hans mentioned, in German for all those assembled to hear, "It is not well known, you know, but the first Iron Cross won in the First World War was won by a German Jew. Sergeant Rosenblum, publish the orders."

Rosenblum spoke just enough German to struggle through the recital, "In the name of the *Kanzler* of the German Republic, and by order of the Commander in Chief, Eastern Front, for conspicuous gallantry in action, and for the saving of human life . . . the Iron Cross, First Class, is presented to Major David Benjamin, Brigade Judas Maccabeus, German Federal Armed Forces."

As Hans, smiling broadly, hung the simple, traditional medal around the Israeli's neck, he spoke quietly, in Hebrew, "I could have given you the Second Class on my own authority . . . but I thought what you have done deserved a bit more. And, with the information you sent back, the Field Marshal agreed."

David whispered back, "What are we going to do about the enemy's plans?"

Still smiling, for what else was there to do, Hans answered, "My friend, we have not the first fucking clue."

Watching on *Anna*'s forward view-screen, and listening with her electronic ears, Krueger simply could not believe his commander's heresy. *Stupid, clueless, Yid-loving bastard,* he fumed. *Traitor to the Fatherland and the* Führer's *memory. Bad enough you saved the kike, but decorating him? For saving some fucking* Untermensch *Slavs? It reeks.*

The world would be a better place without either of them, the Pollocks or the Yids. And if it cost the lives of nine out of ten Germans to make the world so, the price would be fair.

Krueger would have been appalled to learn that, at the level of core philosophy, he, the Nazi fanatic, and Günter Stössel, the Reddish Green fanatic, were not so far apart after all.

Berlin, Germany, 1 February 2008

Everyone in Germany, from the chancellor on down, was pale with the weak winter sun. Even so, thought the chancellor, *Günter looks palest of all.*

"Prison life does not agree with you, I see," commented the chancellor.

"Life as dictator seems to agree with you fully," retorted his former aide.

The chancellor merely grinned and answered, "Let me see; I am a dictator because I would not let you and yours have your very undemocratic way with the fate of the German people? But you, and they, were not dictatorial even though you wished to flaunt the will of that people and wished to turn most of them over to an alien food processing machine? I must admit that I am at a loss to follow your logic, my former associate."

To that Günter had no answer that did not sound hollow. Instead he retreated into an argument against the hated symbols. "You brought back the SS. That makes you nothing but another Nazi."

"Bah! I resurrected a body of fighting men that we *needed* to survive, my doctrinaire friend. And good service they have done, too. If giving them their symbols back helps them fight one iota better, that it offends such as you seems a very small price to pay."

The chancellor held up a hand to stifle further argument. "In any case, I did not call you here to bicker. I called you here to tell you that although your sentence was death, and a damned just sentence I deem it too, I have decided to commute your sentence to life in prison. But you will live out your days in Spandau Prison, Herr Stössel, you and the other four hundred and forty-seven seriously implicated traitors."

Günter asked simply, "Why?"

"Because I think you are less dangerous, locked away and forgotten, than you might have been as martyrs."

Headquarters, Commander in Chief–West, Wiesbaden, Germany, 2 February 2008

Mühlenkampf could not drive the image of the martyred, legless boy from his mind. *Small recompense it must have been to the lad, even had he been able to understand, that I pinned a medal to his pillow. Small recompense too, to the girl he left behind him or the mother who bore him. Jesus, that is the part that I hate, the broken, crippled, dead and dying innocents that war takes.*

I wish I didn't love it so much, or feel like such a damned cheat that it is always the poor boys who suffer and die while I get away scot-free.

Still thinking upon the dying boy, Mühlenkampf mused upon a different kind of world, a different kind of war. *Wouldn't it be nice if only the real professionals, people like me, were the ones who fought and died? Ah, but would the politicians abide by the battlefield's decision? Hah! Not a chance. As soon as they saw their own oh-so-precious hides at stake they'd be grabbing young ones like* Gefreiter[47] *Webber off the street and tossing them into the meat grinder.*

The general shrugged. He hadn't made the world the way it was. And it would not be one whit better for his dreams or for his pretending it was other than it was, either.

In his dream Thomas was little again. But little seemed no bad thing, not when one was warm and safe and pressed to his mother's breasts. He had a full belly and the rosy glow of a glass of wine coursing through his veins. Life was good.

Outside of Thomas' dream, however, life was one continuous nightmare of deprivation, hardship, and mind-numbing terror. The rare dreams now, stolen when he was able to catch some even more rare uninterrupted sleep, were all that remained to him of the lost world of . . . before.

The world of "now," however, intruded on Thomas' pleasant foray into the past. Stealthy as a cat, a new level of cold crept through his thin blanket, nibbling and biting at his consciousness, gnawing at his dream.

Thomas awakened with a shivering start.

❖   ❖   ❖

Mühlenkampf, despite his heated headquarters, shivered himself.

Before him stood his staff meteorologist and his intelligence officer. Both looked as serious as they might have at their mother's own funeral.

"We still have stations in Scandinavia," explained the meteorologist. "And the Americans are still sending us data from Greenland. Iceland, too, reports confirming data. We are going into a deep freeze like we haven't seen in fifty years."

The general nodded, calmly, even tried to keep a confident gleam in his eye. "Will the Rhein freeze over?"

"Yes, likely, sir," answered the meteorologist. "Within ten days at most. And yes, sir, it will freeze solid enough to support the weight of enemy bodies."

"On the plus side, sir, the cold will not support either fog or snow, so if the aliens attack we will have clear fields of fire."

"And that was what *I* wanted to talk to you about, sir," said the intelligence man. "Clear fields of fire are all well and good, but we have this rather frightening report from CInC East...."

Tiger Anna, *Oder-Niesse Line, 2 February 2008*

Hans still maintained, as he so often did, his lonely vigil atop *Anna*'s turret. This night was lonelier than most.

No fog today, so the reports say. No fog and the enemy on the other side is just waiting for daylight. Scheisse!

But cursing fate did Hans no good. Fate was as it was, he knew. In the dim mists of time some meddlers at godhood had played genetic games with a subordinate species. That species had resisted in time and been driven forth. Eventually it had reemerged into the Galaxy, spreading death and destruction across a path that the meddling had made inevitable.

The path had led that enemy species here. Here they had been thrashed enough, and badly enough, that they were forced to think for a change. They had thought upon their problems; they had seen a possible answer.

And now, inevitably... by fate, that answer was massing on the other side

Some part of Hans accepted fate. Some other part rejected it. A large part just wondered at his own.

Am I then doomed? Is my soul forfeit for the part I once played in a great crime? Are my comrades'? Are those of the men I command?

And tomorrow? What will be the better part, to take the burden of evil upon myself by acting alone or to share it out among those who have no guilt for any past crimes?

Unconsciously, Hans spoke aloud, "Anna, I wish you were here to guide me."

"I am here, *Herr Oberst*," answered the tank.

For some inexplicable reason, Hans didn't want to answer in any way that might offend the *tank*. Yes, he knew it was just a machine. Yes, he knew it was not so sophisticated as the Galactics' AIDs. Yet, *Anna* the tank had been home all the long months of this war. He felt she had a spirit of her own, even if she could not articulate it. He had felt as much for the panzers that had carried him though so much of the last war, and they not only couldn't talk, they couldn't even heat coffee.

"*Anna*," he asked, "what am I to do tomorrow?"

The tank answered, "My programmers would have called that one a 'no-brainer,' *Herr Oberst*. As you always have, you must do your best."

Down below, in the battle cocoon, a jubilant Krueger poured schnapps for the rest of the crew. "A great day coming tomorrow, my boys, a great day."

The crew accepted the schnapps. Facing what they soon must, how could they not? But not one of them shared the sergeant major's plain elation.

"How can you do it, Sergeant Major? How can you just . . ." Harz turned away in disgust.

Krueger answered, "Ask Schultz here if it is so hard. Ask him what he felt kicking the barrel out from under that coward at Giessen. It is nothing, boys, nothing. Why I remember a place called 'Babi Yar' . . . in the Ukraine, by Kiev, that was . . ."

The setting sun illuminated the golden onion domes of the great city to the southeast. Kiev, once home to one hundred and seventy-five thousand Jews, would see that population reduced by over thirty-three thousand in the course of two days.

Little seven-year-old Manya Halef, holding her mother's hand, turned around from time to time as they walked. The golden domes looked very pretty, very wonderful in a little girl's eyes.

Manya wasn't sure why she and her mother had to leave their cramped Kiev flat. But she had seen the Germans and—much like her stern-faced teacher in school—they looked like men who had to be obeyed.

Sometimes, as they walked, Manya's mother would pull the girl to her and cover her eyes. At first Manya resisted but, once she had seen what her mother was shielding her from, she sought her mother's shelter. The road to the Jewish cemetery at the junction of Melnikovsky and Dokhturov Streets was lined with bodies of the dead.

Manya had been along this road before, twice. The first time she didn't remember very well. But the last time had been to bury her ancient grandmother, here in Kiev's old Jewish cemetery.

While cleaning his machine pistol, Krueger watched the Jews being herded into the makeshift, barbed-wire-surrounded camp dispassionately. What cared he for their cries? What cared he for their miserable whining? Were they not all enemies of the Reich? Did they not all deserve to die?

Less dispassionately, he watched them strip. Though the Jews had been instructed to come well clothed and with money in their possession, as if for travel, he knew they would not need clothing or money where they were going. It was a useful little lie designed to make them easier to dispose of.

The ad hoc strip show had Krueger's rapt attention. A few of them Jew whores are lookers, he thought. Shame we can't get some use out of them.

Manya just didn't understand it. Here was Mama, always so proper Mama, taking her clothes off here in the open. It was just wrong, wrong, wrong and Manya knew it.

And then—unthinkable!—Mama began tugging at Manya's own clothing, a short, light summer dress. The little girl resisted until someone came by and hit Mama with a stick for being too slow. Then, her face leaking tears, Manya submitted.

But she still didn't understand; she was only seven years old.

✧   ✧   ✧

The fucking Yids have no clue yet what is going to happen to them, *Krueger chortled to himself.* You would think that taking away everything would have been hint enough. But no, they are still in denial, can't believe it is happening. Stupid pieces of shit; be a blessing to the world to rid it of them.

With a click, Krueger seated a full magazine into his Schmeisser.

Manya promised the Germans that she would be a good girl. She promised! *So she could not understand why they were hitting her and her mother to drive them from the camp. Nor did she understand the two lines of soldiers wielding sticks who drove them forward.*

Her mother tried to protect her from the blows as best she could. Even so, sometimes the soldiers hit her. And she had promised, *too. Maybe the sticks wouldn't hurt so much if only she'd still had her clothes on.*

But she *didn't and* they *did and she just didn't understand it at all.*

All she could do was cry.

The Jewish whore wanted to keep her brat with her, did she? Well, orders were orders and Krueger was a man who obeyed orders. The Jews were to be shot in groups of ten, not eleven. He rudely pulled the squalling naked brat out of the harridan's arms, tossed it to the ground, and then spent a few moments to cuff and kick them both into submission.

Manya was stunned by the German's blow as even being forced to undress in public had not stunned her. She sat naked on the bloody ground crying for her mother; a little girl's wordless, endless, wrenching cry. The mother too wept and shrieked.

The squalling brat's noise was irksome. Nonetheless, Krueger enjoyed the mother's shrieks as he raised the machine pistol and, like the professional he was . . . smiling, squeezed the trigger.

"That will be enough, Sergeant Major," said Hans as he placed a firm grip on Dieter's shoulder. "The men will be sickened enough as it is. There's no need for you to sicken them further."

"Yes, sir," answered Krueger, will ill-concealed contempt. "They're just fucking Slavs, after all. It isn't like they're *real* people. I thought the boys should know that."

"Shut up, Sergeant Major," said Hans, eyes flashing and one hand resting on his pistol. "Just shut the fuck up."

The combat cocoon was silent now, as was that of every Tiger along the front, of every other armored vehicle, and every infantryman's trench or bunker. Each soldier, German or Polish or Scandinavian—or on one other front, French—was left alone with his thoughts.

Equally alone, Dieter Schultz pondered on the morrow. He had killed countless nonhumans, and as part of an execution party, one human being.

After many weeks and months of thought, Dieter still didn't know how he felt about that. At the time it had seemed . . . right, somehow. Later on, he had begun to question.

Truthfully, Dieter didn't know what was right anymore. War . . . twisted things, made things inconceivable become real and present. Did that poor bastard of a panzer grenadier deserve to hang? Maybe not. But had what he deserved had anything to do with anything? Again, maybe not.

What was reality? Gudrun was dead. The panzer grenadier was dead. That was reality. There was no sense in wishing that things were any different, no sense in living an illusion.

And tomorrow, Dieter knew, his last illusions would be stripped. Tomorrow he would enter the ranks of the real Nazis, the murderers.

Tiger Brünnhilde, *Hanau, Germany, 2 February 2008*

"Driver Johann?"

"Yes Indowy Rinteel?" Mueller was so tall that the Indowy had generally avoided him to date. Perhaps it was that he was lying on his driver's couch, bringing his eyes down to Indowy level, that made conversation possible now. Then again, that every other member of the crew was sound asleep may have had something to do with it.

"I have read your history, particularly from the last of your centuries. And I do not understand it at all."

Mueller sighed. "Rinteel . . . neither do we."

The little furry alien went silent then, and turned as if to leave.

"Wait, Rinteel," Mueller said. "What part of our history don't you understand?"

The Indowy turned back to face Mueller, lying on his couch. "Those humans you call 'Jews'? What made them the enemy? Why and how did they deserve what your people gave to them?"

Again, Mueller sighed. How to answer such a question?

"Rinteel, to this very day every German bright and knowledgeable enough to be entitled to an opinion goes to bed every night wondering the same thing. The Assyrians murdered cities . . . but at least they had a reason. Marcus Licinius Crassus crucified six thousand slaves along the Appian way . . . but at least he had a reason. The Mongols killed twenty million Chinese to make grazing grounds for their horses . . . but at least that was a reason. But the Jews?"

Mueller stopped for a moment. The very insanity of his country's history weighed down upon his shoulders.

"Rinteel, when we spent a generation getting ready for our *First* World War, our spiritual poet was a man named Ernst Lissauer. He wrote a poem called "*Hassgesang gegen Engeland*," a Song of Hate against England, rousing Germany's sons to what he thought was their true enemy. Rinteel, Ernst Lissauer was a German Jew.

"When we rolled across the Belgian frontier, in 1914, and our soldiers were slaughtered in droves trying to storm the fortresses, the first man to win an Iron Cross for bravery in battle was a German Jew.

"When Adolf Hitler was recommended by his lieutenant for the Iron Cross, the officer recommending him was a Jew.

"They gave of their blood and they gave of their hearts. They fell in battle in droves for their 'German Fatherland.' Ten *thousand* of them fell in battle, Rinteel . . . giving all they had to give for what they thought of as their country. Rinteel, ten times that many served. More than the national average. They *were* us.

"And so, Indowy Rinteel, it is as if God used us, we Germans, to some purpose of his own . . . but we just don't *know*."

The Indowy digested that . . . thought upon the foolishness . . . thought upon the pain in Mueller's voice. Finally he said, "It was a madness then."

Mueller agreed. "Yes Rinteel, it was a madness."

PART V

INTERLUDE

Ro'moloristen thought, *What a magnificent madness is the Path of Fury.* Stretching across the horizon to north and south as far as the God King could see from his lofty tenar, marched wave upon wave of the People.

They marched in knots of twenty to fifty, each knot carrying by main strength a crudely lashed together wooden raft. Half the forests of France and Belgium had gone into those rafts.

Above rode the God Kings, in numbers even greater than the leading ranks of the People warranted. But from each tenar dangled a rope. The tenar would pull the rafts, and drag the People across the river to victory. The plasma cannon and hypervelocity missiles carried by the tenar flashed fire and hate at the defenders on the other side of the great river which fronted the host.

The cannon of the threshkreen were not silent. Even at this distance the thunder of thousands upon thousands of the thresh's frightful artillery was a palpable fist. Their shells splashed down among the People, churning them to yellow froth and splintering their crude rafts.

But always there were more of the People, more of the rafts approaching the river. The artillery could kill many. It could never kill all. Slowly, the People, stepping over the bodies of the slain, reached the near bank of the river.

Ro'moloristen watched the first rank, what remained of it, disappear down into the steep river valley. He knew the People would have a nightmare of a time descending that frozen bank.

But after that, Ro'moloristen expected things to be easier for them . . . once the threshkreen on the far bank saw that lashed to each raft, upright on posts, were anywhere from a half a dozen to a dozen thresh nestlings.

CHAPTER 18

Tiger Anna, Oder-Niesse Line, 3 February 2008

The pit of Hans' stomach was a leaden brick. *Anna's* view-screen told the entire crew more than they wished to know. The Posleen horde advanced to the shallow and now frozen river . . . and about half of the aliens carried or prodded ahead of it a human captive.

Though the aliens and their captives were in easy range, few human defenders—and those mostly the snipers—fired upon them. Here and there Hans saw a Posleen stumble and fall, its chest or head ruined by a well-placed bullet.

There were none of the aliens' flying sleds in the air. Those, Hans was sure, the defenders would have engaged gleefully, even as the snipers shot down any Posleen to which they had a clean shot.

But it makes not a shit of difference, killing those few. Their numbers are, effectively, endless. And their most powerful weapons today are their captives.

Schultz, sitting below Hans' command chair trembled, the commander saw. Glancing around the battle cocoon, Hans saw that everyone in view, from Harz to the operations officer, looked sick. Harz kept saying, over and over, "Oh, the bastards; the dirty, stinking, miserable bastards."

My boys can't do it. They shouldn't have to do it. We never made them that kind of soldier. Shit.

291

"Dieter, sit back from the gun. *Anna*, commander's gun." Relieved beyond words, Schultz sat back from the sight immediately.

"Yes, *Herr Oberst*," the tank replied. From above, a gunner's suite, almost exactly like Schultz's, descended to encase Brasche.

"Sergeant Major Krueger, take control of the bow guns. All others be on watch for enemy flyers but do not engage. Sergeant Major, engage at will."

With a smile, Krueger began raking the mixed formation of humans and enemy. "Fucking Slav untermensch," he whispered. In the view-screen, men, women and children were ripped apart even as were the Posleen. The only difference was that the human's cries could be more readily understood.

The sound was more than Hans could bear. It was as terrifying as the sergeant major's glee, and even more hurtful. "*Anna*, kill external microphones. Operations, pass the word to the other Tigers: only *old* SS will engage. New men are not to fire upon the horde except in point self-defense."

Seeing that the operations officer understood, Hans commanded, "Load antipersonnel. Prepare for continuous antipersonnel."

The loader pressed the required buttons. From *Anna*'s ammunition rack hydraulics withdrew a single canister cartridge and fed it to the gun.

Tiger Brünnhilde, *Hanau, Germany, 3 February 2008*

"Feed it to them, Reinhard, feed it to the bastards."

"Hit!" announced Schlüssel, as a small new sun formed and deformed thirty kilometers up.

"Mueller, hard right."

Even held securely as he was by his straps, Rinteel felt the sudden, jarring turn as the driver twisted the tank and raced forward to get out of the expected Posleen riposte. As always, the Indowy was terrified speechless. As always, he was disgusted at the slaughter his human comrades were inflicting upon the Posleen when he allowed himself to think upon it.

And yet . . . and yet . . . familiarity had dulled the fear. The disgust was severe still, but not the paralyzing force it had been. It was a remarkable thing to the Indowy, to be not so afraid as the situation warranted. More remarkable still was it to be less disgusted by the slaughter his mind envisioned. He was finding he could face both fear of dying and fear of killing a bit better than he had ever imagined.

And, too, Rinteel was discovering that he could kill, *had* killed, vicariously and without any moral dilemma. After all, though it was the crew that fired the gun, it was he, Rinteel, who made sure that gun was in full operating order. And he thought, *And though it is the humans who actually fight the Posleen; it is we, the Indowy, who build them the weapons to fight with. How pure we think ourselves, how above the blood and slaughter. Yet that slaughter would be impossible without us. A foolish people mine, to think that distance from murder turns it into something besides murder.*

Tiger *Anna, Oder-Niesse Line, 3 February 2008*

God, I was a soldier, not a murderer. Do you hate me so much then, that even this *sin I must commit.*

Hans' loader, eyes fixed on the screen before him, announced, "Up!"

Through his helmet's VR, Hans looked upon the frozen-over river. He could see that Krueger's bow guns were having an effect. He could also see that effect was not enough.

Hans' vision fixated on a screaming little blond Polish girl held firmly in the grasp of an alien.

Look at the little girl, Brasche. You have killed hundreds of people in your life, maybe thousands. You tried to think they were all armed enemies. Yes, on how many villages did your fire fall, villages containing little girls like that one? On how many did you call artillery? For how many did the armored spearheads of which you were a part open the way for the Einsatzgruppen? You are already a murderer ten thousand times over.

What are a few thousand more, after all?

Hans thought, *Anna, forgive me. If this causes me never to come to you, forgive me please.* Hans' finger pressed the firing stud.

Wiesbaden, Germany, 3 February 2008

Thomas' hand hesitated over the detonator. He could see the bridge. He could see, too, the horde of aliens crossing on it. But he could also see and hear the mass of French civilians the aliens drove among and ahead of them. Again and again the young French soldier tried to force his hand to complete the circuit. Again and again he failed.

Nearby, Sergeant Gribeauval fired his rifle at the crossing aliens.

"Damn it, boy, blow the bridge!" he screamed.

The boy stammered, "I . . . I . . . I *can't*, Sergeant."

"*Merde*," the sergeant said. He was barely keeping the leading Posleen away from the wires that connected the detonator with the explosives affixed to the bridge, *just* barely. He couldn't get away from his firing position long enough to set off the charges without risking that those charges would be made ineffective in that time. "Boy, drop the bridge!"

"Sergeant, I am trying . . . but . . ."

Gribeauval turned from the firing position. "*Merde!* Just *do* it!"

Thomas looked at the sergeant, wide-eyed and fearful, just in time to see Gribeauval's head explode from a Posleen railgun round. The boy was flecked with the sergeant's blood and brains. Morally frozen as he had been, his terror left him utterly paralyzed.

And, while the boy was so paralyzed, the leading Posleen tore out the demolition's wiring.

Isabelle trembled with fright. People passed by the field hospital, fleeing to the north. The staff was in turmoil, in a shouting, screaming panic.

The enemy was over the Rhine.

With shaking hand Isabelle made a call to the house she lived in with her son. Briefly, she told her hosts the terrible news, then asked them to see that her boy was dressed and sent to her. They promised they would do so.

Medical orderlies carried away on stretchers those wounded that the doctors thought had some chance. As a truck was filled with wounded it headed away to some unknown destination to the north. Yet the supply of wounded was so much greater than the supply of trucks.

Around her was the din of dozens of moaning, wounded soldiers. A doctor walked among them, announcing, "Routine . . . Urgent . . . *Expectant.*"

That was the dread word: "Expectant." *Expected to die.*

"*Mon dieu*, Doctor, what are we going to do for those poor boys we can't evacuate?"

"We have *hiberzine* for some of them, the ones we might have some small chance of saving," he answered. The doctor's mouth formed a moue. "But we really don't have very much of it. Most will have to be abandoned."

Isabelle went white. "Abandon them? To be *eaten*? My God, no, Doctor. We must do something?"

"What do you suggest *Madame* De Gaullejac?"

"I don't know . . . but something, surely. Oh, my God . . . I don't know."

Then her eyes fell upon a field cabinet she knew contained syringes and various medicines, painkillers mostly.

"There are better ways to die, Doctor, than being eaten, are there not?"

Following her gaze to the cabinet he answered, "There are if you are strong enough. I tell you though, *madame*, I am not."

Tiger Anna, *Oder-Niesse Line, 3 February 2008*

I must be strong, insisted Hans as he fired yet another round of canister into the mixed Posleen-human mass. He found that he was unconsciously unfocusing his eyes to spare himself a clear view of the carnage he had been, and was, causing.

They had changed firing positions three times now, *Anna* and her crew. From each position Hans had sent out two to three canister rounds, each shot effectively obliterating most Posleen and human life from an area of roughly one million square meters.

There had only been so many human shields available to the Posleen along this sector. Once Hans cut those down the infantrymen along the river's edge found they were able to do their jobs. In this sector the attack was being stymied.

But a quick glance at the general situation map told Hans that this was very nearly the only sector where that was true. The red-shaded portions of the display showed that the enemy was already in and among the defending infantry over more than half the front.

Other markers on the display showed Brasche that neutron bombs were being expended wildly. Tens of millions of Posleen, and even some humans, were receiving a dose of radiation that would leave them quaking, puking, shitting, choking and all-too-slowly dying caricatures of living beings within minutes.

And none of it would make any difference. This front was broken . . . and all Hans' murder in vain.

Headquarters, Commander in Chief–West, Wiesbaden, Germany, 4 February 2008

Mühlenkampf spoke into a speaker phone lying on his desk. The Posleen had still not succeeded in inconveniencing the *Bundespost*'s telephone system, though the vicious fighting taking place scant miles to the south did interfere slightly with the conversation.

The field marshal's voice held an utter weariness to match that of his civilian chief. "No, *Herr Kanzler*, there is nothing I can afford to send to reinforce the east. Even with what I have here, I am unlikely to hold. *Herr Kanzler* . . . the demolition on the bridge between Mainz and Wiesbaden *failed*. And the enemy has established several dozen lodgments on this bank besides. They pulled the same trick they used in the east, only crossing under a shield of children here. Most of the men could not shoot . . . *would* not anyway."

"Then *alles ist verloren*?" asked the chancellor. *All is lost?*

"There are still tens of millions of our people, and those of our allies, to save to the north and south, *Herr Kanzler*. And the Army will pay whatever price we must to give you the time to evacuate them to the mountains and the snows. So no, *Herr Kanzler*, all is *not* lost, not while we can save our people."

"I will give the orders, Field Marshal Mühlenkampf. Cover the evacuation as best you can."

While his staff worked on the plans for delaying the Posleen advance and moving the headquarters back, Mühlenkampf thought it a good time to visit the front here in the city. Accompanied by his aide, Rolf, and half a dozen guards he set off in a Mercedes staff car.

People were fleeing afoot, by vehicle, and by bus.

Yet not everyone was fleeing. Mühlenkampf noticed a young soldier, sitting in apparent shock on a set of stairs leading from the sidewalk to a house. The boy's eyes seemed fixed on some spot below the surface of the Earth.

"Stop the car," he ordered.

Once the Mercedes had come to a halt by the side of the street the field marshal exited and then walked the few short steps to stand in front of the boy. He saw the boy could not be more than fifteen, at most, though grime and exhaustion would have made him look older to a less experienced officer. The cuff band on the soldier's winter uniform coat said "Charlemagne."

"What is your name, son?" Mühlenkampf asked in quite good French.

Without looking up from whatever private hell he contemplated, the boy answered, "Thomas De Gaullejac."

"Where is your unit?"

"Dead? Fled? I don't know." Still Thomas did not look up. "I just know my sergeant died. And then I was the only one left. And that I was supposed to blow the bridge and . . . didn't." Low as it was already, with those words Thomas' head hung lower still."

"Aha," said Mühlenkampf. *That is one mystery cleared up.* "Why didn't you detonate the bridge, young man?"

Thomas closed his eyes tightly. "There were people on it . . . men . . . women . . . some children. They could have included my mother and brother. And so I just couldn't. I tried. But my hand wouldn't move. I can fight. I *did* fight. But I couldn't kill all those people. Even though I *tried.*"

The boy began quietly to cry then.

"Damned if I can blame you for that, son," sighed Mühlenkampf. *And what you need right now is a chaplain or a psychiatrist. Possibly both.* "Come with me."

Thomas went along, even though some part of his mind wondered if it was only to attend a quick court-martial and slow hanging.

Nothing in Mühlenkampf's demeanor, though, seemed threatening. The field marshal helped Thomas to his feet and led him to the car. "Rolf, take the car and two guards and see this boy to the nearest field hospital for the Charlemagne Division. Can you find that?"

Rolf consulted a laptop that he never left behind. He answered, "Yes, sir. No problem. There's one about six miles from here. Though traffic may be a little tight."

"That will be fine," said Mühlenkampf. "Meet me back here in ... say ... two hours. The guards have a radio for me to communicate with Headquarters. They and I are going to have a little tour of the front lines."

Wounded were still pouring in from the front. Many were fixed, to the extent they could be fixed, on the spot, before being sent back to the slaughter. Others were marked for evacuation or for being left behind.

To these, as to the others she had previously helped, Isabelle brought syringes filled with a powerful morphiate, a guaranteed overdose. For those who were awake she simply left a syringe. For the unconscious ones with an awake comrade nearby she asked if the comrade would assist.

And then she came to a ward tent holding one lone soldier with no comrades ... and no arms. The soldier was conscious though faint, pale from shock and pain and loss of blood. Even so, he understood instinctively what the woman was offering and understood he could not accept it as offered.

"Can you help me?" he asked, weakly.

Her first instinct was to turn around, pretend she was there on some other business. But that would have been cowardly and she knew it. She walked and stood next to the armless soldier's cot.

He was awake enough, if only just, to read her face and the moral confusion drawn upon it. It was a grave and terrible responsibility she had taken upon herself, a responsibility the soldier did not envy her. He tried to help her as best he could. "*Madame*, I am in great pain. Could you give me something ... ?"

She knew as well as did he the game he was playing, but, since it made her task easier, she played along. "Certainly, young man. I have something for pain right here."

Her finger flicked the needle as the thumb of the opposite

hand forced out any air that the syringe might have contained. Then she stopped as she realized she had never given anyone an injection anywhere but in the arm.

He twisted his head slightly in the opposite direction. "They have been using my neck," he advised.

Isabelle searched for a vein, found it, and forced the hair-thin needle into it. A slight withdrawal of the plunger confirmed she had pierced the vein well, as blood from the vein was drawn into the syringe. She pushed some of the syringe's content into the vein.

And then she stopped pressing. *You cannot do this, Isabelle. This is murder.*

The soldier helped her again. "That feels a little better, *madame*, but I am still in great pain. Could I have some more?"

Again, Isabelle pressed another quarter of the syringe's drug into the vein. But again, she stopped before reaching a fatal dosage.

"I think, *madame*, that I will still be in unbearable pain until you give me all of it."

Isabelle looked deeply into the soldier's eyes. She was not sure if she were looking for confirmation that the soldier wished to die then and there, or confirmation that he did not. The eyes gave no answer; between his injuries and the amount of drug she had already given him, they were simply too dull and blank.

" . . . all of it, *madame*, please? The pain . . ."

Shutting her own eyes then, Isabelle slowly forced the rest of the syringe's contents into the young man's neck. She waited there, eyes closed and unmoving, for several minutes as the horror of what she had done washed over her. When she opened them again and withdrew the needle, she saw that the soldier's eyes had closed, that his breathing had gone shallow. In a few minutes, under Isabelle's gaze, the breathing stopped entirely.

Then, eyes full of tears and heart full of sorrow, she fled, leaving behind the now empty ward tent.

Thomas was not alone in the reception tent of the field hospital, but he was ignored by the people bustling to and fro.

That was fine by him; he wanted to be ignored. He did not want to answer any questions, and he did not want any of the people here or in the city to know it was *his* fault that they had to leave their homes and stations and flee for their lives.

Finally an old noncom stood before him, asking, "Grenadier Thomas De Gaullejac?" Seeing the boy's distant nod, the NCO continued, "We are admitting you on the advice of Field Marshal Mühlenkampf's aide. But we cannot treat you here. The psychiatric section has already displaced to the rear. So, for that matter, has the chaplain. You are to go find yourself space on one of the trucks waiting outside and go with them. Do you understand?"

Wearily Thomas nodded again. Then he stood and walked out of the tent to where the trucks awaited.

Isabelle never even noticed the slump-shouldered, filthy soldier leaving the reception tent as she hurried across it on her way to her own ward. She likely would not have even had her eyes not been tear-filled and swollen with weeping. She had to focus on returning to her own place of work to pick up her youngest boy.

Upon her eldest, Thomas, she refused to think. He was almost certainly lost. The same innocent and sweet son she had raised would never have survived alone in the nightmare their world had become.

Mühlenkampf, his party down to himself, a radio bearer, and a single guard, waited at the same place from which he had dispatched Rolf with the young French boy.

Bad, so bad this situation is. Worse than anything I have ever seen, to include the Russian Front. They are chewing through us even faster than the Russians might have. And I need time.

Mentally, he consulted his order of battle and the placement of every unit down to division level. *Hmmm. Goetz von Berlichingen is close.* Jugend *is close, too, but* Frundsberg *is closer.* Frundsberg *is Panzer . . . almost useless in these quarters . . . while* Jugend *is panzer grenadier. And we have two infantry corps within range.*

Then again, Jugend *has an average age of under seventeen, excluding old SS leadership.*

Reluctantly, Mühlenkampf took the radio from its bearer and called his headquarters. "Give me the 1A," he demanded.

After a wait of a few minutes the radio came back, "*Generalmajor Steinmetz, here, Herr Feldmarschall.*"

"Steinmetz? Mühlenkampf. Pass the warning and prepare the

orders. Twenty-first and Fortieth *Korps*, reinforced by SS Divisions Goetz von Berlichingen and *Jugend* respectively, are to attack, *without* regard to losses, to drive the enemy back from the city of Wiesbaden."

"I can do this, sir, but are you . . ."

"Just do it, Steinmetz."

"As you wish, sir."

Tiger Brünnhilde, *Hanau, Germany, 3 February 2008*

The Indowy Rinteel wished desperately to be somewhere, *anywhere*, but here in this tank, shuddering under repeated hammerings of the Posleen landers that pressed in their attack like nothing Rinteel had ever imagined.

There had been no powerful direct hits of course; Mueller's deliberately spastic driving made a kinetic projectile strike a matter of, so far happy, chance. The near misses rocked the tank viciously, however. The Indowy's body had been bruised, bruises over bruises, with every jolt.

There had been plasma hits, more than a few. Yet *Brünnhilde's* ablative armor had been able, so far, to shrug those off. A quick glance at his damage control screen showed Rinteel, distressingly, that that armor was wearing thin in places.

Thin too, the Indowy thought, was wearing the courage of the crew. In continuous action for more than twenty-four hours—for the enemy had come looking for the tank from space a bit before their successful assaults across the river lines, the crew had begun to exhibit signs of something very like the Indowy equivalent of the Darhel's lintatai.

Though with the Indowy it was a cultural and physical issue, not a genetic one.

He looked around the tank's combat cocoon at the crew, trying to analyze those almost inscrutable un-Indowy faces. All glistened of sweat, sweat pulled forth by fear.

Prael, living and fighting under the desperate pressure of a command he had never trained for, but for which he had so far proved more than suitable, had developed a twitch in his cheek. Even to an alien to whom German was worse than a merely foreign tongue, Prael's vocal commands to the crew had acquired a nervous, half-mad tone.

Schlüssel's hands, gripped tight on his gunner's spade-grip, trembled, Rinteel saw. He had not been able to so much as pull his face from the gun's sight for over six hours. The previous break in his concentration? Well, the Indowy couldn't recall it.

Breitenbach, whom the Indowy suspected to be the youngest of the crew, sat shaking. Yet the young man's eyes never left his engagement screen, his hand still stayed fixed to his cannon's control handle.

Henschel, running the loader's station, seemed to retain an old being's calm, as did Nielsen of the humongous feet. The others of the crew did as best they might.

And the Indowy was, wonder of wonders, terrified and disgusted and admiring all at once. He wished himself to be like the humans, too; able to be terrified and brave all at once, to quake at the heart with fear and still to make the hand and eye steady when it counted. *What an amazing species,* marveled the little bat-faced, furry, Indowy. *If we must have an overlord species—and unless we ever learn to fight, and we* can't, *we must—then we could do worse than to serve these humans.*

Tiger Anna, *Southeast of Berlin, 4 February 2008*

In twenty-four hours the crumbling line had been driven back more than twenty-five kilometers. Three times in the last day Hans had ordered his brigade to turn about and lunge back at the enemy. Three times they had driven the Posleen eastward, fleeing in terror. Three times they had carpeted the frozen earth with a blanket of dismembered and crushed enemy bodies.

Yet, each such lunge had also seen the enemy return, in numbers uncountable, pressing at the front and oozing around the flanks. Each such lunge had left a Tiger or two smoking on the East Prussian plain.

The enemy had chosen, so far, not to risk its ships. Hans Brasche smiled grimly for a moment at this mute testimony to the fear in which the Posleen held his much-weakened brigade of Tigers and their lighter comrades.

Out in their vehicles, the lighter troops—Leopard tankers and panzer grenadiers in their Marders—smiled, too. They smiled at being alive, which they would certainly not have been, most of them, had not their brigade commander's tank ignored the Posleen's human shields and blasted both humans and aliens to kingdom come.

On other sectors of the front, so the word had been passed, some units had completely disappeared under the alien wave because no one had been able to bring themselves to fire on women and children until it was too late. Great gaps had been torn in the front, gaps that the Germans and their Polish and Czech allies were struggling to repair.

Each attempt at repair seemed to find the front ever more westward.

Hans was facing eastward when *Anna's* voice called to him, "Emanations from thirty-eight enemy ships heading this way, flying low, *Herr Oberst.*"

Hans maintained his smile after hearing that news. Action, something to take his mind from his recent crimes, was a welcome relief.

Borominskar cursed futilely at his misguided and insubordinate underling. "You foolish *abat*! You incarnate insult to your forebears! You never sufficiently to be cursed, thrice-damned *idiot*! Turn back."

"Up yours, old one," answered the younger God King, Siliuren of Sub-clan Rif. "The enemy is broken and my people are hungry after the long fast you inflicted upon them. I am going to grab my own place in the sun of this world and to the shit-demons with *you*!"

Not bad odds, thought Hans. *Not bad odds at all. We have faced worse in any case, much worse.*

Losses had forced Hans to consolidate his three battalions of Tigers into two. Even those two mustered only ten tanks apiece. Curiously, his Leopard and panzer grenadier units were much nearer full strength. *It was the drawing of the enemy fire away from the lighter units and towards us that spared so many of them, I think.*

The twenty-one remaining Tigers, including *Anna*, waited

patiently under their camouflage foam for the Posleen to enter engagement range.

Hans spoke into his microphone to the entire brigade. "The important thing here, boys, is that there is no ground for us to hide behind. If we engage too soon then the enemy will pull back and just pelt us from out beyond our effective range. So we have to let them come in close. Dial down your antimatter and wait until the bastards are within five thousand meters. Then, when I give the command, fire for all you are worth. There are thirty-eight of the swine coming. I don't want more than two or three to get away to spread the word among the others: 'Don't fuck with 'Brigade Michael Wittmann!'"

Siliuren of the Rif chortled at his defiance of his nominal over-lord. What, after all, meant it to be a God King of the People of the Ships if one couldn't exercise the freedom inherent in that status? If he chose to load his oolt in their ships to a new land on his own, by what right could Borominskar object? It certainly had not been because of the care with which he had fed the people; Siliuren's oolt'os were thin to emaciation by their enforced short rations.

The God King viewed the snow-covered land passing beneath his ship with a certain measure of disgust. *It is a bare place, and inhospitable. Why ever did I leave the world of my birth?*

An honest answer to that question would have been something on the order of, *"You left your world because it was about to be blown to flinders, radioactive flinders at that."* An answer more honest still, though Siliuren was not among either the brightest or the most devout of the People and so unlikely to have read or listened with understanding to the Book of the Knowers, would have been, *You left your world because it was about to be destroyed, but it was about to be destroyed because in eons past beyond clear memory, some people called Aldenat' decided that the universe* ought *to be* a certain way and, *for a while, were able to make it* look *that way.*

God, if there is a God, please, if the aliens look, do not let them see. So Brasche prayed and so, if perhaps using different words, prayed every man of the brigade.

Whether a distant God, scarcely in evidence on the Earth as

it was, was paying attention, or the Posleen ships' masters were not paying attention, the swarm of alien ships flew closer and closer to the irregular waiting line of Tigers, Hans never knew. He only knew that the time eventually came when he was able to order, "All Tigers, Fire. Fire at will."

Siliuren of the Rif barely noticed the voice of his ship's AI. Indeed, the ships *never* put into their artificial voices any intonation that might have been characterized as attention grabbing.

It wasn't until the third time the ship said, "There appear to be twenty-one enemy fighting machines ahead," that the God King asked, "WHAT?"

It was the last question he ever asked.

"First and Third Battalions, bend in your flanks," ordered Hans. "Let's trap as many of the bastards as we can. Little brothers,"—the brigade's panzers and panzer grenadiers—"cover our flanks until we are done."

The Brigade Michael Wittmann, much reduced in strength but not one whit in fighting heart, not one whit in their hate, rolled forward to its last victory.

INTERLUDE

Frankfurt bowed down, weighed to the ground under its own ruins. In its way, the gray, ugly city was more to Posleen architectural tastes than were the brighter, homier of the thresh's dwelling places.

But "more" was a far cry from "entirely." Athenalras was not sorry to see his people tearing the place down and rebuilding it in Posleen style. Especially was he not sorry to see the places which armed the threshkreen stripped to bare earth. His clan had suffered greatly, wounds without precedent and without imagining, from their battles with the humans.

"God how I hate the vile abat," muttered the God King lord.

"My lord?" questioned Ro'moloristen.

"I came here, young one, with a bright and shining host. What have I left? Between the threshkreen's radiation weapons, their fighting machines, and their damned artillery and their infantry which refuses to run unless they see an advantage in it, I lead but a pale, bled-out shadow of a clan. The long body of water the thresh call the 'Rhein' is choked to within a few measures of its surface with the bodies of our people. In the east, their rivers Oder and Niesse overflow their banks for all the bodies of the People deposited in them. Their mountains are ringed with our dead. Their fields are carpeted with the remains of the host, sacrilegiously ungathered."

"But my lord . . . we have destroyed them. The Germans reel north and south to barren wastes."

"We have destroyed *ourselves*. Do not count the humans down, my eson'sora, until the last breeding pair are digested. And that, I fear, we shall never do.

"I wish we had never come to this world," finished Athenalras, lord of the clan.

CHAPTER 19

Lübeck, Germany, 1 March 2008

Seven Tigers, along with a half a battalion each of panzers and panzer grenadiers, reinforced with all that remained of the Brigade's artillery—a couple of undersupplied batteries, stood lonely guard south of the town. To the north and the west, the shattered *Kampfgruppen*[48] of nine *Korps*—perhaps the equivalent of a dozen or fifteen divisions, preinvasion—dug in furiously. A further four *Korps*, or the scraps that remained of them, were turning Hamburg into a fortress to grind the alien enemy. From Hamburg, stretched thin along the Elbe River's broad, deep estuary, what remained of the *Bundeswehr* and a few SS, all bridges before them blown, awaited the final enemy onslaught.

Ferries operated by the *Bundeswehr Pioneere*[49] evacuated what could be evacuated of the millions of trapped civilians and soldiers lining the Elbe's southern banks. All, perhaps, could have been evacuated in a matter of days had the bridges been left standing. And yet all knew, now—at *last*—they knew, that some evils were worse than others, and that killing the helpless was not always the worst evil.

It had been a long, hard and bitterly contested withdrawal for Hans Brasche and his men. They had made stands at Potsdam and northwest of Wittenberge and around Schwerin. Each temporary stand had bought time. Each moment of time had bought human lives moved to safety. The price for the salvation of those civilian lives had always been the same: blood and steel and fire, unmarked graves and fat-bellied aliens, gray- and black-clad bodies left to rot or—more likely—to feed the enemy host.

Each stand was a physical defeat, seeing the Brigade driven back leaving smoking tanks and ruined men behind. Yet each stand had bought the seeds, *O let it be so,* of future victory.

Hans was as proud of his men as ever he had been of the men he had led in Russia . . . or the legionnaires . . . or the Israelis, once he had earned Israeli trust.

Hans' left hand stroked his right lapel, feeling the *Sigrunen* sewn there. *And they are clean, my soldiers. No crimes to their name, not even the crimes of necessity. Their sins, if any, I have assumed. And I was likely damned anyway.*

Well, thought Brasche, *I will find out soon enough.*

Kiel, Germany, 3 March 2008

Most of the refugees had to make the weary trek north on foot with occasional wheeled transportation to assist. Medical units, such as were not needed at the front or, more importantly, *were* needed to care for the wounded, assembled with their charges instead at Kiel on the Baltic coast for movement by sea to Stockholm, Oslo, Helsinki, and even Glasgow, all cities still in human hands and likely to remain that way. Some combat units, those judged too exhausted and depleted, also mustered at Kiel for the northward journey.

In a scene reminiscent of Dunkirk, or the Japanese evacuation of the Aleutian Islands, masses of people waited in tents, or shivering in the cold open air, for word that another ship was loading, and they were to join it.

The Posleen, of course, attempted to stop the evacuation, as a farmer might prevent the escape of a turkey destined for the dinner table. Yet Danish, Swedish, Norwegian, Finnish and British Planetary Defense Batteries were generally successful at keeping the alien ships at bay. Moreover, the Swedes had jury rigged several stout merchant ships with salvaged Posleen railguns. These last gave the aliens fits as they never remained in one place long enough for the Posleen to engage.

Despite the defenses, though, more than one human merchant vessel lay sunken and smoking at its moorings among Kiel's many wharfs and quays. Still, out in the fjord, the city's natural harbor, everything from huge container ships to little two person sailboats bobbed among the waves, awaiting the call to come in and dock. Though Posleen fire occasionally succeeded in pelting the harbor from space, the greatest danger to the ships and boats assembled was each other.

Harbormasters from the usual, civilian, port authorities, supplemented by the sailors of the Germany Navy, kept order as best they could. This best was poor enough, given the density of watercraft in the fjord. More than one crash had occurred, with resulting great loss of life.

This one has lost his will to live, thought the doctor, a psychiatrist trying desperately and, in the case of Thomas De Gaullejac, unsuccessfully, to heal the hidden wounds of war.

The boy had been cleaned up now, his black uniform exchanged for a fresh gown of hospital green. The trench-bred lice were gone; his hair was cut. Even so, his weight was down and continuing to plummet. He ate, when he ate, only on command . . . and then, only if watched.

The doctor had tried everything he knew. When all of that had failed he had even called in a chaplain, thinking, *Where art and science fail perhaps faith may help.* Sadly, the boy appeared not to have been raised to be terribly religious. The chaplain's "God's inscrutable will" had fallen on deaf ears.

The doctor knew the story behind young Volunteer De Gaullejac. This had been drawn out early on, before his disease of the mind had taken him over so fully. Once the course of the boy's guilt had been determined, the doctor had tried a different approach, calling in one of Charlemagne's officers to explain to Thomas that he had not been unique; that almost the entire front had seen men unable to kill the helpless victims of the Posleen's human shield.

"That does not mean that *I* didn't also fail," De Gaullejac had insisted. His condition had taken a turn for the worse then, enough so to make the doctor regret having brought in the soldier to assist. It was at that time also that it had become necessary to watch the boy to ensure he ate.

✧   ✧   ✧

Isabelle watched over her remaining son like a brood hen guarding her last egg. She had seen more than one child, separated from its parents, wandering lost and alone between Wiesbaden and here at Kiel. The fact that she never saw the same child twice spoke grim volumes about the likely fate of many of those children. Though her heart had ached for them, she saw the children only in passing, as the division used its motor transport to race away from the aliens.

Mother and son had boarded ship only a few hours before. Because they were a family unit, however small, the ship's Norwegian crew had found them a small, a *very* small, stateroom for the voyage. Though after the filth she had seen in the last few months the ship seemed almost eerily clean, an unpleasant aroma—residue of recent passengers who could not take a rough sea voyage, perhaps—pervaded the vessel's interior.

Instructing her youngest to remain there in their stateroom, Isabelle had gone to help with loading and billeting the rest of the hospital staff and their patients on the ship.

Her name was *Cordelia* and she was out of Haifa. Once her stern had sported the Flag of Liberia, a ruse that fooled no one but was considered useful in carrying cargos to ports, mainly Muslim ones, that would never have accepted an Israeli-flagged vessel.

Now, however, there were no Muslim ports of any significance left in the world. The little blue-and-white ensign fluttering on her short mast told the world, and any Posleen who dared come close enough, that here was an Israeli ship.

The ensign was the only clean thing about the ship, for she had carried a load of passengers from Haifa before the fall of that town, and had been continuously engaged in ferrying Israelis and Europeans to the north, and war materials to the south, for over a month with no chance for maintenance or even sanitation.

Cordelia stank to the heavens.

She was also, just possibly, the sweetest sight *Oberstleutnant* David Benjamin, Judas Maccabeus Brigade, had ever seen . . . and to hell with the stench.

In command of the remnants of the brigade, some three hundred twelve worn-out and filthy men and women, sans heavy weapons or other equipment, and in control of about fifteen thousand Israeli refugees, Benjamin oversaw the loading of these tattered remnants of his people as they boarded ship.

Benjamin turned his attention from the loading at the approach of a Mercedes staff car bearing the insignia of a German field marshal. He had saluted, something Israeli soldiers did rarely in any case, before he recognized the gray-clad, young-looking man who emerged bearing a white baton.

"Where are your *Sigrunen*?" he asked confrontationally. Hans Brasche was the only man in the world who wore the double lightning flashes that Benjamin could really stand to be around. He and Mühlenkampf had never quite managed cordiality, despite what the Israeli recognized as the German's sincere attempts at amends.

"I didn't need them anymore," the German answered, simply. "I had made my point, given my former followers and comrades back their self-respect. And now, commanding far more regular troops than SS, I have dispensed with them for myself. They were only a symbol, after all, one that meant different things to different people."

To this Benjamin had no response. He could accept that the *Sigrunen* meant something different now—*the lightning sword of vengeance*—to most Germans, to most Europeans, and even to a fair number of Israelis. But to him they were just hateful and nothing would ever change that.

"Your destination is Stockholm, I believe?" queried Mühlenkampf.

"Yes, Stockholm and then by rail north to a Sub-Urb. They are collecting all that remains of Israel at the same place."

"I wonder if that is wise," mused the field marshal.

"Wise or not," quipped Benjamin, "it is still necessary. Mixed in with you lot and you and the Posleen would end up accomplishing what Hitler never could, the extinction of the Jewish people as we all interbred. There are just too few of us left."

"That's what I mean. Maybe we should all be extinguished as separate peoples. Maybe we should become just a *human* race."

The Israeli shook his head in negation, looked the German straight in the eyes and answered, "I remain a Jew."

Mühlenkampf glanced at the Jew's Iron Cross. "You remain, my friend, a lunatic. But I am glad all the same that we are of the same species.

"Good luck to you anyway, lunatic. Good luck and Godspeed." Mühlenkampf held out his right hand in friendship.

For reasons he could not at the time understand, Benjamin— standing not far from the Israeli flag fluttering at *Cordelia*'s stern, and only after a moment's hesitation, accepted.

Isabelle looked over the stern at the receding German coastline. She wondered whether they would manage to get everyone out in time or if, as seemed likely, some other woman might have to wander hospital wards murdering the hurt and sick to save them from a worse fate.

It was a moment of inexpressible loneliness. Part of this was the voyage and the loneliness of the sea. But the greater part was that there was no one she could talk to, not one person to whom she could unburden the sickness in her soul. The chaplain? She had left the church long ago; there was no salvation there for her. The psychiatrists? Her husband, and she was certain now that he was her *late* husband, as Thomas must by now be her late son, had been a *real* doctor. She had picked up his attitudes towards those he deemed "quacks."

The others among the hospital staff were also out of bounds. They all knew what she had had to do. Perhaps they even understood. But she had heard the whispering. She would never find a friend among them. She was *unclean* now.

The sea beckoned to her. A short plunge and the icy waters would clean her. She had no fear of death for herself, not anymore. Yet her remaining son held her to this world as if by chains stretching like an umbilical across the generations.

She shook her head, *no*. The sun was setting, the sea was calm. She thought she might risk a meal. Isabelle turned from the stern, walked the deck, and reentered the ship.

Isabelle barely noticed the slump-shouldered youth being fed by a nurse in the ship's galley. Lost in her own miseries she walked to the line along which food was dispensed. Then she turned, dropped her tray and ran.

She reached the youth and dropped to her knees beside him, wrapping arms tightly around neck and torso. "Oh, Thomas, my son, my baby!"

To the surprise of the nurse feeding him, for the boy had slipped ever deeper into some hell of his own, Thomas' eyes showed a little life for the first time in days. He even turned his head towards this strange woman.

"Mama?"

Tiger Brünnhilde, *North of Hanau, Germany,* *4 March 2008*

"Motherfuckers," muttered Prael as he counted the numbers against him and selected a priority target for Schlüssel. *Brünnhilde's* railgun once again *thrummed.*

"Hit," announced Schlüssel, without energy or enthusiasm.

Prael had no new target for Schlüssel. The enemy had become clever, staying out of *Brünnhilde's* range until they could assemble a group and then driving into to unleash a furious attack. It was hell on the commander to both scan the skies for priority targets and direct Mueller, the driver, out of the likely impact area of incoming Posleen fire.

But that was the intermittent threat. The imminent danger to the tank were the hordes of enemy normals and God Kings roaming unhindered through Germany's heartland. Though *Brünnhilde* and her crew had, so far, crushed and scattered all comers.

The price of that had been the wearing away of the tank's ablative armor to the point where several spots might well permit a high-velocity missile, or plasma cannon burst, to get through.

If the Posleen were not so poor at cooperating, thought Prael, *we'd have all been dead long before now. But, no. The dumb shits come with their ships and they come with their infantry and flyers. But they never manage to do so at the same time. Still, eventually they will do so by chance and then we are dead with our armor in the state it is. Hmmm. Maybe something can be done about that.*

The screens showed blank for the nonce, a condition unlikely to continue for long. Prael said, "Rinteel, we seem to have a little quiet time. Take Schmidt and go topside to see if you can't undo some ablative plates and fix them where they are most needed."

"Wilco," answered the alien, with unconscious irony. More manually dexterous than Schmidt, he unbuckled himself quickly.

"Fifty-seven enemy ships inbound," announced the tank in

her usual monotone. "At current rates of closure they will be in range in six seconds. Several hundred enemy flyers closing as well, in range in fifty-two seconds. I have no information on infantry. . . ."

INTERLUDE

My lord and chief is not the same as once he was, Ro'moloristen thought. *These humans have broken his heart.*

On an intact bridge over the river the humans called the "Elbe" Athenalras advanced on foot to meet Borominskar. Ro'moloristen's chief, though senior as the People reckoned things, walked unsteadily, like an old Kessentai ready to enter "the Way of the Knowers."

Borominskar still stepped briskly. His trunk Ro'moloristen saw to be covered with some kind of blanket seemingly made of mid-length, light-colored thresh fur. The fur seemed very young and fresh, blowing as it did in the early spring sun. Since the People did not have the thresh art of weaving, Ro'moloristen made the logical assumption.

I pity you, Borominskar, if the threshkreen ever capture you alive within a million measures of that blanket. They will not merely kill you; they will cut out your living entrails and roast them before your eyes, then leave your agonized remains for this planet's insects to devour. They will do the same to each of your followers, too, for nothing affects these thresh like the murder of their young.

For you see, lord, that these people are not like us. We kill to eat, with no more pain given than necessary for that purpose. We are not a cruel race, merely a practical one.

But the humans are a cruel species. They can revel in an enemy's agony. I pity you, Borominskar, when the thresh return in strength and break out from their fastnesses.

317

And they will return, O Lord of the east. And they will break out. Our species, as it exists, is doomed.

CHAPTER 20

Tiger Brünnhilde, *the end.*

I survived. How is it possible I survived?

Groggy and disoriented, the Indowy Rinteel arose slowly and unsteadily to all fours from the deck where he had been thrown after the last Posleen hit on *Brünnhilde.* There was a coppery smell in the air, something unique in the Indowy's experience. To Rinteel it seemed to be coming from the thick, red liquid sloshing across the deck. He lowered his head and sniffed at the deck. *Ah, so human blood smells like that.*

There was smoke in the air, bitter and acrid and easily over-whelming the smell of blood once the Indowy managed to drag himself to his feet. Some of that smoke poured from Rinteel's own damage control panel.

If I had been in my chair leaning forward I would be dead now, he thought.

He heard the faint whistle of the tank's blowers, apparently working on automatic once they detected dangerous material in the air. Soon it was clear enough for Rinteel to see around the combat cocoon.

What he saw wrenched his heart. Lining both sides of the cocoon his human comrades slumped in death, hanging loosely against their straps. So many holes had been torn through most of the bodies by the shattering of *Brünnhilde*'s armor that the bodies had gone pale.

Looking back, Rinteel saw that the corpses of Schlüssel, Henschel, and Prael were more torn than most. The Posleen penetration had done its worst work at the rear of the cocoon. Bits of flesh and bone were stuck by blood all over that section.

The horror of the scene seemed to make something go "click" in the Indowy's mind. Rinteel felt a portion of his sanity go gibbering away. With that portion gone, he found, he was able to feel things he had never felt before . . . anger, hate, a desire to punish. At the same time these things crept into Rinteel's mind he felt a deep pain in his body, his people's cultural and philosophical conditioning against violence coming to the fore.

Frantically, the Indowy pushed aside the hateful thoughts. He did not regain his full sanity by doing so.

Then came a low moan from the front of the cocoon, Mueller's driving station.

Perhaps I am not alone after all, Rinteel thought. *Friend Johann may live yet.* He raced somewhat unsteadily on his short legs to Mueller's station and twisted the chair around.

Mueller was alive, though barely. A red foam frothed from his chest as a red stream poured down his face.

"Friend Johann, how may I help?"

"Rinteel, is that you? I can't see you."

"You are badly hurt, Johann."

"Is there anyone . . . ?" Mueller began to ask.

"No, I am sorry. All are dead but for you and me."

With that grim news Mueller sank into a semi-torpor. "All dead. All . . . Rinteel, you must fight the tank. I am dying, and I cannot."

"I cannot either, Johann. My people are not warriors."

"There are warriors and then there are warriors, Rinteel. You must fight the tank." Mueller was overtaken by a spasm of coughing which brought blood and bloody gobbets forth from his mouth. When the spasm was finished he said, so low as barely to be heard, "Use your mind, Rinteel. Find a way . . . perhaps the tank can help you."

Mueller began coughing again. When the fit ended, the Indowy could see, breathing had stopped.

Rinteel had never before lost a friend. A bit more of his sanity departed with the loss.

✧   ✧   ✧

A sane Indowy, Rinteel knew, would have abandoned *Brünnhilde* by now. Yet Rinteel found that he simply could not leave. Between his conditioning and the sense of duty and honor he had learned from the crew, the Indowy was able to put a name to the disease affecting his mind. A human would have called it schizophrenia, though that would not have been perfectly accurate. He had not developed a twin personality so much as he was rapidly developing a twin set of values.

It was in such a state of mental confusion that he asked of the air, "Tank *Brünnhilde*?"

"I am here, Indowy Rinteel."

"What is your condition? My damage control screen is broken."

"Everything critical is operable, Rinteel."

"You can fight then?"

"No, Indowy Rinteel, except in self-defense. And I cannot use my main battery in any case without a commander or crewmember to give me the order to do so."

"Am I an official member of the crew, *Brünnhilde*?"

"You are, Rinteel."

The Indowy stopped then, while different values, new and old, warred within him. He thought that if he gave in to the urge to fight, that part of his now split value system would likely take over all of him. He thought, too, that his body would never survive such a course, that his conditioning would kill him if he gave in to the primitive urge.

And Rinteel did not want to die.

"I do not wish to die, tank *Brünnhilde*," he said, sipping some intoxicant that had miraculously survived the Posleen strike.

"I understand that is common with sentient life, Indowy Rinteel."

"You have instructions, preprograms, do you not, which require you to try to survive?"

"Yes, I do, Rinteel. But this is a matter of programming and not one of personal preference. I have no personal preferences. I am not a person."

To the Indowy this seemed specious. He was, after all, from a civilization in which AI's, notably the Darhel produced AIDs, *did* have personalities. "Refresh my memory, *Brünnhilde*. You cannot engage your survival program while you maintain more than two rounds of your ammunition aboard?"

"This is correct, Rinteel."

The Indowy thought about that, then asked, "Are there Posleen ships about overhead, *Brünnhilde*?"

"There are, Rinteel. I surmise they are not finishing us off because we appear to be dead. The enemy flyers have likewise withdrawn. After the hit that got through I let my close-in defense weapons go silent to fool them. This was part of my survival programming, though I note that it is a war crime under international law."

Dead? Dead? I do not want to die. And yet, if I must . . .

"How many projectiles do you retain for your main battery, *Brünnhilde*?"

"I have one hundred and forty-seven KE projectiles, DU-AM, Rinteel. Plus fifty-nine antipersonnel canister."

"And how long would it take you to expend all but two of the KE?

"Slightly more than one hour, Rinteel."

"And then you will be able to engage your survival program?"

"Yes, Rinteel."

Again the Indowy stopped speaking to allow himself to think. When he had finished he asked, "Can you distinguish the color of the sky, *Brünnhilde*?"

"I can."

"Can you note the color of the earth?"

"Yes, Rinteel."

"Can you change colors in your perceptions? Modify what you perceive?"

"I can."

"Good. I want you to modify your perceptions such that the earth and sky are all green."

"Very well, Rinteel. I have done so."

"Good . . . very good. Thank you, *Brünnhilde*. What colors remain?"

"Just the silver shapes of the Posleen warships."

"Excellent. Now, *Brünnhilde*, I want you to expend all but two of your remaining KE projectiles. But you are not to aim at the green."

Instantly the tank's railgun raised to near vertical, the turret swerved, and the tank itself began to shudder with the pulses of death being sent aloft.

The Indowy smiled then; madness had overtaken him fully despite his philosophical sleight of hand. When the tank was finally destroyed by Posleen counterfire, he would still be smiling.

Spandau Prison, Berlin, Germany, 5 March 2008

The sound of alien claws on the concrete floors and reverberating off of the stone walls and steel doors of the ancient prison filled Günter Stössel with dread.

The guards were gone; had left laughing, in fact, over the presumed fate of the charges they were deliberately abandoning to the Posleen. Neither pleas nor offers moved the warders. Though no *Sigrunen* flashed from their collars they were perhaps more in tune with the mindset of many of those who *had* worn the double lightning flashes in earlier times. Certainly they were pitiless with those of the prisoners who were serving sentences for collusion with the Darhel.

Shivering in his cell, for without the prison staff the heat had shut down, Günter started at the sound of screaming coming from down the corridor and around a bend. The words of the screamer, to the extent there were words, were indistinct. Most of the sound, in any case, was a mindless howl, pleading for life.

The howl suddenly cut off. Günter thought he might have heard the sound of something hitting the concrete floor, but could not be sure. He *was* sure that he did hear a concerto of snarling, snapping feasting. He also heard many more screams and pleas, and more articulate ones, coming from other prisoners.

The sounds of claws on concrete came a bit closer. The screaming pleas, such as one might have heard in some nineteenth-century madhouse, grew ever louder and ever closer.

The Posleen cosslain, when it came to Günter's cell and blasted the lock on the door, found him hiding under a blanket in a far corner of the cell. The cosslain simply removed the blanket and dragged him by the hair to the corridor outside, where all could feed without the jostling that often led to internal fighting among the People.

After the terrified wait, after the growing concert of shriek-ing and pleading and the patter of falling heads, Günter was no doubt quite mad by the time the Posleen arrived at his cell. When the cosslain drew his boma blade and swept it through Günter's neck, severing head from torso, Günter was as indifferent as was the cosslain.

Stockholm, Sweden, 12 March 2008

"All is lost," muttered the chancellor hopelessly.

Mühlenkampf shrugged in his hospital bed. "We have lost a battle, *Herr Kanzler*. But we have not lost the war."

What universe does this soldier live in? wondered the chancel-lor.

Mühlenkampf as much as read the chancellor's thoughts. He answered them with, "A battle is not a war, nor is even a series of battles a war, *Herr Kanzler*. This war will not be over until the last of us is dragged, biting and kicking from the last trench or the last hole after we have expended the last round of ammuni-tion."

"We have saved nearly twenty million of our own people here; a like number have found safety in the Alps. Add to that several million more French and Poles and Czechs and Italians.

"The people we saved, too, are the most precious: women to breed more soldiers in abundance, wise farmers, skilled work-ers. And enough soldiers have been saved to make a seed from which mighty armies will grow. North and south we shall grow again; we shall marshal and build our strength. And the enemy has no chance of digging us out from either Scandinavian snows or Alpine fortresses; they'll starve first.

"But we will not starve, *Herr Kanzler*. Oh, yes, rations may be a little scant and bland until we can break out from our mountain fastnesses. So what? The *Volk* had become pudgy with prosperity, and a lean wolf is a fierce one.

"No, *Herr Kanzler*, the war is not lost, but only beginning."

The remnants of Division Charlemagne had made it to safety; a mere two thousand from a division that had once boasted nearly twenty thousand, and had lost nearly twice that number in action. In a relatively small corner of a huge Stockholm Sub-Urb, the survivors among the French civilians warmed to and welcomed the tiny band that was all that remained of a once great and courageous army. Already, boys and girls as young as twelve were being turned into something their people needed to survive: soldiers.

To Isabelle it was an abomination, to take those so young and twist their hearts and minds to make them killing machines. An abomination it was, but still, she knew, it was not the worst form of abomination. She could not like it; she could not even keep herself from hating it. And yet she knew she could accept it, for the alternative was far worse.

She thought about an old American science fiction series, *Journey to the Stars* or some such title. She had once enjoyed it greatly, though she found few of the plots believable two minutes after a show had ended. Nor had much of the philosophy of the show really moved her.

Yet two things had. The lesser of these was "having is not, after all, so pleasing a thing as wanting." Much more important, especially in her current circumstances, was the simple line, "Survival cancels out programming."

She walked to the small cubicle in her apartment, barely more than a large closet really, where Thomas slept when he had no duties with Charlemagne. Opening the door slightly, she peered in on her resting son.

Sensing that Thomas was asleep, she risked opening the door wide enough to enter. Not wanting to take a chance on awakening him, as she might have had she sat on the bed, Isabelle instead sat on the floor. She was tall enough, and the bed low enough, that she could still reach out easily to gently stroke her son's hair.

"Survival cancels out programming," she thought. *I was programmed by my mother who had seen France lose three wars in a row and thought that the entire exercise was futile. My mother was programmed by her mother who had feared she would never marry because the Great War had created such a shortage of men. And you, my dear son, were programmed by me.*

I made you to be a fine boy, warm and kindhearted and good. And so, when the time came, and you needed to do something horrible to prevent something worse, you could not. But it was my hand that froze yours, my loving mother's heart that pierced your own. The guilt, my son, is all mine. And none of the blame is yours.

And so, tomorrow when you awaken to breakfast . . . and for every morning to come, you will find a mother who will give her heart and soul into making you what I never wanted you to be: a soldier. You will find a mother who will advise you and prompt you and support you in becoming the best French soldier in a century.

For "Survival cancels out programming."

Tiger Anna, *the end.*

Es ist zu ende, thought Hans. It is over: the pain, the war, the struggle. *Well, there are still a few things to do.*

Hans looked around the combat cocoon. Every man turned a questioning face towards him. *We have followed you to the end. Now there is nothing more to do. What now, commander?*

Hans turned his own face from his followers, put on his VR helmet, and said, "*Anna*, situation map please, strategic situation."

"Yes, *Herr Oberst*," the tank answered, and it seemed to Hans there was a deep yet inexpressible sadness in the artificial voice. Perhaps that was merely because the tank's words were filtered through Hans' own, weary and hopeless, mind.

The enemy suddenly appeared on the map *Anna's* VR placed before Hans' eyes, a great red splotch covering Germany from Munich to Hamburg. A thin, irregular line of blue remained at the passes into the Bavarian and Swiss Alps and in Schleswig-Holstein. This line represented the last holdouts among the defenders. All the rest who had not found secure flanks in the mountains were even now drowning under the alien tide.

Passing through the blue line, even as its rear was being overwhelmed and engulfed by the red tide, were the last fleeing million of civilians, showing on the VR map as evaporating pools of green.

"*Anna*, end image."

Hans' removed his VR helmet and turned his attention back

to the crew. "There is nothing more most of you can do. Schultz, Harz, grab your bags and go. Find safety in the north."

Both Dieter and Rudi began to object, but Hans silenced them. "Just go, gentlemen. Your *country*, which is more than a collection of fields and hills and towns and rivers, needs you alive. Find wives; raise families. Bring up sons as good and brave as yourselves, sons that will someday take our homeland back for us. And if you would be so good as to take my hand as you leave . . ."

With similar words, similar handshakes, Hans dismissed all the crew, one by one and two by two, until only he and Krueger were left. Krueger kept his vision carefully fixed on his driver's screen, hoping the commander would find no more use for him and would release him to flee for safety.

But Hans just sat silent in his command chair, his hand stroking a little packet in his left breast pocket, his eyes staring at Krueger's back.

Outside of the tank, Schultz and Harz joined the swelling stream of refugees and scraps of units retreating to the north. It was a sight they had seen too many times before. Yet familiarity had not dulled the pain of watching old men and women struggling to keep ahead of the alien hordes, had never accustomed them to the sight of hungry mothers pushing and leading hungry children for some distant, hoped for, safety.

"We should go back," said Schultz. "No matter what the commander says, he should not be left to die alone. And I am ashamed to be running with these people when we should be standing on the line and fighting to give them half a chance." Dieter turned to go back when Harz's restraining hand gripped his shoulder.

Krueger started when he first felt Brasche's hand on his shoulder. The commander had made no sound in his approach, had made no sound since releasing the last other member of the crew.

"It is just you and I left now, Sergeant Major Krueger, just the old SS. It's fitting, don't you think, that we who were there at the first should also be there at the last?"

What is this fucking maniac talking about? thought Krueger. *I don't want to be anywhere at the last. I don't want there to even* be *a "last" for me. And what is this friendly tone? We both know we detest each other.*

Sensing that the sergeant major would make no answer, Hans removed the hand and walked, no longer trying to be silent, back to his command chair.

"Where you there at the first, Sergeant Major?" Hans asked.

"I was SS from 1938 on, yes, *Herr Oberst.*"

"Really?" asked Hans, conversationally. "I looked over your record of course, when you were assigned to me. It indicated only that you served with *Totenkopf* Division from 1942 onward. What did you do before then?"

"*Sonderkommando, Einsatzgruppe C, Totenkopfverbaende.*[50] Then I pissed someone off and was sent to the front," Krueger answered.

"*Totenkopfverbaende?*" Hans queried. "In the camps?"

"Yes, Ravensbrück," the sergeant major said.

"Ah. I was never there, though I did do a very short time at Birkenau. I had a dear friend who was at Ravensbrück. Tell me, Sergeant Major, were the women there really as pliable as all that?"

Krueger didn't answer. Instead he asked, "Are you going to let me go?"

Dieter attempted to shrug off Harz's iron grip. "Let me go," he demanded. "I am going back."

"No, damn you, you are not going back! If I have to deck you and carry you out over my shoulder you are going to follow the commander's last orders: run, live, breed, return and *fight* for our country again."

"But I don't want to do any of those things," Dieter said, simply. "Maybe if Gudrun were still alive . . ." The sentence drifted off, unfinished.

"And it does not matter a whit what you *want*, old son. What matters is where your duty lies. And it does not lie in getting killed to no purpose. Would your Gudrun want that, do you think?"

"But why would you *want* to go, Sergeant Major? Isn't this what you always dreamed of, a final *Götterdämmerung?*"

"Maybe that is *your* dream, *Herr Oberst.* It has never been mine. I enjoy life too much to want to throw it away."

✧   ✧   ✧

Seeing the confusion on Dieter's face, Harz pressed on that point. "Don't you think she would want you to live? I saw her face, friend, that one night. She was in love with you; don't you ever doubt it. She would want you to live . . . and be happy."

"You are happy with your life then, Sergeant Major? You are happy with yourself?"

"Why should I not be?"

"Oh, I don't know," answered Hans. "I find that I have rarely been so. Though there was a time . . ."

Behind him, Krueger heard the sound of cloth ripping, of stitches being torn. Still he did not turn around. There was something to be feared in the commander's tone of voice now, something he could not quite put a finger to. There was an edge, perhaps, to the commander's words, some bitter undertone.

"I was always under someone's orders, you see, Sergeant Major, all the time of my youth unto my later manhood. Never my choice. Never my will. And there was only the one person, gone now, whose will actually meant more to me than my own."

"Now, however, I find I am free."

Locked in place as if by chains, though the chains binding him were moral rather than physical, Schultz simply stood in place with his head hanging.

What an easy thing it would be, he thought, *to return to the tank and fight and die. Never to feel the loss of a loved one again. Never to have to worry about my mother and father, or my sister. Maybe even, if the priests were right, to find my Gudrun again. How sweet and easy and attractive going back would be.*

How cowardly it would be. Krueger, for all he was a bastard, made me tougher than that. And Oberst Brasche, too, showed me the way of duty and courage that comes from inside. Krueger would despise me for taking the easy way. But Brasche would be disappointed in me and that would be worse.

Dieter looked Harz directly in the eye. "You are right friend. We have much suffering to do yet before we earn our freedom and our rest. Lead on to the north."

✧   ✧   ✧

"Very well then, Sergeant Major, you have certainly earned your reward. You may go and claim it."

In a flash Krueger was out of the driver's chair and grabbing at his pack. He began stuffing some extra necessities into it.

Anna announced, "We have enemy ships coming this way, *Herr Oberst.*"

"I am sure we must, *Anna.* Well, this won't take long. You had best hurry, Sergeant Major."

Krueger stopped stuffing the pack and began to walk the row between the battle station chairs lining both sides of the battle cocoon. Krueger stopped, taken aback, at seeing a square black cloth rectangle lying on the tank's metal deck. A similar rectangle graced Krueger's own lapel, though on his the SS showed.

Krueger looked up to where Hans sat. He saw that Hans' right lapel was bare where the silver SS had once stood. "Why?" Krueger asked.

"I told you, Sergeant Major. I am free now . . . well . . . almost free. I still have my restrictions. And I never wanted to wear that symbol again. For the rest, it was fine. It meant something good. To me it did not. But I felt I had to wear it and try to bring honor again to it for the others."

Hans reached into his tunic's left breast pocket and withdrew a little package. A thin folded cloth something or other he set aside on his chair's armrest, as he did a small folded paper. The last item, a picture, he handed to Krueger.

"Does she look familiar, Sergeant Major?"

"Maybe," he answered with a shrug. "Pretty girl. Your wife?"

"Yes, she was. Look carefully," Hans insisted. "See if you can't remember seeing her before."

"I don't have time for . . ." And then Krueger saw that Brasche had his pistol drawn.

"What the hell is this?"

"I told you to look *carefully.*"

Heart beating fast, Krueger looked down at the picture again. "Okay, yes, I have probably met the girl. I don't know who she is though."

Brasche smiled then and said, "I didn't expect you would know her name, Sergeant Major. My wife was called 'Anna.' This tank is named for her.

A set of memories tugged at Krueger, memories of a little,

emaciated Jewess being used by a squad of men. He dropped the picture and began to reach for his own pistol.

Hans' pistol spoke and then spoke again. Krueger was spun to the floor. He lay there on his back, going into shock, bleeding to death.

Krueger's eyes lost focus for a moment. When focus returned he saw a broadly smiling Brasche standing over him, pistol pointed directly at Krueger's head.

"This is for my wife, Anna, whose name you never asked, you NAZI SON OF A BITCH!"

Beaten in war or not, the Germans were still thorough. Several miles up the road, Harz and Schultz were met by buses, just returning from dropping off one load of refugees to pick up another. The loading was orderly and soon the two were in line on an asphalt parking lot awaiting boarding. Their route, so they were told, would take them into Denmark, across several bridges, and even underwater, before they reached Sweden.

Dieter stopped before joining a line to board a bus. He looked around at a homeland he did not expect ever to see again. Suddenly, without a word, Dieter began walking off the asphalt to the nearest patch of bare earth. There, while Harz looked on without comprehension, Dieter started digging at the earth with his helmet. Soon he had the helmet half filled and another pile of dirt beside the little hole. Dieter reached into his pocket and removed a plastic bag. This he placed onto the dirt in the helmet. Then he filled the helmet with the remainder, tamping it down carefully. He walked back to Harz and the forming line carrying the helmet by its strap.

"And what was that in aid of?" asked Harz.

"At first, when I was digging, I just wanted to bury Gudrun, the only part of her I have to bury anyway, as a human should have been buried. But then I thought that someday, children will ask us, 'What is Germany?' And I thought I might be able to point to this helmet, filled with the rich soil of home and the last remains of as pure a spirit and heart as Germany ever produced, and encased in and protected by a helmet of war as only soldiers ever could have protected Germany. And with that, maybe I will be able to explain."

✧   ✧   ✧

Anna's picture was retrieved from the floor where Krueger had discarded it. Safe in Hans' pocket again, it was joined by his little packet of her hair. He smiled at the nearness, warmly, and thought, *Soon, love, soon.*

"*Anna*, full automation. Prepare for continuous antilander fire. Close-in defense weapons under your control. Engagement parameters Posleen flyers and infantry."

"Yes, *Herr Oberst*," the tank answered.

"*Anna*, call me Hans, can't you?"

"Yes, Hans, I can call you by your given name. Hans, those Posleen ships are almost in range, and there are more of them than I thought. I am loading DU-AM now."

"Thank you, *Anna*. How much time?"

"Two minutes, Hans."

"Very good."

Hans took the small folded cloth something, and began to open it into a yarmulke. "Commander's gun," he announced. His gunner's controls descended around him.

As the first Posleen ship appeared in his sight, Hans began to recite, "Hear, O Israel . . . the Lord is God . . . the Lord is One . . ."

EPILOGUE:
IN A FURTHER FUTURE...

The Heavens twisted. Normal star patterns were distorted and covered as the battle cruiser *Derflinger*, leading the human fleet, began to emerge from hyperspace. *Derflinger* was followed by *Kaiser* and *Kaiserin*, the latest supermonitors *Bismarck* and *Tirpitz*, the heavy cruisers *Scharnhorst*, *Gneisenau*, *Scheer* and *Hipper*. A parsec away materialized a similar fleet, containing *Musashi* and *Yamato*, *Kongo*, *Akagi*, *Kaga*, *Soryu* and *Hiryu*. In between, led by escorts, emerged the combined transport fleet.

Slowly and majestically, the three sub-fleets closed on their target, a major world of the hated Darhel. From below, semirobotic defenses attempted to hold the avenging humans at bay. These were semirobotic in the sense that they required a living operator to release them to fight, but fought on their own. Only this roundabout method saved the Darhel "operators" from lintatai, the catatonia and death that came from actively using violence.

Aboard the transport fleet's flagship, a special vessel on loan from the Americans and named the "*Chesty Puller*," the landing force's chain of command met in the orders room. They had met not so much to consult or plan or even to order as to share a few hours conviviality before the landing.

Shudders ran through this ship as it sent cargo after cargo of kinetic death down onto the Darhel world. In the viewing screen Mühlenkampf and his mixed corps of SS and samurai officers watched with satisfaction as bright lines of dozens of descending KE projectiles ended in actinic flashes before giving birth to clouds of angry black.

Initially a few ships seemed to try to make an escape. Shrieking useless admonitions that they were full of noncombatants, the ships attempted to run the human-imposed blockade. But centuries-old human laws of war held it perfectly legitimate to engage civilians trying to flee a siege. Nothing in those laws required that a siege be intended to have any long duration. The more numerous escort vessels saw to the would-be escapers, while the heavies continued pounding the planet's surface.

Another happy shudder ran through the *Chesty Puller*. Smiling grimly, the shudder reminding him of his last session with a woman, Mühlenkampf lifted his glass in a silent toast, thinking, *and aren't we just giving you a good fucking, you elven pieces of shit?*

The destruction being visited upon the Darhel initially looked carefully planned as one by one their planetary defense batteries were silenced. This actually took several hours to accomplish, hours enjoyably spent in sweet contemplation of revenge, present and future. Though the ship had rung with the occasional hit from the Darhel shore batteries, this too had ceased.

With the defense batteries suppressed, the fleet was able to turn its attention to population centers. LTG Horida, leading a corps of Armored Combat Suits in His Imperial Majesty's Service, grunted satisfaction as one Darhel city after another was beaten to dust. *Just so were our cities scathed . . . at your instigation, evil kamis . . . demons.*

The slightest of smiles informed the face of Brigadier General Dieter Schultz. "Brigadier General" he was, for the SS retained the normal rank system of Western armies and had never gone back to the arcane rank system they had once used, an inheritance of the old *Sturmabteilung*, or SA. The double lightning flashes still glittered on his collar, though, as his silver armband proclaimed "Michael Wittmann." Schultz would lead the heavy armor contingent in the conquest. He looked forward to testing his brigade of E-model Tigers against the Darhel's half-baked pseudo-robots. He was eagerly certain his Tiger, *Gudrun*, would make short work of them.

By Dieter's feet rested a combat helmet of a kind not seen anymore except on parade. That helmet never left his side. Never.

The helmet was filled, apparently, with dirt, a few flowers growing from it.

After one particularly vivid strike, Harz, the Michael Wittmann Brigade's sergeant major, clinked glasses with Toshiro Nagoya, Operations Officer for Horida. Benjamin, of Judas Maccabeus, thinking of his lost homeland, his slaughtered and scattered people, whispered, "An eye for an eye . . . blood for blood."

A ship's chime rang over the intercom. "Gentlemen, time," announced a soft female voice. That was Admiral Yolanda Sanchez, the bloodthirsty Philippine bitch—as she was often referred to, in command of the Combined Fleet, ordering the men to their landing bays.

The revels broke up, officers and senior noncoms moving briskly to join their waiting men and combat vehicles. As each left he used his right hand to reverently tap a pseudo-glass casing containing a folded suede blanket, blonde and still bright after many centuries. Above the blanket, fixed to the wall, was a Posleen head, its face twisted in an agonized rictus.

Last to leave was Mühlenkampf. Still looking at the screen in the view of which a world and a civilization died, he mused softly, but as if the Darhel could hear, "The Aldenata—idiot children— thought they were doing one thing when they fiddled with the Posleen and ended up doing something very different. They were as wrong about their tampering with you Elves. But then, given both those lessons you still thought you were even more clever and that you could change us to suit *your* purposes. Now it is you getting a very different result from any you planned on.

"We, on the other hand, are going to change you and we will succeed. This is because our sights are set lower. We only wish to change you from living to extinct.

"I hope you are pleased with what you have created. . . ."

Far, far away, many parsecs in fact, the ghost of Michael Wittmann, and many another, too, smiled in his bier.

AFTERWORD

"I am, of course, not a lover of upheavals. I merely want to make sure people do not forget that there *are* upheavals."
—General Aritomo Yamagata, Imperial Japanese Army, 1881

This story began on a dare, of sorts.

John Ringo created a very interesting, and very bloody, series called, generally, either the Posleen Universe, The War Against the Posleen, or The Legacy of the Aldenata. The series presupposes an alien invasion—a sort of Mongol Horde in space—and a decadent galactic civilization which is able to give Earth much needed technology to defend itself and which needs humans as soldiers to defend it, the controlling Galactics having been genetically and/or culturally manipulated into a helpless pacifism. Much of the tech described is very neat stuff, of course, but the social ramifications are staggering. This is the major reason why the reader will not see as much Galactic Technology (GalTech to the uninitiated) in *Watch on the Rhine* as one might have expected. The one aspect of GalTech that seems to have the greatest potential social impact is the ability to rejuvenate human beings.

John had solicited contributions from fans, of which Tom is one, for short stories and novellas to deal with areas of the Earth, and of the wider war, that his series was simply not going to cover. These were to be collected, those that met the grade, into an anthology.

Initially, Tom wasn't all that interested, having other fish to fry (like the series John and he are planning on doing . . . hint, hint. Finish the outline, John). But the more Tom thought about it, and the more he considered the twin impacts of both rejuvenation and a war of extermination being waged by these aliens, the more fascinated with the idea he became.

The conversation went something like this:

Tom (who may have been drinking at the time): You know, bro', thinking about Germany, the coming invasion and rejuvenation, they're going to need all the trained and experienced combat soldiers they can lay their hands on.

John (who may not have been drinking at the time): Well, duh.

Tom: Did you ever think about where they are going to get them? Can you say Waffen SS?

John: Cooool. Let's do it. I'd love it. More importantly, Jim would love it.

So we asked Jim. Then we cornered him. Then we started the arm-twisting. He kept twisting free. But we were persistent . . . and the rest was going to be future history.

In the course of writing this collaboration we talked about the nature of the Posleen War, aka the War against the Posleen, by the hour. Tom added a fair bit to John's understanding, and of course John's interactive responses ("No Goddammit, Tom, we can't effing crucify the Greens." "Can we hang 'em? No drop?" "Oh, all right.") added to Tom's basic thought-universe. Of course Tom is a Lieutenant Colonel of Infantry (qualified Ranger, Inspector General, Spec Ops Civil Affairs bubba, etc.) and takes all things related very seriously (Remember, you may not like the effing IG . . . but the IG sure likes effing you). John likes some jokes with his mayhem. Maybe you can tell the difference.

Initially *Watch on the Rhine* was "*Die Wacht am Rhein*" and was only going to be a long short story or a short novella, 45,000 words tops. But Jim wanted a book. Set in the PosVerse. We decided on doing a companion novella, "*Back to Bataan*," that would appear with *Die Wacht am Rhein* and would concern the

Japanese defense of the Philippine Islands against the Posleen. (Which, by the way, we may still do. Time will tell.)

But the story of Hans and Dieter and Anna and Gudrun . . . and, yes, even that Nazi bastard Krueger, kept growing. It grew until it ate all the time and space allowed for both stories. As it turned out, Jim liked that better. And it's good to be king. Just ask him. ("My writers love me . . . pull!" "Arrghhhh!")

"But why the bloody damned SS?" the sensitive reader asks. Put simply, because they would be there in John's universe. Deal. "But what about Malmedy?" Go do a Google search: "biscari sicily peiper." Let ye among you. "But the concentration camps? Babi Yar? The holocaust?" To which we would answer, "Horrible things and the men responsible should have all been hanged. But we fail to see why those things would keep desperately needed soldiers out of action, whatever larger organization they belonged to and whatever symbols they wore."

There is another reason, too. Dear reader, we wanted to shock the hell out of you.

Right now, Western Civilization, however much many of its members may refuse to admit it, is involved in a world war. No, it has seen no entire cities destroyed; no trenches have drawn their scars across entire continents. It is a world war all the same. Moreover, it is a world war that is putting to the test every notion of individual liberty, freedom of conscience, and rule of law that the West prizes. And should we lose we will see, or our grandchildren will, the erasure of all that is good in Western Civilization.

We cannot afford to lose.

Yet winning will have its price, too. Just as the invasion John described is ordained to change humanity into something that one of Hitler's Waffen SS would recognize and call home, so too will this war change us. Because side by side with the virtues of Western Civilization are paired vices that may destroy us: a narrow legalistic mindset, an emphasis on form over substance, and an unwillingness to do the ruthless and violent things we must if we are to survive. This list is not exhaustive. Perhaps worse than these things, however, the West has nurtured at its own breast a set of execrable, vile, treacherous and treasonous villains that seem to seek at every opportunity to do all they can to ensure its destruction.

Yet there is hope. "Survival cancels out programming."

END NOTES

1. Let others speak of their shame,
   I speak of my own . . .
   O Germany, pale mother!
   How have your sons ill-served you
   That you sit beneath all nations
   A mockery or a fright!
2. Federal Chancellor, the chief executive of the Federal Republic of Germany.
3. Germany's World War II armed forces: Army, Navy and Air Force.
4. Guest workers. Think Mexican fruit pickers but in a more regularized system. Many of them are Turks and Kurds. And yes, in 1997 the German legislature voted to ban soldiers from wearing their uniforms in public.
5. Two exemplary former regular officers who entered into, and commanded large formations of the Waffen SS. Steiner is also notable for remaining a staunch and devout Roman Catholic.
6. Hooked Crosses, swastikas.
7. The silver dual lightning bolts of the SS.
8. A contemptuous name for Heinrich Himmler, head of all the branches of the SS, to include the Waffen, or Armed, SS.
9. A Tir is a mid-level Darhel corporate executive.
10. To a large degree German boys get a choice of Army or some form of alternative service.

341

11 "Killers of elves." The Darhel are the elves.

12 "Highest." Colonel.

13 Economic Miracle; the recovery of Germany after World War II

14 Officer Candidate School for the Waffen, or armed, SS.

15 March with us in spirit, with the same step and tread. This is from the strictly forbidden "Horst Wessel Lied."

16 Raise the banner, hold the ranks steady.

17 Our flag flutters ahead of us
Our flag brings a new time
And our flag leads us forward to eternity
Yes our flag means more than our lives
		This is from Baldur von Schirach's *"Fahnenlied."*

18 Center, face

19 Lieutenant General Mühlenkampf speaks.

20 A Kessentai who has forsaken, or for cowardice been driven from, *The Path of Fury.*

21 Forward, forward, Blow the bright trumpets

22 Attention, Attention, anti-tank guns in the direction of . . .

23 As you command, Dieter.

24 Dear God in Heaven!

25 Boys.

26 Though it storms or snows or the sun laughs on us
The day glowing hot or icy cold the night . . .

27 Our faces are dirty but our hearts are happy
Our tanks roar into the storm wind. . . .

28 The wife of a German Army friend of one of the authors, who was once Ribbentrop's secretary, describes him as a "weenie."

29 War economy.

30 Execution place.

31 Little dear.

32 I must then go.
To the little town
And you, my sweetheart, wait here.

33 Attention, Tank. Roll.

34 Armored Recon Brigade, Florian Geyer.

35 Hunters. Think, U.S. Army Ranger.

36 Shit, shit, shit!

37 Don't shoot.

38 Private Genjiro Shirakami was a bugler with the Imperial Japanese

Army during the Russo-Japanese War. Mortally wounded during an assault on Port Arthur's defenses, Private Shirakami continued blowing the charge until he succumbed to his wounds. When his body was later found, the bugle—pointing heavenward—was still pressed to his lips.

[39] Certainly not.

[40] Hamburg's red-light district.

[41] Comradeship.

[42] Mine, alone, she'll be,
Not for anyone but me
And we'll live together through joy and pain
Until God cuts us apart again
Farewell, my love, farewell.

[43] "The Watch on the Rhine." A German patriotic song, almost a second national anthem, as "Stonewall Jackson's Way" was throughout the American South, until quite recently, both.

[44] Hard to translate. *Gemütlichkeit* is a sort of smarmy, comradely, soft and tender good feeling that perhaps only Germans are truly subject to.

[45] In English, perhaps only the word "grunts" carries quite the same connotations.

[46] Rye meal. For many decades, in war and peace, the Germans made a sort of ersatz, or replacement, coffee out of roasted rye meal. Less popular now than formerly, one could still expect them to fall back upon it in hard times.

[47] Private.

[48] Battle groups.

[49] Combat engineers.

[50] Leave it suffice that these were the formations that did most of the really ugly work behind lines on the Eastern Front. The *Totenkopfverbaende*, Death's Head Bands, ran the camps.